SECOND CHANCE

Saint knew he had made a mistake with his young wife the first time he had made love to her. He had hurt her, and he had to take care not to do that again.

Already he had brought her to shuddering pleasure but that was only the beginning.

"Now, don't be afraid," he said.

"I'm not afraid," Juliana said, her body still awash with marvelous sensations. "Not of you."

"I'll go very slowly," he assured her.

She watched his face as he drew her even closer. She saw him hesitate.

"It's all right," she said. "You are so beautiful, like a god. Please come to me."

And he was like a god, she thought. A pagan god. Leading her to paradise . . .

Jade Star

Catherine Coulter

Ⓢ
A SIGNET BOOK
NEW AMERICAN LIBRARY

PUBLISHER'S NOTE

This book is a work of fiction. Names, characters, places, and incidents either are the product of the author's imagination or are used fictitiously, and any resemblance to actual persons, living or dead, events, or locales is entirely coincidental.

Copyright © 1986 by Catherine Coulter

SIGNET TRADEMARK REG. U.S. PAT. OFF. AND FOREIGN COUNTRIES
REGISTERED TRADEMARK—MARCA REGISTRADA
HECHO EN CHICAGO, U.S.A.

SIGNET, SIGNET CLASSIC, MENTOR, ONYX, PLUME, MERIDIAN
and NAL BOOKS are published by NAL PENGUIN INC.,
1633 Broadway, New York, New York 10019

First Printing, May, 1987

3 4 5 6 7 8 9

PRINTED IN THE UNITED STATES OF AMERICA

*To a real-life Jules, daughter of Ildi and
Alex DeAngelis, whose name, Juliana,
inspired the heroine's name.
I will never forget all our good times together
and all the love we've shared.
See you in Tokyo.*

1

Lahaina, Maui, 1854

The warm, coarse beach sand was the odd pinkish color of the squirrelfish, the ocean as deep an aqua as the bluefin trevally.

"Come on, Jules, stop dreaming the morning away!"

Juliana DuPres laughed with the pleasure of a now forbidden swim, tightened her kapa-cloth sarong more tightly over her breasts, and dashed into the swirling waves after Kanola. The tides were strong at Makila Point, but Jules, an expert swimmer, merely relaxed in the grip of the pulling crosscurrents until she was safely beyond them.

"Slow down, Kanola," she called. "There should be a school of parrotfish here and I want to see them." Without waiting for a reply from her friend, Jules drew a deep breath and dove down several feet to the coral reef below. She knew her eyes would be red and swollen from the salt water, but it didn't matter. Not only were there parrotfish, but yellowstrip goatfish as well, a treat. She thought to herself as her head cleared the surface: Father, if you truly believed in the glory of creation, you would open your eyes to the incredible beauty that surrounds you.

She grinned at her thought, and spit out a mouthful of salt water. She could just see Reverend Etienne

DuPres stripped of his sweat-soaked black broad-cloth, cavorting in the ocean and calling out the names of fish. Or lying on his back on the beach, his sallow face becoming healthy and tanned.

"Well, what did you see, Jules? An eel maybe?" Kanola shuddered in distaste.

Juliana swam easily to where Kanola was resting on an irregular outcropping of coral that acted as something of a narrow breakwater. The coral was rough, pitted, and slimy. Jules dug her fingers into a crevice, holding tight to keep from being pulled back into the water. There was room enough for just the two of them.

Jules, her voice filled with enthusiasm as she pulled two soaked hunks of bread from a large pocket on the side of the sarong, told her tolerantly smiling friend, "Now, let's see just how hungry all my friends are. Maybe even that zebra moray who was slithering between my feet." She scattered the bread all about her. Within seconds more fish than she could count—even a whitetip reef shark—were swarming about her and Kanola. Jules smiled when their smooth bodies brushed hers. "More saddle wrasse than anything else," she said in some disappointment.

Kanola regarded Jules with the same affectionate smile she gave her own sister. Jules was only two years younger than she, but she clung tenaciously to her childhood pursuits, and, Kanola admitted, Jules knew more about fish than any haole she'd ever known. She listened to her friend go on about every sort of fish consuming the bread, then interrupted her with a raised hand. She said in English as idiomatic as her friend's, "Your papa has been after you again, I gather?"

Jules sighed, and fell silent for a moment. "Papa is Papa," she said finally. "Everything fun and natural is kapu—particularly," she added on a bitter note, "if one happens to be a female."

"I thought as much," Kanola said. "What has he done now? Forbidden you to swim?"

Jules nodded, a small smile playing about her mouth. "Three years ago," she said.

Kanola was startled. "However have you managed to keep it a secret from him all this time?"

"Thomas helps me, washes me down and all that. I assume that Papa thinks I'm just excessively susceptible to the heat and take a lot of baths, because my hair is usually wet. He doesn't seem to notice my red eyes."

"You are nineteen, Jules, a woman grown. There is more to life than searching out and cataloging fish, birds, flowers . . ." Her voice trailed off when Jules shot her an angry look.

"For instance," she continued at her friend's obstinate silence, "there's John Bleecher." Kanola had been married for five years now and was the proud mother of two children.

Jules stared off into the distance, the endless expanse of ocean blurring before her eyes. "He used to be a friend," she said.

"I'm sure he still is," Kanola said dryly. "And he's not a missionary. He'd give you no orders like your father does, or make you pray on your knees until you're stiff as a board."

"I wish he'd turn his attentions to Sarah. She wants to get married."

"Sarah is a stick," Kanola said, not mincing matters.

"She's also beautiful, fragile, and soft, which is what I've always been told men want in a wife."

"Ha! And you, I suppose, are a hag."

Jules's hair had come loose on her dive, and masses of corky wild curls framed her face. "No, not anymore, I don't guess," she said. "But I'm about as fragile as one of my peacock groupers."

"Well, I think you're lucky you didn't gain your beauty sooner, else your father would have kept a closer watch on you."

"Spoken like a true friend." Jules grinned. "Incidentally, he still thinks I'm a scruffy twit, looks at me like I give him pain. It's the red hair, you know, that I got from my French grandmother, the immoral actress. Come on, let's swim out a bit more. We've the time and I've got a good fifteen more minutes before the sun does awful things to my skin."

That was certainly the case, Kanola thought as she watched her friend dive cleanly into the smooth water. Her skin beneath her sarong was as white as her hair was red, and too much sun, even on her lightly tanned face and shoulders made her not only a blotched mess, but sick as well. Kanola slipped into the water after Jules, and swam lazily after her.

"Would you have a look at that, Captain!"

Jameson Wilkes followed Rodney Cumber's pointing finger. He studied the two very female figures striding cleanly through the water. One was a native, clear enough, but the other . . . Even from this distance he could tell that she was different, a real find.

He was thoughtfully silent for a moment, then said briskly to Cumber, "Take three men and lower the boat. Bring the both of them to me."

"Aye, aye, sir!"

"Beg your pardon, Captain, but the other one . . . she ain't no native gal, sir."

"No, Gallen, I don't imagine she is," Jameson Wilkes said to his first mate. "But then again, Bob, we won't be coming back to Maui, will we?"

Bob Gallen didn't like the direction he knew his captain's thoughts were taking. Plowing prostitutes in Lahaina was one thing, even bringing over those Chinese girls to be sold in San Francisco wasn't too bad, but capturing a white girl was quite another, and it made him feel funny. "What if she's a missionary's girl?"

"Then she's probably a virgin," Jameson Wilkes said. "Don't worry, Bob. If she's married, or is covered with the freckles that usually come along with that color hair, I'll set her quickly back into the ocean. Let's wait and see."

"I don't like it," Bob Gallen said.

Jameson Wilkes knew the moment the two women recognized their danger. He heard one of them scream, saw them flip over and race back toward shore. But his men would be faster, of course.

"Kanola, hurry!" Jules gasped over her shoulder. But Kanola wasn't as strong a swimmer. Jules slowed, and grabbed her friend's hand.

"Go on, Jules!"

"No!" Jules gasped, swallowing a mouthful of salt water. Wild, terrifying thoughts swirled through her head. She'd seen the whaler in the distance, watched it without a great deal of interest until she heard Kanola cry out. Then she'd seen the boat coming toward them.

She grasped Kanola's arm, pulling her with all her

strength. But it was no use. The sun was shadowed by the men and the boat.

"Come on, little girlies," she heard a man's gleeful voice call.

"Dive, Kanola!"

But Kanola was much heavier than Jules, her body no longer as lithe. Jules watched helplessly as one of the men grabbed Kanola by her long, loose black hair and dragged her over the side of the boat. Without another thought, Jules dove deep. She had to escape and get help. It was her only thought as she swam with strong strokes underwater. I must get help! When she could hold her breath no longer, she surfaced, only to see a swarthy grinning face directly in front of her, blocking her way to shore.

"That's enough now, girlie," Rodney said. He and another sailor grabbed for her, one of them clasping her upper arm.

Jules fought silently, but she was no match for the two men. Like Kanola, she was dragged over the side of the boat and dumped on the bottom.

"Would you just fill your eyes with this, Ned," Rodney said. "Not a freckle on that pretty little face. The captain'll be mighty pleased. Oh yes he will."

Jameson Wilkes was pleased. He watched his sailors bundle the two girls up the ladder. He quickly dismissed the native girl, his eyes on the flame-haired wench. He couldn't believe his luck. Even though her thick hair was straggling down about her face and down her back, he knew she was a beauty. She was tall, slender, straight-legged, and those marvelous breasts, heaving beneath the thin covering of her sarong. Like Rodney, he quickly saw that not one freckle marred her lovely white skin.

Jules was brought to a stumbling halt before a tall, very well-dressed man. He looked a bit like her father, she thought wildly, but his face was seamed and swarthy from years spent on a ship. Her father usually carried an umbrella to protect his face from the harsh sun.

"My dear," Jameson Wilkes said, offering her a slight bow, "welcome aboard the *Sea Shroud*."

"Who are you?" Jules blurted out. "Why have you brought us here?"

"My dear," Jameson Wilkes said in his deep voice, "I have but one question for you first. Are you yet a virgin?"

Jules stared at him as if he'd spoken Greek.

"Ah," Jameson said, his eyes glittering. "Come along now, and I'll tell you all you wish to know."

"Kanola," Jules gasped. "She is my friend, she must—"

Jameson stopped in his tracks. Slowly he turned. "Her status isn't in much doubt, but nonetheless, we will see." He walked to Kanola, who stood straight and proud, and with one fast motion he ripped off her sarong. Kanola lunged toward him, her nails aimed at his face, but three sailors grabbed her.

"My dear," Jameson called to Jules. "You see, it is as I expected. The marks on her belly. Childbirthing marks. She hasn't your worth. And like most native women, she's got too much flesh. No, unfortunately, she has no value. Come along, now."

Jules screamed, her voice high and thin, but she didn't have the strength of Jameson Wilkes and he dragged her forcibly toward the hatch. The dim companionway loomed below. She heard Kanola call her name, then heard her cries of terror.

"I suggest you think about thanking me for protecting you from my men," Jameson Wilkes said. "Nor, my dear, do you want to look."

But she did. She saw Kanola on her back on the deck, men holding her arms and legs, and the sailor who had captured them pulling at his trousers. She wasn't stupid or ignorant. One couldn't be, in a whaling town like Lahaina, even if one's father was a minister. "No!" she yelled in fury, and her short fingernails streaked down Jameson Wilkes's face. She escaped him for a moment and dashed back toward the deck.

She rushed like a demon toward the screaming Kanola, cursing with the few foul words she'd heard from drunk sailors in Lahaina. The man turned, and she saw his hairy belly and a huge rod of flesh jutting out from his abdomen.

Jameson Wilkes caught her, pulling her back against him. "You want to watch, my dear? I'm sorry to deny you such an education, but I must." He forced her through the hatch down to the companionway.

He knew his men would ravish the native girl. He also knew that such a sight would probably terrify this lovely creature, and that he didn't want.

"Kanola," Jules gasped. "You must make them stop! Don't let them hurt her."

"I swear to you they won't hurt her," Jameson Wilkes said.

"She's my friend," she cried, still straining against him. "Make them stop!"

"Captain, she got away from us!" Jameson Wilkes didn't acknowledge his man's shout. He said to Juliana, "You see, your friend has escaped. Even now she's swimming to shore."

"She won't make it!" Jules cried, straining hard against his punishing grip. "We're too far from shore."

"Enough!" Jameson Wilkes roared. "I'll send my men after her to save her. Now, stop fighting me!"

But she didn't. She was swamped with terror and fury, and managed to twist about and slam her fist against his jaw.

His head jerked back, and anger filled his eyes. He held her firmly, and hit her jaw with ...s fisted hand. Jules crumpled where she stood.

Jules was aware of the throbbing pain in her jaw before she opened her eyes. The pain held her for a moment, then memory flooded back. She gasped, jerking upright, only to realize that she was quite naked, only a thin sheet covering her. She clutched it to her chin.

"Well, at last. I didn't think I'd hit you that hard. Your jaw isn't broken. I'm not such a fool as that."

"Kanola, my friend," she whispered.

"Quite safe," Jameson said calmly. "My men caught up with her before she drowned and . . . escorted her to shore. You need worry no more about her."

"I don't believe you," she said.

He shrugged. "I have no reason to lie to you, my dear. Believe what you will." Of course the native bitch had drowned, but his men had tried to save her, but not to rescue her.

"Who are you?" she asked numbly, staring at the man who was now sitting at his ease in a chair opposite her.

"Captain Jameson Wilkes, at your service, ma'am. And who are you?"

"Juliana DuPres. My father is Etienne DuPres, a

minister in Lahaina. You will return me, now, sir!"
In her frenzy, the sheet slipped, and she jerked it
upward.

"I wondered when you would realize how very . . .
vulnerable you are, Juliana. That's a lovely name,
incidentally. It suits you." He sat forward, his eyes
intent. "You suit me, you know. Oh yes."

Jules stared at him. She knew all about the evil
men of the whalers, for her father had ranted and
raved about them and their wicked, immoral ways
often enough. But to be faced with one of them, to
be lying in the man's bed without a stitch of clothes
on, was almost too much for her to grasp.

"She's dead," Jules whispered.

"No," he said patiently. "As I told you, your friend
is quite safe now. I suggest, my dear, that you think
about yourself."

"I don't understand," Jules said numbly. "Why
have you done this? What do you want from me?"

"I am, I suppose, a wicked man in your innocent
eyes, Juliana. But you needn't worry. I am first and
foremost a businessman." She knows, he thought,
studying her closely. Deep down, she knows exactly
what I want.

"You're a pig," Jules said.

He laughed at that, but she saw that his eyes remained cold, as icy cold as the sleeting gray winter
rains in Toronto, a place she could scarcely remember.

"My father will kill you."

"Your father? Now, that's amusing, to be sure it is.
Your father, my dear Juliana, is a prig, a weak prig
who can do naught but try to change all the natives
into prigs. Don't you find it ridiculous that many of

the natives that have succumbed to religion now dress like English and American gentlemen and ladies? It's all too absurd, you know. But back to your precious father. Perhaps he and your family will mourn you. For they will believe you drowned, and you will no longer exist for them."

Jules closed her eyes, her captor's inadvertent words careening through her mind. He'd lied about Kanola, of course. She was dead, drowned. If she weren't, then everyone would know that Jules had been taken by a whaler.

"Wouldn't you like to know what I am going to do with you, Juliana? Where I'm taking you?"

She felt her stomach roiling, and slowly she turned her face away from him. Obviously he didn't realize what he had admitted. "No," she said dully, "I don't want to know."

For the first time, Jameson felt a bit worried. The girl's face was deathly pale. He rose slowly, but was wise enough not to approach her now.

"You will rest a bit, Juliana, then we will talk. I would suggest that you remain in this cabin. My men, as you can well imagine, are not always polite gentlemen."

He strode to the cabin door, looking over his shoulder at her before he left. She hadn't moved. He frowned. Then he heard the soft, broken sound of her sobbing, and was relieved.

Excellent, he thought as he left the cabin. She's resilient. She would have to be. He had two weeks to bring her around before they arrived in San Francisco. He wondered, eyes lighting with greed, how much money she would bring him. Then he felt the burning pain in his belly. It came more frequently now, particularly if he were angry or upset, or filled with anticipation, as he was now. He walked from the cabin, kneading his belly and forcing his mind away from the biting pain.

bonising pain in the belly. It came more frequently now, particularly in the very center of his body, and sometimes all the way round. He couldn't the other, therefore, and the doctors: the

2

San Francisco, California, 1854

"Come on, now, Willie, I'm not cutting your arm off, for God's sake! Stop your bellowing!"

"It hurts, Saint, bloody bad."

Saint stared down at the newly stitched gash on Limpin' Willie's arm. Good job, he congratulated himself. He picked up a bottle, saw Willie pale with fear, and began to talk. "Did I ever tell you about this stuff, Willie? No? Well, it's called iodine, and it's better than whiskey for what ails you. And cheaper. Yes, indeed, it was discovered way back in 1811 by a chap named Courtois, but there's controversy even about that, of course." Saint held Willie's arm over a basin and poured the iodine on the wound. Willie yelped and struggled, but Saint had three times his strength and wasn't about to ease his hold.

Saint continued calmly holding Willie's arm in an iron grip while he patted off the excess liquid. "Do you know what 'iodine' means, Willie? No? Well, part of it comes from the Greek word *ion* and it means 'violet.' Just look at your arm, as violet as can be. Now, you've come out of this not only patched up but educated as well."

Limpin' Willie had got his breath and bearings

back. He stared down at his purple arm. "Violet, huh, Saint?"

"The ladies will think you look like a bloomin' flower, Willie."

Limpin' Willie gave him a crooked grin, showing the inside of a mouth that contained only half its complement of teeth. "It still hurts like hell, Saint, but I'll live. Thanks, I owe you one."

"Actually, you owe me five. Dollars, that is. The rest, I'll take in a favor down the road."

"Anything, anytime, Saint." Willie paid his money and prepared to leave.

"Keep that bandage clean, Willie. And no picking pockets or bashing folk around for a while. And don't let the wound get dirty. Come back to see me in three days."

Willie took his leave and Saint stood silently for a moment in the doorway, shaking his head ruefully. Limpin' Willie was a Sydney Duck—one of that group of men from Australia who were criminals to their toes. But he was harmless as a puppy around Saint. At least Willie had had brains enough to come to him immediately. He shuddered to think what would have happened to that wound had Willie waited even a couple of days. He briefly imagined a one-armed pickpocket, and chuckled grimly.

He left his small house on Clay Street and made his way to Montgomery Street to the Saxton, Brewer and Company bank. Delaney Saxton was in conversation with one of his clerks, and broke off when he saw Saint.

"You've saved me, Saint," he called out. "Old Jarvis here is trying to talk me into something mighty suspicious."

"Send Jarvis to see Limpin' Willie. The poor fellow's out of commission for a while, a gash in his arm probably gained while he was trying to rob somebody. It'll do him good to use his brain for a change."

"Patched him up, did you?" Del asked. "I think the Sydney Ducks would elect you mayor if you wanted it. Lord knows there's enough of them, and all of them in your debt, right?"

"Banking and doctoring, we both collect debts, don't we, Del? How's Chauncey?"

"No longer just a mother, thank God," Delaney said, a satisfied grin on his lips.

"You take it easy, Del, you hear? Little Alexandra is only three months old. You give Chauncey all the rest she needs."

Delaney Saxton raised a sardonic eyebrow. "I? You know very well that my wife's insatiable, Saint. I have nothing to say in the matter." He bumped his fist against his forehead and shook his head. "Good Lord, what a man will tell his doctor! You're worse than a damned priest!"

Saint laughed, a rumbling sound deep in his massive chest. "Come on, boy, let's have some lunch. You're looking peaked."

"Boy? I'm the same age as you, old man." Del spoke briefly to his partner, Dan Brewer, then the two men strolled onto Montgomery Street. There was a light blanket of fog, typical for June in San Francisco, and it was chilly enough to appreciate vests under coats. They wove their way through the masses of humanity to Saint's favorite restaurant, Pierre's Culinary Establishment.

They both drank beers while waiting for Pierre's

bouillabaisse. "I wonder how Byrony and Brent are doing," Saint said after a moment.

"Knowing Brent, he won't write. He'll just show up in a couple of months, richer than he was when he left. Fact is, he should, of course, what with his father's plantation to deal with. In Natchez, isn't it?"

"That's what Byrony told me. Named Wakehurst. I wonder how the two of them will deal with all the slaves. I can't imagine Byrony liking the fact that people are actually owned. And Brent's been away from that kind of life for a long time."

"Well, I just hope he and Byrony mend their fences while they're gone. I'd sure like to see them united when they get back." Del paused a moment, shaking his head. "Ira and his dear half-sister, Irene, are still behaving with a bit of nastiness."

"You believe in divine justice, Del?" Saint asked.

"Not particularly. Why?"

Saint shrugged. "I think the Butlers are a bit over-due for it. It still upsets me to think of Byrony married to Ira and considered the mother of his half-sister's child."

"Incest," Del said with distaste, "is something I simply don't understand."

Saint didn't reply, his eyes on the huge serving of bouillabaisse Jacques had set in front of him.

Del said in an aggrieved voice, "I got about half as much as you, Saint."

"Well, you're about half my size, and besides—"

"I know. Pierre owes you favors."

"Yeah. Remember when he burned himself real bad a couple of months ago? I accepted payment in food. My housekeeper's cooking just can't compete with Pierre's."

Delaney laughed and spooned down a bite of the delicious fish stew. They spoke of their mutual acquaintances and compared impressions of new arrivals in San Francisco.

"More and more families, thank heaven," Saint said. "In a couple of years maybe we'll be rid of our rough reputation. Never seen so many horny men as in this city."

"Nor so many happy prostitutes. This is also a town where women can make their fortunes."

Saint grunted something that Del didn't understand, but he didn't ask for enlightenment. Saint didn't approve of prostitution.

"You want to come over for dinner tomorrow night?" Del asked after a moment. "Chauncey would like to see you, and Alexandra, of course."

"Sorry, but I'm kind of committed."

"Ah, the widow Branigan."

"Jane's a good sort," Saint said calmly. "Besides, one of her boys has a bit of a cold."

"Are you going to marry her, Saint?"

"You shackled men," Saint said with mock disgust, a twinkle in his hazel eyes. "None of you is happy unless all us carefree bachelors join you."

"Well, if you had a wife, you wouldn't have to take favors in food."

"Just because a woman has different parts, Del, doesn't mean she can cook."

Delaney laughed, and toasted Saint with the rest of his beer.

"Looks like you're a healthy young horse again, Joe," Saint said, ruffling the towheaded little boy's hair. "Not to worry, Jane," he said to Joe's mother,

23

who was hovering behind him. "The lad's just fine now."

"Thank you, Saint."

But Joe said, "I was hoping I'd get sicker. Mom said you might tell me why you're called Saint if I was sick enough."

"Maybe. No luck this time, Joe. What's that delicious smell, Jane?"

"Bouillabaisse," she said. "I heard you liked it."

Saint, who was filled up to his craw with that particular dish, stifled a groan and forced an agreeable smile.

It was close to ten o'clock before Joe and his older brother, Tyler, were finally tucked into their beds upstairs. Saint leaned back in his comfortable chair, his half-closed eyes resting for a moment on Jane Branigan. She was a fine-looking woman, he thought, with her coal-black hair and chocolate-brown eyes. A bit on the plump side, perhaps, but he was a big man, with big hands. The unbidden thought of his big hands covering her ample breasts and hips made him smile and his loins tighten. A man with big appetites.

"I know what you're thinking, Saint Morris!" Jane leaned down and kissed him lightly on the mouth. "You haven't a subtle bone in your big body."

"Probably not," Saint said with a lecherous grin. He pulled her down on his lap and laced his fingers together behind her back. Her breasts pressed against his chest, and he felt himself harden in response. "You're a fine woman, Jane," he said, the words rumbling deep in his throat, and leaned her back against his arm to kiss her. She responded with endearing enthusiasm, as she usually did, and before long his fingers were caressing her bare breasts. "Nice," he murmured. "Very nice indeed."

He felt her press her buttocks downward against him, and smiled even as he kissed her again, quite thoroughly.

They hadn't enjoyed each other in nearly a week and Jane discovered that she wanted him as much as he did her. In their urgency, they didn't consider going to Jane's bedroom. He took her on the carpet in front of the fireplace, kneading her full hips as he plunged into her warm body.

"Ah, Jane," he said some minutes later as he watched her face contort with her pleasure. "It pleases me so much when you do that." Then his huge body tautened as he surged into her.

Jane pulled an afghan over them, then snuggled against Saint's chest. "It's been too long," she said. "That was very nice."

"An understatement, woman," he growled, gently nipping her earlobe. "Now, Jane," he continued as he felt her hand glide down his chest, over his muscled belly. "I'm only a man, after all."

"Hmm," she said, caressing him in her hand. "Now, that, my dear, is the understatement."

It was close to midnight before they were dressed again and sitting at Jane's small kitchen table drinking tea.

He never spent the night with her because of her boys. Some nights, like tonight, when he was sated and sleepy, he thought fondly of holding her, her arms wrapped around his body.

"How's our little girl doing, Jane?" he asked, dismissing the thought as he sipped the delicious tea.

"Much better. She wants me to call her Mary, which I do, of course. She worships you, naturally."

"Excellent, but is her sewing good enough for you?"

"Yes. She's a bright girl and she wants nothing more than to please. She still likes to stay in the back of the shop, away from the customers, but I expect she'll gain some confidence soon."

"It might take a while, since most of your customers are men," Saint said. "You've got three women working for you now, right?"

"Yes, and business is booming. Lord, I think our little shop has made at least two thousand shirts since we opened last year, not to mention more flannel trousers than I care to count."

Saint pictured the fifteen-year-old Mary—her name in Chinese, he couldn't begin to pronounce—as she had been two months ago when he had saved her from being sold as a prostitute in a filthy crib down on Washington Street. She had been beaten for her unwillingness, and Saint had examined her carefully while she was unconscious. Luckily, she was still a virgin, but he could imagine that her maidenhead was only a technicality. Poor girl. He sighed, leaning back in the chair. So many poor girls, so many victims.

"I know what you're thinking, Saint," Jane said, closing her hand over his forearm. "You've done so much. It's just that the city is so very young and wild and there are so many men and—"

"And many of them rapacious bastards!"

"True, but things are changing, you know. You're not a rapacious bastard, and neither are many of your friends."

"Things won't really change until San Francisco is no longer a city of single men and prostitutes."

"More families are coming all the time," Jane said, making Saint recall his own words to Del Saxton. She lowered her eyes to her lap for a moment. "If only Danny had survived . . ."

"I know, Jane, I know. Your husband was doubtless a fine man. He sure picked a fine wife and made fine boys."

"But *some* gold wasn't enough for him," she said in a voice tinged with bitterness. "If only you'd been in that camp when he came down with pneumonia, things might have been different."

"I'm not a miracle worker. Now, we've talked ourselves into a depression, and that's no good at all, particularly after what you did to my poor body." She laughed, as he had known she would. He rose and stretched. Jane eyed him with wistful yearning. He was such a fine specimen of a man, she thought, her fingers tingling with the memory of his smooth flesh, the soft tufts of hair on his chest and belly. She was so lucky to have found him when she had. She watched him stride over to the sink. She loved the way his chestnut hair curled about his ears, the way his hazel eyes narrowed when he was concentrating. And she knew he didn't love her. They were good together, and, the good Lord knew, he'd helped her more than she could ever repay. Maybe someday, she thought.

"Let me fix this blasted pump, then I've got to get home," he said over his shoulder.

Saint was awakened at three o'clock in the morning by violent knocks on the front door. It was Caesar, from Maggie's brothel. One of the men, a stranger, had beaten one of her girls.

He cursed and ranted all the way to the Wild Star, Brent Hammond's saloon. The other half of the large building was a brothel, called Maggie's.

"Dammit, Maggie," he shouted as soon as he stepped into her sitting room. "How could you let something like this happen? Which girl got hurt?"

"Victoria," Maggie said. "The man is dead. Ceaser slit his throat. Come along."

Oh God, Saint thought as he stared down at Victoria, a pert, vivacious young woman who always had a ready smile for him, except now. One eye was already blackening, her upper lip was split and swollen, and she looked as pale as the sheet covering her.

"Hold still, Victoria," he said gently as he sat on the bed beside her. "It's just me, Saint."

Victoria closed her eyes, biting her lower lip to keep from crying out. His touch was gentle, but she hurt, badly. "Your jaw's not broken," Saint said. He pulled down the sheet that covered her. There were teeth marks on her left breast and an ugly bruise over her lower ribs. He probed as gently as he could, feeling her tense. "Try to relax, Victoria. I'll be done in a minute. Your ribs are fine, but you're going to hurt for a couple of weeks."

He drew the sheet lower, and sucked in his breath. There was blood clotted between her thighs. "Shit," he said very softly. "Maggie, fetch me some hot water and some clean cloths. Now, Victoria, tell me what the bastard did to you."

Victoria drew a shuddering breath and whispered, "He hurt me, Saint."

Dear God, I can see that well enough! "Why are you bleeding? How did he hurt you here?"

He listened to her jerking voice with growing anger. The man had dug his fist into her, tearing her. "He wasn't normal, Saint, and when I started yelling, he got crazy and hit me more." She stopped, and burst into tears.

Saint gently stroked her hair from her forehead, muttering soothing sounds to calm her as he waited for Maggie to return with the hot water. "It will be all right, Victoria. Just a few stitches, and you'll be fine, I promise." As he spoke, he remembered Maggie asking him once, teasingly, why he didn't want any of her girls. "I'd go to hell first," he'd told her, and he meant it. He knew, in all fairness, that Maggie was greatly upset now, for nothing like this had ever happened before. But dammit, something like this should never happen!

"All right, Victoria, I'm going to put you out for a while. It's just chloroform. You understand me? I just want you to breathe in, deeply. Don't fight it, now." She nodded, and closed her eyes as Saint gently placed the dampened cloth with its sweetish liquid over her nostrils.

He carefully stitched the torn flesh, then bathed her and pressed soft cloths against her.

"Thank you, Saint," Maggie said quietly when he rose. He said nothing until he'd pulled a sheet and blankets over Victoria's body.

"Would you like a brandy?"

He nodded, still looking down at Victoria. "She won't be out for much longer. Yes, a brandy is just what I need. Give her a bit of laudanum in water when she wakes up. And have one of the girls stay with her, Maggie."

He followed her from the room.

"This is damnable, Maggie," he said as he accepted the brandy snifter from her.

"I know." He saw the pain in her fine eyes, and just a bit of his anger melted. "I heard her scream, and ran into the room. The man . . . well, I smashed him over the head with a lamp, then called Caesar. The man wasn't really unconscious and he began struggling. He pulled a derringer, and Caesar killed him. Will she be all right, Saint, truly?"

"Yes, in time. I think, though, that you've lost yourself a whore."

Maggie winced at his term, but said nothing. It was true, no matter how one dressed it up fancy in one's mind. She shook her head and sank wearily onto a chair. "I'll see that she's well taken care of. But she's alone, Saint. Like all my girls, Victoria chose to be a . . . whore. Hell, she's getting rich off all the horny men in this city."

"I wonder what her choice is now?"

"I'll take care of her," Maggie repeated. "She's earned quite a bit of money during the past year. She'll be just fine."

And she'll probably go through life now never wanting another man to touch her. "She's going to need some close nursing for a couple of days. I'll see her tomorrow morning. Keep her quiet. I'll take the stitches out in a week or so."

"Thank you, Saint. Lord, I wish Brent were here."

"He and Byrony will be back soon enough. He couldn't have prevented what happened, in any case."

"No, I suppose not," Maggie said. She rose and

shook Saint's hand. "Thanks, Saint, for coming so quickly."

"What did you do with the bastard who hurt her?"

"Caesar dumped him somewhere, I don't know."

"I hope it wasn't in the bay. Wouldn't want the fish to get polluted by such scum."

"I owe you, Saint."

Saint grunted, too weary to argue or preach anymore.

He went home and drank half a bottle of whiskey before falling into oblivion near dawn.

3

Aboard the Sea Shroud

Juliana felt bile rise in her throat as she looked down at the tray of food Jameson Wilkes had brought her. In normal circumstances she would have wolfed down the delicious-looking beef and boiled potatoes.

"You will eat, my dear."

Her head jerked around at his very calm, hated voice. She'd seen him leave but hadn't heard him come back into the cabin.

"I can't," she said.

"I am prepared to make allowances for your shock, Juliana, but not when it comes to your health. I assure you that I will not allow you to become a skinny wraith. Now, eat."

"I'll vomit," she said viciously. "All over your beautiful cabin!"

"If you do," he said very softly, coming to stand beside the narrow bed, "I will let you spend your days up on deck in full view of my men. And you'll be stark naked, my dear."

She took a bite of the potatoes.

"That's better. You will finish all the food on your tray, every bit of it. I will be your dinner companion, so to speak."

"I have nothing to say to you, Mr. Wilkes—"

"You may call me Captain."

"Nothing at all, save to insist that you return me to my parents."

"You know, Juliana, you are really looking quite bedraggled. Your hair is encrusted with salt and tangled like a witch's mop. After you eat, I'll let you bathe. It will make you feel better, and undoubtedly make you appear more appetizing."

"I want to go home," she said, and he heard the break in her voice. She raised pleading eyes to his face. "Please, please, take me home."

"You seem like a bright girl, my dear, too bright to waste your energies begging for what I cannot do."

"Cannot?" she nearly yelled. "You mean you will not! What do you want with me? My parents have no money!" She choked on a bite of beef.

"Your show of spirit does not displease me," Jameson Wilkes said easily. "Would you like me to thump your back?"

Her eyes widened in terror and she shrank back against the headboard of the bed.

"Finish your dinner," he said, sitting back in his chair, his arms folded calmly over his chest.

Kanola, Jules thought, she's dead. He'll kill me too. She'd tried, during the long hours he'd left her alone, to reason out what was happening to her, but her grief and her fear had left her mind numb. She ate mechanically, chewing every bit of food ten times, as her mother had taught her to do.

When Jameson Wilkes removed the tray from her lap, Jules didn't move. She stared straight ahead at his shelves of books, saying nothing.

"Would you like to bathe first or shall I tell you where I'm taking you and why? You've gone mute on me, huh? Very well, my dear, listen well. We are bound for San Francisco, but I believe you already know that. As to your fate, I promise you it won't be so bad. You see, Juliana, I will sell you to the highest bidder at a very special auction. With your looks and your virginity, only a rich man will be able to pay the price. I venture to say that you'll be well treated. Indeed, I would say that the man who purchases you will keep you in some amount of luxury. In short, Juliana, you will be a rich man's mistress."

She looked at him blankly. "What do you mean, a man's mistress? You mean some man would hurt me?"

Jameson Wilkes could only stare at her for a long moment. Then he laughed. "A missionary's daughter," he said more to himself than to her. "How can you be so ignorant, having grown up in Lahaina? You do know what prostitutes are?"

"Yes," she whispered. "Terrible men pay money to debauch—"

"These so-called terrible men pay women money, my dear. And the native women are among the most unrestrained females most men have ever encountered. Now, a mistress is much more prized than a simple prostitute. A mistress is beholden to only one man. If she behaves well with that one man, she in turn is treated well—quite indulged, really. It is not a bad life."

"You would make me a prostitute, then?"

"You have the insistence to cut through euphemism. Yes, plainly, you will be a prostitute."

"But you said that prostitutes are willing to do what they do, that they—"

"Unfortunately, you will not have that choice," he

said abruptly, cutting her off. "But it is not impossible, Juliana, when the man who purchases you, let us say, eventually has had enough of your charms, that you could marry and settle down with children, or even return to Maui, if you wish it."

She heard Kanola's cries, but could only imagine how the men had hurt her before she'd managed to escape them and jump overboard. "I will not do it," she said.

"Ah, more spirit. I repeat, Miss Juliana DuPres, you have no choice in the matter."

"I do! I would kill any man who tried to hurt me!"

"And I, my dear," he said with deadly calm, "have two weeks to change that violent attitude of yours." He rose, staring down at her. "You know, you are almost lovely enough to tempt me. Ah, I see that such a notion repels you. Perhaps you believe me too old. But it is usually older men who are the rich ones. I will return shortly with your bath."

He left her alone. Jules looked toward the cabin door. It wasn't locked. But that fact gained her nothing. She had no clothes, and even if she did find something to cover herself with, there were all those sailors abovedeck. Even if she managed to escape them, what would she do? *Kanola jumped, knowing she wouldn't be able to make it to shore.* The thought was terrifying and impossible. She came up to her knees and stared out the porthole at the endless stretch of ocean. Miles and miles from anywhere.

Jameson Wilkes returned shortly. "Cover yourself well," he said to her, then stood aside as a sailor entered with a stout wooden hipbath, followed by two other men who carried buckets of steaming water.

The men's eyes slid hungrily toward her when they thought the captain wasn't looking.

Jameson closed the door behind them, then turned and said, "Your bath, my dear."

She could only stare at him.

"Come, now."

"Get out," she said.

"No," he said very gently. "This is your first lesson in obedience. Have you ignored the fact that it was I who stripped you? Come, I am well used to women's bodies, and will not lose my head over the sight of you."

"No."

She saw his expression change, and swallowed convulsively. She closed her eyes, humiliation and fear washing through her.

"Don't make me force you."

Slowly Jules rose from the bed, pulling the sheet with her. She walked to the tub, her eyes fastened to the soft Turkey carpet beneath her feet. She felt him jerk the sheet away from her.

Never in her life had another person seen her unclothed. Even her mother. Even Sarah, her sister.

"Get into the tub."

She did.

Although Jameson Wilkes had studied her closely and quite objectively when he'd first brought her unconscious to his cabin, seeing her lithe body in movement made his eyes glitter with pleasure. She was quite, quite lovely. His eyes traveled up the length of her long white legs, slender and beautifully shaped, to her hips. They weren't full and rounded, but he didn't expect that. She was too young and hadn't borne children. She looked coltish, but certainly not sexless. He mentally added another five hundred dollars to the price he'd already decided upon.

He handed her some perfumed soap. "Wash your hair well," he said, and returned to his chair.

Jules tried to hide herself from him, but it wasn't possible. Her breasts were plainly visible, no matter how she tried to curl down into the tub.

After some moments, there was a rap at the cabin door. Jameson Wilkes said quickly, "Don't worry. You will have your privacy. 'Tis just fresh water to rinse your hair."

Privacy, she thought, feeling what must be hysteria welling up in her, a condition she'd always considered the epitome of idiocy.

When he told her to stand up, she obeyed. He rinsed her hair thoroughly, then fashioned a turban around her head. He handed her a large towel and helped her out of the tub. He said nothing as Juliana quickly dried herself, then wrapped the towel around her. Her breasts, he thought, pleased, were nicely rounded and high, enough of a handful for any man.

He handed her a pearl-handled brush and comb.

Jules sat on the edge of the bed and began to untangle her wet hair. This is a dream, she thought, a nightmare, and I'll wake up soon, and shiver, then laugh at my own strange imagination. Then I'll go visit Kanola and play with her children . . .

"You know, your tanned face and shoulders will lighten up quite nicely, I think, after two weeks indoors. You'll be perfectly white all over. Nor," Jameson Wilkes continued, "will we have to darken your brows or eyelashes. All the redheads I've known have had to do so, you know."

Jules thought briefly of the faded daguerreotype of her French grandmother that her own mother kept well hidden from her father. She'd had dark brows, and her eyelashes appeared thick and curling, making her eyes look languid and quite sultry. Jules said nothing.

"Of course, such flame-colored hair as yours is unusual and not always natural. I much enjoyed assuring myself that it was natural."

She stared at him a moment, blankly.

"The very red curls between your thighs, Juliana."

This isn't happening, she thought frantically. It can't be happening!

He saw the horror in her eyes, saw her quickly duck her head down and stiffen. Excellent, he thought. She was no delicate, swooning maiden. She had pride, and backbone.

"I fear the next two weeks might prove a bit boring and confining for you, my dear. But there is no choice, really. I noticed that you were looking at my books. I have a good selection, I believe. Not many young ladies like to read, but I have a feeling that you are different from your sisters. Now, if you will excuse me, I have other duties to attend to."

Jules breathed a sigh of relief, then called out frantically, "I have no clothes! Please . . ."

"No, of course you do not. And you won't."

"But why?"

Jameson paused by the cabin door. "There are two reasons, Juliana. First of all, a gown would make you feel less vulnerable, less malleable, give you a confidence that would be illusory at best. Second, I want you to become used to being naked. You will be spending the majority of your time during the next months in your natural state, I would imagine."

"You are evil."

He quirked an amused brow at her. "Didn't you hear your minister father rant enough about the evil of men?"

"I didn't really believe him."

"Oh, incidentally, Juliana, the trunk containing my clothes is locked. I beg you not to try to pry it open. It is possible that such an act would displease me mightily."

He left her then, sitting on the edge of the bed, wrapped in the bath towel, her wet hair streaming over her shoulders. The pain in his belly sharpened a bit and he rubbed his stomach.

John Bleecher was walking beside her, and Jules knew he wanted to hold her hand. He was a nice boy—no, not a boy, she amended to herself, not any longer. He wanted to marry her. Her father wanted her to marry John. But Sarah didn't, nor did Jules. She would have paired John with Sarah in an instant, but people never seemed to behave as they should. Sarah would worship him, attend to his every word with flattering and sincere attention. Suddenly John turned, grabbed her upper arms, and planted a very wet kiss on her mouth.

Jules gasped, and began to struggle. But John didn't stop. His teeth ground against her lips, and she cried out. But it was no use, he was too strong.

"John, stop it, you idiot! How dare you . . . !"

Jules came suddenly awake, jerking upright in bed. The cabin was utterly dark. Her breathing was jerky, her head still filled with the image of John attacking her. But of course John Bleecher wasn't there. She was alone. John had kissed her once, most inexpertly, she guessed, and when she'd frowned at him, he'd let her be. And her mind had turned him into a monster. Like Jameson Wilkes. Like those sailors who had hurt Kanola. No, she thought, I must face facts. They'd raped her, like animals. And that was what was in store for her. She wasn't certain what that entailed, exactly, and she didn't want to know. She suddenly saw that ugly rod sticking out from the sailor's abdomen, and shuddered. She wouldn't think about it.

She lay back down, pulling the sheet to her chin. What am I going to do? Certainly there was no way to escape from this ship. But when they arrived in San Francisco . . . Surely she couldn't be kept a prisoner all the time. Surely when Jameson Wilkes tried to sell her, she could scream and fight and demand justice.

How many girls had he kidnapped? How many girls had he sold? What had happened to them? Were there more girls aboard his ship right now?

There were no answers, of course.

Jules fell asleep close to dawn. She woke slowly, feeling smooth fingers gliding up and down her bare arm. Her eyes flew open. Jameson Wilkes was sitting beside her, a bemused expression on his face.

"Don't touch me," she whispered, easing as far away from him as she could.

"That's something else," he said calmly. "I *will* touch you, often. You must get used to it. You must learn not to flinch or act terrified. Of course, the man who buys you will want a certain amount of innocence and timidity, but he won't want to have spent his money on a frightened, shrinking little virgin."

He reached for her again. Jules, without conscious decision, flew at him, her nails raking down his face before he could stop her. She pounded at him, her attack more effective because it was so unexpected. He finally grabbed her wrists and bent her arms behind her until she was biting her lower lip in silent pain.

"If you do that again," he said, anger tinging his usually calm voice, "I will bring in three of my most lecherous sailors and let them fondle you and kiss you." He shook her, tightening his grip until she cried out, unable to help herself. "Do you understand?"

She nodded.

He released her. He rose and walked to the small shaving mirror above the commode. "You drew a bit of blood."

"I would kill you if I could," Jules hissed.

He said nothing, merely washed the scratch on his cheek. "I believe I have your punishment," he said, his voice as calm as could be. "I had intended to give you another day or so ..." He broke off and shrugged. He strode toward her, and Jules, with a strangled cry, pressed her back against the headboard of the bed.

She struggled frantically, but soon she was lying on her back, her wrists bound securely above her head to the headboard. He very slowly drew off the sheet.

"There," he said. "How lovely you are, Juliana," he continued, studying her body. Jules closed her eyes tightly, so shamed and humiliated that she wanted to choke from it.

She felt his dry, cool fingers touch her breasts, and screamed, trying desperately to writhe away from him.

Jameson straightened, smiling. "You will remain thus, my dear, until it pleases me to release you. When you are ready to be more cooperative, I will untie your wrists. Now, I have some work to do and I shall stay here in my cabin."

He walked to his desk, sat down, and opened a ledger. She could feel his eyes on her. She wanted to die.

The days and nights blurred in Juliana's mind. She wasn't certain, but she believed it had been four days now since Jameson Wilkes had kidnapped her. It was afternoon, and something within her simply snapped. She would no longer be an obedient, biddable possession. She waited, not moving, until she heard Wilkes's footsteps coming toward the cabin. She knew his sound as well as she knew her own. When he entered, she very calmly struck him as hard as she could with an ivory bookend.

She stood a moment, staring down at his inert body. "Now, you pig!" She stripped him of all his clothes except his trousers. She couldn't bring herself to do that, though she'd planned to. She'd wanted him to feel as she did—humiliated, exposed, helpless. She donned his shirt, hating it because it smelled like him, then tied his hands behind him. In her fury, she kicked him hard in the ribs. Then she stood back, and the realization that what she'd done was for naught struck her hard, and she burst into frustrated tears. She heard the sound of footsteps coming toward the cabin. She raced to the door, but there was no lock. Slowly she backed up and waited.

Bob Gallen, first mate aboard the *Sea Shroud*, knocked on the door. There was no answer. He knocked again, calling to his captain.

Frowning, he opened the cabin door and stood stock-still for a moment, staring first at his unconscious captain and then at the motionless white-faced girl who was wearing his captain's shirt.

"Oh no," he said. He bent down to examine Jameson Wilkes. "He'll be all right, I think," he said, raising his eyes to Juliana. "Look, miss, I'm sorry about all this, but what you've done was utterly stupid. Jesus." Bob plowed his hand through his thick brown hair.

"Please," Juliana whispered, "please help me."

"I can't," Bob said. "Both of us would wish ourselves dead if I did." He quickly untied the captain's wrists and lifted him in his arms. He laid him on the bed.

"Get me into one of the boats, that's all I ask! Please!"

He shook his head. From the corner of his eye he saw the girl race toward the door. He caught her easily and pulled her back. He shook her.

"Don't, for God's sake! You're not stupid! You know what the men did to your friend, don't you, before she jumped?"

"I don't care," Juliana spat at him, struggling with all her might. "I hope he dies!"

"Look, Miss DuPres, I don't approve his taking a missionary's daughter, but I have no say in the matter. For god's sake, even if I managed to get you in a boat and away from the ship, you'd die soon enough."

"All of you are evil! God, I hope you die too!"

Both of them froze at the groan from the bed. As if mesmerized, Jules watched Jameson Wilkes slowly sit up and gingerly rub his head.

"Well, Bob, may I inquire as to the reason for your presence?" Before Bob Gallen could reply—a difficult matter in any case, since he felt strangled with fear—Jameson Wilkes continued, "Ah, I see the problem. You look charming in my shirt, Juliana. Did you strike me?"

"Yes, " she said, her voice shrill with fear. "I only wish I'd killed you."

Jameson Wilkes said nothing until the dizziness passed. "I underestimated you," he said more to himself than to her. "A mistake I shan't make again. Bob, you may leave now. I believe my faculties are sufficiently intact once more."

"Sir, really," Bob Gallen said, but stopped abruptly at the deadly calm threat in his captain's gray eyes.

He turned on his heel, not looking at Juliana again, and left the cabin, closing the door softly behind him.

Jameson Wilkes rose slowly from the bed. "Your modesty prohibited you from removing my trousers, my dear?"

Fear curdled in her stomach, but she knew she had nothing to lose. She would not cower before this evil man. She said with the best sneer she could manage, "After I got your shirt off, I saw how old and ugly you were. Do you think I would want to see more? You are repellent."

Jameson Wilkes was forty-one years old. He didn't consider himself either old or ill-formed. In fact, he prided himself on his body. He was lean, with none of the paunch at his middle that most men his age sported. At her words, he wanted to thrash her, but he controlled his impulse. He saw the fear in her expressive eyes, realized that her speech was all bravado, and reluctantly admired her for it. It had been years, he thought, since he'd thought of a woman as an individual, a being who was separate and distinct unto herself.

It was quite likely that the man who purchased her would be repellent. Probably fat, with sagging jowls. He allowed himself a few moments to feel regret, then quashed it.

He said in his usually calm voice, "Please remove my shirt, my dear."

Jules clutched the fine lawn material to her chest. "No."

He sighed. "If you do not remove the shirt this instant, I will call back my gallant first mate. He, I am certain, no matter what his chivalrous feelings toward you, will be pleased to see all your charms."

Jules felt the pounding in her temples—fear, outrage, determination. "I won't," she said. Quickly she leaned down and picked up the ivory bookend. "You come near me and I will kill you."

She didn't stand a chance, of course. He was on her in an instant, bending her arm in an iron grasp until she dropped the bookend. He practically tore the shirt from her and threw her none too gently onto the floor.

"You deserve to be beaten," he said as he pulled on his ripped shirt. "But I can't mark you. There isn't the time for you to heal. And no man would want to buy damaged goods."

All bravado was gone, stripped away as surely as he had stripped away her only clothing. She covered her face with her hands and sobbed softly.

Jameson Wilkes frowned down at her. Her glorious hair was in wild curls about her face and shoulders. Her white back quivered as she cried. Never before had he dealt with a female like her. For a moment he stood quietly, indecision written clearly on his face. He didn't want to break her, not completely, but he couldn't allow her to be a wild thing, either. He didn't doubt for a minute that she would never willingly allow herself to be raped by the man who would buy her. It would hurt his reputation badly were she to kill the as-yet-unknown man.

Then he smiled, his decision made. Without another word he lifted her from the floor and set her on the bed. He tied her wrists above her head and left her.

That evening when he brought her dinner tray, he said nothing to her of the afternoon's incident. He even allowed her to cover herself with the sheet while she ate.

"Do drink your wine, Juliana," he said. "It is from my own private stock, and quite tasty."

She shook her head.

"You've never tasted wine before?" he asked with mild interest. He rose and poured himself a glass. "Come, now, just a bit to see if you like it."

Jules, her mind numb and empty, raised the glass to her lips and drank. The deep red wine was rich and sweet. It sent welcome warmth all the way to her stomach.

Jameson Wilkes watched closely as she downed the entire contents of the glass. He smiled. "Excellent," he said.

It would take a while, he knew. He had no idea whether the amount of the drug he'd poured into the glass was correct. The old Chinese gnome who'd sold it to him had merely said that the dose "depended." On what? Jameson had wondered. Well, he thought, leaning back in his chair, he would soon see. The drug was a mixture of opium and other things, the old man had said, things that would make women utterly wild. Jameson wasn't certain that such things as aphrodisiacs existed. Certainly the myth about oysters was just that, a myth.

"We will be in San Francisco within a week," he said, cutting through the thick silence. "We're making excellent time, better than I'd expected. Did I tell you, my dear, that this was my last voyage to the islands?"

Jules was beginning to feel odd, somehow detached from herself. She heard his soothing voice, understood his words. She said slowly, her tongue feeling thick in her mouth, "I want to go home. I do not particularly like my father or my sister, but Lahaina is my home." She looked a bit startled at what she'd said, but continued in a soft singsong voice, "I collected flowers, and cataloged fish. I don't want to be a man's whore. I don't want to be like some of the women on Maui."

"You are a smart girl, Juliana. Perhaps the man

who buys you will indulge you in your interests. Perhaps you should consider how best to . . . endear yourself to your future protector."

"No," she said quite clearly. But Jameson Wilkes wasn't very clear anymore, and she blinked to keep him in focus. "My family would know." She realized vaguely that what she'd said didn't make any sense.

She saw he was smiling at her, and wondered at it. She also realized at that moment that she had to relieve herself. Always before, she'd been alone. "I must use the chamber pot," she said.

"Go right ahead, my dear."

Jules shook her head in confusion. "No," she said. "I can't, not while you're in here. Please leave."

This was interesting, Jameson Wilkes thought, studying her face closely. A loss of inhibition, an excellent start. "Of course you can," he said, his voice as soothing as smooth honey.

But still she sat there looking confused, bewildered. He said very gently, "I won't pay you any heed. Go ahead."

Jules eased off the bed and walked to the chamber pot, which was stored beneath a small cabinet. She didn't realize that she was quite naked. Nor did she pay any more attention to Jameson Wilkes. When she was finished, she turned, straightened, and stared at him.

To his complete and utter surprise, Jameson Wilkes felt a powerful surge of lust. He'd believed himself immune to her body—to any woman's body, for that matter. It was a heady combination, her standing so confidently before him, but her eyes dazed and confused.

"What do you feel, Juliana?" he asked, forcing himself not to move.

She shook her head, not understanding what was happening to her. "I don't know."

"Why don't you lie down? Surely what you're feeling will pass quickly enough."

She did, stretching languidly, her eyes closing. Her body felt tingly, strangely alive in places she'd never paid much attention to. But she wasn't frightened of the feelings.

Jameson Wilkes sat down beside her and carefully laid his hand on her breast. He felt her quiver.

He leaned down and caressed her nipple with his lips.

Suddenly she lurched up, crying out in horror. She began striking him with her fists.

I didn't give her enough, he thought as he subdued her. But now I know. Probably, his thinking continued, it was only the opium that had relaxed her so much, sent her into that otherworldly, detached kind of dream state. He'd seen it before.

"What did you do to me?" she yelled, struggling with all her might, even after he'd again bound her wrists.

"Why, nothing, my dear," he said easily. "Perhaps you're really a little whore at heart. Didn't you enjoy my touching you?"

She recoiled from him, from herself. She closed her eyes, not moving even when tears streamed down her cheeks.

Jameson Wilkes walked slowly to the cabin door. He'd won. He ignored the stabbing pain in his belly.

San Francisco

It was near to midnight. There was a quarter-moon, but the fog was so thick that the night looked an eerie gray. Saint had returned to his house thirty minutes before. He had an appointment with Hoot Moon, an unlikely criminal with a personality as unlikely as his name. As he settled down in his favorite armchair to wait for his visitor, he wondered what the man had to tell him. Hoot Moon owed him, as did many other of his friends, for Saint had, through sheer luck, saved the man's life when he'd been shot in the head. He heard a furtive knock on the front door and rose to answer it.

Hoot Moon quickly slipped into the small entrance hall. He was a small man, vicious to his victims but possessed of a strange sort of honor that made him as loyal as a tick to his friends. He counted Saint among his friends.

Saint watched him slip off his thick cloak. "Why all the secrecy, Hoot?" he asked.

"You told me to let you know if any slavers came in," Hoot said in his low, hoarse voice, the result of a knife wound in his throat many years before.

Saint felt himself stiffen. "Who and when?"

"Jameson Wilkes, the old scoundrel, he just got in yesterday. Word's out that he's got something besides just the usual count of little Chink girls for that Chinese madame, Ah Choy. He's got him a missionary girl, Doc, stole her in Maui. I can't say I rightly can hold with that, no siree."

Maui!

51

"I know you spent a couple years there, Doc, in Lahaina. I wanted you to know right away."

Saint felt such a surge of rage, mingled with fear, that he couldn't speak for a moment. He got hold of himself and said crisply, "Come on into the living room, Hoot, and let's have ourselves a drink. Whiskey."

Hoot scratched his ear and followed Saint. He downed the shot of whiskey in one quick gulp, then moved to stand by the fireplace to watch Saint expectantly.

"Now," Saint said, "tell me everything you know."

"He's having an auction tomorrow night, at the Crooked House on Sutter Street. He's really toutin' the missionary gal. He wants plenty of money for her, of course, her bein' a virgin and all."

"Is there a description of the girl?"

"Yep. Flame-colored hair and green eyes. About eighteen, I think, maybe nineteen. Beautiful, according to what I heard, and real white skin."

Saint went utterly still. Oh yes, he knew who the missionary girl was, all right. Juliana DuPres. Jules. Lord, she'd been only fourteen or fifteen when he'd left Maui. His little ruby jewel, he'd called her, ruffling her thick red curls, always out swimming and searching out new species of fish, or hiking to find new plants. She'd quickly become "Jules" after that. And she'd tagged after him like a puppy, that pert little face of hers filled with worshipful infatuation. He could have told her to go to the moon and she'd probably have done her damnedest to do as he wished.

Rage filled him and he felt his stomach heave. He rarely felt the urge toward violence, but he did now. He wanted to kill Jameson Wilkes with his bare hands.

But that wouldn't help Jules.

"Whatcha say, Doc?" Hoot asked after many minutes had passed.

"We've got to save the girl, of course."

"Old Wilkes is gonna ask a fortune for her, I'll bet."

"He'd be a fool not to," Saint said. He suddenly remembered the day he'd left Lahaina. Jules had stood on the dock waving frantically to him. He'd seen tears in her eyes even from that distance. Then he'd seen her father, the damned prig, pull her away roughly.

During the past two years, Saint had managed to buy four young Chinese girls from Ah Choy before they'd been debauched. But of course he didn't have enough money to buy Jules. God, what was he to do?

He said finally, "Hoot, find out exactly what hour the auction starts." He added quietly, "I think it's about time I called in some favors."

After Hoot Moon left as furtively as he'd come, Saint poured himself another whiskey and sat down again in his chair, his long legs stretched out in front of him, his fingers steepled. Until now he'd never involved his friends. There was always the chance of reprisals. Once before, two years ago, a friend had helped him, and had been recognized. He'd been found two days later with a bullet through his brain. But this time was different. He knew he could trust Delaney Saxton. After all, Del had saved his cook and housekeeper, Lin Chou, from one of those filthy cribs. Del, at least, cared. But Del was a new father. If he were recognized, there could be real trouble for him and Chauncey.

The criminal element in San Francisco knew no

social boundaries. Some of the wealthiest men were utterly rotten, and it was impossible to tell who was involved in what. As for Hoot Moon and his sort, they were petty criminals in comparison. And, oddly enough, Saint trusted them.

He could borrow money from Del Saxton and buy Juliana DuPres outright. But the thought of paying, at the very least, a good five thousand dollars to that scum Wilkes made him want to howl. No, he didn't want Wilkes to get a cent. He wanted to smash the man's face into pulp.

Somewhere near three o'clock in the morning, Saint decided he wouldn't involve any of his respectable friends. He'd call in the favors from the Sydney Ducks.

Jules felt calm. When Jameson Wilkes tried to auction her off, she'd scream, fight, tear the place down. Somebody would help her. Not all men were like him.

She was still a prisoner in Wilkes's cabin. After she'd decided what she would do, she spent a good deal of time staring out the porthole at San Francisco. They were docked at the Clay Street wharf, Jameson Wilkes had told her.

He'd put a lock on the cabin door. "Just in case you get any outlandish ideas, my dear," he'd said in that calm voice of his.

She'd asked him two days before, "Isn't there anyone you care about?"

Oddly enough, he'd stiffened alarmingly. But he'd said nothing, merely looked away from her as if seeing someone in the distant past.

It was dark now, and her nose was pressed against

the porthole. There were so many lights, and she could even hear the shouts of men in the distance. She didn't look around when she heard the cabin door open.

"Juliana, it is time."

Jameson Wilkes drew back a moment at the hatred he saw in her eyes. But it was more than that, he realized. There was determination as well. It didn't require a powerful intellect to realize what she planned to do. He shook his head, and there was a flicker of regret in his eyes. He felt a sudden burning pain in his belly and automatically began to rub his stomach.

He handed her a gown, no underthings or petticoats, just a gown that was of a filmy material and a garish crimson color.

Jules only stared at the gown. He'd forced her to bathe that afternoon and wash her hair. She was now standing before him, a sheet wrapped around her. She drew herself up and sneered. "Surely, sir, that gown is in dreadful taste. Won't your gentlemen friends want to purchase a female who looks more a lady than a whore?"

He laughed. "Take the gown, my dear."

"No, I won't!"

"If you refuse," he said, his voice as unruffled as always, "you will go before a roomful of men quite naked. It is your decision."

He calmly laid the gown on the bed, turned on his heel, and strode to the cabin door. "You have fifteen minutes, Juliana, no more."

She had no choice, none at all. She didn't disbelieve his threat. As she struggled to cover herself as best she could with the bright red dress, the memories of that night some five days before again filtered through her mind. Vague images, but they bothered her. She saw herself, as if through a haze, lying on her back, feeling strange sensations, feeling as though she were floating above her body, a body quite separate from her. Until he'd touched her breast—then she'd become herself again. She shook her head. It had made no sense. None at all. She raised her chin and waited for Jameson Wilkes to return for her.

She would best him. Oh, yes, she would.

5

The Crooked House on Sutter Street stood at the end of a cul-de-sac, and was, Saint knew, for all its rumored satanic rites and sexual perversions, nothing more than a whorehouse. A fancy whorehouse with only rich private members.

Members, he thought, shaking his head. That was almost funny.

He thought of Juliana DuPres and what she must be feeling. Terror, no doubt. He wondered if she'd changed much from that pert little straggly girl he'd known five years ago. So bright, she'd been, as bright as her flame-colored hair. He remembered her waiting for him several times outside the Seamen's Hospital on Front Street. If her damned father had known, he would have had a fit, of course, but somehow he'd never learned of those surreptitious visits. No matter how depressed Saint had been, the sight of her had always make him smile.

Saint came out of the shadows at the sound of an owl. Hoot, he realized, was in place, as were, Saint hoped, the other dozen Sydney Ducks. A villainous lot, the bunch of them, but he'd take them over the bastards inside the Crooked House any day.

Saint felt a gentle tugging on his arm.

"Doc, they've already auctioned off three Chink gals. Wilkes ain't to be seen, of course. It's Danvers who's doing the dealing."

Saint adjusted his full beard and his black wig. Because of his height, he could, by standing on a crate, see through a side window. He nodded to Limpin' Willie, eased up onto the crate, which wobbled a bit under his weight, and peered again into the room.

There were at least twenty men, all of them masked, seated in chairs facing a small stage. He'd heard about the anonymity, the major rule, and thus the black masks. It prevented blackmail and a certain amount of embarrassment, he supposed. The curtains behind the stage were black velvet, as were the draperies in the room itself. He felt his blood boil when another quite young Chinese girl was forced out from behind the curtain, her long silken black hair covering her small breasts. He heard muted conversation, heard that sharp-voiced bastard Danvers calling out bids. How many more poor unfortunate girls before Jules? he wondered, concerned that the crate would break beneath him.

Juliana was wrapped in a thick cloak, her hands tied behind her, a gag in her mouth. Jameson Wilkes was seated beside her, his face utterly emotionless. She'd seen around the curtain briefly, seen the masked men seated in the darkened room.

It was some sort of club, she thought, with men here for the express purpose of buying women. But she wouldn't give up. Wilkes had to take off this gag sometime; then she would scream. I'll fight, I'll yell and . . .

Wilkes removed her gag suddenly. "Drink this now, Juliana."

She stared at the glass of wine for a long moment. "Why?"

"It will make everything . . . easier for you."

"You had me drink wine before."

"Yes, and you will again, now."

She looked wildly about her. Two of Jameson Wilkes's men stood behind her. "No," she said, thrusting up her chin.

She felt the rim of the glass pressing against her teeth. She felt the wine seep into her mouth. She collected it, then jerked her head away and spat the wine full into Jameson Wilkes's face.

She saw the look of utter fury contort his features and said very softly, "Why don't you strike me, you bastard? But you won't, will you? You can't. You don't want to bruise your precious merchandise."

Jameson got a hold on himself. "You know, my dear, I'm tempted to feel a bit sorry for the man who buys you. But by then you will no longer be my problem." He looked at the two men. "Hold her head and keep her mouth open."

Jules struggled, but it was no use. She was forced to swallow the wine. She felt Jameson's handkerchief wipe off the drops that fell down her chin.

He stood back and stroked his chin. "Very nice. Keep breathing heavily. Your lovely breasts become all the more alluring."

"I hate you," she whispered. "You drugged the wine, didn't you? With more this time."

"Of course, but you knew that. You will be the most biddable creature imaginable by the time you're on that stage. Now, just sit quietly. I suspect that you'll be as plaint as I wish in another ten minutes." He chuckled a bit. "Do you know, I think I'll give your buyer a bit of the opium. Who knows, perhaps after you've been plowed, you won't need to be . . . convinced anymore." He saw the utter horror in her green eyes, and felt a nagging moment of indecision. No, he thought, he had to sell her. He needed the money, he needed what the money would buy for him. He no longer denied to himself that he wanted her, wanted her more than any woman he'd ever known. But it wasn't to be.

Saint could feel the change in the group of men. There was a surge of anticipation, and the men were speaking to each other in excited whispers, sitting forward in their chairs. He felt his breath catch in his throat. Juliana DuPres was gently led onto the stage. Her beautiful thick hair was loose down her back, a riotous mass of curls. He sucked in his breath at the sight of her. God, she'd changed, she'd become a woman. She raised her head at the instruction from Danvers, and he saw the vague, nearly disinterested look in her eyes. He felt rage flow through him, realizing that she was drugged. He heard excited voices call out:

"Lord, would you look at those breasts—white as the snow in the Sierras!"

"Turn her around and raise the hair off her back!"

"No missionary girl ever looked like that! Wilkes wouldn't lie to us, would he? Lord, she's made to be on her back!"

Saint forced himself to wait just a bit longer, until all the men were completely distracted by Juliana, their attention focused forward to the stage.

He felt sweat break out on his forehead. She looked like a puppet, lifeless and uncaring. Her eyes, glazed and vague, looked remarkably sensual, as if inviting a man to come to her.

He heard Danvers, the auctioneer, call out, "Well, gentlemen, we've a real prize here, a virgin prize. The bidding will start at three thousand dollars!"

The bidding had reached nearly five thousand when one of the men called out, "How do we know that you haven't pushed up those breasts of hers? Let's see them!"

"Yes! Strip her down!"

"Let's see those long legs!"

That was it, Saint thought as he watched the auctioneer reach out to pull down the awful gown from her breasts.

He let out a banshee's shriek, the signal, and slipped off the crate. Within seconds the Crooked House was pandemonium. He himself threw himself against the side door, felt the wood give instantly at his surge of power. From the corner of his eye he saw all the Sydney Ducks pour into the room, yelling obscenities and brandishing pistols and knives. He'd given orders that no one was to be killed. He didn't care about bashed heads or robbery.

He rushed toward the stage. The man who was guarding Juliana was flailing at two Sydney Ducks. Then Saint saw another man, an older man, and he knew it was Jameson Wilkes. He was striding toward Juliana, his face set and grim.

Saint smiled. He reached Wilkes just as he grabbed for Juliana. He looked him straight in the eye, saw his surprise, and sent his fist into Wilkes's jaw. He watched with intense satisfaction as the man crumpled to the floor.

"Juliana," he said, lightly touching her arm.

She looked at him with no recognition at all. He grabbed her hand, and suddenly she began to struggle. He cursed softly to himself, aware that he had to get her out of here quickly. "Forgive me, Jules," he whispered, and sent his fist into her jaw. He caught her against him and quickly lifted her into his arms. Just as he slipped out of the smashed side door, he let out three sharp hoots. Within moments the raiders had fled from the Crooked House, leaving its members staring at each other, some of them bleeding and robbed, their voices bewildered and enraged.

Saint pulled off his cloak and wrapped it around Jules. She felt so slight in his arms, he thought inconsequentially as he ran from the alleyway. He increased his pace, realizing that some heads had been knocked together. With his luck, he would soon have some patients to attend to. He had to hurry.

He made it to his house in just over ten minutes. He nearly laughed aloud with relief as he slammed the front door closed behind him. Moments later, he was carefully lowering Jules to his bed. Quickly he ran his fingers over her jaw. She would have a bruise, but that was all. She was still unconscious, but he imagined it was the drug—opium, likely—that was keeping her under. He had just covered her with blankets when he heard a knock on the door downstairs.

He closed his bedroom door, praying that she wouldn't waken from her drugged sleep. He ripped off his ridiculous disguise and loped down the stairs.

He treated three gentlemen. When they left the

reason for their cut lips, bruised jaws, and cracked ribs delightfully vague, Saint had a difficult time not laughing in their faces. His last patient was Bunker Stevenson, an upright, very wealthy citizen. "Damned misunderstanding over cards, Saint," Bunker said, and Saint forced himself to remain silent and make clucking sympathetic noises. He listened to Bunker go on and on about the poker game, and wondered finally if he weren't, perhaps, telling the truth.

The other two men weren't from San Francisco. Saint wasn't at all gentle in his treatment, and smiled when one of them yelled when he tightly bound his cracked ribs.

It was nearly an hour before Saint returned to his bedroom. He lit a lamp and stood over the bed a moment, staring down at Juliana DuPres. Her hair was in glorious disarray around her head. "You've changed, little one," he said softly, sitting beside her. Very gently he pulled off the blankets. He knew he had to make certain she was all right, and wanted to do it before she awakened. She'd be embarrassed enough as it was.

He drew a deep breath, and for one of the few times in his professional career was very aware that his patient was a woman. Stop it, Saint! You're a bloody doctor, not a rutting bastard!

He stripped off the gown, not surprised that she was naked beneath it. The thought of what would have happened to her made him grit his teeth. I will not look at her, he thought. He gave her a cursory examination, felt his hands trembling, cursed himself soundly, and put her in one of his nightshirts—a nightshirt Jane had made for him that he'd never worn. It was like a huge white tent on her slender body. After he'd covered her again, he gently slapped her cheeks. "It's time to wake up now, Jules. Come on, wake up, don't scare me."

Jules heard a voice, a man's voice, speaking sharply to her, but she didn't want to leave the blessed security of sleep. The voice continued and she felt light slaps on her face.

"No," she muttered, trying to pull away.

"Wake up, Jules!"

Slowly she opened her eyes. She saw a man leaning over her, heard him call her name. He'd called her Jules. That was odd. Jameson Wilkes didn't know her nickname.

She blinked, trying to bring the man's face into focus.

But she felt so leaden, so disconnected. He bought me, she thought suddenly, he's the man who paid for me! She reared up, wildly striking out at him.

Saint closed his hands around her shoulders and pressed her back down. "Don't be afraid, Jules. It's me—Michael. You're safe now. You're with me." She didn't respond for a moment, and he continued softly, "Do you understand, Jules? You're all right now, I promise you."

"Michael?" she whispered, trying to focus her mind on his words.

Michael, he thought. Only Jules had called him Michael, and not Saint, and he'd remembered. "Yes, it's Michael. You've been drugged, little one, but it will pass soon now."

"Michael," she said again. Suddenly she knew who he was, and she felt a bolt of incredible, unexpected happiness surge through her. She nearly gasped aloud with pleasure and relief. "Oh God, it must have been a dream, a nightmare. All of it . . . it was nothing. You're with me again. You've come back to me."

Saint blinked, but had no chance to respond. Jules threw her arms about his chest, burying her face against his shoulder. She said over and over, "You've come back to me. I always prayed you would. You don't know . . . so long since you left me, so long."

"No, no," he said gently, lightly touching his fingertips to her lips. "We're not on Maui, Jules. We're in San Francisco."

But she was clutching at him, whispering, "I always loved you, always. You came back to me."

He grasped her arms and gently drew her away. He looked into her face and told himself that she didn't realize what she was saying. "Listen to me, Jules. We're in San Francisco. I . . . well, I got you away from Jameson Wilkes and that godawful auction. You're safe with me now, in my house."

"You saved me, Michael?" She reached for him again, and he eased her against him, gently rocking her. He pressed his cheek against her wildly curling hair. "You really saved me?"

"Yes, and you're safe now."

Jules felt his large hands stroking down her back, pressing her more closely against his chest. She felt no fear. She felt secure and warm and happy. Her thoughts were tangled, the past intermingling with the present, and all she could grasp was her love for this man. "I love you, Michael," she whispered yet again. "You saved me."

"No, Jules, you don't love me," Saint managed. "Hush, now. Would you like a glass of water?"

She didn't want water. She wanted Michael. She'd wanted him forever, it seemed now. He was holding her, caressing her. His hands were making her feel strange sensations—very pleasant, mysterious sensations that she didn't want to stop. She raised her hand to lightly touch his face. "Michael," she whispered. She raised herself and kissed him.

Saint stiffened, appalled at what was happening. It was that damned drug Wilkes had given her. He had to get away from her. He felt her soft lips and experienced a surge of desire for her.

"Jules, no," he began, but she pressed herself against him and he felt her breasts full and soft against his chest.

"I've always loved you, Michael, and now you've saved me. I belong to you. Please, Michael."

Please what, for God's sake? He struggled for reason. "Listen to me, Jules. You've been drugged, sweetheart. It's the opium that's making you act and feel like this. We've got to—"

Her soft mouth covered his again, and he heard his own low moan. He didn't know how it happened, but he was lying on the bed, Jules clutched against the length of him. "Dammit!" he said aloud. He tried to hold her still, but she was writhing against him, pressing herself more closely, as if she wanted to become part of him. He had to do something, dammit! What had that bastard Wilkes given her? What had been added to the opium?

He drew a ragged breath. He knew she was beyond reason, caught in a dream world of urgent passion. He also guessed that if it had been anyone else who had saved her, this wouldn't be happening. But he was her Michael from five years ago, and it was all tangled in her mind. But none of it was real, none of it.

"Jules," he said, feeling utterly desperate.

She moaned softly. "You'll never leave me, will you, Michael? Promise me that you'll never leave me again."

"I promise," he said.

She became more demanding, more feverishly urgent. He should leave her now, but he couldn't. He closed his mind to his own appalling desire. "I'll help you, Jules," he said, his voice so ragged that he could barely understand his own words. He let her kiss him, let her move against him. Very slowly he eased his hand beneath the nightshirt. Her flesh was warm and smooth under his fingers. He closed his palm over the springy curls and gently pressed. She moaned, jerking against him.

"I'll help you, sweetheart," he said again, his words flowing into her warm mouth. His fingers found her, and he closed his eyes at the pleasure of it. She was warm, and moist, and frantic. Within moments he felt her convulse, felt her legs stiffen, heard the wild cries erupting from her throat. He gazed into her face and saw the bewildered look in her dazed eyes, the confusion, then the release. Then she became still, slumping into him.

He forced himself to ease his hand away from her. "It's all right now," he said against her temple. "Everything is all right now."

And it was, at least for her. She fell asleep in his arms, her breathing soft and regular. Her last softly blurred words were "I love you."

Saint didn't move for a long time. Dear Lord, he thought, I never expected this. He felt his manhood, rigid and throbbing against her belly. Stop it, you ass, he whispered to his enthusiastic member.

I love you.

No, he told himself over and over in the quiet room, she didn't, she couldn't. She was confusing the past with the present. A young girl's infatuation had melded with a woman's needs, and the drug had made her lose all sense of reality, of rightness. But the passion in her ... He knew she'd never felt a woman's release before.

He felt the soft contours of her body, breathed in the pungent, musky perfume Wilkes had made her use. He felt weariness begin to overtake him, despite his still-rampant desire. Before he fell into a light sleep, he realized that he had a very real problem. Juliana DuPres was now his responsibility. What in God's name was he going to do?

On the heels of that thought, he heard again her soft cries of pleasure, and his fingers tingled with the memory of her swollen moist woman's flesh. Would she remember in the morning? Remember what she'd said to him and what he'd done to her?

For his own peace of mind, he hoped she wouldn't.

6

Juliana cried out softly in her sleep when Saint moved away from her, and he whispered, "Just a moment, Jules. I'll be right back, I promise you."

He quickly pulled off his boots, then, unable to help himself, turned to look down at her for a long moment. He wished he could see her as the young girl of five years before, but it wasn't possible, of course. He'd touched her, given her a woman's pleasure, the first time she'd experienced such intense feelings, he thought again, and it pleased him that he had been the first man to bring her to passion. He could still see the dazed astonishment in her eyes when her body began to convulse in pleasure. He closed his eyes against the image, but only managed to see himself holding her against him, caressing her, knowing her. And he'd been involved in her feelings—no way around that, even though he hadn't . . . Well, enough of that thinking, you idiot.

As he leaned down to douse the lamp, his eyes took in the long slender lines of her body encased in his ridiculous nightshirt. If only, he thought, he'd met her for the first time this evening, rescued a stranger from Wilkes, not his Jules. But she was alive in his past, warm and loving and vivid, and his memories of Lahaina were rich because of her. He pulled her under the covers and into his arms, settling himself on his back.

I won't feel guilty about it, he said to himself as he stared up toward the darkened ceiling of his bedroom. I simply did what I had to do. A strange cure for a doctor to employ, he thought, and that made him smile. Then why did he feel a nearly painful throbbing in his damned groin? Sex, he thought, made a man foolish; it overpowered his brain and complicated things. Well, there was going to be nothing complicated about this. But he pulled her closer, and his last thought before he fell into a light sleep was that she had to bathe away that awful pungent perfume.

He dreamed about an afternoon that he'd thought long forgotten, an afternoon some six years before. He was walking along beside his young friend, his step automatically shortened to match hers, not at first realizing that she wasn't behaving normally.

"The bird of paradise is so forceful," Juliana said, stopping a moment to sniff and lightly touch the vivid flower. "All sharp lines, beautiful colors, of course, but it's not delicate like the hibiscus."

This was her fifth stop to admire flowers. He'd had lectures from Jules on all the flora on Maui over the three months he'd known her. He was hot, tired, and wanted to go swimming, so he stopped her.

"Enough about the graceful hibiscus. Let's get into the water and you can show me some blackspot sergeants."

To his surprise, she ducked her head down, and a small "No" barely reached his ears.

"But you always want to go into the water," he said, patting her shoulder.

She raised her face for just a moment, and he was startled at the strange look in her eyes.

"Jules," Saint had said finally, giving her his full attention. "What's all this about? You've been acting strangely, I can't get you to go swimming with me, all you've wanted to do is prattle on about flowers. Now, what's going on?"

To his further surprise, a scarlet flush mounted her cheeks. He waited patiently, watching her pleat her cotton skirt with nervous fingers.

At last he said again, "If you're not going to talk to me, we might as well get me out of my misery and go swimming. What do you say? Want to change your mind? I'll make sure you don't get too much sun. Where is your sarong?"

Her head shot up and she blurted out, "I can't!"

He stared down at her thin, intense face, surrounded with the riotous red curls. She looked as though she wanted to sink into the soft grass beneath her feet. He frowned, curbing his impatience with her; then understanding hit him, and he wanted to laugh. But he said quite gently, taking her hand in his large one, "Come over here and let's sit down a minute. It's a great view, don't you think?"

He felt her hand trembling, felt her pulling back, but paid her no heed. So it was her monthly flow, he thought. Perhaps he should simply ignore it and leave her on the beach while he swam. But she looked so strange; perhaps she wasn't feeling well. Once they were seated on a flat volcanic rock, he said matter-of factly, "I'm your friend, and more than that, I'm a doctor. Your doctor. Now, talk to me."

She wouldn't look at him. "I'm dying," she said simply, her girl's voice high and thin and resigned.

He blinked, looking at her profile sharply. "What the hell does that mean?" Even as he spoke, he realized suddenly that this must be her first time. She was thirteen, and he hadn't realized, hadn't considered that she . . . He felt a fool, a big bungling one.

"Jules, you're not dying," he said. "You're bleeding, aren't you, for the first time?"

She looked at him, aghast, and her tongue flicked over her lower lip. "Yes," she whispered.

In that moment he wished he could see that wilting, pallid mother of hers and shake her until her teeth rattled for being such a damned prude. He proceeded in a calm, practical voice to explain to her the process of becoming a woman. "Do you understand now, Jules?" he finished. "There's nothing to be worried about, I promise. You're just fine. It's all very natural."

"You mean I'm going to do this *forever*?"

He bit his lip at her horrified tone. "Well, not forever, but for quite a few more years."

"But I want to go swimming!" she wailed, very much the thwarted child again.

He laughed and ruffled her hair. "You're just going to have to watch me for a couple more days. You don't hurt at all in your belly, do you?"

"Yes, but I don't care. I don't like this, not at all! It's not fair!"

He hadn't thought about it in that way. "No," he said thoughtfully, "I guess it's not. But then again, Jules, I can't have babies. Do you think that's fair?"

He'd watched her playing with one of the native

women's infants the previous afternoon, and enjoyed her maternal display. But she didn't take the bait, and repeated stubbornly, "It still isn't fair. You can still be a father, and that's almost the same thing. And you can swim all the time, all year around."

So much for that argument, he thought. Thank God, she at least knew where babies came from, at least had a general notion. He supposed he should tell her that she could swim, but he could just imagine what she'd say to that.

Saint turned in his sleep, suddenly uncomfortable, then awakened with a start. There was a soft, pliable body pressed against him, a slender leg, knee bent, flung over his belly. Saint blinked away the dream. It was dawn, dull morning light filtering through the bedroom window. Slowly he raised a hand and smoothed her tangled hair away from his face. She wasn't a child anymore, hating what her body had done to her because it kept her from being a mermaid for five days. Why had that ridiculous dream come to him anyway? Because it was sexual in nature, he realized, even though at the time he'd merely been a good friend talking reassuringly to a young girl. Nothing more.

Saint suddenly realized that he was hard again, his manhood pressing against her thigh. Damned randy goat. He had to get away from her, get things back into proper perspective. As he slowly eased out of her hold, he wondered if she still remembered that long-ago afternoon, and her girl's embarrassed confession, and her outrage at the unfairness of it.

She slept on, murmuring a bit, but not stirring.

Perhaps, his thinking continued as he bathed and shaved in the small bedroom down the hall, he'd had that dream as a guide. Yes, that was it. If she remembered her wild behavior of the previous night, he would simply treat it as naturally as he'd treated her young girl's first monthly flow. He was still her friend, and her doctor. Nothing more.

She slept on even after his housekeeper, Lydia Mullens, arrived. He joined Lydia in the small kitchen, telling her about their guest over a cup of scalding black coffee. He told her what had happened the previous night, omitting only what had happened after he'd brought her here. He also mentioned that he'd known Jules when he'd lived in Lahaina.

Lydia looked aghast. "Wicked," she said finally, shaking her gray head. "I've heard of the Crooked House, of course. You did a fine thing, Saint, yes, a fine thing." She looked toward the ceiling, a frown crinkling her brow. "Poor little mite. What are you going to do, Saint?"

He downed the rest of his coffee, and rose from his chair. "An excellent question. Right now, I want her to wake up. Lord only knows how much opium that bastard gave her.

"I'll cook up a big breakfast for her," Lydia said. "Good food will clear out her system."

Saint nodded, and walked from the kitchen. Lydia stared after him, a thoughtful look in her sharp blue eyes. She was fond of Saint, more than fond, she thought. He was like a son to her, a son to be proud of. She thought of her only son, dead now for three years. Rory had wanted gold so much, too much, and he'd died of dysentery in a wretched mining camp near Nevada City. And she'd come here alone with practically no money. She'd worked in the Stevenson home for two months, until the daughter of the house, Penelope, drove her so distracted she'd simply walked out. She blessed, every now and again, that awful cold she'd gotten, for it had given her Saint. And now there was a girl upstairs, a young girl who had dropped into his life out of his past.

She turned slowly away from the table and began to lay strips of bacon into a skillet. Saint needed a wife, but first she had to get to know this Juliana DuPres.

Jules felt a hand on her shoulder, gently shaking her, heard a soft man's voice speaking to her. She froze inwardly, terror consuming her, until her mind, less dull and heavy now, forced her to open her eyes. She saw Michael leaning over her, his face concerned, his eyes intently studying her. She felt so sluggish, it was an effort to keep her eyes open. Michael, she thought. He was here, with her. It didn't surprise her.

"How do you feel, Jules?" he asked, taking in the physical signs as he spoke. He knew how she felt without having to ask.

"I remember," Jules said, trying to weave her wayward and tangled memories together.

He tensed, afraid to say anything.

"Is Jameson Wilkes dead? Did you kill him?"

He was relieved at her tone—angry, aggressive. "No, but I did slam my fist into his face. I don't imagine he'll feel very well for a while."

"Yes," she said again. "I remember. He drugged me, forced wine down my throat when I refused to drink it." She fell silent, her brow furrowed in concentration. "I remember now that you hit me. My jaw hurts."

"I'm sorry, Jules, but I had to get you out of there fast. I think you believed I was one of those bas . . . rotten men, and you fought me."

"Well, I just hope that you hit Wilkes much harder." She yawned, and raised her hand to cover her mouth. She paused, staring at the long sleeve that fell over the tips of her fingers. She looked at him, puzzled.

Saint became all professional. "I'm a doctor, Jules. I had to make sure you were all right. That's one of my nightshirts, my only one, in fact. It's yours until I can buy you something else."

His very bland, cool tone would have worked if she hadn't spent two weeks faced with what men did to women. He'd stripped off that awful gown. He'd seen her naked. She'd seen Wilkes's leering looks when she'd been without any clothes in front of him. How had Michael looked at her? It was too much. Tears shimmered in her eyes and began to course down her cheeks.

"Jules! Come on, now, sweetheart. That's no way to greet an old friend after five long years."

He wanted to hold her, to comfort her, but he held himself still. He said roughly, "Buck up, Jules, the world hasn't ended. Nothing happened. You're safe here. Don't turn into a watering pot on me now." *God, at least I pray nothing happened.*

She sniffed, trying to swallow the tears, and dashed the back of her hand across her eyes. "You're right," she said. "You're not like Wilkes."

"No," he said very gently, "I'm not."

"I don't understand how you saved me," she said, her attention wandering inward even as she spoke. Something was gnawing at the back of her mind, but she couldn't remember what it was.

"I was told by one of the Sydney Ducks that Wilkes had a missionary's daughter from Lahaina. When I heard the description, I knew it had to be you. The rest was planning, that's all."

He saw that she was frowning at a point beyond his shoulder. He waited patiently, knowing that if she remembered the happenings of the previous evening, he would simply have to deal with it.

Jules said abruptly, her eyes suddenly intent upon his face, "You haven't changed at all, Michael. You're still large and hard and handsome, and your eyes still crinkle."

He wished she'd used some word other than "hard." "I'm nearly an old man now, Jules."

"Ha! You're ten years older, that's all. I remember you used the same argument on me when I asked you to marry me at the advanced age of fourteen." She flushed at her words. A child's words from the past. Something nibbled insistently at the edge of her thoughts, but she couldn't seem to grasp it, to understand. It was frustrating and disconcerting. Slowly she raised her hand to touch his face. "You still feel like you used to," she said. Then suddenly she said, her voice intense, "I dreamed you came back to me in Lahaina, and we were together again."

"A dream," he said cautiously. "And I did come back to you, in a sense."

"Yes, I suppose. Your eyes are so beautiful. The hazel is so much nicer than my . . . slime green."

He laughed at that. "Oh no, not slime, Jules. Don't you remember how you got your nickname?"

She smiled, two dimples deepening in her cheeks. "Yes, but it's you who have forgotten, Michael. My nickname is from my awful hair, not my eyes."

He remembered the young girl telling him that she hated the name Juliana, and he'd said, looking at her glorious, wildly curling hair, "Why not 'Jules' then? That's close enough to 'jewels,' and that's like your hair. All right?"

"Not slime," he repeated, smiling gently at her. "Your eyes, like your hair, are jewels, green jade in this case."

"You make me sound like a gawdy piece of jewelry. Rubies and jade!" She paused a moment, then said, nodding, "I like the jade. That makes me sound exotic."

He heard Lydia call up and frowned. They'd spoken of nothing really. But at least she was responding to him normally. He said, "There's the sterling voice of my housekeeper, Lydia. I told her about you, Jules, and she's made you breakfast. Are you hungry?"

"Yes," she said, surprised. "You know, I really am. For the first time in a long while."

He saw a flash of pain in her eyes, but for the moment he ignored it. "Let me invite Lydia up to meet you. You'll like her."

Jules did like Lydia, but the housekeeper clucked over her until finally Saint sent her out of the room.

Some minutes later, Saint was thinking between bites of fluffy scrambled eggs that she was responding much better than he'd believed possible. And her eyes were brighter; she was more alert.

And she was so damned beautiful that it made him ache just to look at her. And she was in his bed, and not fourteen years old anymore.

When Lydia came back to remove the breakfast trays, she looked closely at Jules. "Good, you did justice to my food. You let Saint take care of you, young lady."

"You and that crazy name," Jules said.

"No one else calls me Michael," he said. He reached out his hand to touch her jaw. To his consternation, she jerked away from him, her eyes widening in terror.

"I'm sorry, Jules," he said, immediately dropping his hand. He forced a rueful grin. "I just want to feel your jaw. I did smack you pretty hard."

Get hold of yourself, and stop acting like a ninny! He's not Jameson Wilkes! "I'm being stupid," she mumbled, trying to make herself relax.

"No, you're being very brave. I'm proud of you."

She gave him a pitifully hopeful look that made him flinch inwardly. "I'm glad you haven't changed," she said. "You may feel my jaw. I won't be silly anymore."

She leaned forward and watched his face as his fingers, long, blunt, yet so gentle, touched her sore jaw. Without conscious thought, she leaned against his fingers, years of absolute trust inherent in the simple movement.

Saint felt a treacherous weight descend. She was so vulnerable, so unsettled and confused, and he was her anchor. He looked at the gentle arch of her slender neck. So delicate, he thought, so fragile. He drew his hand away, appalled at himself. Again.

She smiled at him, a dazzling smile. He sucked in his breath. "You've turned into a beautiful woman, Jules," he managed.

"Me?" She laughed incredulously. "Well, maybe passable. John Bleecher did want to marry me, you know," she added on a mischievous grin.

"Bleecher? The planter's son? That gangly boy who had pimples?"

"Yes, but now he doesn't. And besides, I didn't want to marry him, so I'm not certain if that counts or not."

"Just why didn't you want to marry him?"

Jules frowned. "Kanola asked me the same thing . . ." She broke off abruptly, memory flooding her. Kanola was dead. She felt tears well up. She turned her face away.

"What's wrong, Jules?"

"Kanola's dead. Wilkes's men . . . hurt her, I know it. I saw them holding her down and she was fighting them. She's dead."

He closed his eyes a moment against her pain. Had Jules seen her friend raped and murdered? He wanted to ask her how Wilkes had captured her, but at that moment he heard a knock on the front door. A patient. Damnation! "Jules . . ." he began.

It was someone sick to see him, she thought. I've got to stop acting like a helpless child. She swallowed the bitter bile and forced a smile. "I'll be all right."

"I'll be back up as soon as I've seen my patient." He rose. "I want you to rest, Jules. We've got to clear the opium out of your system."

"Can I have a bath, Michael?"

"I'll send Lydia up," he said, and left the bedroom, gently closing the door.

He felt a spurt of rage to see Bunker Stevenson waiting for him in his surgery. He still wasn't certain that Bunker hadn't been one of the men at the Crooked House. He said shortly, "I'll be with you in just a minute, Bunker." He pulled Lydia into the hall. "No one is to know she's here. Can you help her bathe, Lydia? I'll figure out what we're going to do."

Lydia looked at him sharply. "Bunker wasn't one of those men, was he?"

"I'm not sure," Saint said tersely. "I can't very well ask him, I suppose."

"I'll see to the child."

Child, hell, Saint thought as he walked back into his surgery.

7

"It's jasmine," Lydia said as she poured a bit of liquid into Juliana's bathwater.

"Anything would be better than what I smell like now." *Gentlemen like this scent, my dear. But don't use too much. It's very potent.* When he'd turned away, she'd poured nearly the entire bottle on her shoulders and chest and the skirt of the gown. She'd thought he would strike her, but he hadn't. He'd pulled the gown to her waist and bathed the heavy musk from her body.

The girl's words were true enough, Lydia thought. She wondered if Jules had been raped, but didn't ask, of course. She helped her out of Saint's nightshirt and into the porcelain tub.

"You need more flesh," Lydia said.

Jules winced, remembering all the food Wilkes had tried to tempt her with. "Yes," she said in a clipped voice, but it didn't occur to her to try to cover herself. He's changed me, she thought. She wasn't at all embarrassed that Lydia was helping her, seeing her with no covering but her hair.

"You'll need some clothes," Lydia said as she helped Jules lather her long tangled hair.

"Yes, Michael said he'd get me some."

"Michael?" Lydia asked, a brow raised.

Jules smiled a bit at that. So he was still close-mouthed about his given name—Ulysses Michael. "That's his real name, at least part of it." When he'd told her his name one afternoon so long ago, she'd announced that she preferred "Ulysses" and burst into gasps of laughter. "Michael," she thought now. Such a kind name, a full name with depth and complexity. "Does everyone call him Saint?" she asked Lydia.

Lydia smiled. "Yes, and I'll just bet I can blackmail him now. You see," she continued at Jules's puzzled look, "everyone wants to know what his real name is and he won't tell. Nor will he tell anyone how he got the nickname Saint."

"I know," Jules said. I'm acting normally, she thought. I'm sitting in a bathtub in Michael's house in San Francisco, and I'm acting like nothing at all happened to me.

"Well, if you decide to tell me, I'll doubtless become a rich woman by selling that tidbit," Lydia said. "Here, dear, let me rinse your hair."

When Juliana was tucked back into bed, she said to Lydia, "Michael told you about me?"

Lydia heard the shame in the girl's voice, and patted her hand. "Yes, he did. I hope you don't mind, for I'll never tell a soul. Saint will take care of you, my dear, you mustn't worry. He is a very responsible, thoughtful man."

"I know he is," said Jules, and closed her eyes. She wasn't worried. My family believes me dead, she thought. And Kanola's children have no mother now, her husband no wife. All Wilkes has is a broken jaw. She felt hatred, pure and raw, flow through her. She was so locked into her private misery that she didn't hear Lydia leave the bedroom.

She fell asleep and dreamed. Wilkes was laughing, watching her intently as she drank some wine. Then she began to feel heavy, and dull, and very strange. She saw him lean over her and kiss her breast.

"No!"

She heard her own scream, and jerked upright. "Jules!"

"No!" she screamed again, seeing a man striding toward her. She scurried frantically to the far side of the bed.

Saint stopped cold. He'd been outside the bedroom when he heard her cry out. He drew a deep, steadying breath and said very quietly, "You had a nightmare, Jules. You're with me—Michael. Do you understand?"

She stared at the wall, mute. She swallowed convulsively as her mind cleared. She whispered, "He made me drink some wine and he touched me and kissed me and . . . fondled me." She gulped, hating him, hating herself, hating her shame. *His mouth was cold and dry and alien.*

Saint saw her fingers lightly press against her breasts. He should have killed Wilkes. For a long moment he couldn't speak. He pictured her naked, terrified, drugged, and Wilkes touching her. He fought down his own rage. She didn't need his fury, she needed to be reassured.

"Jules, it's all right. Come, look at me."

Slowly she turned to face him. She saw the compassion in his hazel eyes, and hated herself even more. He was being kind to her because he pitied her. She probably disgusted him. Thank God she hadn't told him any more.

"I'm all right now," she said in a tight voice.

Saint forced a smile. "You certainly look fine," he said. "I like the damp hair. It makes you look like the little mermaid I remember so well. Do you remember all those times I helped you dry your hair so your father wouldn't get into a snit?"

That drew her out the way he'd hoped it would.

"I remember. I escaped most of the time, but once I didn't. It wasn't my hair, it was the sunburn. He didn't forbid me to swim until I was sixteen. I ignored him, of course. Then it was my brother, Thomas, who helped me sneak out."

Saint also remembered all the times he'd had to drag her out of the ocean and the bright sun so she wouldn't look like a broiled lobster. "How is your brother, anyway? I always liked Thomas."

"He is fine," she said. *And he's probably the only one of my family who's sorry I'm dead.* "He's a man now, Michael."

"Time has a way of adding years," Saint said.

To his immense relief, she suddenly giggled, a sweet, fresh sound that warmed him and made him relax a bit.

"I'm remembering what you always wore when you went swimming," she said.

So did he. He should have had more sense, he thought now. Being half-naked in front of a child was one thing, but as he'd learned, it was quite another in front of an impressionable young girl. It had finally struck him when he'd seen her staring with very different eyes at him one afternoon as he'd walked out of the surf.

"You looked like Adonis," she said now. "Do you still have those frayed, cut-off sailor's pants?"

"You're embarrassing me, Jules," he said. It had seemed so natural to wear only those meager pants when he was swimming with her.

"Why? You're so beautiful."

He flushed. The last thing he wanted her to remember was a half-naked man. "Enough," he said, trying to sound cool and unconcerned. "After lunch, little one, I'm off to buy you some clothes. Unfortunately, I can't take you with me."

"Because of Wilkes," she said flatly.

"Yes. Until I find out what he's up to, I can't risk him finding out where you are, or, for that matter, who took you away from him."

"He doesn't know it was you?"

Saint grinned. "You should have seen my disguise. I probably looked like a huge black bear, and the most villainous creature imaginable."

Over lunch they spoke more of their shared past. He knew she had to talk about what had happened to her, but he didn't want to rush her. Not yet, anyway. And, dammit, he had to figure out what he was going to do with her. But he knew what he had to do. He had to take her home. Oddly, he didn't want to face that prospect just yet. He realized he wanted to enjoy her company for a while longer. That, he added to himself, and see that she healed inwardly, that she was cleansed of her fears and nightmares.

He ended up sending Lydia out to do some shopping for her, because Delaney Saxton called. The Saxton's four-month-old daughter was on her deathbed, according to a frantic Del.

Saint was relieved to tell Chauncey Saxton that her daughter was just colicky.

"New mothers," Saint said, grinning at Chauncey, "and new fathers. I'll bet when Alexandra starts teething, I'll be spending most of my time here reassuring you that she's not expiring."

"I can't wait until you have your own child, Saint!" Chauncey retorted. "Then we'll just see how calm you are!"

Unbidden, Saint saw a baby with bright red hair and green eyes. He blinked.

"What's wrong, Saint?" Del Saxton asked. "You sick too?"

"I'm an old fool," Saint said. "Now, if you two nervous parents will excuse me, I'll be off."

"Before you go, have a brandy with me in the library," Del said.

"That sounds like I'm not invited," Chauncey said.

"No, love, not this time. I need to calm my weak man's nerves. Come on, Saint."

Over delicious French brandy Del said in a pensive voice, "I heard the strangest thing just this morning."

"Oh?"

"Yes. It appears that someone rescued a very pretty girl last night from the Crooked House."

"Good for that someone," Saint said in a bland voice.

"I agree. It's just that someone is probably in a very precarious position now."

"I can't imagine why," Saint said easily.

"I met Jameson Wilkes some two years ago," Del continued. "He is not a nice man, which is an understatement. Evidently, according to my source, he's on a rampage. One can but hope that the someone who rescued the girl can trust all the men who helped him. If one of them spills the beans, there'd be trouble, real trouble."

"It sounds like one of them already spilled the beans," Saint said, looking at his friend closely.

"No," Del said. "I discovered what happened from Maggie. It turns out that one of the members of that little club at the Crooked House showed up at her brothel late last night. He told one of her girls, Lisette, what had happened, and she told Maggie."

"And Maggie told you. So now Lisette, Maggie, and you know."

"That's right. You may be certain that Lisette and Maggie won't say a word."

"That's a relief, certainly," Saint said.

"I'm here if you need help, Saint."

Saint met Del's eyes. "Thank you," he said. "I've got to go now." He turned at the doorway. "How did Lisette and Maggie know the someone was me, if I may ask?"

"Size."

"Ah."

"Well, not just size. Maggie guessed because she knows how you feel about enforced prostitution."

"Let's hope no one else guesses."

There was no real choice, Saint knew. He had to get her back to Maui as soon as possible, for her own safety.

He said as much to her that evening over dinner. She was wearing a simple gray gown that Lydia had bought for her, and her glorious hair was pulled back from her face and tied with a black ribbon. She looked fresh and beautiful.

She didn't look like a fourteen-year-old girl.

He saw her bucking and writhing in his arms, her face pagan with pleasure. He felt the softness of her, the moist swollen woman's flesh. I've got to stop this, he told himself. But he wondered if her husband, that mythical man whose face and name he never wanted to know, would pleasure her as he had, revel in her pleasure as he had despite his best intentions.

"I don't want to go back there," Jules said calmly after a long moment of silence. She laid down her fork. Lydia had already returned to her boarding-house and they were alone. "I want to stay here, with you."

That took him aback. "Jules," he said, "your parents must be frantic about you—"

"My parents believe me dead, drowned."

"Then their grief will cease shortly. It's your home. It's your life, it's—"

"I don't like my parents," she said, a stubborn lift to her chin. "Certainly you remember my father. He is just more so now. My mother is still fading like a wilted plumeria, my sister, Sarah, is such a prig, and she's become more and more insufferable and snob-bish."

"And Thomas?"

"My brother is the only one I care about. You know that. He will escape soon enough—after all, he's a man and he's free. He can't stand our father either."

"Jules, you're young. No, don't interrupt me. Hear me out. You were brought here under terrible cir-cumstances. Wilkes is looking for you. It's not safe for you. Besides, there's John Bleecher at home, and he no longer has pimples. You'll marry, Jules, and have babies, and eventually you'll forget all this."

"I thought you said I was young," she said, staring him down.

He had, dammit. He shook his head.

"I don't want to marry John Bleecher. I told you that." She shuddered, unable to help herself. "I don't want to marry anyone." But that wasn't true. She wanted to marry Michael. She'd wanted to marry him since she was twelve years old . . . well, maybe thirteen. He didn't love her, of course. He still thought of her as a silly little girl. He'd saved her, but now he wanted to be rid of her and continue with his life. From beneath her lashes she gazed at him, feeling herself grow warm. His face wasn't classically hand-some like the princes in fairy tales. It was strong, and rugged, and filled with caring, determination, and kindness. But his eyes were beautiful, and his mouth. One could lose oneself in his eyes. She was being a fanciful fool, she knew it, but he was everything a man should be, she thought. And he'd saved her and she wanted him, only him.

"I don't want to go back," she said again.

But Saint was still hearing her say she didn't want to marry anyone, and he'd seen her unconscious shudder.

"Jules," he said very gently, leaning forward to grasp her slender hand in his. "You will marry. You mustn't allow your experience to make you . . . hesi-tant about marriage. A man who loves you, who cares about you, will make you forget. He'll under-stand, he'll help you."

She felt shame and humiliation wash over her. "You know nothing about my experience!"

He released her hand and sat back in his chair, his arms folded across his massive chest. "Why don't you tell me, so that I will understand."

He'll hate me, despise me if I tell him. He'll look at me like I'm the lowest sort of female.

It was as if he'd read her mind, and, indeed, he guessed very closely, for he saw the pain, the loss of innocence in her eyes.

"Tell me, Jules. I have always admired you, cared for you. Nothing could ever change that. You're a fool if you think it could."

Her throat felt dry and scratchy. She wanted to cry. She wanted to scream. She did neither, merely stared at him like a lost child.

Saint couldn't help himself. He was out of his chair in an instant. He pulled her upright and cradled her in his arms. He stroked his fingers through her thick hair, savoring the feel of it, savoring the fresh, sweet scent of her body. "Nothing matters," he said, pulling her closer. "Please, don't continue to think what you're thinking. You did nothing wrong. You must believe that, Jules."

Suddenly, as if she were staring through a soft veil, she saw him holding her like this, stroking her, speaking to her softly. She felt his strong hands moving over her. Then the veil thickened, receded, and she saw nothing more. She leaned her cheek against his shoulder.

I love you, Michael. I've always loved you.

The words rang clear in her mind. She'd said those words to him. But when? She raised her face and whispered, "I don't understand."

"What? What is it you don't understand?"

"I just saw you holding me as you're doing now,

but not really. And you were ... touching me and speaking softly to me."

He stiffened, and she felt it. She went cold all over. For an instant she saw herself quite clearly, writhing, crying out, feeling sensations that were alien and wild and ... And he was there.

"No, Jules," he said, shaking her a bit. He hated that bewildered look in her eyes. "It's not what you're thinking."

She raised her eyes to his face, arching her back against his strong arms to see him better. "Was it only a dream?" she whispered.

She saw the truth in his eyes, and he knew it. "Let me explain," he said finally. "Come into the sitting room."

He released her, took her hand, and led her into the small parlor. "Sit down."

She sat.

He walked to the fireplace and leaned his shoulder against the mantel. "Wilkes drugged you. You remember that."

"Yes, I remember."

"When I brought you here, you were very much under the influence of the opium. And when you recognized me, you thought we were in Maui again. The past became the present, Jules, and you were ... confused."

I love you, Michael. I've always loved you.

She'd embarrassed him horribly. She was embarrassing him now.

She rose to her feet. "I don't want to know any more."

She nearly ran to the doorway.

"Jules! Stop!"

He caught her at the bottom of the stairs. He pulled her around and shook her. "Don't do this, dammit! You were not yourself, not really. You didn't know what you were doing."

Her eyes went wide, and he knew that she was remembering now, remembering in vivid detail.

"You . . . touched me," she whispered. "Between my . . ." She choked, feeling for an instant the touch of his fingers on her flesh, feeling the wildness, the urgency, the frenzy, but she couldn't capture the actual feelings. They flitted away from her consciousness, leaving her more confused.

"Yes, dammit, I touched you and I gave you a woman's pleasure. I had to. You were . . . confused, and I had to." *Like hell! You were a wild thing, crazy for it.*

She became very still, trying desperately to clutch at something that made sense, that made her herself again. She said in a lost voice, "I don't know what a woman's pleasure is. I can't remember exactly."

"Oh God!" He pulled her against him roughly. "I'm sorry, Jules. I didn't mean to say it . . . like that."

"Did you take my virginity?"

"Did I what?" His mind was reeling.

"Jameson Wilkes said he was glad I was a virgin because the man who bought me would know it and be pleased. That was why he could charge so much money for me. But how would a man know? Did you know?"

"I didn't take your virginity. I'm not an animal, for God's sake! I wanted only to help you, to make you . . . calm again. How could you ever believe that I would hurt you?"

"No, I know you wouldn't hurt me. It's just that I don't understand how a man could take something from me. I know that men can hurt women . . . is that what he meant about taking my virginity?"

"Yes," Saint said, gritting his teeth. "Well, no, not really." He released her, running his long fingers distractedly through his hair. "It's complicated, Jules." *Complicated, hell! It's the easiest thing in the world!* "It's something . . . well, it's something that your husband will explain to you."

"Then I will never know, will I?"

But you know a woman's pleasure, if you could but remember it. "Yes," he said firmly, "Yes, you will."

She was silent, her eyes cast down. He hugged her gently to him as a father would a child. "Would you like to sleep now?"

"Yes, I suppose so."

He took her to the small guestroom. "If you hear any knocking during the night, just ignore it. It's probably someone who needs a doctor. All right?"

"Yes, Michael."

8

"We're leaving on the *Carolina* Friday."

Jules dropped the collection of Lord Byron's poetry to the floor and started to rise from her chair.

Saint raised his hand to still her. "No, stay there, Jules, and let me finish. I will escort you, of course. It will take us about two weeks to reach Lahaina."

"I know exactly how long it takes," she said, her voice bitter. She clutched the arms of the chair until her knuckles showed white.

"Yes, I guess you do. Then you will be reunited with your family."

And you will leave and I'll never see you again.

She watched him stride into the small parlor, making it seem even smaller with his presence, and for an instant, saw him wearing his ragged, cut-off pants. His legs were tanned, and long and thick with muscle. She saw him diving after her, dunking her, laughing with her. She felt a spurt of warmth deep in her belly. She felt his eyes on her and kept her face down. Maybe she should look at him straight, she thought. Maybe he would see into her mind and keep her with him. But no. He was giving her his very patient look; he was prepared to calmly demolish her every protest. But she wasn't a child any longer. But how to make him realize that?

Jules drew a deep breath, and plowed forward. "I would like to stay in San Francisco, Michael. I could find a job. You wouldn't have to be responsible for me."

Saint raised a brow at that. "Just who would be responsible for you, then?"

"I am not a child, even though it pleases you to think so—still. I am a grown woman and I will—"

"No," he said, looking at her fisted hands, "you're not a child. But you are returning to Lahaina, Jules, and that's an end to it. Your family . . . it's where you belong."

"Michael, I could help you, really I could. Please, won't you just listen to me—"

Again he interrupted her, unable to bear her pleading. "Jules, please try to understand. I am doing what is best for you."

"I could be your mistress."

His breath flew out in a sharp hiss. "My *what*?"

"Your mistress," Jules repeated in a steady voice. "Jameson Wilkes explained to me that a mistress belongs to only one man and he takes care of her. So I could continue to live here, and you could take care of me and I could do whatever it is a mistress is supposed to do."

Saint simply stared at her. He supposed he should be glad that Wilkes hadn't rid her of all ignorance and innocence during the two weeks he'd had her. "Jules," he asked her very carefully, "he did tell you what a mistress was supposed to do, didn't he?"

"No, not really. I told him that a mistress sounded like a whore to me and I wouldn't do it." Jules ducked her head, realizing that she'd just done herself in. "Not with just anybody," she hastily amended. "Just you."

"I see," Saint said. Handle this with kid gloves, he thought, and with some humor, if I can dredge up any. "Jules, I can't afford a mistress. I'm only a poor physician, remember? And if I could, you would have to parade about in awful gowns like the one Wilkes made you wear, and douse yourself in that smelly perfume. Surely you wouldn't want that?"

"I couldn't just be me?" Her voice was so hopeless that a smile tugged at the corners of his mouth, and he saw her as a young girl again—questioning everything, innocent of guile, and stubborn as a mule when she wanted something. He kept his voice light, teasing. "Indeed not. A mistress is a bird of very different plumage—a simple, elegant cormorant is not allowed. There are different rules about mistresses, you know."

She looked at him suspiciously. "I don't believe you. Just what are these rules?"

"First of all, a mistress is not a lady. She isn't allowed to be around ladies. She's an outcast, if you will, and she has no rights, no security. She's taken care of only as long as the gentleman she lives with wishes it. It isn't pleasant, Jules."

"It would be pleasant with you, Michael," she said, and he sighed at the upward thrust of her stubborn chin.

Saint walked to her, drew her out of her chair, and gently stroked his large hand down her arms. "I don't want a mistress, Jules. And you are not mistress material. You're beautiful, vibrant, and you're meant to have a husband and a home of your own and children. The rest is nonsense and not at all for you."

"Do you already have a mistress?"

He thought of Jane—not a mistress, not Jane—but Jules saw the expression in his eyes and wanted to strike this unknown woman. "No," he said firmly, "I don't have a mistress."

Jules stared up at him, not really believing him, but knowing that Michael had never lied to her. What would he do if I kissed him? she wondered. She raised her hand and lightly touched her fingertips to his cheek. "I'm glad you don't wear a beard," she said.

He felt his body leap in response. It wasn't her touching him, or her words. It was the look in her vivid emerald eyes that made his loins tighten. She'd had the same look when he'd stroked his hand between her thighs and felt her and caressed her. It was a vivid image in his mind: her long lashes sweeping down as she moaned softly, arching against him in a frenzy, as if she wanted to become part of him.

He released her abruptly, disgusted with himself. He tried for a smile. "I'm glad you don't wear a beard either."

Her smile was as forced as his. "You said that I would get married and have babies."

"Yes, I said that."

"So I'm not too young for that."

"No, you're not."

"Then I'm an adult."

"Yes, an adult."

"Then, Michael, you have no right to tell me what to do. I'm a woman grown and I will make my own decisions. I want to stay in San Francisco. And if you don't want me, I'll just have to—"

"Wilkes would have you within twenty-four hours."

Her chin went up. "I'll buy a gun and shoot him."

He looked at her as if he wanted to throttle her. "You've become quite a talker in the past five years, haven't you?"

"I've always been a talker, and you know it. And don't think you got away with throwing in a cormorant to distract me. I wasn't distracted and you don't know anything about cormorants."

"Jules, the subject is closed. You will do as I say."

"But—"

He placed his fingertips over her lips. "No. Trust me, please."

He was implacable and she knew she'd lost.

Lahaina

Lahaina didn't have a natural harbor, only an open roadstead. Ships could always approach or leave it with any wind that blew. No pilot was needed. The *Carolina* approached through the channel between Maui and Molokai, then let the trade winds carry it close to Lanai and in toward Lahaina. Saint and Jules stood on deck watching the harbormaster climb aboard to give Captain Rafer a copy of port regulations. Chase boats and tenders waited to take the few passengers and sailors into the town and to sell goods to those who remained aboard.

"I'd forgotten how beautiful it is here," Saint said, gazing at the lush green hills that rose behind the town of Lahaina. Jules said nothing, but now he didn't expect her to. "And there's the taro patch. Is it true, Jules, that Kamehameha worked there to show his subjects the dignity of labor?"

"Not that I ever heard," she said, her voice clipped,

"but I suppose it's a nice story. Makes him sound noble and all that, which, I suppose, he was."

He fell silent. He'd tried every ploy he could think of to make her less resentful of coming home, but nothing worked. His laughing, bright girl had withdrawn into herself.

He felt the now familiar surge of impatience with her. It was as if she'd built a very firm, impenetrable wall between them. During their voyage, she'd been firmly polite, and a stranger.

And she'd said not a word about the two weeks she'd spent with Wilkes, even when he'd asked her three evenings before, following the only storm they'd experienced during the two-week voyage. He hadn't seen her for nearly twenty-four hours, his services as a doctor in demand from the moment the storm hit. "I'm tired as hell," he'd said, joining her at the railing.

"You look it," she said, not turning.

"Thanks for your concern," he said dryly.

Jules turned to face him, and shrugged. "I hope all those green-faced, vomiting passengers paid you well. Will you be able to buy yourself a prostitute when we reach Lahaina?"

He stared at her, and automatically shook his head.

"But it's just one night, doctor. Nothing expensive or demanding, like having a mistress."

"Do you always turn sarcastic and nasty when you don't get your way?"

She saw the weariness in his hazel eyes, but bit down on the tug of concern she felt. "Yes," she said, "I do, particularly if the *man* making the decision is a blind ass."

He smiled, just a bit, and forced himself to look away from her, out at the endless expanse of ocean.

"I think the last woman to truly enjoy insulting me was my mother. Of course, she did it with humor."

"I'll just bet she was laughing after she birthed you. That's why she called you Ulysses—revenge."

"Can't say I blame her," Saint said easily. "I weighed eleven pounds. Poor woman used to tell me that the real Ulysses—from what she'd read—searched and searched for nigh onto twenty years before he came home, and that's how she felt after nine months hauling me around inside her."

"As I said, revenge."

"Ah, but she tempered it with 'Michael'—that's innocuous enough, surely."

It wasn't innocuous, it was the most beautiful name she'd ever heard. She said, "Lydia told me that she could make a fortune in blackmail if only she could find out what your real name was and where you got the nickname Saint."

"My friends never give up. It's like a contest now. They come up with all sorts of ploys to make me cough up the facts, and I sidestep." He turned around and leaned back against the railing. "God, I'm tired. And a doctor is supposed to be able to cure anything and everything. As if I could do anything about seasickness!"

"I would have helped you if you'd just asked me," Jules said.

"Thank you, but it took all my resolution not to throw up, given the stench in the cabins. No reason for you to turn green, and you would have, I guarantee it."

"I never get sick," Jules said with all the confidence of a young person who thought of illness as weakness.

"I hope you never do," Saint said. There would probably not be a better opportunity, he thought, silent for few moments. "Jules," he said very abruptly, hoping to throw her off balance, "your friend Kanola—did Wilkes's sailors rape her?"

She stiffened as if he'd shouted an obscenity in her ear. She heard Kanola screaming, saw that awful man with that thing sticking out from his belly, and tried to shut off the awful memory. "I don't know," she managed after a moment. "Wilkes dragged me to his cabin, said he would protect me." She wanted clarification of exactly what rape was, but was too embarrassed to ask.

Thank God, he thought, she hadn't seen it. He had absolutely no doubt that Kanola had been raped, repeatedly.

"Then what happened?"

His voice was matter-of-fact, and she tired to keep herself calm and in control, but it was difficult. "She managed to escape the men and jumped overboard. She couldn't have made it to shore. We were too far away."

"I'm sorry," he said, wishing there were something a bit more he could say. He continued calmly, as if discussing the present sunny weather, "I know that Wilkes drugged you once before you arrived in San Francisco, and that he touched you and kissed you."

"No!"

"You told me that, Jules."

"No," she said again, hating the dank chill that crept over her flesh at his words.

"I don't want what happened to eat at you, Jules. I don't want you to bury it deep. It truly helps to tell a friend. Tell me what he did to you. Then you can forget it."

She jerked away from him and snarled at him, her voice vicious, "What do you care what he did to me? You want to hear all the marvelous details? Friend, ha!"

"What did he do, Jules?" he asked again, not allowing her to anger him. He heard the remembered fear in her voice and knew that her spate of words was bravado—no, more like protection, self-protection.

"I think," she said finally, getting a hold on herself, "that I should begin to call you Saint. That's how you're acting, of course. A saint—so full of human caring and kindness, so anxious to make the poor little creature forget her nightmare. You can go to hell, Saint!"

Saint was not a violent man. In fact, once, when he was only fourteen years old, he'd gotten into a fight with another boy and broken his jaw with one blow. He'd been appalled. Now, he thought, looking at her set face from beneath lowered lashes, he wouldn't mind at all breaking his rule. A good thrashing would, at the very least, make him feel a hell of a lot better. He'd said nothing more, for there was nothing to say.

Jules said now, pointing toward a small knot of native women on the dock, all of them dressed garishly, "There are the prostitutes. But I don't see my father or any of his friends—many times he goes to the dock when a whaler comes in and rants and screams about Satan, and evil, and disease."

"I don't know much about the Satan or evil part," Saint said calmly, ignoring the bitter irony in her voice, "but I sure as hell know about the disease." He saw that the two sailors who were at the oars of the tender were already waving and shouting toward the women.

There were about a half-dozen other ships, most of them whalers. The long, narrow dock was bustling with local people hawking wares, and here and there in the distance Saint could see a black frock coat. Either a businessman or a preacher, he thought, or one of those useless diplomats from Oahu.

"Come," he said, and helped her out of the tender. Her hand was cold and clammy, and he added gently, "I'll be with you, Jules."

She allowed him to assist her, then pulled her hand away. They walked into Wharf Street. Saint glanced briefly toward the fort, built in the early 1830's and now used mostly as a prison. It was looking a bit the worse for wear, he thought. Dwight Baldwin's home looked as neat as a pin, set back from Front Street, its paint fresh, its garden neat and green. He and Baldwin, a Protestant medical missionary, had been good friends during Saint's stay in Lahaina. He started to ask Jules about him, when she suddenly pulled off her bonnet and shook her head. Her bright flame hair drew several glances, then a loud gasp.

"Juliana! My God, it is you!"

Saint turned to see a young man staring at Jules as if looking at a ghost. It was John Bleecher, the planter's son. He wasn't pimple-faced now, Saint noticed. Indeed, he was a handsome young man, well-formed, open-faced, and at present, pale as death.

Jules was very still. She moved closer to Saint, saying only, "Hello, John. How have you been?"

John roused himself. "Saint? Dr. Morris? Yes, it *is* you. Juliana, what happened? Everyone has believed you dead. Kanola's body . . . well, it washed up on shore, and since you had been seen with her, we all thought—"

"Yes, I know," Jules said, interrupting him in a curt voice. "She's dead, but I'm not. I . . . well, I survived."

"I don't understand," John said helplessly, wishing he could fling himself upon the pale, beautiful girl he'd wanted for two years now. But there was something terribly wrong. What was she doing with Saint Morris? He'd been gone for a long time now, five years.

"John," Saint said pleasantly, "why don't you help us with the luggage? I want to take Jules to her home."

"Jules . . . ? Oh, yes, certainly."

Saint watched the young man pick up Jules's one small valise. No, he thought, she couldn't marry him. He wouldn't suit her; he wouldn't understand her. He would stifle her spirit without realizing what he was doing. He would also paw her endlessly and scare her witless.

Saint shook his head at the direction of his thoughts. It was none of his business, after all. He would stay the two days the *Carolina* would be in port, then return to California. He would never see her again. Something inside him rebelled at the thought.

Etienne DuPres's house was on Luakini Street, just one block behind the Baldwin house. It was set back from the busy street, its white clapboards gleaming in the sun. Saint heard Jules draw in her breath when she saw her brother, Thomas, clad only in trousers and an open white shirt, turn onto the street and wave to John Bleecher. Saint saw the shock on his face, but Thomas, unlike John, showed no hesitation. He gave a loud whoop and ran full tilt to his sister and swung her up into his arms.

"Thomas," Jules whispered, burying her face in her brother's neck.

Saint saw the front door to the DuPres house open and Aurelia DuPres slowly walk onto the narrow veranda. Saint saw her clutch at her flat bosom, then faint dead away. He'd forgotten how damned vaporish the woman was. Doubtless all the wretched clothes and tight corset she wore didn't help matters.

By the time he reached her side, there were people everywhere, and pandemonium.

Saint had also forgotten how much he disliked Etienne DuPres. There was no joy in the man, only grim, unremitting purpose. He was tall and very thin, his black broadcloth suit making him appear gaunt. His eyes were not sparkling and alive like his daughter's, but a pale cold gray. His hair was thinner now, the black streaked with white.

They were all seated in the small parlor, Jules's mother fluttering her hands, Sarah, Jules's older sister, silent and stiff, watching her sister, her lips pursed. Thomas was carrying on in his exuberant fashion, seated cross-legged on the floor beside Jules's chair. Even though he was dark-haired and tall like his father, he had Jules's openness and joy.

Etienne DuPres stood tall and silent next to a fireplace that was never used. He'd hugged his daughter briefly, then set her away. For a moment Saint thought he looked to be in pain—a good sign, he thought, that he'd missed and grieved for his younger daughter. Etienne DuPres said now to Saint, "How did you get my daughter?"

Saint smiled toward Jules and said pleasantly, "You are the luckiest family alive. Your daughter is safe and well."

Before he could explain further, Reverend Du-Pres said, his voice even colder, "We understood that Juliana had drowned. She was forbidden to swim, but that is another matter. I would like to know what happened to her, and how you got her."

"I was taken by a man who wanted to sell me," Jules said. "In San Francisco. Michael saved me."

There was a moan from Mrs. DuPres, and Saint prayed the damned woman wouldn't faint again. Sarah said in a shrill voice, "Taken? Whatever do you mean? Why would anyone do that?"

Jules said in her clear, sweet voice, "His name is Jameson Wilkes. I believe you've met him, Father. He decided I was well-enough-looking, and took me to San Francisco. He wanted to sell me to a man so I would be a mistress."

Thomas DuPres roared, "Damnation, Jules! That miserable bastard . . . God, I'll kill him!"

"You will be silent, Thomas," Reverend DuPres said. "So," he continued, looking down at his daughter, "you were in the company of this evil man for two weeks, and he debauched you."

Jules paled. "If you mean by 'debauched' that he . . . hurt me, no, he didn't. He wanted to save me because he would get more money for me if I were a virgin."

"How dare you speak like that in front of your mother and sister! Merciful Lord, to be cursed with such—"

"That's quite enough." Saint rose, his very size intimidating, his quiet voice instantly reducing Reverend DuPres to silence. "Your daughter is safe and well. She was not debauched. And even if she had been, I don't see that it would matter. What matters, sir, is that your daughter is with you again."

Etienne DuPres said nothing. He'd done his best by the girl. But she was willful, just as her scarlet-haired grandmother had been. She shouldn't have come back. He felt rage flow through him, rage and shame. He looked at her again, then walked from the room.

Jules sat before the small dressing table, slowly brushing her hair. She didn't look up when Sarah came into their bedroom.

"I am glad you are alive, Juliana," Sarah said.

Then why do I want to shiver at your tone? Jules wondered. "Thank you," she said, not breaking count with her hairbrush.

"You've been gone well over a month. Everyone was very upset. Father preached a marvelous sermon for you. He touched but once on your disobedience and your perfidy in swimming in the ocean."

"Now he can unpreach it," Jules said.

Sarah, as was her habit, stepped behind the narrow screen to undress. "John is going to marry me."

Jules raised her head at that, looking toward the screen in the mirror. His affections were short-lived, she thought. But she wasn't angry at him; she was immensely relieved. "I am glad for you," she said. "John is very nice."

Sarah fingered the buttons on her long nightgown. "I saw how he was looking at you this afternoon. But he won't go back to you. Not now. Not after what you've done."

"But I didn't do anything," Jules said.

"So you say," Sarah said. "As for Saint, well, you're better off with him. You should have stayed with him."

I wanted to, but he didn't want me.

Jules turned on the stool and eyed her sister silently for a long moment. She would be pretty if only she would smile— not just her mouth, but her eyes. Her hair, unlike Jules's, was a soft brown and didn't fly about her head in wild curls. "Sarah," she asked quietly, "do you love me?"

"Yes, I suppose so," Sarah said finally, "but I want John."

"But you said you're marrying him! You have him, Sarah. He has nothing to do with me!"

Suddenly Sarah seemed to collapse. She covered her face with her hands, and wrenching sobs broke from her throat.

Jules, appalled, quickly went to her. "What's wrong, Sarah?"

The sobs continued, and Jules stood helplessly, watching her sister's slender body shake.

"John means nothing to me, please believe that," Jules said. "He loves you. Why else would he marry you?"

"You fool," Sarah whispered, raising her tearstained face. "He went crazy when Kanola's body was discovered and we were told that you'd been with her. Crazy, do you hear? But I wanted him, Juliana. I've always wanted him. He grieved. And I . . . well, I comforted him."

"Well, of course you did. I'm certain he comforted you too."

"You stupid fool!" Sarah nearly screamed at her. "I let him have me! That's why he's marrying me now. He has to! Dear God, I could be pregnant right now, and here you are, back again. I hate you!"

Jules stepped back, her face white. Very slowly she stripped off her white nightgown and began to dress. It didn't occur to her to step behind the screen, and her sister's shocked gasp only made her smile, a small, bitter smile.

"What are you doing now?"

"Nothing," Jules said.

"He did debauch you, just like Father said. Taking off your clothes without a thought! It's disgusting."

Jules turned a puzzled look to her sister. "Didn't you take off your clothes with John?"

Sarah shuddered. "No, of course not. It was dark. I just let him . . . well, I know that *you* understand what he did." She shuddered again, and Jules suddenly felt very sorry for John Bleecher.

She finished dressing in silence.

"Where are you going?"

"Out," Jules said, and quietly slipped from the room. The house was dark. Everyone was in bed. Jules carefully propped open the back kitchen door and walked quickly toward the beach along the back streets. She could hear sounds of revelry—men's laughter and women's giggles—and now it had a new meaning to her. She saw not a soul. When she reached the deserted beach, she stripped off the hot, restricting gown and walked slowly down the beach toward the ocean, clad only in her short chemise. There was a half-moon, and as usual, the sky was clear, the stars dazzlingly bright. Gentle waves crested with barely a sound and slithered onto the wet sand. She didn't wade into the water, but skirted the waves and sat on an outcropping rock, hugging her arms about her knees.

She'd been gone for such a short time, really, but everything had changed. And everyone. No, that wasn't true. She saw her sister's contorted face, the streaming tears. Priggish Sarah had made love to a man. She'd obviously disliked it.

Jules saw her own life as series of days spent in silent despair and nights spent thinking of what she couldn't have, and swallowed down the hated tears.

It was as if she'd conjured him up. She sat very still, watching Michael, magnificently naked, stride through the surf toward the beach. He was running his hands through his thick hair, then shaking himself like a mongrel dog.

As he came closer, Jules let her eyes fall down his body. She had never before seen a naked man—only Michael when he'd worn those meager pants. Now he wore nothing. The hair was thick on his chest, narrowing as it snaked down over his flat belly. She knew that men had things on the front of their bodies, and that's where babies came from. Men stuck themselves into women. For a moment she stared at him objectively, wondering how it would work, and how it would feel to touch him there. How it would feel to have him pressed against her, naked.

He turned a moment, looking back over the water. Her fingers tingled as her eyes traveled down his back to his buttocks, to his long legs. Old Lanakila carved figures in smooth, glowing wood. Michael looked as sculptured and perfect as the most beautiful of Lanakila's statues. Suddenly he twisted about and his eyes met hers, and held.

He made no move to cover himself, merely stood there, the water lapping over his feet, gazing at her.

9

She was staring at him, staring intensely at his manhood, now swelling and jutting out beneath her gaze. Before he'd seen her, he had been thinking that Maui was indeed a Garden of Eden, so lush and warm and vibrantly beautiful. Jules fit into his image as naturally as the moonlit waves lapping over his feet.

Very slowly he walked toward her. Her bright hair was in wild disarray, flowing down her back and over her shoulders. She was wearing only a simple white cotton chemise that came to her knees.

He said nothing, merely stopped in front of her. She sat very straight on the edge of the rock, her hands folded primly in her lap, her emerald eyes wide upon his face. He dropped to his knees in the sand, feeling the coarse grains against his legs. He stretched out his hands and placed them on her thighs. Slowly he pulled her legs apart. He slid his hands upward beneath her chemise, his fingers wet and warm on her smooth thighs. He clutched her buttocks, lifting her, and brought her down against him.

She cried out softly, and Saint shook himself free.

He was reeling with the vividness of the fantasy that had held him for many moments. He knew that what he'd imagined could easily happen—right now. He felt his manhood swelling, responding to her yearning gaze.

He forced himself to stand rigidly, and called out, his voice cold and distant, "What are you doing here, Jules?"

"I didn't know anyone else would be here," she said, her voice high and breathless.

"You didn't answer my question."

"I . . . I had to get away from the house, from Sarah."

Had priggish Sarah been tauting her? "I see" was all he said. He walked briskly up the beach, aware of her eyes following his progress. He found his clothes and quickly dressed himself. He managed to pull on his boots, then straightened. The bulge in his trousers had diminished, thank heaven.

When he turned, she was standing very quietly, watching him. Soft moonlight flowed over her face.

"I'm staying with the Baldwins," he said. "I'm going back now. I will probably see you in the morning."

God, he sounded like a cold, uncaring bastard. He stopped in his tracks. "Jules," he said, his voice gentle now, "don't let Sarah hurt you. She doesn't understand." *No one does, least of all your damned father and your wilting mother.*

"Sarah is Sarah," Jules said. She raised her chin. "I shall be quite all right, thank you." *You want to go, so go!*

It was as if she'd spoken aloud. He merely nodded, turned on his heel, and strode from the beach.

He felt a great shudder go through his body.

*   *   *

I should paint a picture, Jules thought, and call it *Family at the Breakfast Table with Prodigal Daughter.* She nearly laughed aloud at the thought of Koli bringing in a fatted calf so everyone could rejoice over a feast at her return. Her father was sitting stiff and unyielding in his high-backed chair. Her mother was pulling apart a soft piece of bread, her thin fingers nervous and anxious. Sarah said not a word, merely toyed with the fresh papaya. Thomas, sensing the tension, kept his head down and wolfed his breakfast, as was his wont.

I don't belong here. I don't belong anywhere.

"Today is Saturday," Etienne DuPres announced. "Will you be going to the plantation, Thomas?"

"Yes, Father. John and I have some business to discuss."

Jules saw Sarah's head come up at Thomas' words, saw the desperate yearning in her eyes as she asked, "Will John come back with you for lunch?"

Thomas flashed a quick glance toward Juliana. "I imagine nothing could keep him away."

"John is going to marry our Sarah," Aurelia DuPres said in her thin, high voice. "Of course he will come."

Etienne gazed a moment at his younger daughter. She looks like a wanton, he thought, just like her damned grandmother, even with her hair plastered against her head and tied securely.

"Juliana," he said abruptly, shoving his chair back and rising, "you will come with me to my study. I wish to speak to you."

Juliana escaped the house long before noon. She didn't want to see John Bleecher. She didn't want to see anyone. She kept to the back streets, but she saw many people she knew. The missionary contingent merely nodded to her and kept going. The natives were open, friendly, and glad to see that she was still alive. She knew she should visit Kanola's husband and children, but she couldn't bring herself to do so yet. The pain was too fresh. She walked south along Waine'e Street today, past the Episcopal cemetery. She didn't turn toward the ocean until she reached Shaw Street. It was narrow, and muddy after a brief morning rain. She lifted her skirts, kept her head down, and continued walking. Her mind kept returning to the conversation with her father that morning. Not really a conversation, she amended to herself silently. He had stood on high, like God, and made a pronouncement.

When she reached the beach, she pulled off her shoes and stockings without hesitation, set them on a rock, and walked toward the water. Men were out on their canoes fishing, and two young children were playing in the waves. Naked-masted whalers were farther out in deep water. She walked farther down the beach, pausing every once in a while to examine an interesting shell that had been washed up. She didn't pay any attention today to the birds, nor did she even spare more than a passing thought to the fish.

The hem of her skirt was soon soaked, but for the first time in her life she simply didn't care. What else could her father do in any case?

She turned away from the water and walked barefoot to Maluuluolele. She stared at the small island in the center of the pond. It was a tiny island, Mokuula. How many years had it been a home of

Maui chiefs? She couldn't remember. Even King Kamehameha III had received visitors here in the recent past, showing them the large burial chambers holding the ornate coffins of those long-dead chiefs.

"Juliana."

She froze in her tracks at the sound of John Bleecher's voice.

She turned slowly to face him. "Hello, John. I thought you would still be at my father's house."

"No, I left. I . . . I had to see you, talk to you."

I will not hurt Sarah, nor will I hurt John, Jules swore to herself. "I will be leaving Maui soon, John."

"I know," he said. God, she was beautiful. His fingers itched to touch her, to feel her beautiful wild hair.

"I really want to be by myself, John, if you don't mind."

He said nothing, merely walked toward her, stopping but inches from her. She looked up at him and was taken aback at the unfamiliar look in his blue eyes. She cocked her head to one side, silent.

"We're alone," he said more to himself than to her.

"I suppose so," Jules agreed.

Suddenly, without warning, he grabbed her, hauling her against him and pressing his mouth against hers. Jules was too startled for a moment to struggle. "John!" she cried out, and felt his tongue thrust into her open mouth.

She began hitting him then, twisting to free herself from his hold. She hadn't realized before that he was so strong.

"Stop it, Juliana," he snarled at her in a voice she'd never heard. "Damn you, you know I've always wanted you, not Sarah. And now I know the truth. You've given it to how many men now?"

"Given what, for God's sake? Let me go, John! How dare you do this?"

But he didn't let her go. He seemed wild. She felt pain in her ribs, but didn't cry out. "Don't act the innocent with me, Juliana! I know now, all of it! Sarah told me what you've done. It won't make any difference to have one more man, will it? God knows, you've been flat on your back for Saint!"

For a moment Jules lost her burgeoning fright in sheer shock. What had Sarah told him? "You think I'm a whore?" she asked in bewildered surprise.

He answered her with a groan and buried his face against her throat. She felt his hands grab her breasts, and she cried out, seeing Jameson Wilkes over her, his fingers stroking her naked breasts, squeezing, hurting. She went crazy in that moment, clawing, kicking at him, her breath coming in loud, jerking gasps. John hurled her to the ground and slammed his body down on top of her.

He was hard and punishing against her belly—she could feel him through the layers of clothing. Dear God, he was going to hurt her, and she knew now that this was what rape was.

Saint washed his hands and wiped them on the white towel Dwight Baldwin handed him.

"Thanks for coming in with me, Saint," Dwight said. "We've only the twelve patients right now, but just you wait a couple of months."

"My pleasure. You still treat more syphilis than anything else?"

"Lord yes, it never ends. The poor fellow you just examined, what do you think?"

"You've got to take the leg off today or he'll be dead tomorrow."

Dwight Baldwin sighed. "That's what I thought too. Dammit, it was a stupid, needless accident. It happened on the taro plantation, and Elisha Bleecher didn't bother to bring him in until yesterday evening."

"Exhort him with hellfire and brimstone tomorrow from the pulpit," Saint said.

"Won't do a bit of good, I'm afraid, but you may be certain that I shall. Come, let me walk you out."

"Have you got ether around?"

"No, but I do have chloroform. Thank God we no longer have to put our patients through such agony. Didn't you tell me that you were an actual witness to the first use of ether in 1846? At Massachusetts General Hospital, wasn't it?"

"Yes," Saint said, "I was. It started out a circus, with all the other doctors and medical students laughing derisively, and ended in complete and utter silence. I'll never forget Dr. Warren's face when he made his first incision. The patient didn't move, didn't utter a sound. When it was all over, he turned to the audience and said in the most bewildered voice I've ever heard, 'Gentlemen, this is no humbug.' "

"I remember hearing that one doctor walked up to the patient and began slapping him, still unable to believe that he wasn't faking."

That hadn't happened, but it made a good story, so Saint only nodded to Dwight. "Now, if only we can get our colleagues to use ether on women in labor." Saint knew Dwight Baldwin as a man of infinite compassion and caring for his fellowman, but like many men, religious or otherwise, he believed firmly that it was the scheme of things for a woman to undergo childbirth with nothing to ease her agony.

Today Dwight didn't take the bait. He was silent for many moments, then said calmly, "I heard about Juliana DuPres."

"Yes," Saint said. "I told you about her adventure and mine last evening."

"That's not what I meant," Dwight said, sighing.

"I know. I bet everyone has heard things," Saint said. "It will pass. She'll be all right."

Dwight gave him an incredulous look, but Saint had turned to speak to an old man who used to bring him fresh fish at least three times a week. He'd set the old man's broken leg and taken the fish as payment. Old Kama had simply never stopped bringing him fish.

Saint and Dwight Baldwin parted some minutes later. Saint made his way to the DuPres house, only to be told by Mrs. DuPres that Juliana had left. Saint thanked her, frowned, and set out to find her. He tracked her to the south of town.

When he heard her screaming wildly, frantically, his guts twisted. "Jules!"

He ran toward the sound, and broke through the bushes that blocked his view. He saw Jules on her back, thrashing and screaming, with John Bleecher on top of her, grinding his pelvis against her as he ripped at her clothes.

His mind went blank with rage. With a loud roar he launched himself upon the younger man.

"You goddamned little bastard!" he yelled, and grabbed John bodily off Jules. He smashed his fist into John's gaping mouth, and the force of his blow sent the slighter man staggering back.

"You filthy pig," Saint growled, "I'm going to break your bloody neck!"

Jules managed to pull herself upright. She saw Michael strike John, heard John's yowl of pain. He would kill him! She saw her brother running toward them, and shouted at the top of her lungs, "Thomas! Help! For God's sake, hurry!"

It was like trying to halt a train, Thomas thought frantically as he threw himself on Saint's back. "You'll kill him, Saint!"

Saint came out of the black, ungoverned rage as quickly as it had initially consumed him. He saw John Bleecher's bloody nose, heard his moans of pain.

"What the hell is going on?" Thomas demanded.

Saint very slowly straightened, closing his eyes a moment. He said in an emotionless voice, "That little bastard was trying to rape your sister." He smiled grimly. "I think he needs cooling off."

Saint picked John up, one large hand grasping his collar, the other the seat of his breeches. He carried him to the ocean, waded in, and tossed him out into the waves, facedown.

He was still smiling when he came back to where Jules and Thomas were standing. It was a ghastly, grim smile.

The smile disappeared at the sight of Jules's white face. She was standing rigidly still, her eyes staring at him but not really seeing him. "She'll be all right," he said more to himself than to Thomas. "Jules," he said softly. He reached out for her, only to see her shudder and stumble backward.

Jules sank slowly to her knees. She raised wide, bewildered eyes to Saint. "He said I gave it to every other man and I should give it to him. He said Sarah told him what I'd done."

"That stupid, jealous bitch!"

"Enough, Thomas," Saint said, turning briefly toward the young man.

Suddenly it was too much. Jules saw herself sprawled naked on Wilkes's bunk, saw him touching her, leering at her. She felt John grinding his body against hers. She clutched her arms about herself and rocked back and forth on her heels. "No, no, no," she said softly, her voice singsong.

"Oh God, Saint," Thomas whispered, terrified. "Do something!"

"Take John away from here, Thomas," Saint said quietly. "Leave me alone with her. Don't let anyone else come along, all right?"

John was staggering toward them, and Thomas quickly turned to run to him. Saint saw Thomas grab John's arm none too gently and drag him off. Thomas said something, but Saint couldn't make out his words.

He waited a few more minutes, then dropped to his knees in front of Jules. He clasped her chin in his hand and lifted her face. Her eyes were wide and unseeing, her lips still moving, her only words "No, no . . ." He slapped her hard, and caught her so she wouldn't fall. He saw her blink, shudder, then cry out softly. Gently he drew her against him, rocking her in the circle of his arms. "It's all right now, Jules. Everything is all right. No man will ever hurt you again. I promise."

And he included himself in that promise.

He drew a sigh of relief when she slumped against

him and began to cry. He was becoming stiff in the kneeling position, and slowly sat down, pulling Jules down beside him. He kept her face pressed against his chest, his arm supporting her.

"He's sending me to Canada," she whispered in a deadened voice, "to Toronto, to live with his older sister Marie, who's a spinster and does good works. He said he wouldn't abide my shame here, wouldn't abide all the shame I've brought on *his* family."

Saint closed his eyes a moment. God, what was he to do now? He said, "I will speak to your father, Jules. He will not send you to Canada."

Jules wanted to tell him that there was absolutely nothing he could do, but she didn't say it. He'd already saved her; he'd already done much too much for her.

"John said that I'd given it to you."

What a way to talk about sex, Saint thought, so angered at John Bleecher that if the young man had appeared, he would have started beating him again, with great relish. He clamped down on his anger and said quietly, "John Bleecher is a spoiled, thoughtless little rich bastard. I don't know what your sister said to him, but I fully intend to speak my mind to her!"

He felt Jules's head shaking against his chest. "No, please, Saint," she said. "Sarah loves him and she . . . let John have her. He's got to marry her. She's just afraid that he won't, now that I'm still alive."

"She deserves to be horsewhipped."

To Saint's relief, he heard Jules laugh. It wasn't much of a laugh, but it was a start. She was resilient, his Jules. "I agree," she said. "And you may be certain that I'll blister her ears."

"Good. And you may be certain that I'll speak to your father. Canada, for God's sake!"

Saint faced Reverend Etienne DuPres across the man's huge mahogany desk. What a paltry, mean-spirited specimen he was, Saint thought. No humor, no love, just the kind of fanaticism that kills the spirit, doesn't save it. He said without preamble, "I've come about Jules."

"Her name is Juliana," DuPres said, distaste plain on his face.

"Fine. In any case, I've come to speak to you about your younger daughter. She told me that you intend to send her to Canada."

"Yes, that's right. I will not abide her presence here any longer than I must. She is a blight on her family. My sister will take her in hand."

"May I ask why you consider her a blight?" Saint asked calmly, too calmly.

"Come, Dr. Morris," DuPres said, his hands shaking with disgust, "I have no doubt that you, along with many others, have enjoyed my daughter's body. I will abide no harlot in my house."

"Didn't you listen to her? Didn't you hear what she had to say? None of it was her fault, and, I might add, she is still a virgin. She is the furthest thing from a harlot. She is pure and innocent."

And she's been hurt, God, hurt so much.

"Dr. Morris, I understand that many men, once they've taken a woman, don't wish to be bothered with her anymore, you included, evidently. I am her father, more's the pity, and I shall do what I believe best. Now, sir, you will excuse me."

Saint wanted to hit him, but he remembered John

Bleecher's bloody face and moans of pain. He remembered how he'd sworn never to hit another who had not his strength. He stared a moment at Jules's father, wishing he could fathom the way the man's mind worked, but he couldn't, of course. He also realized that there was nothing more he could say. He knew now what he had to do. He knew he had absolutely no choice in the matter. He said nothing more, merely turned and strode out of the man's study and his house.

Etienne DePres stood quietly for a long time, staring at nothing in particular, his mind working furiously. He had absolutely no doubt, just as he'd said, that Saint Morris had debauched his daughter. And Juliana, with her grandmother's wild blood . . . well, he knew her for what she was, had known since she was a little girl what she would turn out to be. And now, he thought, nodding at himself in approval, he knew what he would do. He sat down at his desk and began to write.

10

Saint quietly slipped into the back of the Waine'e Church. It was cool inside, for the building was of stone. It could seat nearly three thousand Hawaiians, most of them packed together on the floor. There were calabash spittoons for the tobacco-chewing chiefs and ships' masters on the far side of the huge room. This Sunday morning, however, there were only about three hundred souls waiting to hear the Lord's words. Saint thought cynically that the souls gathered were so few because Dwight Baldwin, who normally preached at the Waine'e, was across the island ministering to a dying woman, leaving Etienne DuPres to exhort the flock.

He spotted Jules with her family at the front of the church, her face, beneath her plain bonnet, pale and set. He sat back, crossed his arms over his chest, and prepared himself to be bored.

But he wasn't. He was enraged.

After two hymns were sung, Reverend DuPres walked to his pulpit, read from the Scriptures, and spoke briefly and generally of the sins of the flesh. Nothing new in that, of course. It was one of Reverend DuPres's favorite sermons. Then he paused a moment, and Saint could have sworn that he smiled.

"It is difficult," Reverend DuPres said, his voice rising and filling the large room, "for a man of God to be cursed with an offspring who has no moral responsibility, despite all the pious teachings she's received, despite the model of a virtuous mother and father." He paused a moment, aware of the gasps of surprise, aware that he had everyone's attention. Saint tensed. No, he thought, DuPres won't, he wouldn't, not to his own daughter!

"As most of you know, particularly those of you who know my family well, we believed my younger daughter dead. Just as that virtuous woman Kanola is indeed dead, and with our Savior in heaven. The difference between these two women is obvious. The one chose death rather than submit to the wanton evil of the flesh. The other chose to debauch herself, to wallow in sin."

Saint heard a snicker from one of the sailors. He looked at Jules and saw that she was rigid as a statue. Her mother's head was bowed, but Sarah, curse her, was smiling. Thomas' face was red. Saint was barely aware that he had risen and was slowly walking the long distance toward the pulpit. He felt his rage pound through him like storm-tossed waves to the shore.

"My daughter Juliana DuPres," Reverend DuPres continued, his voice stern and cold, "has debauched herself. Indeed, she has a true sinner's disregard for what is good and Christian, and dared to come back to Lahaina—in the company of one of the men who taught her the way of the flesh."

"You goddamned bastard, shut up!"

"I will not shut up!" Etienne DuPres shouted back at Saint, slamming his fist on the wooden pulpit.

"No, I will speak the truth, Dr. Morris! My daughter has proven herself to be a harlot, a slut! And you, sir, have added to her sins! Even yesterday, she tried to seduce, yes, seduce, my virtuous daughter's fiancé, John Bleecher! A fine upstanding young man who was appalled and who would have none of her, of course!"

"Father, that's a lie!" Thomas DuPres roared, jumping to his feet. "He tried to rape her!"

"She is to be reviled, cast out—"

Reverend DuPres got no further. Saint rushed to the pulpit, grabbed him by the lapels of his black frock coat, lifted him a good foot off the floor, and shook him as he would a rat. "You miserable lying worm!" Saint hissed at him. He drew back his arm and slammed his fist into his jaw.

Etienne DuPres collapsed unconscious to the floor.

The place was pandemonium.

Saint turned and very calmly walked to where Jules was sitting, both the white community and native Hawaiians scurrying out of his way. "Jules," he said very gently, "come with me now."

She raised wide, empty eyes to his face.

"Come," he repeated, taking her hand.

"Juliana, no, you can't," her mother whispered, but Jules ignored her. She placed her hand into Michael's and he led her unresisting from the church.

His heart was pounding against his ribs, and he could feel himself trembling. He closed his eyes a moment against the bright sun, unaware that he was squeezing Jules's hand painfully.

When he opened his eyes, he didn't look down at her beside him, merely kept walking toward the beach. The sound of the breaking waves usually soothed him, but not this time. He led Jules to a palm tree and said quite calmly, "Sit down, and stay out of the sun. It's quite strong today. I don't want you to get sunburned."

"I have my bonnet on," she said vaguely, but she moved to stand beneath the palm fronds.

"All within the space of twenty-four hours I've wanted to kill two men," he said in that same unnaturally calm voice. "I, a physician, a saver of life."

She raised her head and saw the pain in his hazel eyes.

"It is my fault," she said simply. "You mustn't blame yourself. You are ... too good and kind. Perhaps he was right— my father, that is. I did choose to live instead of end my life as Kanola did. I suppose I would have allowed myself to be ... debauched to survive. No, Michael, don't blame yourself. I am truly sorry."

Saint shook himself. He was a damned fool, carrying on about himself when it was Jules who was suffering. "God forgive me, I'm sorry." He pulled her against him, comforting the both of them. She was utterly passive, unresponsive.

"Jules," he said quietly after some moments, his breath warm against her temple, "I was there only because I wanted to speak to you after the service, away from your family. I arranged with Reverend Baldwin yesterday to marry us. When he returns from tending his patient, he will."

Jules wanted to howl and laugh at the same time. She knew what her father had said to Saint the day before; her mother had told her. She knew why he wanted to marry her. He was honorable; he felt responsible for her; he felt pity for her.

"I should have killed myself," she said. "Then no one would hate me and revile me now."

His arms tightened painfully around her and she cried out, unable to help herself.

Saint didn't apologize. He said furiously, "Don't you ever say such a stupid thing again! Listen to me, Jules. Even if you had been raped by a dozen men, it wouldn't have been your fault, and I wouldn't feel any less respect for you. For God's sake, if a woman dies in childbirth, is she to blame?"

"But it's true, Michael. All of them, except for Thomas, wish I were truly dead."

"You are not to die. I won't allow you to die until you're well over eighty. You will forget your damned father, your weak, silly mother, and that mean-spirited sister of yours."

She pulled away from him and he let her go. She said over her shoulder, her voice utterly without emotion, "It isn't fair that you feel constrained to make me your wife. I will go to Canada."

"No, you will go nowhere, save back to San Francisco with me." He paused a moment, then asked thoughtfully, "Did you guess that your father would treat you as he has? Is that the reason you wanted to stay in San Francisco?"

"I . . . I don't know. I can't see that it's particularly important now. I do know that my father was closeted with John Bleecher last evening. Michael, how could John lie like that?"

"Forget the little bastard," Saint said sharply, uncomfortable with the renewed rage he felt. "Jules, will you marry me? Will you do me the honor of becoming my wife? Will you come home with me to San Francisco?"

She said, in an attempt at humor, "Wouldn't you prefer me as your mistress? Isn't a wife more expensive?"

"No, I wouldn't, and frankly, I don't remember how expensive a wife is."

Jules blinked at that, distracted. "You've already had a wife, Michael?"

"Yes, in Boston. Her name was Kathleen and she was an Irish girl. Only seventeen, but I was a wordly twenty-year-old. She left me to return to Dublin to fetch her mother. She died there of cholera, as did her mother." Saint paused, aware that he'd spoken emotionlessly. He was also aware that he felt nothing but a faint regret now. Indeed, he could no longer see Kathleen's face in his mind's eye.

"I'm sorry," Jules said, and quickly lowered her eyes. She felt guilty suddenly because she was glad Kathleen was dead and out of Michael's life.

"It was many years ago, and there's no reason for you to be sorry. She wasn't part of your life." Saint's voice was natural now, and he was in firm control again. "Now, Jules, your answer, please."

It wasn't really a question, she knew, but she didn't say that aloud. She wanted to ask him if he loved her, but she didn't ask that either. He didn't. She also knew, in that moment, that she had enough love for both of them. The Lord moves in mysterious ways, she thought blankly.

"Yes," she said. "Yes, Michael, I would be honored to marry you."

He felt as if a great weight had been lifted from his shoulders. His friends had teased him many times about taking a wife. They would doubtless be delighted. And she wasn't a stranger to him. He had watched his own wife grow up—at least he'd known Jules in her most formative years. And liked her and enjoyed her company.

"Come here," he said, "and let me kiss you."

As soon as the words were out of his mouth, he felt another, equally heavy weight descend. He couldn't and wouldn't force her to be a wife in more than name, not after what she had been through.

To his surprise, Jules walked back to him, stood quietly in front of him, and raised her face. He quickly placed a chaste kiss on her pursed lips. They had been friends, and they would continue to be friends. Nothing would change that. He would never hurt her.

Jules opened her eyes. "Thank you, Michael," she said.

"Certainly," he said abruptly, misunderstanding her words. What did she think, he wondered—that he would ravish her here on the beach, like John Bleecher?

He caught her hand in his and they walked from the beach together.

Dwight Baldwin wished he'd been present at the church that morning. Certainly he'd been appalled to hear that Saint had physically assaulted a man of God, but he was willing to make allowances when he heard what Etienne DuPres had said. He smiled at Saint now as he stood beside his new bride. He looked immensely relieved, and he was smiling, thank the Lord. Poor Juliana looked numb. Perhaps everything would work out well between these two very good people. He would send many prayers heavenward to that end.

"You may kiss her now, Saint," Dwight said.

Saint dipped his head and gently touched his closed lips to hers.

Mrs. Baldwin, a placid, plump woman, hugged Jules, and to Dwight's surprise, Jules said with some of her old enthusiasm, "I'd forgotten how beautiful your garden is, ma'am. The kukui, bananas, guava, kou—"

"Don't forget the grape arbors," Saint added, giving her a tender smile. "Surely, Mrs. Baldwin, you remember what a naturalist Jules is. Have you any new plants to show her?"

"Figs," said Mrs. Baldwin. "If you like, Juliana, we can serve you some at the wedding dinner."

Jules turned wide eyes on her hostess. "Wedding dinner? But there is no one to come."

Dwight said easily, though he thought he actually felt her pain for a moment, "Of course we're having a celebration dinner, my dear. You and Saint have many friends here. True friends, you know, remain just that."

"I do not wish," Jules said to Reverend Baldwin, "for you to be in disagreement with my father. It could not be comfortable for you. You have already done so much for me . . . for us."

He wanted to tell her that he thought her father was the most unnatural creature imaginable, but he didn't. There was no reason to upset her further. "I will be just fine, Juliana. You are not to worry about anyone save your new husband, and I think the poor man is becoming faint from hunger."

"I agree," Saint said. "You are to talk about me, my empty stomach, and not about the Baldwins' garden."

Jules took him at his word, and to his consternation, began to tell the Baldwins about his fine and selfless work in San Francisco.

"I think that soon you will be as noble as your nickname, Saint," Dwight said with a crooked smile sometime later in the crowded Baldwin parlor. "You've got yourself a fine woman."

"Yes," Saint said, looking over to where Jules stood speaking to several local Hawaiian families. "I never thought this would happen, even two days ago." He shook his head. "Life is bloody strange."

Dwight laughed. "I'm just glad you weren't already married. Then we would have been in the stew!"

Saint said before thinking, "No, marriage wasn't for me. I . . ." He broke off suddenly, a flush rising on his cheeks.

Dwight patted his arm. "You'll think differently—quite soon, I would imagine. My, my, look who is here."

Thomas DuPres, dressed in his Sunday black suit, stood uncomfortably in the doorway, his hands nervously picking at the rim of his hat.

Saint, without another word, strode to his new brother-in-law and extended his hand. "Thank you for coming, Thomas," he said.

Behind him he heard Jules's soft voice. "Thomas!" He stepped aside and watched brother and sister embrace, Thomas awkwardly patting Jules's back.

Saint said quietly, "After everyone has left, Thomas, why don't you stay awhile? We can talk. As for you, my dear," he continued to his new wife, "would you care for a glass of punch? I'm sure Thomas is also very thirsty."

Before the evening was over, Saint was approached by two ships' captains. Captain Richards of the *Occidental* said, "Wilkes has been a thorn in my side for years, Saint. David Gascony and I were talking. When we get to San Francisco, we've decided to look the bastard up and—"

"And what?" Saint asked, touched and amused by their concern. "There's nothing any of us can do, unfortunately. If you and John made a fuss in San Francisco, my wife's reputation would be seriously damaged, and she would be hurt even more than she has been here."

"Damn," said David Gascony. "I hate to think the bastard will simply get away with it!"

"At least," Mark Richards said, stroking his full whiskers, "you didn't let her bastard of a father get away with his rotten words, blast him."

Dwight Baldwin said, humor lacing his deep voice, "I agree completely, Mark. Would you believe it? Etienne called me to his house to take care of his jaw. I tell you honestly, I was sorely tempted to finish the job. I covered the entire side of his face with iodine, Saint, and told him in all seriousness not to talk for at least three days."

The men laughed. Jules looked up at the sound of Michael's rumbling laughter, and blinked. She thought it was the first time he had truly laughed since she'd seen him again. It was a wonderful sound. He's my husband, she thought. My husband.

"I'll tell you something else, Saint," Dwight said a little while later. "Etienne knew I was going to marry the two of you. He just looked at me, didn't say a single word, and I swear to you, I think he was delighted. In fact, it occurred to me that he may have perhaps denounced his daughter to force your hand."

"Then he is indeed a despicable creature," Saint said, his lips thinning. "I tell you, Dwight, if heaven is populated with a congregation like him, I don't think I want to get past Saint Peter."

"One saint telling another saint to remove himself? Impossible, my dear fellow!"

Dwight arranged with his friends the Markhams to lend a small house to the newlyweds. It was located near Makila Point, only a fifteen-minute carriage ride south of Lahaina. Saint didn't want to be alone with Jules, but there was nothing he could do save accept the Markhams' offer with good grace. He waited until Jules went upstairs with Mrs. Baldwin to pack her few things before speaking to Thomas. Dwight, a gentleman of great understanding, left them alone in the parlor.

"I hate him," Thomas said without preamble. "I hadn't realized how much until I saw how he treated Juliana. And John Bleecher—dammit, Saint, the fellow's paltry, a coward! He and Sarah deserve each other!"

"I agree with everything you've said, Thomas," Saint said, lowering his body into a comfortable chair. "The question is, what are you going to do?"

Thomas DuPres drew a deep breath and blurted out, "I want to go to San Francisco with you and Juliana."

Saint saw the pleading and defiance in the young man's eyes, and slowly nodded. "Yes, I think that would be a good idea. Unfortunately, Jules and I won't be leaving until next Wednesday, aboard the

Oregon. Where will you stay until then? I assume you know that your sister and I are expected to be alone."

"I've already asked my friend Hopu. Hell, Saint, I'd sleep on the beach if I had to."

"Have you thought about what you want to do when we reach California?" Saint held his breath, fearing he'd hear Thomas spout off about finding gold and becoming rich overnight. He was blessedly surprised when the younger man said, his voice rich with determination, "That's easy. I want to be a doctor, like you."

Saint said on a slow smile, "Excellent, Thomas," He rose and firmly clasped his hand. "Will you say good-bye to your parents?"

"I don't know," Thomas said truthfully. "Perhaps by Wednesday I'll be able to, but not now."

"I know just what you mean. Indeed I do. Now, let's drink a bit of Dwight's excellent brandy."

"Father has always hated Juliana," Thomas said, swishing the amber liquid in his glass some moments later. "She's so different, you know."

"I've often wondered about that," Saint said.

"I overheard him talking to my mother about Juliana some years ago—complaining, of course. I think it's all because—and you won't believe this—my mother's mother was a French actress, and Juliana is the very image of her. Evidently my grandmother called my father a petty bourgeois, told my mother she was a stupid twit to marry such a pious prig. My father, of course, could just barely overcome his scruples to marry my mother. And he quickly removed her from all sinful influences."

"I begin to understand," Saint said. "Hair as red as sin and eyes just as wicked, is that it?"

"Yes, I suppose that's it. But it's paltry, Saint, to dislike a person—your own child, for heaven's sake—all because she resembles someone else."

It was more than "paltry," Saint thought later; it was an illness that no physician could cure.

It was a beautiful, calm evening, the waves breaking gently onto the shore, their white crests gleaming nearly silver under the half-moon and brilliant stars.

"We're married," Jules said, staring out over the water from her perch on some volcanic rocks.

"Yes," Saint agreed, wishing she weren't sitting so close to him, "yes, we are. Is it all right with you, Mrs. Morris?"

"Yes," she said, turning to face him. "I promise I won't be very expensive, Michael. I like that—Mrs. Juliana Morris."

There was humor in her voice and it pleased him inordinately. He took her hand in his without meaning to. Her flesh was warm and soft. "That's a relief," he said, smiling at her, "because I don't have that much money. It isn't unusual for my patients to pay me with favors."

"I'm fortunate then," she said with great insight, "else you might have had more trouble rescuing me, isn't that so?"

"Yes, that's so," he said, releasing her hand. A strand of thick hair blew across her face, and without thinking, he reached up to smooth it back. She grew very still, her large vivid eyes unwavering on his face.

He rose abruptly, keeping his back to her. He looked down at his enthusiastic member, now bulging against his trousers, and cursed softly. "It's late,

Jules," he said, his voice sounding harsh. "Go to bed."

Jules stared at his rigid back. "I think I'd rather go swimming," she said softly.

He quivered at that, remembering that night on the beach, her eyes on his naked body. He closed his eyes a moment, but he saw her in his vivid fantasy, saw his hands widening her legs, saw his hands stroking up her thighs to clutch her hips, to bring her down upon him.

"Go to bed," he repeated.

"But don't you want to—?"

He whirled around. "Damn you, Jules, get into the house! I am your husband, and you'll obey me. Now!"

11

Jules woke up abruptly, disoriented for several moments. She stared about the small bedroom and for a brief instant thought that Wilkes was here, and she was again his prisoner.

When she read Michael's brief note, propped up on the kitchen table, telling her he had gone into Lahaina to fetch some food, she felt at first profound relief, than a spurt of anger.

Why hadn't he awakened her? She felt as if she were in some kind of quarantine. Was he afraid that she would be stoned for a harlot if she were to show her face again?

She stripped off her modest cotton nightgown, wrapped her swimming sarong around her, and left the house.

"Jules! I'm back!"

There was no answer. Saint saw her rumpled nightgown on the floor and shook his head. He knew where she was. He closed his eyes a moment. Please, he prayed, she wouldn't, couldn't, swim nude as he had done that night.

He strolled onto the beach, shaded his eyes against the bright morning sun, and searched for her bright head. He felt his heart pound uncomfortably for a moment when he finally spotted her. Dear heavens, she was out so far! Did she want to kill herself? He turned cold at the thought.

He was standing on the beach when Jules, having caught a big wave, was carried nearly to his feet on her stomach. She was laughing. He watched her stand and wring out her hair. The sarong molded her young body, leaving very little to the imagination—at least to his imagination.

"You swam out a good mile," he said, his voice rough, hands on hips.

Jules smiled at him. "Good morning. Yes, I did. I had to, you know. The reef sharks like the deeper water on the far side of that coral reef." He followed her pointing finger.

"I see," he said. "Come along, I've got our breakfast. Can you cook, Jules?"

"I can try," she said, giving him a sunny, guileless smile. She'd determined a good hour ago that she wouldn't make him feel guilty for leaving her alone. She wouldn't nag him or make him sorry he'd married her. She wouldn't say a word about spending the night by herself. She would be the perfect wife.

"That sounds ominous. Perhaps together we can keep ourselves from starvation."

She wanted to tell him how very handsome he was in his loose white shirt and black trousers. But he looked preoccupied, so she merely nodded and trotted after him into the small house.

He said, not looking at her, "Why don't you change first?"

"Actually, I'd like to get the salt water off me.

There's a fresh spring just a few hundred yards away."

"Go ahead, then. I'll see what I can do about feeding us."

When Jules returned some thirty minutes later, Saint realized that he had grown concerned not ten minutes after she'd left. "Next time," he said curtly, "I'll go with you."

"All right," she said agreeably. "This looks delicious!"

They feasted on eggs, fresh papaya, and bread. "You, Michael," Jules said, sitting back in her chair and patting her stomach, "are an incredible man. You can do everything."

"Your hair is dry," he said, disregarding her praise as he eyed the riotous curls.

She touched her fingers to her hair and sighed. "I'll have to tie the mess down with a ribbon."

"No, leave it the way it is. I like it."

She looked so pleased with the meager compliment that Saint flinched. He added, "Your hair is beautiful. I've always thought so."

She actually flushed with pleasure, and he rose abruptly from the table, turning away. He closed his eyes. Lord, he didn't want the responsibility for this fairy creature. She could be too easily hurt. "What would you like to do today?" he asked. Three days and two more nights, he thought blankly. He'd slept outdoors the previous night. Thank heaven they weren't in Massachusetts, in the winter.

"I wish we had time to go to the volcano and see the sunrise. It's very spectacular."

"We don't, unfortunately. Any other ideas?"

She was silent for a long while, staring thoughtfully down at her folded hands. "Kanola and I were swimming off Makila Point when Wilkes kidnapped us. I thought I would be frightened to swim here again, but I wasn't. Is that . . . unnatural?"

She was such a curious little thing, he thought, staring at her. "No," he said finally. "It means that you've got lots of common sense."

"That or no sensibilities," she said. "When Mrs. Baldwin took me upstairs last evening, I told her about it—Makila Point, that is. I thought she was going to faint."

"You didn't tell her any of the rest of it?" he asked carefully.

"No, of course not." She lowered her eyes. "She asked me if there was anything I wanted to know about my wedding night."

Saint swallowed convulsively. "And?"

"I already know everything, Michael! I just asked her if men stuck that thing into . . ." She broke off, her face as red as if she'd been in the sun too long.

He smiled, unable to help himself. "I understand. What did Mrs. Baldwin say?"

"She said yes, that was true, and that it wasn't too bad, not really, but that she was certain that you would be very careful. I told her that it sounded very strange to me."

"Did she say anything else?"

Jules nodded. "Yes, she said that it wasn't strange really and that you were a doctor."

"Those two things go hand in hand? I'd never considered that before."

She saw the amusement in his eyes, and grinned. "Now that you mention it, it doesn't make much sense, does it?"

"Not an ounce," he agreed. "Now, Jules, since

you haven't any ideas to speak of, I think I'll go swimming."

Saint decided that Jules's idea of the male thing that was stuck into women had originated with him. At least Wilkes hadn't paraded about in front of her naked. He suddenly remembered her few words about the sailors. She'd seen a sailor's penis—the sailor who had raped Kanola, probably. He also wondered a few minutes later as he was stroking through the water if Jules would mind lovemaking with him. She certainly seemed interested. He hadn't seen a patch of fear in her eyes when they'd spoken of her conversation with Mrs. Baldwin. Yes, he thought, she had all the frankness of a child, a child who had been desperately hurt. Despite the chill of the water, he felt himself harden. "Damned randy bastard," he snarled at himself.

That evening, they strolled to the beach to watch the sunset. "I'll miss this," Jules said as the sun dipped finally over the horizon, casting the sky in vivid red for a few moments. "I feel a bit like Eve being tossed out of the Garden of Eden."

Saint, who was wearing only a shirt and his cut-off pants, dropped down on the sand and leaned back on his elbows. "Do you cast me as Adam?" he asked.

"I don't think so," Jules said, turning to stare down at him. "I didn't corrupt you."

"I don't think you could corrupt anyone, even if you tried your damnedest."

"I looked at you, very closely, Michael."

He knew immediately what she was talking about. He said, "Yes, I know. Am I the only man you've ever seen with no clothes, Jules?"

She shook her head, a quick, dismissing gesture, and said, "You're beautiful."

"That's a novel thing to say about a man, particularly a huge hairy beast like me. But I thank you."

Jules looked away from him, out over the water. "You changed, even while I was watching you."

Deep waters, he thought, shifting his weight a bit. "A man," he said very carefully, "is very simple in terms of function. When he wants a woman, he becomes larger."

"Yes," she said, "you did." She suddenly turned her large emerald eyes to his face. "Did you want me?"

"I think I just hoisted myself on that evil petard," he said, striving for some humor. "What I should have said is that sometimes a man's body reacts even when he doesn't want it to. Sometimes a man can find himself very embarrassed, and for no reason at all."

In the darkening evening light, he couldn't make out the expression on her face, but he knew she'd stiffened.

"Jules," he said quietly, "do you want me to make love to you?"

"You mean kiss me and touch me and stick—"

"Yes, all of that."

"I . . . I don't know." She sighed, hugging her arms around her knees. "I guess I speak so openly to you because I know you won't do anything to hurt me. Like John Bleecher."

"No, I would never hurt you."

"When I woke up this morning, I thought for just a moment that Jameson Wilkes had me again. And sometimes when I close my eyes, I can see John, and

I feel that awful fear. Of all of it, I guess it's the feeling of absolute helplessness, that because I'm a woman and not as strong, a man can do whatever he pleases to me. I hate that. It's not . . . right."

"No, it isn't. But not many men are like that, Jules. Most men admire and respect women, just as I do. Shall I tell you what I would like?"

"Yes, I suppose so."

"I would like for you to trust me enough to tell me what happened to you during your time with Wilkes."

He saw the frisson of distaste and fear contort her face, barely heard her whispered "No, oh, please no." He made a vow to himself in that moment that he wouldn't touch her until he could be certain she wouldn't be disgusted by him, and afraid. He rose to his feet and dusted the sand off his clothes. "I think I'll go for a walk. Jules, if ever you do want to talk about it, I'll be around to listen."

"All right," she said in a small, thin voice. She watched him stride down the beach. She almost called him back. But she didn't. Slowly she lowered her face and sobbed softly against her hands. If she told him, she knew he would hate her. He wouldn't denounce her as her father had done, oh no. He would remain polite to her, and very kind. But she would disgust him, and she didn't think she could bear to see the distaste for her in his eyes.

The next morning, Saint watched Jules speak to Kanola's husband, a tall, sleek man who worked at the Government Market selling fresh meat. His name was Kuhio, and it was soon obvious to Saint that he blamed Jules for his wife's death. They were speaking Hawaiian, but Saint could make out a few of

Kuhio's words: *hoomanakii, ino, hookumakaia.* And Jules saying over and over the word *minamina, minamina.* Something about her regret, her sorrow.

But Kuhio kept repeating that she was vain, wicked, sinful, a mistress of betrayal.

Finally Saint stepped between them, bowed to Kuhio, and took his wife's limp hand. "Come," he said.

"He told me that he wouldn't let me near his children after what I'd done."

"He's grieving, that's all. It is convenient for him to have you to blame."

She raised wide, strained eyes to his face. "He told me that I was more wicked than my father had said on Sunday."

"Stop it, Jules! . . . Oh, damn!"

"Well, if it isn't my innocent little sister," Sarah said, closing her parasol with an abrupt snap. "Were you speaking to Kuhio? You needn't worry, Juliana, Father has given him money to recompense him for you killing his wife."

We're leaving tomorrow, Saint said over and over to himself. Jules won't have to put up with this anymore. His hands clenched, but he couldn't very well hit Jules's sister, though in his mind, she deserved it.

Jules simply stared at her sister, her eyes bewildered and pleading.

Saint said now, his voice bland, "How well you're looking, Sarah. I do hope that you and John Bleecher marry before your belly swells."

Sarah gasped, then gave her sister a look of utter hatred. "You had to malign me too, didn't you? You evil, wicked girl!"

"Of course," Saint continued, smiling, "after you marry John, I imagine you'll have to keep a keen eye on him. I do hope he doesn't give you syphilis, Sarah."

"You filthy creature! You deserve each other!"

"And I think, my dear, that you and John Bleecher will make the perfect couple. He can make love to you in the dark, then go find himself a helpless girl to force. Do send your sister a letter announcing the birth of your first child."

"John will kill you for that!"

For the first time, Saint felt his rage get the better of him. "I would like to get my hands on that worthless little bastard," he said, his voice evilly pleasant. "Again. Is he hiding his black-and-blue face?"

"Please, please, stop," Jules whispered, grabbing her husband's hand. "Sarah, you can't mean all those things you said—"

"Shut up, Jules! No apologizing to this jealous bitch! Good day, Miss DuPres."

Saint pulled her away with him, ignoring the startled, curious glances cast their way. Let them all gossip, he thought, it wouldn't matter. Tomorrow they'd be gone.

They'd walked into Lahaina, and now they began their walk back to Makila Point. Jules didn't say a word.

Neither did Saint. What could he say?

Saint jerked awake, jumped to his feet, and ran into the small house. Jules was screaming, sobbing as if her heart were breaking.

"Jules," he nearly shouted at her as he sat down beside her on the narrow bed. She was writhing, her body twisted in the single sheet that covered her. She cried out again, whispering, "No, oh God, no!"

He grabbed her shoulders and shook her. "Jules, wake up! Come on, sweetheart, wake up."

Jules felt his hands on her, heard his man's voice, and struggled wildly. "No, don't touch me!"

He didn't want to slap her as he'd done before, but he didn't see much choice. He drew back his hand, then paused. He saw her eyes slowly open in the dim light, saw her blink. "Michael?" she whispered, her voice hoarse.

"Yes, Jules. It's all right now. You're safe, with me." Had he repeated the same words to her before?

She drew a shuddering breath, but she couldn't seem to stem the sobs erupting from her throat. She couldn't seem to break away from the awful dream.

"Jules, tell me. Tell me what you were dreaming." He felt only a moment of guilt, using her vulnerability against her. But it was for the best, dammit. "Tell me."

She gulped down the tears, and buried her face against his bare chest. "He tied me down on his bed, my arms and legs apart. He took all my clothes. He touched me and told me how lovely I was. He told me that he would keep me naked so I would get used to being looked at. He told me that the man who bought me would want me like this. Oh, God!"

"It's all right," Saint repeated, stroking her hair. "It's all right now."

It seemed as though the dam had burst, he thought, listening to her gasping little breaths, seeing through her eyes what had happened to her.

"He threatened me. He told me if I didn't behave for him, he would bring in some of his men and let them play with me. He made me walk about in front of him naked. Then that night he drugged me, and put his hands on my breasts, and kissed them, and I felt so strange, and so frightened. He kept touching me . . . he never let me wear any clothes until that awful red gown. He told me he wanted to take me, but I was worth too much money to him as a virgin." She suddenly reared back in his arms, her eyes wild. "I laughed at him and told him he was an ugly old man!"

"Good for you," Saint said. "Well done, Jules."

"I did it only once," she said, more calmly now. "I was too frightened of him to put up much of a fight after that." She buried her face against his chest again. "He even made me relieve myself in front of him, and bathe. I felt like a cheap, worthless . . . nothing. He wouldn't stop fondling me! God, I hated his hands, and how he looked at me when he was touching me."

He held her tightly against him, rocking her slightly. At least it was all out now. He knew the moment she got a hold on herself and came completely awake. He felt her stiffen.

"Jules," he said sharply, shaking her, "no, don't think what you're thinking."

She sniffed, then very slowly pulled away from him. He let her go and she sank back down on the pillow. She closed her eyes, thinking that even in the dark she could make out the disgust and distaste on his face. All because of a stupid nightmare. She turned her face away.

"Jules," he said quietly, lightly touching his fingertips to her hair. "Do you feel better now?"

Feel better! She wanted to die.

He repeated his question.

Say something, you spineless idiot! "Yes," she managed. "Please, Michael, I want to go back to sleep."

She heard the bed creak as he rose. There was absolute silence for several moments, except for their breathing. He was staring at her—she knew it, she could feel the condemnation flowing from him to her.

Saint sighed, turned, and left the bedroom.

The next morning when he called her for breakfast, she sidled out of the bedroom as if she'd been hiding. She wouldn't meet his eyes.

"We're leaving this afternoon on the *Oregon*," he said, toying with his bread.

She said nothing.

"Is there anything you would like me to fetch for you from your parents' house?"

She raised her head, but still didn't meet his eyes. "My surfboard is hidden behind the house."

"Unfortunately, the water is too cold for surfboarding in San Francisco. I remember you were quite good at it."

"Yes, I am. I will miss that wild feeling." Her voice broke on a sob. "Kanola taught me when we were very young."

This is no Garden of Eden, he thought. This is more like hell we're escaping. He said sharply, "Enough, Jules. Your life has changed—neither you nor I can deny that. But everything will work out. I promise to be a good husband to you. I promise you'll never starve."

"If we're ever on the edge," she said, "you can always sell me to the highest bidder."

He stood abruptly, his chair falling to the floor,

and placed his splayed hands on the tabletop. "If you ever speak like that again, I will thrash you." His anger was immense, but when he saw her flinch, it dissolved immediately. "And if you ever cower away from me, I'll thrash you. Damn you, Jules, I am not Jameson Wilkes, nor am I John Bleecher!" She didn't reply, but then again, he didn't expect her to. He straightened, a bit chagrined by his display, and said more calmly, "Your brother will meet us at the dock."

But Thomas wouldn't meet them at the dock. Later that morning, Dwight Baldwin rode his swaybacked mare to the small house on Makila Point. "Saint," he said. "Juliana."

Saint shook his hand, saw the troubled look in his gray eyes, and said quietly, "What's wrong, Dwight?"

Reverend Baldwin sent a worried look toward Jules.

"What's wrong, sir?"she asked in a shrill voice, her body tensing.

"I'm sorry," Dwight said. "Thomas was beaten up last night. No, no, he'll be all right, but he's in no shape to travel for a while."

"His injuries?" Saint asked in a tight, controlled voice.

"No internal injuries, as best I can judge," Dwight said. "But he's got a couple of broken ribs, and a broken leg. He'll need to stay in bed for several weeks."

"Who did it?" Jules asked.

"John Bleecher and some of his friends. The bunch of them left the island early this morning, bound for Oahu. I suppose they'll stay away until it's forgotten. John's father, when I spoke to him, claimed that his son was conducting some business for him on Oahu. He said his son had nothing to do with any of this and

Thomas is a liar." Actually, Elisha Beecher had been far more colorful in his speech.

"Is Thomas at home, sir?" Jules asked.

"Yes. Reverend DuPres is in something of a quandary," he added. Saint knew exactly what he meant, but Jules, who was concentrating on her brother, didn't seem to hear his words.

She said, "I must see him, Michael, before we leave."

"Yes," he agreed. Jesus, the last thing he wanted was to face her damned father again, but there was no hope for it.

He heard Jules whisper, "It's my fault, all of it."

12

Unfortunately, Saint saw, there were no signs of iodine on Reverend Etienne DuPres's jaw.

"Get out and take my harlot of a daughter with you!" he shouted, and tried to slam the front door.

Saint, without much effort, pushed him back.

"It's your fault," Jules's father yelled as he fell back, shaking his fist at Jules. "Your poor brother, beaten because he tried to protect you!"

"Ah, so now you will admit that John Bleecher attacked your daughter and not the other way around?"

"I admit nothing!"

"Father," Jules said calmly, "I would like to see Thomas."

Saint saw the man's face flood with rage, and quickly said, "We will both see Thomas. After all, he was to accompany us back to San Francisco today. Come, Jules."

"No!" DuPres shouted. Saint shoved him aside as if he were naught to be bothered with. "You little slut—you should have been destroyed the moment you emerged from your mother's womb!"

Saint turned at the foot of the stairs and said very calmly, "If you do not keep your mouth shut, sir, I will break your jaw. This time, I will ensure it is broken. Do you understand?" He took one menacing step toward the man.

"This is my house!"

"Fine," Saint said. "Remember that this is also your daughter and that I, sir, am your son-in-law. I assure you, that fact is the only blot I know of in my family history." He shook his head. "You really are quite a paltry man."

He felt Jules's hand on his sleeve, and turned to walk up the stairs with her. "Easy, sweetheart," he said quietly. "You knew it wouldn't be pleasant. Ignore him. He is not . . . well."

"I have come to realize that he is rather narrow," Jules said. She gazed up at him a moment. "Even if your children were awful, you wouldn't treat them like he treats me, would you?"

"If they looked like you, I'd give them huge bear hugs."

Thomas managed a travesty of a grin when his sister and Saint came into his bedroom.

"Good Lord," Saint said on a whistle, "you look colorful enough to become a country's flag!" He walked to the bed, lifted Thomas' hand, and took his pulse.

"I'll live, Saint," Thomas said. He winced slightly when Saint gently placed his hand on his belly and pressed here and there.

"Yes," Saint said, "you most certainly will—we need more good doctors. I'm taking Jules away today, Thomas. You of all people understand that she must leave. I am leaving money with Reverend Baldwin. When you are well enough, you will book passage and come to San Francisco. All right?"

Thomas closed his eyes a moment and choked down his tears. "Yes, Saint," he managed. "God, everything has been such a muddle, and now this!"

"I know. Now, tell your sister that you're going to live." Saint rose and stood aside.

"Stop looking at me as if I were on my last legs, Jules," Thomas said to his white-faced sister. "Don't be a fool . . . come on now. I'm fine, just fine. Don't you believe your husband? I'll be with you in a month, you'll see." The spate of words exhausted him, and he laid his head back heavily on the pillow.

"Thomas, I'm so sorry," she whispered.

"Women," Thomas scoffed, biting down on the awful pain in his ribs. "Watering pots and silly twits, all of you. Cut line, Jules. You heard Saint—I'll be fine." He was beginning to feel like a parrot, dammit! But birds didn't want to kill, he thought, and to kill John Bleecher would give him the greatest pleasure at the moment.

Jules leaned down and kissed her brother's pale cheek. She stroked her fingertips over his bruised jaw. "I love you, Thomas. We will both build a fine life, you'll see."

"Lord, I know that," he scoffed. Anything to keep away those damnable tears.

Jules kissed her brother again, and stepped back.

"You take care, Thomas," Saint said, shaking the boy's hand.

"Yes, Saint, I shall." He lowered his voice. "Please take good care of my sister. She is so . . . hurt."

Saint felt an unaccustomed lump in his throat. "I will, Thomas, I will."

They were not to escape Reverend DuPres's house with no more confrontations. Sarah, her eyes puffy from crying, her face pale as wax, was standing in the hall below, waiting for them. When she saw her sister, she screamed, "You miserable bitch! God, I hope you die, you don't deserve to live!"

Saint squeezed Jules's hand. He wanted to feel some sympathy for Sarah, but couldn't seem to find any within him. He said in a mocking, cold voice, "You are a bore, Miss DuPres. Let's just hope you aren't a pregnant bore."

"Shut up, damn you!"

"Such language from a missionary's daughter," Saint said in that same mocking voice. "So, John Bleecher has left you high and dry, so to speak. After he tried to kill your brother. And before that, he tried to rape your sister. You have excellent taste in men, it would appear."

"I hate you," Sarah hissed, her hands fisted at her sides.

"Were I you, Miss Sarah, I should be careful what my dear father overheard me say. I wouldn't put it past him to toss you out on your ear for your . . . lascivious leanings. After all, how much is a father expected to take? Two sluts for daughters? Come, Jules. We have a date with the *Oregon*."

Jules followed him silently from her father's house. She paused a moment in the road and stared back. "So much unhappiness," she said in a low voice. "Poor Thomas."

"Yes and yes," Saint agreed. "You are well out of it, sweetheart. And Thomas will be out of it soon."

It was evening, and Saint knew he couldn't tarry any longer on deck. He was alone now, the other few passengers having retired sometime before. As he stared out over the endless expanse of ocean, he remembered the first time he'd ever seen the sea. He'd been with his Uncle Rafe fishing on the Chesapeake Bay. Then they'd ridden to the Atlantic and the thirteen-year-old Saint had wanted only to sit on a rock and stare at the savage beauty of the crashing waves. He pulled away from the railing and sighed. He'd seen the small cabin, the single narrow bed, and gulped. Well, he would simply have to deal with it. After all, he was a man, not a randy boy.

"Damn you, shut up," he said to the randy boy as he strode along the companionway and quietly opened the door to their cabin. He pulled up short. Jules stood in the middle of the small space, her hands clutched around her stomach, bent over.

"Jules, what's the matter?" He was at her side in an instant, his gut wrenching in sudden fear. To his surprise, she straightened immediately and flushed a vivid red. He cocked a brow at her. "I'm waiting," he said. "What's wrong? Do you hurt? Are you feeling seasick?"

"No," she whispered, looking utterly miserable. "I'm not seasick. You know I'm never seasick."

"Then what's the matter?" At her continued pained silence he said sharply, "If you don't talk to me now, I'm going to poke and prod around."

"My . . . stomach hurts," she said in the thinnest voice he'd ever heard.

"Your stomach? Was it something you ate at dinner?"

She shook her head, mute.

"Jules . . ." he said, his voice threatening.

"My stomach is cramping," she said finally.

"Ah," he said, relief flooding through him. "You've

begun your monthly flow." He saw that she was ready to sink through the floor in embarrassment. "It's all right, sweetheart. I'll give you some laudanum in water. It will make you sleep, and when you wake up you'll feel just fine. All right?"

"All right," she whispered.

Now, he thought as he pored several drops of laudanum into a glass of water, he wouldn't have to worry about his body behaving in a reprehensible fashion. He had five days of enforced nobility. He silently handed her the glass of water. She drank all of it, and just as silently handed back the glass.

"Now," Saint said, "why don't you get into your nightgown? You'll be very sleepy soon." *And the last thing I want to do is undress you myself.*

There was no screen, and he left her alone for a good five minutes. When he walked back into the cabin, she was sitting on the side of the bed, swathed neck to toe in a white nightgown.

"Do you feel any better?"

She shook her head, not looking at him.

"Do you have bad cramps every month?"

She shook her head, still not looking at him.

"Does your back hurt?"

"No," she said, looking now at her toes.

There was a single chair in the small cabin. Saint sat down and patted his thighs. "Come here, Jules."

She looked at him, horrified. He only smiled at her encouragingly.

Slowly, color fluctuating alarmingly in her face, Jules padded over to him. He held out his arms, and she sank down onto his legs. He gently pulled her against him and held her.

He felt her tense with cramp.

"It will be gone soon," he said, lightly kissing her hair.

"It's . . . it's nothing to you," she said in a muffled voice.

"Nothing? What it is is natural. However, I do not believe in pain when it can be alleviated. Now, you just relax, and I'll tell you about Louis XIV."

"He was a French king," Jules said.

"Yes, in the seventeenth century. He was called the Sun King. In any case, when he was born, he came into the world with two teeth. The queen, his mother, was appalled, and very wisely refused to put him to her breast. You can imagine the wariness of the two wet nurses. I remember reading that they were well compensated for their stoicism."

He felt her ease, felt her head fall against his chest. He continued, his voice growing softer, "There's another story about poor Louis. It seems that he had a rather embarrassing problem that involved his backside. He had what's called a fistula. The surgeons operated successfully, and the courtiers, to show their sympathy for their king, proceeded to have similar operations!"

Her breathing was even and soft. She was asleep.

"For a while very few gentlemen in the court were able to sit down." He eased her back into the circle of his arm. Her thick dark lashes were fanned against her pale cheeks. He hadn't really noticed before that her brows and lashes were a dark brown, not a washed-out red as one would expect. And not one single freckle, even on the bridge of her nose. A nice straight nose, he thought. And a lovely mouth, a passionate mouth, the randy boy within him added. He continued to study her, perhaps really seeing her for the first time. "You've grown into quite a beauty," he said softly, lightly touching his fingertips to her soft throat. "And now you're my wife . . . and my problem." No, he amended to himself, his responsibility.

He carried his sleeping wife to the bed and gently laid her on her back. He looked thoughtful for a moment, then shrugged. He stripped off his clothes and slipped in beside her. The damned bed was so narrow he could feel the warmth from her body.

When he awoke the next morning, he realized that he was precariously close to falling off the bed. Jules, he saw, turning to face her, was sprawled on her stomach, her arms and legs spread, as if she were floating in the water. He was normally a light sleeper, but he'd never stirred, even when she'd begun her takeover. He smiled, then rose and bathed.

Dressed, he returned to the bed and sat down beside her. "Jules," he said, gently shaking her shoulder.

A very heavy sleeper, he thought, and shook her again.

"Hmmm?" Jules pulled up to her elbows and slewed her head around. "Michael? What's the matter? Where . . . ?"

"We're aboard the *Oregon* and it's morning, and how do you feel?"

Jules ducked her head and said in a muffled voice, "I'm just fine, thank you."

"Good. Why don't you get dressed and join me in the dining room?"

When Jules entered the long, narrow dining room on the main deck of the *Oregon*, she saw a knot of men, her husband in the middle of it. As she neared, she heard laughter, then Michael's voice saying, "To this day, it's called 'burking.' "

"Good God," one heavily whiskered gentlemen laughed, "and to think I'd believed medical science had advanced to the point of curing people, not killing them!"

Saint laughed, then spied his wife. He excused himself. "Hi, sweetheart."

"You're quite a storyteller," she said, remembering his outrageous tale about Louis XIV. "What's all this about 'burking'?"

"In Scotland, not very long ago, a man used to supply the medical school with dead bodies for dissection. Unfortunately, he got into the deplorable habit of strangling people to get corpses. And that was called 'burking.'"

"His name was Burk, I presume?"

"Yep, and he was hanged, finally. After some sixteen-odd folk ceased to exist due to his greed. The medical school paid handsomely for bodies."

"You have quite a talent," she observed.

"It comes in handy, like last night," he added, smiling down at her. "Patients, in my experience, need to be distracted. You're sure you feel fine this morning?"

"Please . . . yes."

"We're married, goose," he said, tucking her hand through his arm. "And I'm a doctor. Two valid reasons why you should never be embarrassed with me."

"If you say so," she said doubtfully.

"I do say so. Now, onward to food. I have a lot of body to maintain."

The day was warm, the weather calm and clear. Jules became acquainted with the remainder of the passengers, met Captain Drake, and listened to her husband charm everyone who came into his orbit.

She felt little or no embarrassment until Michael left her again that night so she could change into her nightgown.

She wasn't asleep when Saint slipped into the bed beside her. She reached out to touch his arm, and realized he was quite naked. She gulped.

"Michael? Would you tell me a story?"

He laughed and turned onto his side to face her. It was probably a fine idea, he thought. He himself needed to be distracted this time. "Well," he began, "let me see. Did you ever hear the story . . . ? No, I think I'll tell you about some of my friends in San Francisco. You've probably heard me mention their names— Delaney and Chauncey Saxton."

She nodded.

"Well, Del is a very rich man. He wasn't, not at first. He was one of the argonauts—that means he came to California in 1849 with the first group of men to search for gold. He found it. Unlike most others, he used the gold he'd discovered wisely. He owns a bank, is a partner in many other businesses in the city, and owns three or four ships that go to and from the Far East. He'll make you laugh within three minutes of meeting him. He's very witty, you see, and gives his witty wife, Chauncey, quite a time of it. She's English, beautiful, and now a mother. She's also very rich in her own right. You'll like her, I'm sure of it."

"Won't she think I'm . . . well, not a very nice person, after what happened?"

"Jules, if you don't stop that foolishness, I'm going to beat you!"

He reached out his hand to touch her shoulder, but instead connected with her soft breast. He sucked in his breath and drew back his hand as if burned.

"I'm sorry," Jules gasped.

"No, no," Saint managed. He grinned ruefully into the darkness. "You see, Jules, I'm not in the habit of sleeping with my wife." *In fact, I'm not in the habit of sleeping with anyone, much less lying in the same bed and not making love.* "Are you sleepy now?"

"Yes," she said, lying without hesitation.

She lay awake a long time, listening to her husband's deep, even breathing.

Saint, the light sleeper, awoke the next morning aware that something was very strange. Jules was lying on top of him, her head resting against his throat. His manhood was hard and throbbing against her soft belly.

"Damn," he said very softly. He realized then that he was lying in the middle of the bed, and in her sleep, she'd just tried to find some space. "Damn," he said again. Very slowly he eased her off him.

"Michael?" she said in a sleepy, slurred voice.

"Yes, sweetheart. Go back to sleep." *Please!*

To his relief and regret, she did, curled up on her side, her hand fisted beneath her cheek.

When he rose from the bed, he cursed himself, even as he turned again to look at her. Her nightgown was bunched about her thighs—long, slender legs, so white and so soft-looking. He pulled a sheet over her.

13

Saint learned in the next several days that his young wife was quite a storyteller in her own right. He came into the dining room one afternoon after treating a fellow passenger for an abscess on his leg, and saw Jules sitting at a table, her hands gesticulating while she talked. He moved closer, saying nothing, his eyes intent on her vibrant face. When he'd known her as a young girl, he'd thought her fascinatingly aware of everything around her, but in the endlessly curious manner of children. Not so, he had come to realize. She'd managed to nurture her curiosity, her complete excitement with life itself. Even the events of the previous month and a half had only dimmed her spirit for a while.

"The whole thing about the *kapus*, you see, was to curtail the native women's freedom. They couldn't eat with the men, couldn't eat certain foods—bananas, coconuts, pork, even baked dog!"

"Good heavens," said Miss Mary Arkworth, "what was there to eat then?" Miss Arkworth, who had lived on Oahu for a number of years and who knew the answer very well, could have added that all the *kapus* were supposedly religious in nature, but she didn't. She was enjoying the very bright Mrs. Morris' enthusiasm too much to dampen it.

"Sounds fine to me," said Nathan Benson. "Let them eat cake if they're not allowed baked dog."

"Well, Mr. Benson," Jules said in a tart voice, "it's all well and good to joke about it, but there was a story about a little five-year-old girl who ate a banana. Instead of killing her, which was the punishment for breaking a *kapu*, they ripped out her right eye."

Amid the gasps of outrage, Saint asked, "Weren't all the eating *kapus* gotten rid of by a woman?"

She smiled at him, as if he were a very bright pupil, and nodded. Her audience quieted, leaning forward to listen. "You see," she said in a confidential voice, "after King Kamehameha I died, his queen, Kaahumanu, announced to her young son that she would be his *kuhina-nui*, or vice-king."

"Smart lady," said Mr. Benson.

"Indeed," said Jules. "And she was a very brave woman. To break the eating *kapu*, she ate a banana in front of the king, Liholiho. He, dear boy, ignored it. Then she had the temerity to eat a meal in his presence!" Jules paused dramatically.

A natural storyteller, Saint thought, smiling at her.

"What happened?" Miss Arkworth demanded.

"Nothing, not a single thing. Kaahumanu broke him down. Finally, at a banquet, the king went to the women's table and began piling pieces of food into his mouth. The vice-king—a woman—won!"

"What became of her?" asked Mrs. Benson.

"She died of old age," said Jules.

"Odd," said Saint. "I thought she died from overeating."

Jules shot him an impish grin. "Well, like most Hawaiian women, she was immensely fat. That, you know, is what is considered beautiful on the islands."

"Now, Jules," Saint said when they were alone a few minutes later, "Victorian prejudices have started taking hold. Many of the Hawaiian women are forcing their healthy bodies into those awful whalebone corsets. You didn't tell all the truth."

She nodded and said sadly, "Civilization is not always such a wonderful thing, I think. And," she added, grinning up at him, "I didn't want to ruin the impact of my story."

Saint cupped her face between his large hands. "You, Mrs. Morris, are a natural."

"A natural what?" Jules asked, her eyes coming to rest on his mouth. She felt a bit breathless and somewhat strange, as if his fingers and his palms were warming her from the inside out.

Saint felt her lean toward him and immediately dropped his hands, saying lightly as he did so, "A natural teller of tall and not-so-tall tales. Now, would you care to stroll on deck?"

"I suppose even naturals must have exercise," she said.

His dreams became vividly erotic, jerking him awake to stare into the darkness, his body covered with sweat and pounding with painful need. He rose several mornings before dawn, unable to lie quietly next to Jules, listening to her even breathing, the soft sighs that made him wonder what her dreams were made of. Certainly not of sex, he told himself. Perhaps of fear and dread of men, but not of sex, not of him.

They were but four days out of San Francisco when he could bear it no longer. He stayed in the small parlor where the gentlemen smoked and gambled until very late, unable to face lying down in that damned narrow bed beside his young wife. He drank too much, lost one hundred dollars at vingt-et-un, and made his way to the cabin well past midnight.

Jules was on her side, facing away from him, the sheet pulled to her chin. He sighed with some relief, eased out of his clothes, and slipped in beside her. She didn't stir.

He slept fitfully, until finally he was lost in that vague, blurred state that seemed so real, so very vivid. Jane Branigan was beside him, touching him, laughing and teasing him, and he was in such great need of her he thought he would die. Then they were lying together and he was stroking her body, calling, "Jane, my God, Jane." He felt her soft breasts, felt her nipples tauten from the teasing of his fingers. God, he wanted her, and now.

"Jane," he whispered, nuzzling against her throat. She wasn't naked, as she should have been. She was wearing something, and the starchy material scratched his mouth. He felt nothing but urgency, and rose over her, pulling the offending nightgown up above her breasts. The touch of her warm flesh made him crazy. His hands and mouth covered her breasts, her smooth, soft belly. He lay atop her, moaning aloud. His manhood, throbbing, urgent, pressed against her closed thighs.

"Jane," he whispered, moving restlessly over her. "I can't wait, Jane."

He pulled her legs apart and felt his manhood surge

forward. But she wasn't ready for him, wouldn't let him enter her. He was frantic now, not understanding.

"Jane," he said again, "what's wrong?"

Jules came abruptly awake. She heard Michael's voice repeating a name. Not her name. Jane. She was suddenly aware that a man, a huge man, was covering her, pressing her down into the mattress, and she cried out, her mind, blurred with sleep, thinking it John Bleecher or Jameson Wilkes. Then something deep within her cried out, refusing to accept the terror of a dream. No, she was with Michael. It was he covering her, pressing against her.

She tried to rise, bewildered, not understanding. She heard him moaning deeply, telling her between gasping breaths to relax, to give in to him. But something was terribly wrong. *Telling Jane to relax!* Suddenly she felt his hand probing against her, felt that male part of him pushing forward against her.

Saint felt wild with need, frustrated and angry that he couldn't enter her body. He felt Jane trying to push him away; then he heard a sharp cry of pain.

"Michael! No . . . please!"

He came awake with jolting awareness. "Jane," he said stupidly, then drew in his breath sharply. In the dim light of dawn, he saw Jules sprawled helplessly beneath him, and he was trying to force himself inside her.

"Oh God, no!" He pulled himself up and rested on his haunches, his head in his hands. He'd very nearly forced his wife without realizing what he was doing.

Jules lay very still. He was on his knees between her widespread legs. "Michael?" she whispered.

"I'm sorry," he managed, hating himself more at

that moment than at any other in his entire life. "I'm sorry, Jules. I didn't hurt you, did I? Are you all right?"

She frowned at him, uncertain, becoming more bewildered by the moment. "I don't understand."

He retreated quickly, rising from the bed and shrugging into his dressing gown. Of course she didn't understand. Lord, it was difficult enough for him to comprehend.

"Who is Jane?" he heard her ask.

He turned slowly to face her, and was relieved to see that she'd pulled down her nightgown and was leaning against the pillows.

He walked to the bed and sat down beside her. "I know you don't understand, Jules." He paused a moment, uncertain what to say. Finally he continued. "I was dreaming, a result of all the damned whiskey, I suppose." *Liar! You're randy as hell and supposed to only* sleep *with your wife, not rut her!* "I didn't realize what I was doing. Jules, I didn't hurt you, did I?"

"Jut a bit. I was surprised. Who is Jane?"

He slashed his hand through the air. "It's not important. Look, sweetheart, I can't continue sleeping with you. I can't trust myself not to . . . well, take advantage of you. You were frightened, weren't you?"

Of course she'd been frightened! What could one expect? But he hadn't been trying to make love to her; it had been another woman he was dreaming about. She closed her eyes against the awful hurt. She turned her head away from him. She had to know, even though it hurt so much. "Who is Jane? Who is this woman you were dreaming about?"

How could he tell her that in a dream he could act

out what he wanted, that his immense desire for her, to be justified even in the recesses of his mind, had to transfer itself to another woman, a woman he wouldn't hurt, a woman he knew wanted him?

His head was aching abominably, and he needed to clear his mind. He rose and began to dress. He knew Jules was watching him, he could feel her eyes on him, but he said nothing. All his concentration was on escaping, both from her and her question and from himself and his repehensible behavior.

He sat down in the single chair and pulled on his boots. "I'm going out for a while, on deck." He was out the door and gone before she could gather two words together.

She didn't cry. She didn't do anything, save lie there looking up at the darkened ceiling of the cabin. He didn't return by the time she fell asleep, the sun rising brightly in the morning sky.

Jules saw him immediately when she came into the dining room late that morning. He'd returned to bathe and change while she'd still slept, she realized from the wreckage in the cabin. He was avoiding her.

Who was Jane?

She drank a cup of coffee and nibbled on a slice of bread and butter. He made no move to separate himself from his cohorts and come to her.

Saint was aware of her the moment she walked into the dining room. She looked a bit pale and tired. He himself felt like the proverbial piece of cow dung, but he'd refused to dose himself to ease the hangover. God, he deserved every shard of pain that sliced through his damned head. This can't continue, he thought sometime later, so weary of pretending to listen to his fellow passengers that he couldn't bear it. He rose finally and managed to escape. He made his way to their cabin. She wasn't there.

With a lagging step he went on deck, finding her seated beneath the mainsail on a pile of coiled rope.

"Jules," he said, greeting her.

She looked up at him but only nodded.

He ran his fingers through his windblown hair. "Look," he said abruptly, "I've come to . . ."

"To apologize?" she supplied when he faltered. "You have already apologized. It isn't necessary for you to do so again."

"Perhaps 'explain' is the more apt word."

"Is Jane your mistress?"

He said sharply, "I told you I don't have a mistress."

"I don't know any other word for it. You make love to her, don't you? You care for her."

"Yes and yes, but it's not the same thing."

"Does she live in San Francisco?" *Is she there now, waiting for you to come back?*

She was speaking so calmly, with far less enthusiasm than she used discussing the dolphins they'd seen yesterday.

"Yes," he said, frustrated, "she does. She is a very nice person, Jules."

"Why didn't you marry her?"

"Because I don't love her, dammit!"

You don't love me either. "I see," she said aloud. "A pity you didn't rescue her. Then perhaps you would have—married her, that is."

"I did rescue her, but not in the same way."

She arched a questioning brow, saying nothing.

He eased down beside her on the coil of rope. The mailsail flapped overhead and the wind whipped through his hair. The smell of salt permeated everything. He wanted to tell Jules to get into the shade, for her fair complexion was turning a distinct red, but he didn't. "Her name is Jane Branigan, and she's a widow with two boys. Her husband died in one of the gold camps and I simply helped her to get started on her own. She owns a seamstress shop and is doing well now."

"Does she know about me?"

"She knows that I was taking you back to Maui."

Jules closed her eyes, fighting against the burdensome pain. He'd more than likely made love to Jane Branigan while she, Jules, was staying in his house.

"She will be . . . upset?"

"I don't know. We are good friends, Jules."

Will you still go to her when we arrive in San Francisco? Will you make love to her? . . . Where's your pride, you stupid twit! She raised her chin. "Perhaps I shall have some good friends who are men."

"Perhaps you will," he said in a light voice.

"Perhaps I shall even dream about them and call out their names and not yours."

He sucked in his breath. *You are twenty-nine years old, you stupid bastard. Have a little sense and wit. She's lashing out because you frightened her, then called out another woman's name.*

"Jules," he said slowly, "I am truly sorry for what happened. It is difficult for a man to be very close to a woman and not . . . well, respond to her. It is also very common for a man to dream about sexual things so vividly that they almost become real. Women do it too."

"I don't."

You haven't because you don't know what to dream about! "Perhaps someday you will understand what I mean. In any case, it won't happen again, I swear it to you."

Jules wished at that moment that he hadn't awakened, that she hadn't cried out. It would have been over with, and she felt now that she could deal with any fear better than this. She said, "When we are home, you will continue to see this Jane?"

He hadn't thought about it. It was the kind of thing that shouldn't happen. A man married, his wife a virgin, and he so damned randy . . . She was so beautiful, his Jules, so bright and vivid, and so very vulnerable. He would simply have to become a monk. He had no choice in the matter. A saint who was also a monk. He supposed it fit.

"No," he said finally. "I will see her, of course, as a friend, but I won't have sexual relations with her again. Marriage, for me, means fidelity."

"Fidelity seems to have no bearing on anything," Jules said, and quickly rose, beating down her skirts as the ocean breeze swirled around her.

"Just what is that supposed to mean?"

She ignored his question, merely shrugging. "I must fetch my bonnet."

"Yes," he said, his voice showing his weariness. "Yes, you should. You're becoming quite red."

14

San Francisco

"Now, Molly, you're an old hand at this. Breathe slowly, light shallow breaths. That's it." Saint gently wiped Molly Tyson's sweating brow with a cool damp cloth.

"I was so scared you wouldn't be here," Molly said as a contraction eased. "I heard you'd gone off to those Hawaiian Islands."

"Yes, I did, but my timing is always exquisite, and so, it appears, is yours. That's it, Molly . . . no, don't tense up. Here, squeeze my hand. That's it."

"Damn, it hurts," Molly gasped. "How could I have forgotten how bad it hurts?"

"I know. Scream if you want to. I know I would." Saint winced as she wrung his hand, her back arched up, her body rigid, in a contraction. "All right, Molly, the pains are coming closer now. Let me see how far along this little fellow is."

He rose and walked to the basin of hot water that Molly's eldest daughter, Elizabeth, had provided. He washed his hands, then returned to the bed. He wished there were another woman to be with her, but there wasn't, and he wasn't about to let twelve-year-old Elizabeth in here. As for Ranger Tyson— the man was useless as a fish flopping on the beach when Molly had a baby. As Saint eased his hand into her, he was grateful that Molly wasn't embarrassed or a prude. Lord knew, he'd had to deliver babies when the women were suffering as much from embarrassment at his presence as from their labor pains. "Things are coming along just fine," he said after a moment. "Not much longer, Molly." He returned to the chair beside her bed and took her hand into his again.

"In a little while I'll give you some chloroform. No, don't tense up. Incidentally, did I tell you that Queen Victoria had chloroform used when she birthed her seventh child last year? If the Queen of England allows it, it's sure to spread."

"I don't know, Saint, Ranger isn't so certain, and Father O'Banyon says that the Bible preaches that women should have pain with childbirth and—"

"To hell with Ranger and Father O'Banyon," Saint said, interrupting her. "Neither of those blessed gentlemen has to do any of the hurting. I've heard that ridiculous argument about women and sorrow until I'm ready to kill. Now, you just think about this new little tyke. You're lucky you aren't an Indian wife, Molly. Did I tell you about the Indian tribe—I can't remember the name—but if a woman in labor wasn't birthing quickly enough, they tied her to a stake out in a field. Yes, indeed, it's true." He grinned at her incredulous look, knowing she was now distracted. "Then, Molly, a brave would ride full tilt toward her, veering away only at the last instant."

"Oh God, that's awful!"

"Yes, but you can imagine that such a fright would do something. Evidently it worked, or I can't imagine that they'd continue scaring the woman out of her wits. That's it, Molly, pant."

He administered the chloroform about ten minutes later. The birth of Molly's third child, a boy, came quickly after that. The chloroform didn't stop all pain, but it certainly lessened the utter agony a woman felt in the last minutes of labor.

"You just get your breath, Molly," Saint said, grinning down at her, "and I'll take your beautiful baby out to Elizabeth."

"Tell Ranger, if he isn't too drunk, Saint. He wanted another boy."

Over an hour later, Saint mounted his horse, Spartan, and rode north back to the city. Ranger Tyson was partner in Hobson's Stables in San Francisco. Instead of money in payment for his services, Saint had bargained himself free stabling and feed for Spartan for six months.

Saint breathed in deeply the crisp, fog-filled air. It was near to dawn, and streaks of crimson had started to slash across the horizon. Why, he wondered, rubbing his jaw wearily, did women always tend to start their labor at night? He'd left Jules asleep, at least he hoped she'd been asleep.

They'd arrived in San Francisco three days before on a foggy, chill afternoon. Jules, used to the balmy weather of the islands, was shivering violently by the time they'd gotten to his house. Lydia Mullens, bless her, had wrapped Jules up and poured hot chocolate down her. He remembered clearly his feeling when he'd stepped into his surgery. It was as if he'd been living out of time. Everything was again as it had been, as it should be, except that he had a shivering wife upstairs. She hadn't been cold before, he remembered, but then, she'd spent all her time in his house.

"Damn," he said aloud with no particular heat, rubbing his hand over Spartan's satiny black neck.

Spartan nickered.

Saint grinned, staring between his horse's ears. "Well, old boy," he said to his horse, "life isn't the way we left it, is it? The question is, what the hell is going to happen now?" Spartan wasn't obliging enough to nicker again.

Saint was tired to his bones, but it was a comforting physical weariness that he appreciated. At least he wouldn't have to endure those damned draining erotic dreams for a while. As for Jane Branigan, she'd behaved with great understanding when he'd visited her the day before. It was almost as if she'd expected it, he realized, thinking back to her words.

"She isn't all that much a child then, I gather," she'd said, pouring him a cup of coffee in her small kitchen.

"She's nineteen," Saint had said. "Not a child, no." Had he given her the idea that Jules was still in puberty?

"And I don't suppose, you being as you are, that we'll be seeing much of you anymore."

"Of course you'll be seeing me. I'm fond of the boys, Jane. It's just that—"

"I know, Saint," she'd said quietly, "I know. Honor, fidelity, and all that."

"I suppose so," he said. He remembered that dream he'd had aboard ship, and clenched his fists at his sides.

His thoughts veered again to his young wife. Jules

had withdrawn from him after that last damned fracas aboard the *Oregon*, and he supposed he couldn't blame her. Lord, how should she have reacted when he'd very nearly forced her and called out another woman's name? Later, when he'd found Lydia unpacking Jules's clothes in his bedroom, he hadn't known what to say. He didn't want to sleep in the spare room—the damned bed was too short for him.

And he couldn't sleep with her. It was simply too much.

To his surprise and silent relief, Jules had taken the matter out of his hands. He'd been called away to treat a broken hand—the result of a fistfight, of course—and when he returned that evening, he saw that she'd moved all her things down the hall to the spare bedroom.

He didn't know what to say to her. *Thank you, wife, for not forcing me to sleep with you.* It was odd, he thought, frowning slightly. He'd never in his life been so damned obsessed with sex. Sex was just something that went along naturally with everything. *I guess not having it makes my mind weird,* he concluded, hoping it would go away.

And there was Jules, smiling, chattering gaily, primarily with Lydia, until his—no, *their*—housekeeper had left for the night. Then she'd become quiet and withdrawn again.

He'd settled quickly back into his routine. As for Jules, he wasn't certain exactly what it was she did when he wasn't there.

"Spartan, what about Jameson Wilkes?" he said aloud to his horse. Spartan nickered, but at their entry into the city, and not in response to Saint's profound question. Already, men were up and about.

He returned greetings and continued toward Hobson's Stables on Market Street.

"The bastard," he continued to his horse after a moment, "is bound to discover that Jules is married to me. What the hell will he do?" *He won't believe she's a virgin anymore. She won't have any more value to him.* "True enough," he said in response to his silent observation.

He left Spartan at the stable in the capable hands of John Smith, an unlikely name for an unlikely gnomelike individual, and walked the short ten minutes to Clay Street and his house.

He suddenly thought of Jules pregnant with his child, of Jules giving birth, and he felt a knot of fear. He hadn't exaggerated his birth size to her. He'd been enormous, but his mother, bless her humorous soul, had been a large-boned woman, capable of carrying him and birthing him without too much danger to herself. Jules wasn't large-boned, and he realized he didn't know how wide her pelvis was. He closed his eyes a moment, tripped over a discarded piece of pipe in the street, and cursed roundly. He let himself in quietly, and eased into his bed.

"You have some visitors, Jules," Lydia Mullens said to her young mistress the following afternoon.

Jules quickly bounded to her feet, her book dropping to the floor beside her chair in their small parlor. "Vistors?"

A bright feminine voice said behind Lydia, "Please forgive us for just barging in like this, but we couldn't wait for an invitation from Saint! Married! Agatha and I had to meet the new Mrs. Morris."

A very lovely young woman with high-piled chestnut hair came gracefully into the parlor and thrust out her hand. "How do you do? I'm Chauncey Saxton, and this, my dear, is Agatha Newton. Oh, how beautiful you are—not that any of us doubted it for a moment! Saint has the most stunning taste."

Jules took the gloved hand. "My name is Juliana, but Michael calls me Jules."

"Michael?" said Agatha Newton, arching an eyebrow. "Lordy, so the dear man does have a real name! I'm Agatha, my dear."

"Hello," Jules said, a bit dazed. Agatha Newton was an older woman, massive-bosomed, with a booming, very kind voice.

"I'll bring in some tea, ladies," Lydia said. "You just sit down, lovie, and entertain the ladies."

"Mrs. Mullens," Chauncey Saxton said, "must think she's died and gone to heaven. A lady, finally, in Saint's house."

"Please," Jules said, waving her hand, "please do sit down. Michael told me about the Saxtons and the Newtons, of course. He said you were all dear friends."

"Yes indeed," Chauncey said. "Jewels, huh? You mean like diamonds and emeralds?"

"No, actually, J-u-l-e-s," she said, spelling out her nickname. "Michael didn't want to distort my real name too much."

"Just wait until I tell Horace—my husband, you know—Saint's real name! Lord, the dear boy is in for a thorough razing."

Jules smiled, relaxing for the first time. "Actually, 'Michael' is only one of his real names," she said with an impish smile.

"Both ladies leaned forward in their chairs, questions on their faces.

Jules laughed. "No, I must have loyalty to my husband."

"Where is Saint, or Michael, by the way?" Chauncey asked.

"There was a problem of some kind. He said something about having to go see Maggie."

"Ah," said Chauncey. Her husband, Delaney, had told her about the new Mrs. Morris' experience. Now wasn't the time to bring up Maggie's profession, or the probable profession and sex of his patient.

Lydia Mullens came into the parlor at that moment, carrying a rather tarnished silver tray. "I didn't have time to polish the thing," she said apologetically to Jules. "In fact, Saint's never used the tray before."

"Things are very different now," said Agatha with great complacency.

"Now, Jules," Chauncey said after sipping the delicious jasmine teas, "Agatha and I are here to invite you to a small dinner party at our house. Saint has already accepted, but we wanted to meet you and invite you in person. It's time you met some of San Francisco's fair populace."

Jules felt a bolt of excitement. "That would be wonderful," she said enthusiastically. "Oh dear, I must buy a new gown, and I must ask Michael if . . ." She broke off suddenly. "Michael said it was all right?"

Chauncey paused a moment, suppressing the frown that threatened to crease her brow. What had this poor girl been through? What indeed was her relationship to Saint? She said finally, in a very firm voice, "Of course Saint agreed. He's very proud of you and wants you to get out and about. Why don't you accompany me tomorrow, say, to Monsieur David's? He's an excellent modiste—but that's a woman, isn't it? Well, whatever he is, he's quite good and has a marvelous selection of lovely gowns, many of them from Paris."

I'm blabbing like an idiot, Chauncey thought, bringing her flighty monologue to a halt.

"I should appreciate that," Jules said. But she was worried about money. Clothes were expensive, she assumed. Perhaps Michael didn't wish to spend money on things like that.

Agatha and Chauncey stepped into Chauncey's open carriage some thirty minutes later after a thoroughly satisfactory visit. Chauncey said to their driver, Lucas, "Let's go to the Newtons' home now, please."

"She's very . . ." Agatha broke off, shaking her gray head.

"Vulnerable? Frightened? Wary?" Chauncey said.

"Yes, I suppose all of those things."

"I shouldn't care if she were a wretched individual," Chauncey said. "We must take care of her, for Saint's sake."

"Don't you mean Saint Michael?"

Jules felt excited, yet very tense. Michael didn't return home until late in the afternoon, and by that time she was nearly incoherent with anxiety.

"Hi, Jules," he said, striding into the parlor. "How was your day?" He shrugged out of his light coat and tossed it to a chair back. "What's wrong? Do you feel ill?" He'd looked at her only a moment, but he was so aware of her that he sensed almost instantly that something was different. He watched her glide her tongue over her bottom lip.

It affected him as strongly as if she'd thrown herself naked upon him. This has simply got to stop, he told himself. I will not be a slave to my damned randy body.

"Michael, do we have any money?"

He blinked at that. "Enough. Why?"

She said in a tumbled rush of words, "Mrs. Saxton and Mrs. Newton were here and they invited us to a party and Chauncey said she'd take me to Monsieur David's for a new gown and I didn't know if you would mind or if you would want—"

He held up his hand to stem the flow of words.

"He sounds very expensive," she said, ignoring him in an effort to get it all out at once, "and Father, well, he never . . ."

Saint felt that damned elusive pain at the pathetic trailing off of her voice. She looked up at him, hopeful as a child, but certain that a treat was to be denied. But she wasn't a child, dammit.

He said very gently, "Jules, of course you must have a new gown, several in fact. Do go with Chauncey. And don't worry about money, all right?"

"But—"

"No buts. Don't worry."

"But Lydia told me how, many times, you have to barter for things, and how people owe you favors, and I don't want to be a burden to you, at least more than I already am."

That made him angry. Damn Lydia anyway for her big mouth! "Enough, Jules," he said sharply. "You are not a burden, and don't you ever speak like that again, do you understand me?"

She wilted at his anger. "I'm sorry," she whispered, her head bowed. "It's just that I *am* a burden. I don't do anything, nothing at all, and I'm—"

He couldn't bear it. He strode swiftly to her and

gathered her against him. She was rigid for a moment then leaned against him. He breathed in the sweet scent of her hair, felt her small bones beneath his fingers. He closed his eyes and held her. "I want you to be happy, Jules," he said finally, his warm breath against her temple. "There is enough money, I promise. I could have ten burdens like you and it wouldn't matter. In fact, I'd like it very much."

He could still feel her uncertainty, her resistance, and said in a teasing voice, "I think you would look lovely in pink."

"Pink?" she squeaked, looking up into his grinning face. "With my hair?"

"That's better." Without thinking, he quickly kissed her pursed lips. She flushed. Get her mind off you attacking her again, you ass! "How about an emerald necklace, then? To match your sparkling eyes?"

She smiled at that, naturally this time. "You truly don't mind, Michael?"

"Idiot," he said, squeezing her. "Now, would you like to ride out to the ocean with me? There are a number of birds I would like to have you identify for me. Talk about ignorant—all I can recognize is a gull and sometimes a cormorant. They've got long, skinny necks, don't they?"

She gave him a brilliant smile and he thought: She's my wife, she belongs to me, and I want her to be happy. He remembered so vividly that single night when he'd brought her pleasure, the convulsive rippling of her slender body, the soft cries that erupted from her throat, the taste of her. Damn, he wished he could stop thinking about it, forget it. He released her abruptly, knowing that if he continued to hold her, she would feel his hardness. He wouldn't frighten her. Never again.

He bundled her out of the house before he could be trapped by another patient. He rented a mare for her from Ranger Tyson, the proud new father of another Tyson, and they made their way to the ocean, very slowly, for Jules wasn't all that used to riding.

"When you go with Chauncey tomorrow, be sure to buy yourself a riding habit, all right?"

Jules pulled her cloak more closely about her. "I've never had a riding habit," she said.

"In royal blue," Saint said firmly. "Now, sweetheart, what is that damned bird over there on that sand dune?"

"That, I believe," said Jules with great concentration, "is a snowy plover. And that one," she said, excitement and fun in her voice as she pointed to another bird, "just might be a wandering tattler."

He grinned over at her. "I know quite a few wandering tattlers, and they all speak English. You wouldn't be making that up, now, would you?"

"No, sir. I love the name, don't you? I've really never seen one in the flesh-and-feathers before, but it does look like a bird in one of my books."

"Books?" he asked. "I don't recall seeing any."

She was silent for a long moment, saying finally, "I have two of them. They're in Lahaina in my father's house. I had hidden them under my bed and forgot about them in all the . . . excitement."

"Tomorrow," he said, "or the day after, we will replace them for you. Also any more books you want. My library is rather meager." He saw that she would argue with him, and added quickly, "If you see a small plant, maybe it's a yerba buena, which is, just in case you don't know something I do, the original name of San Francisco."

Jules nodded, knowing his intent, and said in a forced gay voice, "I will look. And perhaps we'll see a Bonaparte gull."

15

"Now, Dan Brewer is my husband Del's partner at the bank," Chauncey was saying to Jules. "We're trying to find him a wife, but the pickings here in San Francisco are still quite slim. Another gentleman you'll meet is Tony Dawson, part-owner of the *Alta California*, another one of those bachelors. You recall that young lady I introduced you to before lunch? The one who treated me like I had the plague, and looked right through you?"

At Jules's nod, Chauncey continued, "Well, my dear, that is our own lovely Penelope Stevenson. A more snobbish, gossiping, ill-humored female you'll never meet. Her mother looks like a ship under full sail and her father, Bunker ... well, he's jovial enough, I guess. Ah, there's Lucas with the carriage. I must get home to feed Alexandra now. Would you like to come with me?"

But Jules had just spotted a small bookstore, and remembering Michael's promise, said, "No, I think I'll browse a bit more." She pointed to the bookstore across Kearny Street.

"That's Mr. Jointer's shop. You'll like him. Very well, Jules, I'll see you Thursday evening. It was such fun, and you'll look exquisite in all your new clothes."

Jules thanked her once again, her hand not too steady as she thought about the awful amount of money she'd spent at Monsieur David's.

"Give my love to Saint."

Jules watched Lucas, a pirate of a fellow if Jules had ever seen one, help Chauncey Saxton into the open carriage. He was, Chauncey had told her, married to her longtime maid, friend, and housekeeper, Mary. "And therein lies a story!" she'd said, shaken her head, and laughed.

Jules waited on the sidewalk, waving her hand until the carriage was swallowed up in the incredible traffic along Kearny Street.

She gathered up her skirt and began to weave her way among drays, beer wagons, lumber wagons, and myriad types of men, who all stared at her to the point of embarrassment. She remembered Chauncey's words. "There are so many lonely men. We have more and more women and families moving here all the time, but still so many men have no one. For the most part, you needn't worry, they're quite respectful." And they seemed to be, she saw.

I'll just see what Mr. Jointer has in stock, Jules told herself. I won't buy anything, not today. She had reached the shop when she chanced to look up. Her body went rigid. Jameson Wilkes was striding toward her, looking every inch the successful businessman in a dark gray suit. Jules grabbed for the doorknob, but it didn't turn. She looked blankly at the small sign in the window: "Closed until 2:00." Oh God, what was she to do?

He saw her. She saw him stare a moment at her,

not at first recognizing the girl dressed in the dark blue muslin gown, her wild hair held firmly in place beneath a small bonnet. She knew the moment he realized who she was. *He can't do anything to you, idiot! There are dozens of people about. He can't do a thing!*

Jules squared her shoulders and gave him her most insolent, contemptuous look.

"Well, well," Jameson Wilkes said, giving her an appraising look as he drew to a halt only a foot away from her. "As I live and breathe. If it isn't the new Mrs. Morris." He swept off his hat and gave her a mocking bow. "I must say, my dear, I think I prefer you in your natural state, sprawled on your quite lovely back on my bed. But then again, ladies' clothes tend to drive men's imaginations wild. Oh yes indeed."

She felt a searing pain in her stomach and vaguely recognized it as fear. *He can't do anything to you!* "Well," she said in the coldest voice she could find within herself, "if it isn't that dishonorable, filthy pig of a man. Mr. Wilkes, your clothes bespeak a civilized man. How strange and how disturbing that appearances are so deceiving."

He sucked in his breath, wanting nothing more than to fling her over his shoulder, perhaps beat her senseless, and remove her to his house. He wouldn't force opium down her, oh no. He wanted her to know everything, feel everything he would do to her. Instead, he said with a short, humorless laugh, "How very brave you are, my dear Juliana. And so very insulting."

"It is quite easy to be so with you, sir. Although *sir* denotes a gentleman, doesn't it? How silly of me to make such a mistake."

"You think you've won, don't you?" he said very

softly. "You think yourself safe from me, don't you? You and that damned husband of yours."

"Well, of course," she said, hoping her voice sounded confident and contemptuous at the same time. "I am married to a man, an honest man, and—"

"And he saved you that night. Ah yes, I found that out, but not until you'd returned from Maui with him, married. He and his Sydney Ducks, the worthless scum—"

"Certainly like should recognize like! But in this case, Mr. Wilkes, their actions were noble and honorable. I should prefer any number of them to you."

Jameson Wilkes got a hold on himself, but it was difficult. The smart-mouthed little bitch! God, he wanted to touch her! "And how do you like marriage, my dear? As I recall so well, you didn't know at all what it was men did to women. Do you like your husband plowing your little belly with that huge rod of his? Ah yes, I know he's a huge man—heard it from many of our more colorful ladies in this city. They're pining for his return to their respective beds, you know."

Jules sucked in her breath, her face going white. She knew he was lying, knew Michael wouldn't touch another woman, knew . . . Get a hold of yourself! "You are a pig and a bastard," she managed to say, her voice almost pleasant. "If ever you speak to me again, my husband will kill you. Or I will."

"Such language from a missionary's daughter," he said, his eyes glittering down at her.

"One must be appropriate at all times," Jules said. "Unfortunately, I do not know appropriate language to fit your character. Perhaps the Sydney Ducks do."

With that parting shot, she turned on her heel and

marched away from him, her head held high. She didn't pause even when she heard his mocking laugh behind her.

"We will see, Juliana!" he called after her. He found that his muscles were knotted with tension, and he forced himself to take slow, deep breaths. The thought of Saint Morris taking her, sating himself in her lovely body, made him want to spit, which he did. He suddenly remembered how very pale she'd become suddenly when he'd spoken so mockingly about her husband plowing her belly. Why? he wondered. Or had she turned pale at the thought of Saint Morris fucking whores? He strode thoughtfully across the street. Could it be, his thinking continued, that the bloody doctor was soft, had listened to his young wife's pleas, and hadn't yet taken her? He was, after all, a doctor, a man reputed to be kind and gentle, despite his great size. The stupid sod! It was something to think about, indeed it was. After all, he had married her out of obligation, nothing more. Wilkes's lips thinned. It was impossible to believe she was still a virgin, even though he wanted to, very much. No matter. He would still have her. He rubbed his hand over his stomach at the familiar burning pain.

He had all the time in the world, and he knew he must go very slowly and carefully now. Saint Morris was a highly respected man, with powerful friends. But Wilkes would find a way, he certainly would. He was smiling when he entered the El Dorado saloon some ten minutes later.

James Cora was leaning against the long mahogany bar, a thick cigar in his mouth. "Looks like you just won yourself a pot of money," he observed.

"Not yet," Wilkes said smoothly, "but one never knows. How about a whiskey?"

"If I tell Michael," Jules said in an agonized whisper to her pale image in the mirror, "he will go after Wilkes. But Michael is honorable, and Wilkes isn't. He would hurt Saint, I know it. He would hire men and they would hurt him, maybe even kill him."

She turned slowly from the mirror, not knowing what to do.

"And it would be all my fault."

"Did you say something, Jules?"

Jules whirled around at the sound of Lydia's voice. "Oh no, I was just thinking out loud."

Lydia frowned at her young mistress. She didn't look well, not at all. She said, "Saint's downstairs taking care of a Chinese who got his arm cut open. If you want to talk to him, he'll be done in ten minutes, I'd say."

"Yes, thank you, Lydia."

Saint was gently suturing Ling Chou's thin forearm. "Did you know that old Bonaparte wanted to march on China after he'd gotten Russia?"

Ling Chou, who was gritting his teeth, not making a sound, because a man shouldn't complain, blinked at Saint. "No hear that," he managed.

Saint hadn't either, but he continued, "Yes, sir. Way back in 1811—*was* it 1811? he didn't remember—"when he was making his plans, he said to his military advisers, 'After Moscow, it's on to Peking, to make myself emperor of the world.' " Saint set the last stitch. "Of course with men like you there, Ling Chou, the little man wouldn't have stood a chance. Sometimes I think it's a pity that he didn't go to

China first—would have saved a lot of trouble for England and France. I'll just bet there wouldn't have been a Waterloo. You men would have taken care of him just fine."

"You think so, Saint?"

Saint deftly tied off the last stitch. "Sure do," he said cheerfully, "and I'm all done here. Good job, if I say so myself. Now, I'm going to clean this off real good and bandage it. You come back in three days and I'll change it. Don't get it dirty or wet, you hear me?"

"I hear," said Ling Chou. When Saint finished the bandage, Ling Chou paid him, counting out the five dollars in meticulous fashion, bowed, and walked slowly to the door. "Bonaparte, huh," he said, turning. "Who is Bonaparte, Saint? And who is this Waterloo?"

Saint grinned. Hoisted on my own petard, he thought. "Just a fool general, Ling Chou, long dead, and a place that won't ever forget him."

"I see," said Ling Chou with great dignity.

"I've got to come up with some stories about real Chinese people," Saint said to himself as he straightened up his surgery. "That one was off the mark entirely."

He nearly knocked Lydia down as he strode out of his surgery. He caught her arm to steady her. "What's this? Sorry, Lydia, but where's the fire?"

"I just wanted to talk to you before you see Jules."

A thick brow went up. "What's wrong?"

"I don't know, but she's upset about something, and she wouldn't say anything to me. She looked pale as a clean sheet."

Saint was silent for many moments. Finally he said, "I'll take care of it, Lydia."

But there was another patient at the door, this time one of Jane's boys, Joe, and he had a black eye as impressive as any Saint had ever seen.

"Won't you come back with me, Saint?" Joe pleaded. "Mom won't get mad if you're there."

"Coward," Saint said, grinning at the boy. "You've got a while to come up with a heart-wrenching tale to tell her. She'll still probably tan your butt, boy."

Joe looked glum. "You never come by for dinner anymore. Mom doesn't say much, but I know she misses you. All of us miss you, Saint."

At the door, Jules paused a moment at the boy's words. Oh, damn, she thought, wanting to escape, but knowing she couldn't, not now.

"Hello," she said just before Michael and the boy saw her. "I'm Jules." She thrust out her hand to the boy, and he took hers automatically. "My, what a beautiful assortment of colors! Reminds me of the moorish idol—that's a fish, you know—yellow and black and some white thrown in for good measure. I do hope you gave a good account of yourself."

Saint saw Joe staring at Jules as if he couldn't believe his eyes. He cleared his throat. "Joe, this is Jules, my wife. I'll tell you what. Both Jules and I will come over to see your family sometime soon. All right?"

"You're awful pretty," Joe said. "I didn't know Saint got hisself married."

"Hisself is very married," Saint said, grinning at his wife. "Of course she's pretty, Joe. Now, you run along home and face your medicine. Sorry, but there's no way I can hide that eye."

"Not even a black patch?" Joe asked hopefully.

"Now, that's a fine idea," Saint said, appearing much struck. He thought of Jane's face when her son walked in looking like a miniature pirate. "Hold on a minute, Joe. I think I just might have one lying about."

"I've never seen hair that color before," Joe said as Saint disappeared into his surgery. "It's awful red."

"Yes indeed," Jules said. "I'd much rather have hair your color."

"Nah, I'm a boy. Girls don't want to look like boys."

Don't think it for a minute, she thought, staring at the thick thatch of dark blond hair. Did his mother have the same color hair? Was she as pretty as her son was handsome? Probably. Hadn't Chauncey Saxton said that Saint had exquisite taste in women?

"Here you are, Joe." Saint carefully fitted the black patch over Joe's eye. "Lordy, what a swashbuckler you are! Do you like it, Jules?"

"Most impressive," she agreed. "You look a bit like Lucas, the man who works for the Saxtons. Your mother will be so taken aback, she just might forget to chew a strip off you."

"I doubt it," Joe said, staring at himself in the window. "Thanks, Saint. A pleasure, ma'am," he added awkwardly to Jules.

Saint chuckled after the boy had left. "Cute lad," he said, eyeing his wife from the corner of his eye.

"Yes, he is, very."

Saint gently clasped Jules's hands, and brought her close to him. "Now, what's wrong, Jules?"

"Wrong?" she repeated in a shrill voice. "Whatever do you mean, Michael?"

"You went out with Chauncey Saxton, and now you've got a long face. Didn't you find any gowns you liked?"

"Certainly, but they needed altering and will be delivered tomorrow." *I'm not going back to get them—not alone, in any case.*

"Did someone say something to you?" She was so guileless, he thought, her eyes gave everything away. He could see her trying to manufacture a quick lie, and gently shook her. "What happened?"

"I met Penelope Stevenson!" she said.

"Oh no, not that godawful twit! Did she say something unkind to you?"

Penelope hadn't, but Jules nodded vigorously.

"What?"

"She said I was a . . . an adventuress!"

"Jules," Saint said very patiently, "I am still the master storyteller in this house. Don't try to outmaster the master. If you don't tell me the truth, I'll . . . well, I don't know what I'll do. Maybe beat you, or lock you up and not feed you for three days."

I'd rather starve and be beaten than have Wilkes hurt you, she thought in silent misery.

"I'm waiting."

She shook her head, stubborn as a mule. He looked at her, his frustration mounting. There came a knock at the front door. Another damned patient. He released her, a frown furrowing his forehead. "Don't you dare try to make up another story before I get back to you, Jules."

"Michael," she called after him, "would you like me to assist you? I've got a very steady stomach, you know." What an inspiration, she thought, inordinately proud of herself.

"No, certainly not," he called back when he saw who his patient was. One-armed Johnny. The last thing he wanted was for Jules to meet one of the most dishonest little bastards in the city.

"Saint, I've got a friend who got coshed on the head. He's bad, Saint, real bad."

"All right. I'll be right along. Jules, don't wait dinner for me. This might take a while."

"Good-bye," she said. "Take care!"

With One-armed Johnny to protect him, he didn't have a thing to worry about, he thought, giving his wife a reassuring wave of the hand.

Her shoulders drooped when the front door closed behind Michael and that disreputable-looking man. She walked slowly into the parlor and stared about her. At least back home she could have spent hours wandering the beach and swimming. Identifying birds, feeding the fish, just enjoying the sun on her face . . . playing with Kanola's children. But Kanola was dead. So much had happened in such a short time. Too much, and yet not enough. Not only did she now have a husband, she was also a prisoner.

She decided to write to Thomas.

"Well, if it isn't Saint Michael and his lovely bride! Come on in, both of you."

Saint shook his head ruefully. "You've done me in," he said to Jules. "All right, Del, have your sport, but my wife is sworn to silence."

"You mean silence about your other name?" Jules asked innocently, and he squeezed her until she squeaked.

Del Saxton grinned as he led Saint and Jules into the parlor. "Here's our guest of honor, Chauncey," he said. "Lord, you picked a beauty, Saint," he added, giving Jules an appreciative look.

"Don't show your true colors just yet," Chauncey said, buffeting her husband lightly on the shoulder. "Remember you're a very married man with a child to boot. Lovely, Jules, really lovely. The gown is perfect for you."

"I agree," Saint said. "The green nearly matches your eyes, sweetheart." He'd had the strong urge, when she'd come downstairs to join him, to rip that lovely gown off her. Her shoulders were bared, milky white above the lace. "Lovely" wasn't the word he would have chosen for her. Her waist looked minuscule and he guessed that Lydia had pulled her stays very tight. He disapproved of that, but Jules had looked at him with such eagerness, such hopefulness, that he said nothing about the damned corset. "Beautiful," he'd managed in a choked voice.

"Truly? You're not just saying that?"

"No, I'm not just saying that."

She'd fluttered about for a moment, then blurted out, "It cost so much money! And all the underthings, and the gloves—"

"Don't be an ass, Jules. I thought I told you to leave the money to me."

Even now, in the middle of the Saxtons' parlor, knowing he should have himself well under control, he wanted to lean down and kiss her white throat, and her shoulders, and the soft swell of her breasts. Lord, he wanted . . .

"You're looking lost to this world, Saint," Chauncey said. "Come, have a glass of sherry."

He pulled himself together and forced himself to

look at his wife without the greed of desire in his eyes. "Would you like some sherry, Jules?"

"I've never tasted it before," Jules said, looking shyly up at her husband.

I want you so much, he wanted to tell her. Instead he said, "Just a little, Chauncey. I don't want a drunken bride."

The Newtons arrived a few moments later. Horace eyed Jules with an experienced connoisseur's eye and nodded. "Well done, my boy. Aggie here told me what a pretty filly she was, but she didn't go far enough."

"I feel like a racehorse," Jules said, and everybody laughed.

Agatha hugged her briefly. "You'll have to get used to all the gentlemen looking at you like you're a new dessert, my dear. Just wait until Tony and Dan arrive."

Tony Dawson, a journalist to his fingertips, hadn't, unfortunately, heard about Jules's background, and asked her over the first course of terrapin soup how she'd managed to tie herself to a big oaf like Saint.

Saint felt her stiffen beside him. She sent him an agonized look, her tongue frozen in her mouth.

"Jules comes from one of the Hawaiian Islands, Tony," he said easily. "I knew her when she was a skinny little girl. I must admit, age has brought some astounding changes."

"Hawaiian Islands," Tony repeated, his interest aroused. "However did you get together again?"

Chauncey said brightly, "Haven't we some champagne, Del? Agatha, won't you try one of Lin's delicious rolls? Dan, some more peas?"

I can't sit here like a puppet, Jules thought, and let

everyone protect me. "I came to San Francisco and we met again, Mr. Dawson," she said in a clear voice.

"I see," Tony said. "Call me Tony. Everybody does, you know."

"My father is a minister in Lahaina, Maui," she continued, seeing that he was as confused as ever, but too polite to probe. "Michael was a doctor there."

"Michael?" Tony said, clearly startled, and thankfully turned his attention to that new tidbit.

Saint sighed. "That's right, Tony. But please, I feel more comfortable with 'Saint.' "

"It fits so well," Del said.

Dan Brewer, Del's partner, who had been told of Jules's experiences, said quite gently, "You're a fortunate lady, Mrs. Morris. We hope you will be happy here. The weather, I'm certain, isn't as Edenish as Maui, but nonetheless, I think you'll find it pleasant most of the time."

"Edenish?" Tony repeated, a brow arched. "I'm the writer at the table, Dan. Please confine yourself to simple words and lending out money."

There was general laughter, and Jules relaxed. So did Saint. He would speak to Tony later. In fact, he thought, he'd been a fool not to realize that something like this was likely to happen. He caught Tony's eye and gave him a simple nod.

Saint found himself looking again and again at his wife's lovely throat and shoulders. He said suddenly to Jules, "You need a necklace—emeralds, I think. Del," he continued, "tell me where I can find some jewelry for my wife."

"Oh no," Jules said, aghast at the thought of the cost. "I don't want . . . that is, I don't need—"

"Certainly," said Del Saxton. "Emeralds, with perhaps some sapphires, would look lovely on you, Jules, particularly with that gown."

"I agree," Chauncey said. "Diamonds are too harsh, I think. Yes, emeralds and sapphires. Vibrant and warm."

"It's settled, then," Saint said, reaching under the table to squeeze his wife's hand. "I'll come see you in the morning, Del."

Agatha said to the table at large, "It's nearly September. Do you think Brent and Byrony will be home soon?"

"The Hammonds," Saint said to Jules. "Brent owns the Wild Star and he and his wife went to Mississippi to take care of the plantation he inherited."

"Brent is a handsome devil, and usually quite charming," Agatha said. "I have a feeling, though, that Byrony has him well in hand by this time."

"He was out of hand?" Jules asked. "I thought you said he was quite charming."

"Let's just say, love," Saint said, "that Brent Hammond was like a fish wriggling on the line, and Byrony . . . well, she's got spirit, that girl."

"And grit," added Horace.

The talk continued for a while about the Hammonds, and Jules chewed thoughtfully on her baked chicken. She was very aware of her husband, the way he used his hands when he spoke, his long, blunt fingers, the deep, full laugh. She remembered Wilkes talking of Michael and all the women he'd slept with. It wasn't true, she knew it wasn't.

You should tell him about meeting Wilkes. She shook her head at her own thought, and felt miserable.

After dinner, Chauncey brought Alexandra downstairs to be admired. Jules held the baby, such a beautiful child, and her eyes met Michael's.

"I love babies," she said softly.

Saint felt his guts twist. He watched her as she spoke soft, meaningless words to the baby, watched her eyes light up with pleasure when Alex grabbed her finger and held it tightly. And he laughed when Jules blinked and said, "I think I'm wet, Chauncey."

"Oh dear, indeed you are. Come with me and we'll make sure your gown isn't ruined. Del, do take Alex up to Mary for repairs."

When Jules followed Chauncey from the room, Saint joined Tony Dawson. "I should have told you, but I forgot. It isn't for publication, of course."

When he finished, Tony Dawson whistled softly. "Jesus, Saint, I'm sorry. I didn't mean to embarrass her."

"You didn't know. Forget it, Tony."

"That poor girl. Thank God you were here, Saint, and put a stop to it."

Del joined them shortly thereafter, laughing a bit. "The joys of fatherhood," he said. "Ah, I see you've told Tony. There is something else, Saint. Wilkes is entrenching himself quite thoroughly here. One sees him everywhere. Are you worried that he will try to make things difficult for you and Jules?"

Saint said without thinking, "If he knew she was still a vir—" He broke off, appalled. "I think I'll have some of your whiskey, Del. Excuse me."

Tony started to say something to Del, but Del shook his head and said very softly, "Shit."

Brent Hammond, Jules thought, was probably the most beautiful man she had ever seen. He was tall, lean, and his incredible dark blue eyes glistened with pleasure and pride as he listened to his wife, Byrony, telling the Saxtons and Michael about Wakeville.

"So you see," Byrony concluded, "not only are we shortly to be real parents, but we've also got an adopted family of about four hundred former slaves. And that's why it's taken us so long to come home."

"Wakeville, huh?" Del Saxton said. "It has quite a ring to it. Now, my dear Mr. Hammond, I have a feeling that we need to talk of finance, don't we?"

Brent Hammond grinned. "Well, maybe just a bit, Del. Many of our people are quite skilled, but I'm afraid I'll need a loan to buy seed and machinery and lumber. Buying all the land, and tents to keep everyone out of the rain, about wiped me out. The land is so rich—Lord, I think you could grind any kind of seed in the world into the earth with the heel of your boot, and you'd end up in three months with—"

"The largest tomatoes," Byrony continued, "the largest cabbages, heavens, every kind of food! We'll be self-sufficient in no time at all—"

"And of course we'll need to build houses and stores and a church," Brent finished.

"That's quite an act you two have," Saint said, grinning back and forth between Brent and Byrony Hammond. "I even forgot to buy a ticket."

Jules found herself simply staring at the couple. They'd actually transported former slaves to California and were planning their own town! "I wish I had some money to donate," she said to Byrony. "But I do have a lot of time and I could do something to help."

Byrony patted her hand. "I appreciate that, Jules, and you may be certain that I'll be knocking on your door." Suddenly Byrony blinked, then broke into surprised, bright laughter. "Brent, he moved!"

Brent Hammond gave his wife a long, lazy look. "He always kicks up a dust when we're in company. What do you think, Saint? A spot of brandy to quiet him down?"

"Nope, let the little devil move about. You feeling all right, Byrony?"

She nodded happily. "Not even one moment of nausea. But I'll tell you, Saint, Brent is driving me crazy! You would think that this is the first child ever to be conceived."

"By me, at least," Brent said. "I'm still not convinced that the rest of you could manage it half as well."

Jules's eyes flew to her husband's face, and she swallowed a knot of unhappiness. He was smiling from his great height at Byrony Hammond.

"Brent," Chauncey said to Jules, "believes the rest of the male population adheres to the medieval paintings showing conception through the ear."

"Really, love," Del said over the laughter, "a most unladylike observation. Even Saint is blushing, and Jules's face is as bright as her hair."

Unabashed, Saint said, "I was just trying to picture in my mind how that would work."

Jules gasped. "You're terrible!"

"I have to be somewhat outrageous to keep up with Chauncey, sweetheart." He continued to Brent, "Are you going to keep the Wild Star?"

Brent looked thoughtful. "We haven't decided yet. I think Maggie's interested in buying me out, but it's such a steady stream of income. I don't want us to starve in Wakeville."

"Byrony," Saint said, "before I forget, do come see me tomorrow. I want to make certain everything is all right."

It was the first time Jules realized that her husband, who was a man, was also a doctor, and that he would actually see and touch other women. It was most disconcerting. She heard him continue to Brent, "It occurred to me that besides medical help, your folk are going to need clothing. Tell you what, Brent, I'll contract with Jane to make clothes."

"I'll get Horace to pay half," Del said.

"Don't forget Bunker Stevenson, Sam Brannon, and I'll bet we can even enlist James Cora to help."

"A ball," Chauncey said suddenly. "A subscription ball, that's what we need."

"With costumes, love?" Del asked. "Like the first time we met?"

"Yes, indeed, and I'll thank you, husband, not to remind me of that evening!"

"Ah," Del said, "but there was such wit flowing, at least from this poor soul." He held his hand dramatically over his heart.

"We could invite all the upper crust, charge them a fortune, and Wakeville would shortly be on the map," said Saint.

"We can even ensure that Lloyd Marks is there," Chauncey said. "He draws the maps," she added to Jules.

"I think," Del said, "that the Stevensons would be delighted to hold the ball at their home."

"Yes indeed," said Saint. "You can hint to Bunker that we'll all do our damnedest to find Penelope a husband out of the flock of men who will be there."

"If," Byrony said, "we could just convince Tony Dawson to be a bit mean, he'd make a perfect husband for Penelope."

Planning the Wakeville ball went on for several more hours. Lydia served all the food in the house and cleaned out Saint's liquor supply. When the last of the guests had left, Jules sighed and walked back into the parlor.

"What a scene of devastation," Saint said ruefully, following her.

Jules was silent a moment, then turned to her husband, blurting out, "What will you do to Byrony?"

"Do? What do you mean?" He cocked his head to one side in question.

"I mean, she's pregnant!"

"Ah," he said. He walked to his now thoroughly embarrassed wife and took her hands in his large ones. "Yes, she is pregnant. Yes, I will examine her, thoroughly. She is a patient. I want her to go through childbirth with as little difficulty as possible, and I want her child to be as healthy as possible. That's all there is to it."

"You don't . . . that is, you won't touch—"

He broke off her pitiful string of words. "Come sit down, Jules." She did as he bid her, and he moved to stand by the fireplace. "You may be certain that I am not a slave to lust, my dear. As I said, Byrony, outside my office, is a good friend. Once inside my office, she is a patient."

"But she's so beautiful!"

"True. And it bothers you that I will be touching her intimately?"

"Yes."

"Well, that's straight talking. In medical school, a long time ago—"

"Not more than nine years!"

"Well, then, nine years ago, when I ws a young man rather than a doctor, I got terribly embarrassed, more than my female patients, I'd wager, when I had to examine them. Embarrassed, not lustful. I remember once that my hands were actually shaking, and my face was red as a beet. But, you see, Jules, that young girl I was examining was very ill. She hurt. She trusted me to make her feel better. The fact that I was a young man made no difference. Pain tends to dissolve embarrassment, you know."

Jules lowered her head. "You must think I'm an awful fool."

"Not at all . . . well, just a bit, sweetheart. As my wife, I realize it must be difficult for you to understand that a female patient has no more sexuality to me than a male patient. But it's true."

"But I'm not your wife," she said, and bit down hard on her lower lip.

"Of course you are," he said sharply, disregarding the true meaning of her words. "Now, do you believe me? Trust me?"

"Yes, of course. I'm sorry, Michael." She fingered the beautiful emerald necklace about her throat that he'd give her two weeks before. He was so generous to her, so kind, and here she was questioning him like a silly shrew. She wanted to apologize again, but instead she heard herself asking, "Have you gone to see Jane Branigan?"

"Yes," he said simply. "I would have taken you with me, but I wasn't certain that it would be wise."

Jules swallowed a bit painfully. "Did you kiss her?"

"No."

"Did you want to?"

Yes, he thought, he had wanted to. He hurt from need. And he didn't know what to do about it, because he'd promised Jules he'd be faithful. He lied easily: "No."

"And if Jane got sick, you wouldn't feel anything if you had to touch her?"

"Of course I'd feel things. I am fond of her, Jules. I would be frightened that she would be too ill for me to help her."

"And if I were ill?"

He smiled at that. "I'd be scared silly. So don't get sick, all right?"

Jules felt as though she'd dug a hole a good ten feet deep and leapt into it. She fought to get out. "Thomas should be here soon," she said.

"Yes, he should," Saint said, relieved at her abrupt change of topic. "I've been thinking about him, and probably the best thing for him would be to go back East, perhaps to New York, to medical school."

"But he's so young!"

"Not at all. He's twenty-two, isn't he?"

She nodded.

He found himself looking at her closely. She looked beautiful, he was used to that, but she also looked a bit pale and too thin. He frowned. Surely she couldn't be lonely. Chauncey and Agatha both spent a good deal of time with her—she was always visiting Chauncey to play with Alexandra. Now that Byrony and Brent were back, he was certain she would become friends with Byrony.

He had forced himself not to touch her. He couldn't bear it. When he went to bed at night, he was careful to keep his door closed. It was another tangible barrier that kept her safe from him. Even when he woke up during the night, his breathing harsh, his groin aching, he'd see that closed door.

"Jules," he said suddenly, "are you happy?"

He saw her quiver, but she didn't look up at him. *No, I feel like I'm living a half-life. I'm frightened that Wilkes will take me every time I leave the house. I'm afraid that Wilkes will send men after you.*

"Of course," she said, forcing her head up. He flinched at the haunted look in her eyes, but he didn't know what to do. Dammit, he thought, so frustrated that he wanted to yell. How much longer could they continue living like this? He knew she had to have time, time to forget, to heal, but God, it hurt. He heard himself say in a tight, very controlled voice, "I want you to be happy."

"Yes," she said, "I know that you do."

The day before the subscription ball, Thomas Du-Pres arrived in San Francisco. He looked fit, handsome, and darkly tanned, and Jules didn't want to let him out of her sight. He limped only slightly. Saint, pleased to see his wife laughing, chattering like a magpie, her face flushed with pleasure, sat back drinking a brandy, watching the two of them. Unlike Jules, Thomas had brownish-red hair and his eyes were brown. But, he saw, they both were possessed of the same stubborn chin.

"I must say, Thomas," he said during a brief lull in the conversation, "you're looking much better than I thought you would. No more pain?"

"Narry a bit, Saint. Reverend Baldwin gave me a clean bill of health three weeks ago, said my leg was mending just fine, then told me to fatten up before I came here. He said you'd blame him, Saint, if I showed up on your doorstep looking like a scarecrow. Jules," he continued to his sister, "we've both been disowned by our father, but I didn't think you'd mind particularly."

"No, not really," Jules said. "Thomas, is Sarah happy now? Is she all right?"

"If you mean by that is she pregnant," he said in a hard voice, "the answer is no, she isn't. She is the most godawful female, and now with John Bleecher gone, she's become a total shrew."

Saint saw that Jules was upset, and said quickly, "Perhaps things will be better for her soon."

Thomas threw his brother-in-law an incredulous look, but said nothing.

It was nearly midnight when Jules yawned loudly. "Time for you to go to bed, sweetheart," Saint said, rising with her. "Thomas and I will be up shortly. You can take him about tomorrow." He gave her a chaste kiss on her cheek. Thomas squeezed her tightly, and held her a moment.

"I'm so glad you're here, Thomas," she said. "Oh, you'll be in the spare bedroom, second door on your right upstairs." With those words, she left the two men alone, one smiling, the other staring after her, the meaning of her words like a death knell in his mind. He'd been an idiot not to realize that Jules would have to move back into his bedroom. He closed his eyes a moment, picturing her in a pristine, virginal nightgown, curled up beside him.

"Saint, you want another brandy?"

He shook his head. Thomas kept him up another hour, discussing medicine. If Thomas noticed that his brother-in-law was distracted, he was polite enough to ignore it.

Please let her be asleep, Saint thought when he very quietly opened the bedroom door. She was, and sprawled in the middle of the bed on her stomach.

He sighed, undressed quickly, and slipped in beside her. Too late he realized he should have worn one of the nightshirts Jane had made for him. She didn't awaken, but before he fell asleep, she was curled up next to him, her slender arm thrown over his chest.

Saint, a light sleeper, awoke immediately at the sound of knocking on the front door. It was barely dawn. He rose instantly, and dressed more quickly than he ever had in his life. He took one last look at his sleeping wife, now curled up on her side, before he slipped out of the bedroom.

There were three scruffy-looking individuals, two of them supporting the third, whose face was pale and drawn with pain. "Limpin' Willie told us to bring you old Sam here, Doc. He got hisself knifed in the back."

Saint sighed, wondering if the knife wound, which turned out not to be too bad, was the result of a victim fighting back. Sam pressed fifty dollars in his hand an hour later, and staggered out again, supported by his friends.

Jules was so excited she could scarcely sit still in the swaying carriage. Thomas, his costume that of a pirate, complete with a black eye patch, looked dashing. Saint wore a black broadcloth suit and a long black velvet cloak and a black velvet mask.

"Your stays too tight, little sister?" Thomas asked her. "You're jumping about like one of those Mexican beans I read about."

"Oh no, I just can't wait to get there. Michael, we've never waltzed together before. And Chauncey told me that the orchestra is all the way from Sacramento. Do you really like my costume? Agatha said I look the perfect shepherdess, and if she had any sheep, she'd give—"

"Lord, do you run on, Jules!"

Saint took her hand into his. He wanted to tell her that she looked so exquisite in the draped white gown that he wanted to touch and kiss every inch of her, dressed and undressed. "You are perfect," he said in a light voice. "I also like your hair piled up like that—most effective. Ignore your brother. Brothers aren't supposed to appreciate their sisters."

"Everyone will know who you are, Jules," Thomas said, eyeing her hair, "even with your mask on."

And everyone did, of course. But Jules didn't care. Even if she'd been completely disguised, Saint's size would have given her away.

They waltzed, chatted with friends, admired costumes, mentally counted the money the ball was bringing in, and drank champagne. Saint had watched

Bunker Stevenson very closely when they'd arrived. If he had been one of the men at the Crooked House that night, he didn't show it. Even when Saint looked him straight in the face, his eyes hard and flat as he introduced Jules, Bunker showed no sign of recognition or embarrassment. He hadn't been at the Crooked House, Saint thought. As for the others, doubtless many were here and they would recognize Jules. But they would say nothing. They wouldn't dare. He grinned at Penelope, gowned in a dampened Regency-style dress, her very nice nose in the air, as was her wont.

But Penelope was excited, even though she had no trouble disguising the fact.

Until she met Thomas.

"Well," said Penelope, eyeing Thomas without much interest, "I understand that you are Mrs. Morris' brother. Good evening, Mrs. Morris."

Jules merely nodded.

"Yes," Thomas said pleasantly to Penelope, "quite a curse, wouldn't you agree? But then again, she's such a beautiful curse and she makes me laugh."

Penelope, who had been ready to dismiss the young man, retrenched, deciding to give him just a bit of her attention. "I have decided I will waltz with you, Mr. DuPres," she said, offering him a dazzling smile.

"Your decision is gratifying, Miss Stevenson, but I haven't asked you, ma'am. I do believe I'm thirsty. Jules, would you like a glass of champagne?"

It required all Jules's efforts to keep from bursting out laughing. Penelope, red-faced, was staring at Thomas, her hands clenched at her sides.

"That was marvelous, Thomas," Jules said softly as they moved away. "Chauncey Saxton told me Penelope was such a snobbish twit, and so full of herself."

"True, but she's very pretty," said Thomas. He tossed down his champagne. "She just needs a man to teach her manners. Now, Jules, I want to do some dancing."

"With Penelope?" she asked in an impish voice.

"Not yet. Let the girl suffer for a while. By the time I ask her, she'll be appropriately chastised, and eager."

Jules, who had never seen this side of her brother, blinked up at him. "Pretty sure of yourself, aren't you, brother?"

Penelope didn't appear to be suffering at all, Jules thought. As usual, there were many more gentlemen than ladies, so her hand was claimed for each dance. Still, her eyes sought out Thomas, and glittered. Thomas ignored her.

"Finally," Brent Hammond said to Jules a while later. "A waltz, ma'am?"

"I'd like that," Jules said.

He was a graceful dancer, and Jules quickly found herself following his lead with ease. "Michael said your wife is in fine health, sir."

"Yes," he said, his eyes searching out Byrony in the throng, "but I told her not to tire herself. It appears, however, that she's doing just that."

"It's so exciting! I can't blame her. I've never been to a ball before," she added.

Brent looked down at the lovely girl in his arms, really seeing her for the first time. "You're a natural dancer," he said, smiling at her. "Saint's a lucky man."

"That, sir, is what I keep telling him!"

"I don't suppose I can convince you to tell me

Saint's other names? 'Michael' is inoffensive enough. Come, tell me."

Jules laughed, shook her head, and inadvertently stepped on his toes.

"How about where and how he got the nickname Saint?"

"Your wife is waving at you, sir," she said gaily as the music came to a halt.

Brent watched her glide into another dance with Dan Brewer. He made his way through the crowd toward his wife. To his surprise, he saw Penelope Stevenson standing with Jules's brother, Thomas. She looked absolutely furious, and Thomas, interestingly enough, was looking ready to yawn with apparent boredom.

Jules released her husband, but only for five minutes, she told him, to speak to several men. The orchestra was not playing, and she looked about for Chauncey or Agatha. They must have gone upstairs to the ladies' receiving room. She walked to the French windows along the side of the ballroom. It was a beautiful, clear fall evening. She slipped out onto the balcony and leaned her elbows on the railing. It was nice to be alone for a bit. But only for five minutes, she added to herself. She wanted to dance with Michael again. She wished desperately that she'd managed to stay awake the previous night, but she hadn't. She didn't even know if he had come to bed, for when she'd awakened in the morning, he'd been gone. She sighed, and for once didn't admire the beautiful azaleas on the balcony. Something had to be done, but she simply didn't know . . .

"Ah," a soft voice came from behind her, "the little lamb left alone to the wolf."

Jules whirled about to face a man wearing a light gray cloak and a gray mask.

"Who are you, sir?" she asked, not at all concerned.

"I've been watching you all evening, my dear. You seem very sure of yourself, surrounded by all those people. I had almost despaired of finding you alone. It would appear that you've made quite a few friends."

"What," Jules said, suspicious now, "are you talking about?"

"I must also tell you that you look more beautiful than I had imagined. Is it possible, my dear, that you occasionally miss me, think of me?"

"Your jest, sir, is wearing a bit thin," Jules said sharply. "Have you perhaps visited the punch bowl too many times?"

"Really, Juliana, don't you recognize me?"

She did, very suddenly, and felt herself go cold. He didn't have to remove his mask. "Get away from me!"

He lunged for her, grabbed her arm, and pulled her against him, away from the open windows. "No!" she shrieked, and felt his hand slap down over her mouth.

She struggled wildly and bit his hand.

He sucked in his breath, and for an instant his hand eased and she jerked her head back and screamed.

"You damned little bitch," he hissed in her ear. In the next moment she felt searing pain as his fist crashed into her jaw. Flashes of stark white exploded before her eyes, and then there was nothing.

17

Thomas DuPres, quite satisfied with his latest skirmish with Penelope Stevenson, strolled through the chattering groups of people toward the long bank of French windows. He'd seen Jules going in that direction a few minutes before, and decided he wanted to talk to her. Lord, it was an opulent house, he thought, and like Jules, he'd cataloged and duly appreciated all the flowers arranged in huge pots throughout the ballroom. He saw Penelope waving imperiously to him, grinned to himself, and quickly eased out onto the balcony. It was no wonder the girl was spoiled rotten; he just might be also had he been raised as she had been, doubtless given anything she wanted. For the moment, he would let her suffer.

He looked about for Jules but didn't at first see her. He called her name softly—just in case, he told himself, there were any lovers out here.

He suddenly heard a man curse viciously. He whipped about and searched the shadows at the far end of the balcony. He saw his sister struggling wildly with a man wearing a long cloak and mask. He watched in shocked horror as the man struck Jules and she crumpled where she stood.

He yelled as he sprinted forward, "You bastard! What the hell are you doing?"

Jameson Wilkes saw the young man running full tilt toward him. He gave Jules one final look, so furious he wanted to howl. He started to draw out his derringer, but decided it was too risky. He'd heard her strike her head when she'd fallen, and for an instant he felt tearing fear that she was terribly hurt or even dead. "Dammit, no!" He wasn't certain if it was a cry to her or a cry to some unhearing god. He wrapped his cloak tightly about him and vaulted gracefully over the balcony railing.

"Jules!" Thomas was only vaguely aware that the man had disappeared. He knelt beside his sister, saw that she was unconscious, and quickly lifted her into his arms. He drew to an abrupt halt just outside the French doors. No reason to cause a riot, he thought. Gently he eased her down and slipped inside. He found Saint speaking to Del Saxton.

"Come quickly," he said. "It's Jules. She's been hurt."

Saint felt fear ripple through him, tensing his muscles. He said nothing, merely hurried after Thomas. When he saw her, pale and small, lying unconscious against one of the long windows, he forced himself to be calm. *I'd be scared silly*, he remembered telling her when she'd asked him what he'd feel if she were ill. And he was.

He gently took her wrist and felt for her pulse. Strong and steady. He heard Thomas saying to Del, "I think he struck her jaw. When he saw me, he jumped over the railing."

Saint lightly ran his fingers over her jaw, relieved, for it wasn't broken. But why was she still unconscious? He turned on his heel to look up at Thomas. "Did she fall?"

"I think so."

So she'd hit her head on the stones. He lifted her just a bit and quickly found a growing lump behind her left ear. "Damn," he said very softly.

"Wilkes?" Del Saxton said.

"I don't know," Thomas said. "Of course, I've never seen Wilkes before, and this man was wearing a mask—a gray mask and a cloak. Is she all right, Saint?"

Saint closed his eyes a moment, trying to get hold of himself. "I'm getting her home right now," he said, his voice harsh. "Thomas, stay here, and you too, Del. No reason to upset the guests."

"I'll have Lucas bring around our carriage," Del said. "It will be quickest."

She was still unconscious when Saint lifted her into the carriage some five minutes later. "She'll be all right," he said to Thomas and Del. God, he hoped he was right!

"Are you certain—?" Thomas began.

"Stay here. I'm the doctor, remember?"

Lucas whipped up the horses. Saint pulled Jules onto his lap and pressed her head against his chest. The short ride was the longest in his memory.

"Thanks, Luc," he said over his shoulder. "Don't worry."

Saint carried her upstairs and eased her down onto the bed. Our bed now, he thought. He undressed her as gently as he could. "Damned women's corsets," he muttered, pulling the stays loose. He left her in her shift and methodically examined her.

Enough was enough, he decided a few minutes later. He slapped her face, saying as he did so, "Come on, sweetheart, wake up now. I'm scared silly, and you don't want your husband a dithering idiot. Wake up, Jules."

Jules heard a man's voice, but it made her head hurt, a dull, pounding pain. "No," she muttered, trying to pull away from the hands on her shoulders. "No."

"Come on, love."

The light was dim, and he was shadowy, just as the light had been on the balcony at the Stevensons' ball, and she thought he was Jameson Wilkes. She cried out and tried to push him away. "No!" she shrieked.

Oh God, Saint thought, not again. From her fear, he was quite certain that it had been Wilkes.

"It's me, Michael. Michael," he repeated, not touching her. He waited patiently for her to quiet and regain her wits.

"Michael?" Jules managed to focus on him. "Wilkes," she gasped. "He tried to—"

"I know. But he didn't. Thomas saved you, sweetheart. You're home with me now. And safe."

Of course, he'd said that before. And he'd lied.

"My head," she whispered, for the sound of her own voice sent waves of pain through her entire body.

"When you fell, you hit your head. You've probably got a concussion, but you'll be all right. How does your jaw feel?"

"I don't know, all I can feel is my head." She shivered in reaction and Saint quickly pulled a blanket to her chin.

"I imagine it hurts quite a bit," he said very softly. "I can't give you any laudanum, at least not yet." he held up three fingers. "How many, Jules?"

"Three."

"And now?"

"Six."

"Good."

"The ball," she wailed softly. "I wanted to waltz with you again."

"We will again, soon, I promise. God, you did scare me silly." He took her limp hand in his and brought it to his mouth. He kissed her fingers.

"He's crazy," Jules said, watching her husband holding and kissing her hand through a haze of pain.

"You're certain it was Wilkes?"

"Oh yes. He mocked me and taunted me. Just like the other—" She broke off, biting her lip, appalled.

Saint was silent for many moments, studying her pale face. "What other time?" he asked.

She wanted to lie, but the tone of his voice wouldn't brook a lie. "A while ago, that first day I was with Chauncey."

"Would you mind telling me why you didn't inform me of this?"

He sounded so controlled, so very calm, that she said honestly, "I was afraid that he would hurt you."

He went rigid.

Jules didn't notice. She was trying desperately to control the pain. "I knew he couldn't hurt me—there were so many men about on the street. But I thought if I told you, you would go after him. You're so honorable, but he's a snake. I couldn't bear it if he hurt you."

"Jules, look at me."

"Yes," she said, his face clear before her eyes.

"Do I look like a fool, an idiot? Do I look like a man who could be hurt?"

"He would hire people! He would—"

"I think you'd best be quiet now. God in heaven, I don't believe this!"

Saint rose, ripped off his black cloak, and hurled it to the floor. He was so furious he couldn't think straight. He forced himself to take slow, deep breaths. "Jules," he said, very calmly now, "I am your husband. You are my responsibility. If you don't trust me to take care of you, you reduce me to nothing. Do you understand me?"

"No," she managed, then cried out softly.

"Oh damn," he said, angry with himself now for upsetting her. Some doctor you are, idiot! He sat down beside her and gently probed the lump behind her ear.

'I don't want to cry," she gasped, but her head felt like a melon being battered against the ground. Tears seeped from the corners of her tightly closed eyes. Saint wanted to find Wilkes and kill him. But he couldn't leave her. He cursed again very softly, pulled off his boots, and eased into bed beside her. "Come here against me," he said. "In a little while I can give you something for the pain. But not yet, sweetheart. I'm sorry, but I can't take the chance." The chance she'd never wake up.

He could feel the waves of pain each time she tensed. Very quietly, his voice soothing and low, he started to speak. "Did I ever tell you about the Siamese twins I saw born in Boston? They were male, and attached from their waists to their knees." No, no, he thought frantically. That story had a ghastly ending. "They lived happily ever after. But there was this man, way back in the fifth century. Actually, he was the Emperor Justinian, and his wife was the Empress Theodora. Interestingly enough, the empress had been a prostitute before she married Justinian and won a crown. In any case, the both of them wanted to eradicate prostitution. Her way didn't work, of course, but it was quite an interesting approach." Saint paused a moment, and Jules said in a sleepy voice, "Yes? Go on, Michael. What did she do?"

He smiled slightly, and continued, "Well, what she did was to build a beautiful palace-prison, and she had five hundred prostitutes taken there. They were treated very well. In fact, they could have whatever they wanted, with the exception of one thing: no men allowed. It is said that most of the women committed suicide in their despair, and the remainder soon died of boredom and vexation."

He heard her giggle. She said in a blurred voice, "Vexation? I love you, Michael, but I think you made that up."

He swallowed, unable to think of anything to say. She didn't know, didn't realize, what she'd said. "I didn't make it up," he said.

She didn't answer. She was asleep.

"It was vexation. I know the feeling well," he said, and kissed her very lightly on the cheek.

He woke her during the night, forced her to tell him who she was, who he was, and how many fingers he was holding up. At last, early the next morning, he gave her some laudanum in a glass of water, and watched her fall into a deep, healing sleep.

Thomas was waiting for him downstairs, still dressed as a pirate, pacing furiously. He was so angry he couldn't speak, and Saint, after reassuring him for the tenth time, sent him to bed.

Lydia was furious and appalled, and Saint winced at the sound of her crashing the pots and pans about in the kitchen, each of them probably a substitute for Wilkes's head.

Then Del Saxton arrived, his face grave and worried. He said without preamble, "How is she?"

"She will be fine. I gave her some laudanum just a while ago and she's sleeping soundly now."

"I've put a search out for Wilkes. Apparently the man's not a complete fool. It appears he's left the city. I also ran into Limpin' Willie early this morning. He's ready to spit nails and will get the Sydney Ducks out scouring for him."

"Thank you. I had intended to . . . well, it's done. Thomas is still asleep." He stopped and drank some strong black coffee, offering some to Del.

After several moments, Saint said more to himself than to Del Saxton, "Wilkes approached her before, but she didn't tell me." He gave a bitter, mocking laugh. "She was afraid he would hurt me. *Me*! The little fool was worried about protecting me!"

Del studied his friend for many moments. "You can thank me for keeping Brent away, at least for a while. He's of course rather upset with you because you didn't tell him about Wilkes."

"What the hell was there to tell, for God's sake?"

"Calm down. Don't you want your friends to be concerned? No, don't answer that. I've been thinking," Del continued after a moment.

"And you're going to dose me with your damned advice whether I want it or not!"

"Yes, I suppose I am. Listen, Saint, I assume that Jules is still a virgin. If you'll remember, you let that fact slip."

Saint winced.

"It seems to me," Del continued quietly, "that there are two ways to protect her. The first is to find Wilkes and kill him. That would be difficult, because he's gone to ground. The second—and certainly more pleasurable—way would be to consummate your damned marriage and get her pregnant."

"Pregnancy doesn't necessarily follow sex, Del," Saint said, trying to make light of his friend's words. "Indeed, if you will recall, Chauncey didn't become pregnant for a number of months, and I imagine that you kept her quite busy during those months."

"True, but beside the point. You've got to try, Saint. No matter this weird obsession Wilkes has for her, I can't envision him wanting to kidnap a pregnant woman."

"No," Saint said very softly, utterly serious now.

"You can't continue playing the benign father to your wife! Chauncey tells me that Jules is crazy in love with you. What the hell is going on, Saint?"

Saint rose and walked to the fireplace. He looked down into the empty grate. Crazy in love with him? What utter nonsense. A young girl's infatuation mixed with a strong dose of gratitude—fleeting, ephemeral as the San Francisco fog. He said without turning, "Jules has been hurt very badly. Whatever feelings she thinks she has for me, if I tried to make love to her, she would be terrified. I had hoped she would forget, and perhaps . . ." He shrugged. "Last night, when she regained consciousness, she thought I was Wilkes. If you had seen her face, you wouldn't suggest such a thing. I will not hurt her. I will not force myself on her."

*　　*　　*

Jules looked blankly at the partially open parlor door. She felt dizzy, her head fuzzy. Slowly she tied her dressing gown more closely about her. It was odd, but she didn't remember thinking Michael was Jameson Wilkes. Had she truly looked terrified? The men's words wove in and out of her mind, fighting with the laudanum. She heard Michael's low, intense voice, "No, no more, Del. I know you mean well, but—"

"You're my friend, dammit! You of all men leading a celibate life! How much longer do you think you can stay sane living like this? And face it, Saint, you can't keep Jules a prisoner, and you simply can't be with her all the time."

"I'll think of something," Saint said.

She heard Del Saxton rise from his chair and move toward the door. She pulled herself upright, and wobbled back up the stairs. Her head began to pound again and she curled up under the covers, closing her eyes tightly.

When she woke, Thomas was sitting beside her.

"Michael?" she whispered.

"Sorry, love, he's with a patient. How do you feel?"

"I had this strange dream," she began, then closed her mouth. It hadn't been a dream. Her mouth felt full of dry wool. "Can I have some water, Thomas?"

"Certainly, love. A moment, there isn't any up here. I'll be right back."

Of course there wasn't any water here. That's why she'd dragged herself downstairs earlier. And heard them talking, Michael and Del Saxton.

After she'd drunk her fill, Thomas said, "You look like one of those skinny little lizardfish, all pale and limp."

"Thank you, brother," she said.

"Saint filled in all the things I didn't know about Wilkes," Thomas said. "There have been a good dozen people in and out of here all morning. I think half the male population of San Francisco is looking for that bloody bastard."

She looked at him hopefully. "Do you think he's really gone for good?"

"I don't know, Thomas said thoughtfully. He gently stroked her hair back from her forehead. He tried a crooked grin. "How he could want you—a tangled little raggamuffin—well, it's beyond me."

He wouldn't want me if I were pregnant.

She said, "Tell me about the ball. Did you have a good time?"

"After what happened to you, very little. Del and I kept it under wraps, so not many people know."

"I thought you said people were trooping in and out all morning."

"I mean friends, not acquaintances."

"Michael has a lot of friends," Jules said.

"And so do you, love."

"Thomas?"

"Yes?"

"Have you ever made love to a girl?"

"Good grief, Jules! ... Ah, Saint, you're just in time to save me from embarrassing questions!"

"What embarrassing questions?" he asked, smiling from Thomas' rueful expression to his wife's flushed face.

"I asked him if he'd ever made love before," Jules said, thrusting up her chin, "to a girl."

"Shall I leave, Thomas, so you can say what you will to this inquisitive wife of mine?"

227

Catherine Coulter

"No," Thomas said hurriedly. "Actually, Saint, I think that knock on her head must have addled her wits."

"I think that happened a long time ago," Saint said, and sat down on the bed beside her. "How is my impertinent patient?" Why, he wondered, had she asked such a question of her brother? He decided that he really didn't want to know.

Jules managed a shy smile. "I'm all right," she said. "Truly, even though I do look like a tangled raggamuffin."

"That sounds suspiciously like a brotherly description."

"Sure was," Thomas said. "Now, Jules, you behave yourself and do as Saint tells you. I'll leave you to her, Saint. I'm off to see Bunker Stevenson. Of all things, the old buzzard wants to talk to me about my future."

"Bunker? What future? He's not a doctor."

"Lord only knows," Thomas said, grinning. "If I'm not here for dinner, don't miss me, all right?" He strode from the room, whistling, his walk cocky.

"That young man," Saint said, "is going places."

"I think this must have something to do with Penelope. Thomas was marvelously nasty to her last night."

"Intrigued the little twit, huh?"

"Thomas did say that she needed a man to teach her manners. It seems he's decided he's just the man to do it."

Saint laughed. "What a pair you two are. Now, Jules, let's see how that lump is doing."

She expected an explosion of pain, but there was only a dull throbbing at his touch. He was very close

228

to her, his eyes intent—his doctor's look, she thought. She felt his warm breath on her cheek. "I'm sorry," she said.

"So you should be," he murmured, still intent on his examination. "But we won't speak of it again for a while. Not until you're back in top form."

"I'm going to be twenty next month," she said.

"Are you, now? I'd forgotten."

"I'm not fourteen anymore, Michael."

His hand stilled for a moment. He said slowly, "No, you're not. You want to know something else, sweetheart? You've got a very colorful jaw."

She didn't want to talk about her wretched head or jaw, she wanted to talk about being celibate, but she was so drowsy, her head fuzzy. "When I'm in top form," she said, her voice slurred, "then I'll do . . ."

Saint pulled back and looked down at his sleeping wife. "What will you do, imp?" he asked softly. He gently smoothed the riotous curls from her face. Twenty years old. His mind leapt forward without pause. So many women had children by the time they were twenty. He frowned to himself even as his hand slid beneath the cover and rested lightly on her belly. He stretched his fingers, measuring the distance between her pelvic bones. He whipped his hand back, furious with himself, but he couldn't stop the thought. She wasn't as small as he'd believed she'd be. He left the bedroom, not looking back at her.

"It makes me so bloody angry I want to yell!"

Jules smiled at Chauncey. She was sitting up in bed, feeling quite marvelous, really, despite Michael's insistence that she remain off her feet for another day. "Michael says Wilkes has disappeared," she said.

"It's true, if all of Saint's criminal friends say so," Chauncey said. "Thank God Thomas was there."

"Indeed," Jules said. She added, tired of speaking of Wilkes, "I understand your dear friend Penelope is in the throes of a transformation."

Chauncey giggled, clearly distracted, as Jules had hoped she would be. "Lord, how I would love being a fly on the wall in the same room with your brother and dear Penelope. As to any transformation, I should live so long! What do you think?"

"Oddly enough, Thomas likes her. He says beneath all those layers of shrewisness beats only half a shrewish heart."

"I wish him luck. Oh, incidentally, the most ironic thing has happened. I suppose it's divine justice and all that. Did Saint tell you about the Butlers up and leaving San Francisco just yesterday?"

"Who are the Butlers?" Jules asked.

"Oh dear, I should have known Saint wouldn't say a thing about it."

"The cat's escaped, Chauncey, you might as well tell me."

"It's a rather long story."

Jules groaned. "Not another storyteller."

"All right, it's a very short story. You see, Ira Butler married Byrony DeWitt, who is now Byrony Hammond. He married her because, in truth, his half-sister, Irene, was pregnant with his child."

Jules could only stare at her.

"My sentiments exactly," Chauncey said. "In any case, Byrony agreed to pretend that she was pregnant and that Irene's child was hers. She didn't know then that the child was the result of an incestuous union. She found that out later. Del had the marriage annulled, and Byrony married Brent. It always bothered me that the Butlers got away with their deception, for Byrony was hurt very badly. Just a couple of days ago, if what I've heard is right, a new maid walked in on them, in bed. Their house of cards collapsed. I understand they've left to return to Baltimore. Now, that wasn't too long or too involved, was it?"

"What it is is amazing. Poor Byrony, I had no idea—"

"Not many people do. Just our little group, I suppose you'd say. Now, my dear, I think I'll leave you alone. Saint told me not to tire you."

"Oh, Chauncey. How much money did the ball make for the Hammonds and Wakeville?"

"Nearly fifteen thousand dollars," Chauncey said, preening a bit. "Both Brent and Byrony are esctatic, needless to say. Now, you rest, and I'll see you tomorrow."

Jules wondered before she indeed fell asleep why people's lives were never so simple as one would imagine. Her first thought upon waking several hours later was: Tonight I'm going to seduce my husband. I'll prove to him that his nobility is no longer necessary. The next time I see Jameson Wilkes, if there is a next time, I'll stick my pregnant stomach out at him.

She giggled.

18

"Jesus, I'm tired."

Jules looked at her husband and smiled. *You won't be soon.* She said, "I'm sorry. A difficult patient?"

"Make that plural. How do you feel, sweetheart?"

"Just fine, top form and all that, and you aren't going to sleep downstairs tonight, are you?"

Saint swallowed, automatically drawing back from her. "I don't want to disturb your sleep," he said.

"But what if I wake up during the night, ill? Do you want me to crash a chair against the floor?"

Saint sighed. "I suppose I could sleep in the guestroom with Thomas."

"In that case, I could simply shout, I suppose," Jules said calmly, watching him closely. "Of course, that might hurt my head dreadfully."

Saint floundered about for reasons, any reason in fact, to stay away from her. Finding none for the moment, he said, eyeing the tub, "You had a bath."

"Yes, and Lydia washed my hair for me."

"I see," he said, beginning to inch toward the door.

Jules played her ace. "Please don't leave me alone, Michael. It's nightmares . . . and I'm frightened." *Please forgive me for the fib.*

She thought she heard him curse very softly, and kept firm control over the smile that threatened to break free. "Very well," he said, and his voice sounded like a condemned man's.

He turned off all the lights and undressed in the dark. Jules didn't mind. She rather hoped he wouldn't wear one of those ridiculous nightshirts. But he did.

"Good night, Jules," he said as he slipped in beside her, hugging the far side of the bed.

"Good night," she said softly, and prepared to wait. Not too long, just enough time for him to relax.

"Michael?" she said finally, not moving.

"Yes?"

He sounded too alert, she thought. Well, there was no help for it. "What do you think of celibacy?"

She heard him suck in his breath. "Go to sleep, Jules," he said, his voice harsh.

"Do you think it's more difficult for a man to be celibate than a woman?"

She was going to drive him crazy, he thought, inching even closer to the far side of the bed. She was so bloody innocent, so guileless . . .

"I don't like being celibate."

Guileless, hell! "All right, Jules," he said, turning toward her, "what the devil is going on?"

She said very calmly, "Aren't we married?"

"I repeat, what the devil is going on?"

She sought the word Del Saxton has used. "I think we should consummate our marriage."

"No!"

"Why not?"

"Jules, please, no. I am not such a monster, and you are hurt, and I won't add to it, do you hear me?"

He continued, his voice jerky, about how he didn't

233

want her to be afraid of him. She said nothing, merely waited until he had gotten it all out of his system.

When at last he fell silent, she smiled into the darkness and squirmed over to him. She took his face between her hands and kissed him. She missed at first because it was so dark, but then she felt his mouth beneath hers. "No," he said, trying to shove her away.

She clung like a leech. She wanted to tell him that she loved him, but knew that he didn't want to hear that. It would make him feel guilty because he didn't love her. She said in the most seductive voice she could manage, "I want you, Michael. You are my husband. I am a woman, not a child. Please."

Saint felt her words crash through him. His body was taut, on fire. Lust, you damned bastard! "Jules," he began, "I will not hurt you."

"Why would you hurt me?"

He'd turned to face her, his strong hands clasping her shoulders. "Any man would hurt you—if not physically, then . . ."

"You think my weak woman's mind would snap or something?"

She managed to slip one hand free, and with unerring instinct let her fingers rove down his belly. He gasped, now trying to escape her. "Stop it," he moaned.

Her fingers found him, hard and throbbing through the nightshirt. "No," she said, "I won't stop. You are my husband, and you owe me certain things. You keep telling me that I'm your responsibility. Well, be responsible."

"Get your hand off me, Jules, or I won't be responsible for—"

She laughed.

"You damned little . . ." He had no time to search out the right word, for she pressed herself against him, her hand between them, holding him gently but firmly.

"I am not afraid, Michael. Not of you, in any case. Please, be my husband."

"Oh damn," he said, still not moving. Suddenly she released him and moved away. He drew a jagged breath, aware of relief and dreadful disappointment.

He reached out his hand, not really meaning to, thinking that perhaps she was upset and needed reassurance. His hand met bare flesh. Her shoulder. She'd pulled off her nightgown. Very slowly he rose from the bed. He lit one lamp, turning to face her.

A sheet was pulled just barely over her breasts. She looked very beautiful, her eyes luminous, her hair tousled about her face, her shoulders white and slender.

She was smiling at him.

"You look silly in that nightshirt," she said.

"Yes," he said finally, "I suppose I do." He pulled it off, standing very quietly at the end of the bed, naked. He was aware that she was studying him, and his member, the focus of her attention, thrust outward.

"Have you had enough yet?" he asked, his voice hard.

He watched her lick her lower lip. "Oh no," she said, holding out her hand to him. "Please, Michael, don't be afraid of me."

"I am afraid *for* you, Jules. Look at me, for God's sake!"

"I have, and you're beautiful. You were perhaps more romantically beautiful that night on the beach when you came out of the water—"

"I am not beautiful. I am a big, hairy man, and you know very well that if I touched you, you would hate me."

"And be terrified of you?"

"Yes, damn you!"

"Aren't you getting cold standing there with only your hairy chest on?"

She was goading him, and doing it very well, he thought, frowning at her. She let the cover slip, on purpose of course, and obligingly he dropped his gaze.

"Jules," he said finally, reaching for his dressing gown, "you don't know what you're asking. I would touch you and caress you, and I would come inside your body. It would bring back all the pain and fear you felt with Wilkes."

She felt a surge of warmth at the very graphic image his words created in her. Wilkes and her experiences with him were a million miles away. As were those with John Bleecher.

"Please, Michael." She wanted to touch him, wanted to feel his body covering her. She wanted him to kiss her and tell her how much he wanted her, how much he loved— Her thoughts broke off at that. He didn't love her, at least not yet he didn't. She would make him love her.

"Please," she said again. "Come to bed, Michael."

"You're my wife," he said very quietly to himself.

He chucked aside the dressing gown and climbed into bed beside her.

He lay quietly, still uncertain. Then she was pressed against him, her soft breasts against his chest. He swallowed, and without further thought, he clasped her to him. "Oh God," he whispered, gently pressing her onto her back. He lowered his head and lightly touched his mouth to hers. A bolt of searing need shot through him, and he trembled with the force of it. He had to go slowly, very slowly. If he frightened her, if he hurt her, he would never forgive himself. He called on every bit of experience he had. He remembered his wedding night with Kathleen, her pain when he entered her that first time. It was a pity that women couldn't be like men in that regard. No maidenheads, no pain. He drew a deep breath. Very slowly. He merely kissed her, gently, giving her time to decide, to pull away from him, or to react to him. He felt her hand stroking down his back, caressing his buttocks.

"Jules," he whispered into her mouth. "Let me love you, it's better that way."

"Why? I want to touch you."

"Because I won't be able to control myself," he said, his voice raw. He clasped her hands and drew them above her head. The cover came only to her waist, and his eyes were drawn to her breasts. "You are so white . . ." He said his thought aloud: "You are a man's dream."

"And you are my dream," she said, looking at him while he studied her. She felt his warm breath on her breast. Would he touch her there, as Wilkes had done? Make her feel ashamed and somehow dirty? *Stop it! He is not Wilkes!*

But when his mouth closed over her, she felt a moment of utter terror. She didn't move, didn't make a sound. He was so very gentle, his tongue playful and teasing. He raised his head and looked at her in the dim light. "I don't know where to kiss you first," he said. "I want all of you at once."

He came back over her and clasped her to him. He kissed her ears, the tip of her nose, smoothed her eyebrows with a fingertip, told her over and over how beautiful she was. "Now, you must learn how to kiss properly."

She smiled at that, and waited, willing her mind to ease, to allow her pleasure with him.

"Part your lips," he said, and she did. She felt his mouth, firm and warm, felt his tongue glide slowly over her lower lip. "Breathe through your nose, Jules," he said, and tested the waters. "Excellent, little one," he said, smiling warmly down at her.

"Now, I want to feel your tongue. Yes, that's it." He thought he would explode with the intense sensations swamping his body. She was so giving, so trusting. . . .

He released her wrists and she brought her arms about his back. When he thrust his tongue into her mouth, then quickly withdrew, she sucked in her breath in surprise. He laughed softly, and said into her mouth, "I will come into you like that, Jules." He grinned ruefully. "But I doubt I'll leave you so quickly. I'll probably want to stay inside you—" He broke off—he had to. Odd how his own words, his own images, were making him crazy.

"When?"

He closed his eyes a moment, willing himself to control. But he couldn't help himself. He eased on top of her, balancing himself on his elbows above her. "When you are ready for me," he managed, and kissed her again, slowly, thoroughly.

Jules felt his swollen member against her closed thighs. She wanted to feel him, and tried to open her legs.

"No," he said. "Not yet, sweetheart." Saint wanted to caress and kiss every inch of her, but he held back. The thought of her freezing in embarrassment made him stop cold. But if he didn't bring her pleasure, he would hurt her, he knew it. Slowly he eased off her. "No," he said softly when she tried to press herself against him, "no, just lie still." His fingertips stroked lightly over her bruised jaw, downward, feeling the soft flesh of her shoulders, the silken flesh of her breasts. He took a taut nipple between two long fingers. "You feel so soft . . . and so pink."

Jules giggled nervously. "How can I feel pink?"

"You do, don't argue with me." He lowered his mouth and suckled her breast. He felt her stiffen just as she'd done the first time he'd touched her breast, but he continued, praying that she would ease. She did, a bit. He let his hand move slowly over her ribs. Keep talking to her, he told himself. It would distract her. "I've got to fatten you up," he said, pressing the palm of his hand over her ribs. "Did I ever tell you about that young boy that I—"

"Michael," she said, cutting him off, "can I touch you? Can I feel your ribs?"

"Yes."

Jules swept her hand over his hairy chest, downward, reveling in the feel of him. So different from her, so incredibly powerful. She pressed her fingers against his flat belly, but before she could forage

239

lower, he let his own palm rest lightly on her woman's mound. She froze, rigid as a stone.

"Don't be afraid, sweetheart," he said.

"I'm not, not really," Jules managed. "It's just that I didn't think that you would touch . . ."

His fingertips lightly probed and found her. Her soft flesh was somewhat moist. Familiar territory, he thought, caressing her more deeply, that first night he'd given her release clear again in his mind. He loved the feel of her. He closed his eyes at the sensation, wishing only that his mouth could replace his fingers. But it was too soon for that intimacy.

"What's wrong?" Jules asked in a high, thin voice. She didn't know what to do. She felt exposed, vulnerable, and his fingers made her feel pleasantly strange, yet embarrassed.

"Nothing, little idiot. You are perfect."

"Are you certain? You're not just saying that?"

"No," he said, raising his head to kiss her again. "I'm not just saying that." He wanted desperately to draw her upward and kiss her, and taste her, and bury himself in her sweet flesh. But he knew he couldn't. Not yet. He let his fingers find a rhythm that seemed to please her, for she gasped suddenly, digging her fingers into his shoulders.

"Michael," she cried, "please, I don't know . . . I can't— "

"Yes, love," he said. "Just lie still." He continued to caress her as he raised himself over her. Slowly he parted her legs. He sat back on his heels a moment, watching her squirm at the touch of his fingertips. He studied the long white legs, sleekly muscled, unlike those of many young women of her age, whose greatest exercise had been to walk from the living

room to the bedroom. He gazed at her female softness and felt his control desert him.

"Jules," he said, his voice agonized. "Please, hold
still."

She felt bereft when his beguiling fingers left her,
but she was tense with anticipation as she watched
him guide himself toward her. She felt his fingers
gently parting her. She didn't know what to do. He
would come inside her. Yes, she wanted that. She
felt that male part of him pressing aginst her, felt
the incredible heat of him. She could hear Michael's
ragged breathing, knew that he needed her, needed
her now, this moment. She tried to relax, to open
herself to him. He entered her, his fingers still parting her to ease his way, and she felt herself stretching painfully. She felt his hands on her thighs, holding
them apart, and he came deeper into her.

"Jules, love," she heard him say sharply.

She opened her eyes and stared at him. His face
was pale, taut, tension radiating from him.

"You've a maidenhead, and . . ." He groaned deeply
in his throat, and thrust forward.

Jules cried out, she couldn't help it. He was deep
inside her, and it hurt so badly she sobbed. She
stuffed her fist into her mouth, not wanting him to
know.

"No, Jules, hold still!" She was squirming under
him, trying to rid herself of the dreadful pain. She
felt his fingers find her again, and stroke her, but
the very nice sensations didn't return. He groaned
suddenly, arching his back, and thrust forward until
she took all of him. He felt his seed spew deeply
within her.

He balanced himself on his elbows when he had

enough strength to do so, and looked down at her. Her face was pale, her eyes tightly closed, her eyelashes wet spikes on her cheeks. He cursed vividly. He'd given her very little pleasure, he knew. Slowy he drew out of her, feeling her shudder with pain.

"God, I'm sorry," he said, pulling her against him. He stroked her back, eased his hand up beneath her thick hair to knead the muscles of her neck. "Jules, are you all right?"

She thought about it. She felt very sore, as if she'd been battered inside, which, she supposed, she had. But he'd tried to be careful with her. It hadn't been all that bad. "I'm fine," she said finally. "Truly, Michael."

But he felt her tears against his bare shoulder. God, he'd forced her, given in to his own need. He was no better than Wilkes. "Never, never again," he said to himself, unaware that he'd whispered the words aloud.

Jules felt as though he'd slapped her. No, please, no, she wanted to scream at him, but she said nothing. Her head was beginning to throb, just like the rest of her, she thought grimly. She wanted to talk to him, but her mind was whirling with the burgeoning pain, and she gulped, burying her face into his shoulder.

Saint felt her shudder, and hated himself. He lay awake long after he heard her even breathing and felt her body relax against him. He eased away from her, rose and doused the lamp. He slipped into bed again and drew her back into his arms. He could still feel himself tearing through her maidenhead, feel her struggling against him. But he hadn't stopped.

No, he'd continued hurting her, letting his lust rule him. She was so precious to him, he realized. So fresh and vital. He couldn't bear the thought of her awakening and flinching away from him, fear and wariness in her eyes. It brought him nearly physical pain. Why, he wondered, on the vague edge of sleep, had she wanted him? Seduced him?

When he heard the pounding on the front door, drawing him quickly from a fitful sleep, he knew relief that he wouldn't have to face her in the morning and see her fear of him. He was out of bed and downstairs within moments.

It was a fisherman from Sausalito, whose wife was vomiting, blood coming from her mouth and from her bowels. Saint dressed quickly, flinching at the sight of blood on his member, looked at his sleeping wife, and left the house. She would be fine, he thought, striding beside the fisherman, his black medical bag tightly held in his right hand. And he was the last person on earth she would want to see when she awoke.

Jules woke early the following morning, and reached for her husband. His pillow was cold. He was gone. A patient, she thought. He'd had to leave to take care of a sick person. She rose gingerly from the bed, aware of soreness between her thighs. Then she saw the blood, and gasped aloud. There was also blood on the sheets.

She knew it wasn't from her monthly flow. She forced herself to be calm, and bathed away the blood. It seemed to have stopped, and she felt an overwhelming relief. She dressed and went downstairs.

"Good morning, Jules," Lydia said, eyeing her

young mistress closely. "No head problems this morning?"

Jules shook her head, and forced a smile. "No, I'm fine, really. Is Thomas up yet?"

"Up and gone. That young man has more energy than a hungry mosquito."

Jules wasn't very hungry herself, but she managed a cup of coffee and a slice of bread. "Did you see Michael?" she asked finally.

"No, he must have been called away."

"Did he leave a note or anything?"

Lydia shook her head. She saw the pained look in Jules's eyes and wondered about it. A short time later, she had no more reason to wonder. She saw the bloodstains on the sheet. That damned fool man had better get home soon, she thought, pulling the sheets off the bed.

Jules paced the parlor. She realized she was terrified at the thought of leaving the house by herself. She could see Jameson Wilkes waiting for her. Where was Michael?

Saint was very gently drawing a sheet over the fisherman's wife. She had died, and there was nothing he could do. She'd been ill more than a week, her husband had admitted to him on the boat ride across the bay, and now she was dead, never regaining consciousness in the last two hours.

And she had been young, not much over thirty, Saint guessed. He left the small house, the husband sitting at the kitchen table, a bottle of whiskey in front of him.

Saint wandered along the one dirt street of Sausalito. Life seemed particularly burdensome. There was one saloon, the Little Willow, and even though it was early afternoon, he walked into the dim, rather smelly room and ordered his own bottle of whiskey.

He knew rationally that the woman's death more than likely couldn't have been prevented, even if he'd seen her sooner. Damn, doctors didn't know a thing. He took a long pull on the whiskey. He hated death. He hated pain and illness, but even more than hate, something embedded deeply within him forced him to do what he could. And now he'd given his wife pain, gratuitous pain. He'd known better, but he'd allowed her, in all her sweet ignorance, to seduce him.

And he'd left her alone to face her thoughts.

He drank deeply, telling himself yet again that he was the last person she would want to see after the debacle of last night.

Jules wandered up to their bedroom late that afternoon. She paused in front of the long mirror and stared at herself. She remembered his words: *Never, never again.* Was she so unattractive, then? Slowly, after she'd locked the bedroom door, she undressed. Naked, she approached the mirror again and studied herself. She had never seen another woman naked, so she had no comparison. She didn't think she was ill-looking. She wasn't fat or bowlegged, or flat-chested. He had touched her, everywhere. She lightly placed her hands over her breasts. There wasn't the same feeling of warmth she felt when he touched her. She stared at her belly, at the cluster of red curls between her legs. He'd even caressed her there. She didn't flush with embarrassment, she simply continued staring at herself. She'd probably made him feel guilty, acting like such a watering pot. He hadn't hurt her all that much. *Never, never again.* But she had hurt him—that, or he hadn't enjoyed her body, taking her only because she'd demanded it of him. How could he have enjoyed it when she'd fought him, and cried like a stupid fool?

She felt tears sting her eyes now. Everything had gone awry. She'd hoped that he would change toward her, but not this way. Slowly she sank to her knees in front of the mirror and buried her face in her hands.

Saint pulled himself together when he heard a man talk about all the bloody fog rolling in. "Unusual this time of year," the man said to his companion. "No way out now."

That brought Saint to instant sobriety. "Fog?" he asked the man.

"Yep. You're from the city, ain't you?"

"Yes, and I must get back."

"Ain't nobody going out in that damned soup. Sorry, mister, but you're spending the night here."

Saint paid his shot and went outside. The man was right. He couldn't see a foot in front of him. San Francisco could be a thousand miles away, and in any direction. He thought of Jules and cursed. He should have left her a note, dammit. She would worry, and there was nothing he could do about it.

There were no inns in Sausalito, so he walked back into the saloon.

19

Saint didn't get back to San Francisco until late the following afternoon. He felt dirty, tired to the soles of his boots, guilty, and he didn't want to go home. As he strode along Clay Street, his eyes on mud puddles that could bring the unwary low, he imagined the look on Jules's face when she saw him. Disgust, revulsion—God only knew. For a moment he allowed himself to remember the intense pleasure he'd experienced, but of course, the pleasure had been all his. He kicked a stone viciously out of his way. Life, he decided, had become bloody hell.

He drew a deep breath and opened the front door to his house. "Jules," he called.

Jules, who had talked herself into fatalistic calm, heard his voice and forced herself to walk slowly from the parlor into the entrance hall.

"Hello, Michael," she said, not meeting his eyes. Somehow his presence made her feel dreadfully vulnerable and exposed. "Are you hungry? Lydia made a delicious beef stew, and there's freshly baked bread. Thomas isn't here. I believe he is again with Penelope Stevenson, teaching her manners, no doubt." She ground to a pained halt.

Saint wanted desperately to take her in his arms,

to stroke her bright head, to comfort her, but he was afraid to. He thought ruefully that he needed comforting himself. He smiled painfully, knowing she was putting on an act for him, trying to behave naturally, hiding her true feelings about him.

"I need a bath first," he said. "I'm sorry, Jules, about a lot of things. I should have left you a message, but I expected to be home soon. I was called over to Sausalito, across the bay, and couldn't come back any sooner because of the fog. Please forgive me—a doctor's lot and all that."

She raised her eyes to his face. For a brief instant his expression was unreadable; then she knew she saw pity in his eyes. She rocked back on her heels, hating him, hating herself. He'd found her lacking, found her still to be a child, not a woman, and now he was stuck with her. She wanted to yell, but she didn't. She said nothing, merely looked away from him. "Yes," she said finally, "yes, there was fog." She hadn't known the fog was all that heavy, but of course she hadn't been out of the house. She'd been too afraid to leave. No, she amended to herself, not really afraid. She hadn't wanted to leave because he might return at any moment.

"What happened to your patient?"

"She died," he said, his voice clipped. "I could do nothing for her."

"I'm sorry," she said.

He slashed his hand through the air. "There was nothing to be done for her, as I said. Now, I think I'll go up. I won't be long, Jules."

He wasn't long and the dinner was indeed well prepared. Saint said nothing more about his trip to Sausalito. He didn't want to burden her with particulars. In fact, he said very little, not knowing what to talk about to her. He was drinking a cup of coffee, screwing up his courage, and finally said, "Jules, I want to apologize, to tell you how sorry I am for what happened, for what I did and—" He broke off suddenly, seeing her flinch.

He very nearly sighed with relief when there was a loud knock on the front door.

It wasn't a patient. It was Brent Hammond.

"You stupid bastard," Brent said as he strode into the house.

"Good to see you too, Brent," Saint said. "Come in, won't you? Would you like a drink?"

"Nope. I want to talk to you."

Brent saw Jules from the corner of his eye, and quickly turned to smile at her. "Good evening," he said. She looked pale, Brent thought, and no wonder.

Jules nodded, and looked a question at her husband.

Brent answered for him. "I need to speak to your husband for a little while, Jules, if you don't mind. Incidentally, Byrony sends her love."

"Not at all," Jules said, and went upstairs. She'd never felt so alone in her entire life. She hated the house, the bedroom, hated the wretched mirror that showed her looking miserable.

In the parlor, Brent said, "Now, my friend, I've had a talk with Del."

Saint walked to the sofa and sat down, his arms behind his head. "Go ahead. I doubt I can stop you unless I plant my fist in your face. Since Del has said his piece, do feel free to dose me with your marvelous advice."

Brent smiled. "Touchy, aren't you, Saint? No advice. I've come with an offer for you."

"Lord save me! Look, Brent, why don't you just go back to your beautiful wife and leave me the hell alone!"

"If I recall correctly," Brent said, unperturbed, "you were very involved in my affairs not too long ago."

"That was different," Saint said, irritated. "You were acting the fool, wearing blinders, and poor Byrony . . ." *Oh God, that sounds like me.*

"Like hell," Brent said pleasantly, cutting off his thoughts. "Now, just listen." He sat forward in his chair, his hands clasped between his knees. "You are my wife's doctor. You will deliver our child when the time comes. In return, I wish to begin payments to you on sort of an installment plan. Your wife needs protection. I will provide that protection. His name is Thackery, and he's very smart, strong, and loyal. He's a black man, a former slave from Wakehurst, and a fine marksman. He will live here until Wilkes is taken care of. He will be with your wife when you can't be. He will be her bodyguard and protect her with his life. Now, what do you say, Saint?"

Saint wanted to tell Brent to take this Thackery and throw him in the bay, but he didn't. Brent was right. And he was a good friend. Saint sighed. "All right."

Brent cocked a dark brow. "My, my, marriage seems to have mellowed you a bit. Made you more reasonable, more amenable. Thackery is waiting outside, of course. Would you like to invite Jules down to meet him?"

"Probably," Saint said, rising. He wondered how Jules was going to react to having a bodyguard. "Let me fetch her." He turned in the parlor doorway. "Brent, thanks."

"My pleasure, old son," Brent said.

Jules gave Thackery her most winsome smile. She had to take him off guard, a difficult task at the very least. In their first week together, he went everywhere with her, never interfering in what she wished to do, merely staying stolidly with her, his presence forbidding to strangers and a relief to friends. Jules liked him. But now she had to distract him. Ah yes, the dress shop owned by Monsieur David. The perfect place.

"I would like to look at some gowns, Thackery," she said, waving toward the shop.

"Certainly, Mrs. Saint. I'll be right here when you come out."

Mrs. Saint! She'd tried to make him call her Jules, but he merely smiled at her and continued with "Mrs. Saint." Jules nodded brightly and walked, shoulders back, into the store. She pretended to be interested in the new shipment of gowns from France. Every few minutes she peered out the window. Damn, Thackery hadn't moved an inch!

She spoke briefly to the dapper Monsieur David, then slipped out the back of the store. The gun shop, run by Marcus Haverson, was just a block down Kearny Street. She'd stolen some money from Michael's strongbox just that morning. No, she amended to herself, it was her money too. After all, wasn't she Mrs. Saint?

Ten minutes later, she was the proud owner of a derringer. In another ten minutes she had rejoined Thackery.

Thackery arched a black brow. His young mistress looked awfully smug, and there wasn't one package in her arms. He wondered what she was up to. This jaunt of hers into a dress shop, looking all sorts of innocent and guileless, was unusual, and he was suspicious. She was a handful, but he didn't mind that. She was never boring. But she was unhappy. He was quite certain of that, even though she never said anything particularly unhappy. She was bright, chatty, interested in everything they saw. They'd visited the Russ Gardens, the old Dolores Mission, even the racetrack. But still . . .

He supposed it natural for her to be wary of that bastard Wilkes. But he would see to that man if he ever dared to show his face. No, it wasn't all Wilkes, he didn't think. He wished he could figure it out. Her husband was a very nice man who, as far as Thackery could tell, treated his young wife like one of those pieces of Dresden china Mrs. Hammond loved so much.

"I didn't like anything," Jules said, which was true, she supposed. She twisted her hands a bit nervously, aware of Thackery's suspicious look. To her relief, he didn't say anything. It didn't occur to her until later that she didn't know a single thing about guns. She eyed the long-barreled gun tucked into Thackery's belt, realizing she had to trust somebody. It was late afternoon, but she said to Thackery, "I would like to ride to the ocean. We're very close to the stables. All right?"

Thackery merely nodded. He would have preferred a visit to the Saxtons. He and Lucas were becoming friends, and he was fascinated by Lucas' tales of the gold fields.

When they reached the ocean, he listened with half an ear to Mrs. Saint carrying on about some long-legged birds that were skittering across the sand dunes. A bird was a bird, for God's sake.

When Jules saw that they were quite alone, she paused a moment, drew a deep breath, and blurted out, "I bought a derringer, Thackery. I want you to teach me how to use it."

"So," Thackery said on a deep breath, "that's what you were up to."

"Will you teach me how to use it?" Jules asked, her eyes steady on his face.

Thackery scratched the black woolly hair on his head. "No, ma'am," he said finally. "That's *my* job. Ain't nobody going to get to you while I'm here."

"If you don't teach me, I will sneak away and practice by myself. You know I can do it, Thackery."

"You need to have your bottom thwacked, Mrs. Saint," Thackery said, his dark eyes calm on her upturned face.

Jules said nothing, trying to stare him down. But Thackery was made of stern stuff. "I'll tell Dr. Saint," he said.

"He won't care!"

Thackery looked thoughtful. "Why not?"

She looked to him as though she wanted to cry and spit all at the same time. She said finally, "I am his cross to bear. You must know that he saved me, Thackery, then had to marry me because my father kicked me out. He didn't want to, but he's honorable. He really doesn't care what I do or don't do, just so long as I don't bother him."

Thackery heard the pain in her voice, and his reaction to it shocked him. He knew loyalty, indeed he did. Both the good Lord and Thackery knew how much he owed Mr. Hammond. But he'd sworn he'd never again trust another white. Until Mrs. Saint. Poor little mite. When he'd been a slave, it had never occurred to him that a white man or white woman could know a moment of unhappiness. Whiteness seemed to him then to be the key to all that was pleasant on this damned earth. Well, maybe white folk in California had more problems than those in Mississippi. He looked at Mrs. Saint, saw the pleading and defiance in those vivid green eyes of hers, and knew he had to say something, do something.

He temporized. "I could just take that little thing away from you, Mrs. Saint."

"You try it, Thackery," she said flatly, her eyes narrowed, "and I'll . . . well, I'll make you very sorry."

"You just would, wouldn't you? No, don't answer that. I ain't going to help you, and that's that."

He wouldn't budge, and after another few minutes of fierce arguing, Jules gave up. She refused to speak to him all the way back to San Francisco. His last words before he left her at home were, "I'm going to the Wild Star to see Mr. Hammond. You just keep that damned toy put away, you hear?"

"I hear," Jules said, and stomped into the house.

"What are you doing here?" Jules asked Thomas a few moments later. She was surprised to see him at home.

Thomas gave her a big smile. "I came home to ask Lydia to make something special for dinner. Penelope is coming."

Jules groaned. "Does she have manners yet, Thomas?"

"If she throws her peas at you, I'll put her bottom

in the air," he said, grinning widely. "Oh, yes, the Hammonds are in the city, and Saint invited them also. Seven o'clock. All right?"

Jules nodded. "Where is Michael?" she asked.

Thomas scratched his head. "I think he said something about seeing a Mrs. Branigan."

Jules sucked in her breath. His mistress! No, she amended, not his mistress. His lover, his former lover. "Why?" she asked, and immediately regretted asking.

"How would I know, sis? He's a doctor, isn't he?"

But Saint wasn't being a doctor, not on this visit. He sat in Jane's parlor, a cup of tea balanced on his knee. The boys were outside playing at last, and Jane was fidgeting about, straightening the pillows on a chair.

"Well?" Saint asked finally.

"It's your wife, Saint," Jane said, watching him closely. She saw him close his eyes briefly, a look of pain crossing his face.

"What about her?" he asked harshly.

"Joe saw her today. She bought a gun at Haverson's. I thought you should know."

Saint stared at her, disbelieving. "He's wrong," he said flatly. "There's no earthly reason for her to buy a gun. Thackery is with her all the time."

"Joe assured me it was true," Jane said. "That boy likes to fight, but he doesn't lie. You know that, Saint."

"Hell and damnation! Sorry, Jane." He set down the teacup and rose to his feet. "I don't bloody believe this!" He began pacing in ferocious silence, his brow knit.

"You should also know," Jane continued carefully

after a few moments, "that she visited Maggie the other afternoon. I heard it from a man who came to pick up his shirts. He didn't understand why Saint Morris' wife was visiting a whorehouse."

"Shit," said Saint very softly. "Sorry, Jane."

"There appears to be a serpent in paradise."

Yes, he thought, the serpent was his damned manhood! Such a ridiculous thought brought a momentary smile to his face. A rigid serpent. He laughed, a harsh, grating sound.

"Saint," Jane said, moving quickly to him and laying her hand lightly on his shoulder, "I'm sorry, but I thought you should know." She regretted her sarcastic comment, and wanted to make amends. "Please, Saint, if you want to talk about it, you know I'm a good listener."

"There's nothing whatsoever to talk about," he said. "I suppose I knew things weren't going all that well, but there's nothing like keeping one's eyes closed, is there? No, don't answer that, Jane. I've got to be going. I have the dubious pleasure of having Penelope Stevenson to dinner this evening."

"Good luck, Saint," she called after him softly, but he didn't hear her.

Saint entered their bedroom close to an hour later. Jules was splashing like a happy, unconcerned child in the tub. He paused in the doorway, wondering whether or not to retreat. She saw him and fell instantly silent.

"Hello, Jules," he said awkwardly.

Jules felt a wave of color wash over her cheeks. She sank down a few inches in the water. Why should I be embarrassed? she thought, suddenly angry. He knows . . . everything. "I shall be finished in just a moment," she said, raising her chin.

Saint made the mistake of allowing his eyes to leave her face. He felt an instant tightening in his loins at the sight of her soft white shoulders, the tops of her breasts. He swallowed, and backed up. "I'll be downstairs, Jules. I need a bath also. Just call me when you're finished."

He disliked her so much he couldn't bear to be in the same room with her! She was sorely tempted to climb out of the tub and hurl the water at him. But she didn't. She said only, her voice nasty, "How sorry I am that you had to work so very hard this afternoon. What was wrong with Mrs. Branigan, anyway?"

He forced his eyes back to her face. He thought of the damned gun, of her visit to Maggie. Here she was attacking him like a shrew for his visit to Jane! For God's sake, he'd told her he wouldn't sleep with Jane anymore! His eyes darkened, and he said coldly, "Why, nothing at all was wrong with Jane. Nothing at all. Not everyone I visit is ill, you know."

She wanted to yell at him, but she pressed her lips together and lowered her head. She heard his harsh breathing, heard the bedroom door slam, then listened to his retreating footsteps down the corridor.

"He's a miserable man," she whispered, and hated herself for the wretched tears that trickled down her cheeks. "I guess that makes us about even, since I'm a miserable woman."

Penelope had never before been in Saint Morris' house. It was dreadfully small and not at all well-appointed. Well, she was here and she supposed she must make the best of it. After all, Saint was Thomas' brother-in-law. She greeted Saint with cool politeness and tried her rarely used charm on Thomas' sister. What wild red hair, she thought, thankful of her own smooth flaxen tresses.

"How nice to see you again," Jules said, wondering for perhaps the dozenth time what Thomas saw in this dreadful girl. Her voice could chill the wine.

"Yes," Penelope said. "Dr. Morris," she added, gracefully inclining her long neck. "My parents send their regards."

"How about a glass of sherry, Pen?" Thomas asked.

Jules watched Penelope turn a beguiling smile on her brother. Pen! Penelope's voice softened as much as her eyes. "Oh yes, Thomas, that would be very nice."

Saint was markedly silent until the Hammonds arrived, full of good cheer and laughter. Byrony's stomach was well-rounded now, and her skin had that glowing, almost translucent look that some women gained when pregnant. "As I live and breathe," Byrony said in a very sweet voice. "Penelope! How very delightful. How I wish the Saxtons were here also."

Penelope didn't know what to do. She felt Thomas' hand on hers, squeezing, and she forced a big smile. "Hello," she said. "It is very good to see you both again. Mother is so pleased with the amount of money we raised for your slaves, Mr. Hammond."

"There are no slaves in California," Byrony said sweetly.

"Yes, Pen," Thomas added, "you must begin to listen and perhaps read the newspaper. It would give you all sorts of useful information."

Brent Hammond was watching this interplay with

some interest. He said quietly to Saint, "Your brother-in-law has more guts that I. Does she always roll over and play dead when he tromps on her?"

"He does handle her," Saint said, "and very well, it appears. I doubt you'll hear too many sly innuendos out of her tonight."

"How is Thackery?" Brent asked abruptly.

"Fine," said Saint. Brent followed his friend's gaze to Jules. She looked inordinately lovely in a dark green silk gown that was fashioned low on her white shoulders. Her flame-colored hair was intricately arranged in thick coronet braids atop her head. Curling tendrils framed her face.

"I spoke to him briefly before we came in," Brent said. "He informs me that your wife is a handful. But when I questioned him further, he became as closemouthed as a clam. I fear he's shifted his loyalty to your little one there. He is, I suppose one would say, firmly in her pocket."

Saint didn't want to talk about it. He didn't even want to think about it, at least not this evening. "Does Byrony have any more nausea in the mornings?" he asked.

Brent arched a questioning brow, but allowed the shift in topic. "No, she informs me she's healthy as I am, but fatter. You don't expect any problems, Saint?"

Saint did, but he didn't say anything. No sense in making Brent worry. If the child grew large, Byrony would have difficulties, for her pelvis was narrower than Jules's. "No problems," he said aloud. "Just make certain I'm around a couple of days before she's due to deliver."

"We'll be settled in Wakeville for the winter. You

don't mind trekking down? You'll stay with us as our guest. Jules also, of course."

"That would be fine. And don't worry, Brent."

"If you insist. Incidentally, Maggie was telling me that Jules—"

Saint raised his hand. "No, I don't want to hear it. I've already been informed. I intend to speak to Maggie tomorrow. Now, let's join the ladies and masterful, romantic Thomas."

To her profound surprise, Penelope found that she was enjoying herself. Certainly the fact that Thomas squeezed her hand in a meaningful way occasionally under the table made her smile, but she hadn't imagined that she would actually enjoy having dinner with a gambler and a girl from Maui and a doctor. And a pregnant lady!

". . . and then Limpin' Willie told me that he returned the hundred dollars to the man's pocket and sent him on his way," Saint said. "He told me the fellow had one of my bandages on his arm. Thought I'd be upset if he did him in after I'd fixed him up."

He paused a moment to let the laughter die down.

"I think you should run for mayor, Saint," Byrony said. "You would gain more votes than any man in the history of San Francisco."

"Saint," Thomas said, sitting forward in his chair, "tell us the story about Napoleon and his one experience with a cathartic."

"In front of the ladies, Thomas? And I believe you've already told it. Needless to say, he refused any further treatment of that sort."

"What's a cathartic?" Penelope asked.

"The opposite of an emetic," Thomas said, hooting with laughter.

"Thomas!"

"Yes, Pen?" Thomas asked, his face as innocent and guileless as his sister's was when she wanted to fool Thackery, Saint thought. Which evidently she had. She hadn't spoken one word directly to him all evening. He wanted to be alone with her. He wanted to yell at her and shake her. He wanted . . . Oh no, you damned randy bastard! Not that, not again.

He sat back and pretended to listen to Brent describe their progress at Wakeville. Lydia's roast beef sat like leather in his stomach, as had her attempt at Yorkshire pudding. He sipped at his wine, his gaze going to his wife's face.

What the hell was he going to do with her? He'd hurt her badly, but that didn't excuse her recent behavior. He supposed he would have to speak with Thackery, have the man keep a closer eye on her.

"Michael?"

He was jerked out of his fog. "What?" he said, turning to Jules.

"The ladies will be in the parlor," she said, rising. He quickly stepped to her side and politely held her chair. She didn't look at him.

"We won't be long," Saint said.

Another two hours passed before they were alone. Thomas left to drive Penelope home, and Brent, his voice light and amusing, claimed his fat wife needed her rest, which gained him Byrony's elbow in his ribs.

Saint said without preamble, "I want to talk to you, Jules."

"I'm tired," she said, moving toward the parlor door. "I'm going to bed. You know, Michael, it's that rather large piece of furniture up in the bedroom. Good night."

"Jules!"

He jumped to his feet and strode after her. "You come back here!" he shouted to her retreating back on the stairs.

Jules paused at the top of the stairs, curled her lip at him, and said coldly, "Oh no. It seems that the parlor has become your bedroom. I have no intention of speaking to you there."

"Damn you," he growled, and stalked up the stairs after her.

20

Let him come in, Jules thought, stomping into the bedroom. She stopped in the middle of the room, turned, and faced the open doorway.

Perhaps she should begin taking off her clothes—that would stop him in his tracks!

Her fingers went to the long row of buttons.

"Don't you dare," Saint said, coming into the room. He paused a moment, then slammed the door closed behind him. "Leave those buttons alone!"

"Why?" she asked, unfastening yet another. "Would you find it so very repulsive? I thought doctors were quite used to seeing naked women."

"I want to talk to you, not see you with nothing on but your hair." What game was she playing, damn her!

Jules sat down on the swivel chair in front of the dresser, folded her hands primly in her lap, and began to twiddle her thumbs. "Yes?" she asked.

We used to be such good friends, he thought, staring down at her, his frustration mounting. She used to trust me, to . . . love me. No, not that, you ass! She loved you as a child would an older brother. He said, "Why did you buy a gun today?"

She started to deny it, but knew it would do no

good. "So," she said coldly, "I cannot even trust Thackery. When did he tell you?"

"He didn't."

"Then how do you know?"

Saint shrugged. "It doesn't matter. Now, where is it?"

She looked mulish, and he grabbed her reticule from the dresser and riffled through it. She said nothing, merely stared at him tight-lipped.

There was no gun in the reticule.

"Where, Jules?"

Now was the time for a lie, she thought, squaring her shoulders. Otherwise, he would tear the room apart looking for it. "I decided that Thackery was right. I don't need a gun. He will protect me."

Saint stopped, turned very slowly, and looked at her. "Are you telling me the truth?"

She shrugged pettishly. "Why shouldn't I? I told you, I realized it was silly for me to have it. Besides, I don't know the first thing about derringers."

"I see. Just what did you do with it, Jules?"

She held his gaze steadily. "I threw it in the ocean this afternoon." She lowered her eyes quickly. That wasn't a good lie at all. All he had to do was ask Thackery.

"If," he said, "I discover that you aren't telling me the truth, I will thrash you."

She said nothing, merely twiddled her thumbs.

"What I should do is buy Thackery a leash. A short one."

She shrugged, still saying nothing, and kept her eyes on her thumbs.

"Another matter," Saint said after a moment. "I understand you paid a visit to Maggie the other day.

No, let's not repeat how I found out. Suffice it to say that I did, quite by accident. Would you care to tell me why you went to a brothel?"

"I wanted to meet her. Chauncey Saxton told me how very nice she was."

"She runs a brothel," Saint said. "It doesn't matter how nice Maggie is. If you wish to make a friend of her, you will invite her here, you understand?"

"She won't come here."

"Then that's an end to it."

"No."

"What?"

"I said," Jules said very calmly, "that I shall do as I wish. And *that's* an end to it."

"Jules, listen to me." He stopped, knowing that nothing he said would make any difference. He knew she was stubborn. He simply hadn't guessed how stubborn. And she thoroughly disliked him, so why should she care what the hell he thought about anything? He suddenly remembered Victoria, her body viciously beaten by a mean drunk. God, he hated prostitution. Even willing women could be brutalized, just as Victoria had been. "Several months ago, Maggie called me to the brothel. One of the girls, Victoria is her name, had been badly hurt." He paused a moment, realizing that he didn't have her complete attention. "Actually," he continued, his voice hard, "the man had not only beaten her, he had used her unnaturally, and torn her." Should he be more graphic? He couldn't bring himself to be. "I had to stitch her up, Jules. She was ill for several weeks."

"Why are you telling me this? It is terrible, of course, but it has nothing to do with me."

He frowned. "I don't know. I don't want you hurt, Jules."

"Then why did you go visit Jane Branigan?"

"She wanted to speak to me, that's all. Nothing more."

"About what?"

"It's not important."

"Are you going to sleep here tonight?"

"Your mind," Saint said, clamping down on his body's instant response to her words, "jumps about more unpredictably than that strange animal in Australia. No, I'm sleeping downstairs. I'm expecting a patient, he's coming up to see me from San Jose." That was a bloody lie, but what else could he tell her? No, I won't sleep here or I'll strip off your nightgown and force you. Again. And this time you wouldn't be asking me to, since you know . . .

"Good night then, Michael."

He merely nodded, and turned to leave.

"You needn't be quiet when you leave to see Jane Branigan," she called after him. "I'm a very heavy sleeper."

A muscle moved convulsively in his jaw. "Good night, Jules," he said, and strode from the bedroom.

Jules heard the front door open and close some fifteen minutes later. She turned off the lamp beside the bed, flipped onto her stomach, and cursed into the pillow.

It was only a week until Christmas, and the days had shortened drastically. It was only a bit after four in the afternoon, and Jules had to move to the window to read the letter. It was from her sister, Sarah. It was a taunting, rather petty letter, in which Sarah described in great detail her wedding to Tory Dickerson, a visiting planter from Oahu. "Good for you, Sarah," Jules said aloud to the silent parlor. "Now maybe you'll be just a little bit happy." She folded the letter, then took it up to Thomas' room, propping it up on his pillow.

She was alone, Lydia having left an hour earlier to buy some Christmas presents.

She wandered about the house, gazing into Michael's surgery. There were several glass-fronted cabinets, two chairs, a desk, and a long table, where, she supposed, he examined people. She studied the bottles in the cabinets, but without much interest, for she recognized only a few of the labels. He'd been gone most of the day, called by David Broderick's servant to come to his house. Broderick, it seemed, had broken his leg.

She grabbed her cloak, gently placed her derringer, now loaded, into her reticule, and stepped out into the growing darkness. She didn't see Thackery. Perhaps he was off visiting Lucas. She had told him at noon that she wasn't going out today. Well, so much for him. She would take care of herself.

She would go visit Maggie. Certainly it was too early for Maggie to be entertaining men. Her eyes narrowed as she walked toward Kearny Street. Where are you, Mr. Jameson Wilkes? I'm not a virgin, not anymore, but I certainly would like to see you!

She became aware of the number of men staring at her. She raised her chin. There were catcalls and whistles and some lewd comments tossed her way, but she ignored them, staring straight ahead. She saw some women, gaily dressed, and knew they were prostitutes. She had nearly gained Portsmouth Square when she heard an astonished voice from behind her.

"Good God! Jules, is that you?"

She turned slowly, recognizing Brent Hammond's voice.

"Hello, Brent," she said. "How are you this fine day? No fog, but Michael tells me there's not much during the winter. It's getting dark so much earlier now, isn't it? How is Byrony?"

"What the hell are you doing here?" Brent said, eyeing her speculatively. Where was Thackery?

"I'm visiting Maggie."

"Like hell you are!"

"Your language is foul, sir, and it's really none of your business. It was nice seeing you. Now—"

"Stop, Jules! Does Saint know what you're up to?"

"Up to?" Jules raised a supercilious brow. "I am a free person, Mr. Hammond. I am out walking and visiting, just as I suspect your former slaves can now do. Good day, sir."

Brent ground his teeth. Then he smiled, his charming, seductive smile. "Very well. Do allow me to escort you to Maggie's apartment. I'm certain she's very anxious to see you, particularly here."

Jules was nonplussed. Finally she nodded. Brent took her arm and led her through the alley to the back entrance of the Wild Star. When they reached the top of the stairs, he steered her to the left.

"A moment, Brent. Maggie is—"

"I imagine that Maggie is visiting Byrony," Brent said smoothly. "Come along."

Of course, Maggie wasn't in the Hammonds' apartment. Byrony was seated in front of a glowing fire, reading. She looked startled, then pleased, greeting Jules warmly and offering her a cup of tea.

After the amenities, Brent said to his wife, "I will come back in a little while, love. You and Jules can visit."

"How lovely. Give us at least an hour, Brent."

Jules was in a quandary. The major reason she'd wanted to visit Maggie was her husband's taboo. But how could she tell the glowing Byrony Hammond that she didn't want to stay? She gave Brent a crooked smile.

"Just so," Brent said softly to her. "Later, ladies."

He tracked Saint down in front of his house, Saint having just returned from the Brodericks'.

"How nice to see you, Saint," Brent said blandly. "My, do you happen to know where your wife is?"

Saint waved a hand toward the house. He paused, seeing no lights in the windows. He frowned. "All right, Brent," he said in a resigned voice. "Where is she? What has she done this time?"

"Why, she's with my wife," Brent said. He added, "Of course, when I just happened to see her, she was on her way to see Maggie. Thanks to my perfidy, she is with Byrony, her guns spiked, as it were."

"Damn," said Saint.

"Yes. I guess my next question is, where is Thackery? Your wife was quite alone, trying her best to ignore all the very interested men."

"Jules very probably lied to him and told him she wasn't going out of the house. Thackery will have a fit when he finds out."

"And you, Saint?"

"I don't like fits."

"No, you don't, do you? But marriage seems to

have brought you as many confusions and complications as it brought me. I don't know what's going on, Saint, and you're probably dying to tell me to go to hell—"

"Why?" Saint asked, sighing. "You did well by my wife, and I thank you. Lord knows, *I* can't seem to handle her."

Brent eyed his friend closely. "You might try thrashing her," he said.

Saint laughed. "Yes," he said, "yes, I just might. Well, I'm off to fetch my errant wife. Thanks again, Brent."

Before he could leave, Thackery returned, a laughing Thomas with him.

"Hi, Saint," Thomas said. "What's going on? There aren't any lights in the house."

Thackery said very quietly, "Tell me where, Dr. Saint, and I'll go fetch her."

Perhaps it would be better, Saint thought, if Thackery got her. "She's at the Hammonds' apartment, above the Wild Star."

Thackery nodded, touched the brim of his hat, and strode off into the growing darkness. Saint turned to his brother-in-law. "Lydia should be back soon. You hungry, Thomas?"

"Yes," Thomas said. He laughed suddenly. "I won't be seeing Penelope this evening. She tried to give me orders about a certain something, and I informed her . . . well, I told her she could spend some time alone to think about her woman's modesty."

"Good God, Thomas," Saint said as they went into the house. "Whatever did the girl want you to do?"

Thomas looked thoughtful as the two men went into the parlor. Saint lit the lamps and took off his coat. He looks tired, Thomas thought. Damn Jules anyway. Whatever is that little twit up to?

"Drink, Thomas?"

Thomas nodded. "Sherry, please, Saint."

The two men relaxed a moment, drinking in silence. Saint said again, "What did Penelope want you to do?"

Thomas raised twinkling eyes to Saint's face, and Saint started. There was a good deal of similarity between that impish look and Jules's.

"She wanted me to make love to her."

"Penelope? Good God!"

"Exactly," Thomas said. "I told her she should be ashamed of herself." He grinned in fond memory. "She is, of course, quite desirable."

Saint could think of nothing to say.

"She wants to marry me, you know, and since I'm as elusive as hell, I suppose she thought she would compromise me."

"And what did you say?"

"I told her no, and that this evening I was going to spend the night making love to a woman who expected nothing from me. For a while there, I thought she would expire with hysterics."

Saint shook his head. "Thomas, the gentlemen of San Francisco salute you!"

Thomas sat forward in his chair, his glass between his knees. "Bunker wants me to come to work for him in the foundry. I'm not certain that's what I want."

"Doing what?"

Thomas shrugged. "Probably a glorified office boy to start with. Somehow, working for my father-in-law doesn't seem too smart a thing to do."

"No, I would agree."

"I want to be a doctor, Saint."

Saint leaned back, his arms behind his head. "I think," he said finally, "that you should determine if that is really what you want by working with me. I could teach you a goodly amount. If you decide in, say, six months that you wish to continue, I think you should go back East, to Boston or New York, for your formal training."

They continued discussing the pros and cons until Lydia arrived. Ten minutes later, they heard Jules's voice. Thomas watched Saint's face harden, his eyes glitter.

"Well," Thomas said, rising quickly. "I think I'll be going out now. I've got to spend some time with Morton David, an interesting man. Of all things, he's an actor, Shakespeare and all that." Thomas paused a moment in the doorway and said quietly, "Good luck, Saint."

Saint heard him greet his sister with an affectionate "You look like hell, Jules. Go comb your hair, you look a fright."

Jules knew Michael was in the parlor, but she didn't want to see him. She went upstairs and stayed there until after Lydia had left. She heard him call to her.

She eased into her chair at the foot of the dining table. He handed her the several dishes, saying nothing.

"I trust you had an interesting day," Saint said finally, laying down his fork.

"No, not really," Jules said.

"Oh? You found Byrony boring?"

"No, she was quite charming. She wanted me to ask you if she could come by tomorrow."

He nodded. "Certainly."

He wasn't angry and it made her very wary. "Michael," she said, taking the offensive, "I am bored! I do nothing except sit around and brush my hair!"

"Fine, I'll dismiss Lydia and you can take over her duties."

That shut her up, Saint thought, but only for a moment.

She thrust her chin upward. "So, if I can't be anything else, you'll allow me to be your housekeeper!"

"What else do you want to be?"

"Would you pay me what you pay Lydia?"

Elusive chit, he thought. "Probably not—you haven't her experience or skill."

He sat back and watched her, knowing he'd spiked her guns.

"You think I'm afraid to work?"

"Jules, I don't think you're afraid of a damned thing, more's the pity."

Yes, she wanted to tell him, she was afraid of more things than she could count. Why wasn't he angry with her, yelling at her, for going to see Maggie?

She blurted out her last thought, "Aren't you angry with me?"

He nodded. "Yes, of course."

But he didn't care enough to yell at her, she thought. She didn't know what to say. She watched him rise. He'd opened his shirt at the neck and she coud see the silken tufts of hair on his chest. He was so handsome, she thought, her eyes going down his body hungrily. But he didn't love her, he didn't even like her, not anymore. She gave him nothing but trouble.

"I'm going out," Saint said. "Incidentally, Jules," he added, halting a moment in the doorway, "Thackery will be here."

"Ah yes, my jailer. Give my regards to Mrs. Branigan."

He paused and said, his voice hard, "You will cease using Jane as a bone of contention between us. She is a fine woman. I admire her and respect her, but that is all."

She lowered her head, saying nothing.

21

January is a brooding month, Jules thought, pulling her cloak more closely about her. The air was thick with swirling fog and a chilling drizzle that made her bones ache with cold. She thought of Maui, pictured herself running along the beach, the warm trade winds in her face. She wondered if she'd ever become accustomed to this bitter climate. She supposed with a shake of her head that she should count her blessings. After all, she could have ended up in Toronto.

She'd managed to lose Thackery. She'd gotten quite adept at it over the past couple of weeks. She was hunting again. It added excitement to the game to think she was also the hunted. Wilkes was there, waiting for her, just as she was searching for him. She knew it, she could practically feel his presence.

It was odd, her thinking continued, even as her eyes darted about her as she walked, but Wilkes had become the focal point of her life. It was odd and, she realized, rather pathetic. But she had nothing else.

Both Thomas and Lydia knew that Michael slept in the parlor. Lydia had said nothing, but Thomas had not been so reticent. Indeed, she thought, seeing his face in her mind's eye, he'd been appalled and angry.

"What the hell is going on, Jules?"

She'd merely looked at him, not at first understanding his attack.

"Saint," he nearly shouted at her. "Your husband, little sister. I find to my chagrin that my brother-in-law, the owner of this damned house, is sleeping like some sort of extra guest downstairs! What is wrong with you?"

"Nothing," Jules said.

That had brought him up short. His features softened just a bit. "Look, Jules, I realize that all is not well with you two, but you don't even allow him to sleep in his own bed?"

"He doesn't want to," Jules said.

"Oh, come on, Jules." Thomas said in disgust. "You're not exactly a troll. I don't understand any of this."

"It's very simple, Thomas," Jules said, her voice hard. "Michael didn't want to marry me in the first place. He had to, if you'll remember. In terms of sleeping with me, he's not interested." That wasn't precisely true, but all the rest of it was hardly Thomas' business, after all.

Thomas looked shocked. "He's never slept with you?"

"Once. That, it appears, was more than enough. Now, Thomas, is there anything else?"

He saw tears sparkling in her eyes, and without another word gathered her in his arms. "This isn't right, love," he said quietly, stroking her hair. "I'm sorry, Jules. Damn, after all that happened to you, well . . . is there anything I can do?"

She shook her head against his shoulder. "Don't embarrass Michael, please, Thomas. He doesn't deserve it, it's not his fault. He's making the best of a bad bargain."

But there was something Thomas could do, and he had done it two days later. He'd moved out. The short note he'd left his sister simply said that it was time to make his own way. And he'd thanked her for her hospitality.

Thomas had been gone a week now, Jules thought, starting momentarily at the shadow of a man in an alley to her right. Nothing. Jules had moved that same day back into the guestroom.

And the siege of polite indifference had continued.

That voice, Jules thought, freezing. It was Wilkes! She was certain of it! She clutched her small derringer, fear trickling through her, fear and excitement. At last! Her eyes glittered in anticipation, her fingers tightened about the trigger.

But it wasn't Wilkes. It was a man, a very dirty man, dressed poorly, and he was drunk.

"Little girlie," he said fondly, staggering toward her. "My Anna had red hair, like a flame, she did."

"Get away from me," Jules said, backing up a step.

"Anna?" he said, his eyes bleary, his voice shaking.

"No, I'm not Anna!" Jules said, and tried to pass him. He let her go, and she heard him make a whimpering noise behind her. Poor man, she thought. She turned slightly to look at him, worried that he might hurt himself. She jumped as two hard hands grasped her shoulders, jerking her around. This man was neither drunk nor dirty, and his eyes were alight with unexpected pleasure.

"Well, well, you're dressed awful nice, ain't you? Awful pretty, too. How much?"

"I am not a whore," Jules said, her heart beginning to pound painfully. "Go away."

"How much?" the man repeated. She saw in a detached manner that one of his front teeth was gold. "I'm rich and you're just too pretty to let go. Come now."

"Go away," she said again, and pushed her hands against him. He didn't even notice that one hand held a gun.

"It'a almost dark," the man said, tightening his grip. "I don't mind the alley. Do you like it standing up? I won't pay you as much as I would if I could stick it in you in a nice bed. Come on now, little honey."

She tried to jerk away from him, but it was no use.

Suddenly his hand was flattened over her mouth and he was dragging her backward toward the filthy, dark alley.

"Stop fighting me," he hissed into her face. "I'll pay you, and you'll like it."

He was strong, Jules thought blankly. Oh God, what had she done? She felt her heart pounding wildly, felt her mouth go cotton dry. He was going to rape her!

She felt his mouth pressing wet kisses on her face, felt his hands tugging at her cloak to get to her breasts.

"Stop it!" she screamed against his hand.

She felt his hand wild on her breast, kneading, pressing her back against a brick wall.

"You just hold still," he growled at her, and lifted his hand from her mouth. She yelled, a high, thin sound that broke off abruptly when his hand yanked up her skirts.

His hand was pressing against her stomach, jerking at her underthings. She started hitting him, and the derringer struck the side of his face. He drew back in stunned fury.

"You little bitch," he said in utter astonishment. "Why'd you do that? You ain't nothing but a—" He stopped abruptly, seeing the derringer. He grabbed her wrist and jerked it forward. But she wouldn't let it go. There was a loud popping noise.

Jules watched as the man spun away from her, clutching at his shoulder. Blood oozed from between his fingers. He stared at her, his expression disbelieving. She dropped the derringer into her reticule and sagged against the wall.

"Mrs. Saint! What the hell—"

Thackery, whose practice was to keep well behind her, came bursting into the alley.

"My God," he whispered, "you shot him!"

"He thought I was a whore," Jules said, her voice calm, too calm, Thackery thought, eyeing her white face.

"What did you expect? Walking about by yourself, daring someone to come along . . . Oh damn!"

Thackery gathered the moaning man and hauled him upright. "Mrs. Saint, fetch me a carriage, now!"

Jules dashed into the street and yelled at a passing beer wagon. It cost her all the money she had to convince the man to drive them back home.

When Lydia opened the front door, she gasped.

"Get Dr. Saint," Thackery said, and carried the man to Saint's surgery.

Saint was daubing iodine on a miner's leg. "Now,

there, Lewis, you'll be—" He broke off when the door burst open.

"Later, Lewis," he said, and motioned for Thackery to put the man on the table. Saint said nothing, all his attention on the bullet wound. It was high on the man's shoulder, and the bullet had gone clean through. The man moaned and began to struggle. "Hold him, Thackery," he said, not looking up.

"Damned little whore shot me," the man muttered. He stared up at Saint, confusion and pain on his face. "Why would a whore shot me? I told her I'd pay her. I ain't no liar."

"Maybe she didn't like brown eyes," Saint said, his hands busy. "Just hold still, you're not dying, for God's sake!"

"She shot me," the man repeated blankly, his eyes dazed now from shock.

Saint got the bleeding stopped. He bathed the wound, spread on a thick layer of basilicum powder, and tightly bandaged the shoulder. "You'll be good as new in a week."

The man merely regarded him vaguely, and Saint asked Thackery, "Do you know who he is?"

"With that beautiful gold tooth? Maybe the president," Thackery said dispassionately.

Saint lightly slapped the man's face. "Name. What is your name?"

"Avery. I made me a good-sized strike. I was here celebrating, at the Oriental Hotel, and the little whore shot me."

"At least he won't have to spend the night in the parlor," Saint said. "Thackery, hail a hack for him and get him back to his hotel."

"Dr. Saint," Thackery began, knowing the time for reckoning had arrived.

"Well, what?"

"Before I get him out of here . . ."

Saint pulled his attention from the man and eyed Thackery.

"It's Mrs. Saint," Thackery said. "She shot him."

Saint said nothing. He didn't move. His face was an unreadable mask.

"She didn't mean to, but he was trying to force her."

"Don't defend her, Thackery," Saint said very calmly. "It isn't necessary. Get him out of here, please."

Thackery lifted the man in his arms. Saint followed him silently, not looking at his wife, who was standing quietly in the entrance hall, watching.

When the front door closed, Saint walked calmly into the kitchen. Lydia was pounding at some bread. "I want you to go home," Saint said. "Now."

Lydia wiped the flour from her hands, her eyes studying Saint's face. She wasn't blind, nor was she deaf. "I don't know if I should," she said.

"Leave, Lydia," Saint repeated. "I won't kill her." He gave a short, harsh laugh. "I'm a physician, remember?"

Lydia sighed. At least, she thought, he would speak to his wife. That, she supposed, was better than the deadening silence that pervaded the house.

Jules watched Lydia slip out the front door. She felt numb, blessedly numb.

Saint looked at her a moment, then said, "Come here into the parlor. You need a brandy."

She followed him, standing quietly in the middle of the room until he pressed a glass in her hand.

281

"Drink. All of it."

She did, and fell into a paroxysm of coughing.

He didn't touch her. Her face was red when she caught her breath.

"Finish it."

She did, then thrust the empty glass at him. Very carefully Saint set it down.

He held out his hand.

Jules simply stared. She loved his hands, she thought vaguely. The fine sprinkling of hair, the long fingers, their blunt tips. She had loved it when he'd touched her, caressed her.

"Give me the gun," he said.

She opened her reticule and looked at the very small instrument that could very easily have killed that man. She couldn't bring herself to touch it. She shuddered, unknowingly, and thrust the reticule at him.

Saint took the derringer, opened the chamber, and took out the second bullet. He then dropped the gun to the floor and stomped on it. Once, twice. It broke into three pieces, Jules saw.

"Now," he said, "I believe it's your turn, Juliana."

"Juliana?" she repeated.

"I believe," he said, his voice as cold as Toronto winters must be, "that 'Juliana' is more appropriate than 'Jules' for a whore. 'Juliana' is also more appropriate than 'Jules' for a liar."

His words broke over her, filling her with his disgust, and she began to shake; she couldn't help it.

"You might consider trying tears," Saint said, making no move toward her. "Though this time, Juliana, I promise you they won't work."

"No, no, I won't cry," she said.

"Refreshing," he said. He walked away from her—he had to—to the fireplace. He leaned his shoulders gratefully against the mantelpiece. "Would you care to tell me what happened?" he asked, his voice very polite, very calm.

"Nothing, not really. He pulled me into an alley." Jules drew a deep breath. "I was frightened and we struggled. The gun went off by accident, Michael."

"Such a short, almost boring tale," he said. "Fortunate for your conscience that the man, Avery—not a bad fellow really, I imagine—won't die because you're a stubborn, witless little fool."

As if drawn by a puppet's string, her chin went up.

"Would you mind telling me why you were out alone?" He waved a hand toward the window. "It's dark, and was almost dark when you were out there. Obviously you thought you'd lost Thackery."

"Yes," she said, "that's what I thought."

"I believe I asked you a question, Juliana."

What could she tell him? When she really didn't understand her own motives? "Wilkes," she whispered, her eyes on the toes of her shoes.

"Wilkes? What the hell does he have to do with anything?" At her continued silence, he added in a mocking voice, "Have you changed your mind about him? Do you want to find him, give yourself over to him?"

"No!"

"No what? I would appreciate some specificity."

"I was out . . . tracking him."

He could only stare at her. "Tracking him," he repeated. "If you managed to find him," he continued after a moment, "you wanted to kill him?"

"Yes," she said. "I'm tired of being a prisoner! I'm tired of being a helpless victim."

"But you're not tired of being a damned fool. Tracking Wilkes—dear God, I don't believe this!"

"Why not? And I'm not a fool." She saw that he was regarding her as if she had suddenly announced that she was going to jump into the bay. "At least," she muttered, now more angry than numb, "he wanted me!"

Saint felt himself stiffen, his hands fisting at his sides. "What did you say?"

"Nothing, I didn't mean that! It's just that . . ."

"That what?" he asked when she faltered.

"I don't know what to do!"

"Charming," he observed. "So blatant stupidity is the answer. Your woman's mind—well, I should have faced it sooner, shouldn't I?"

"What do you mean my 'woman's mind'?"

"I was wrong to say that. Rather, it's more the case that you're still an ignorant child. Selfish, reckless, silly, and so uncaring of anyone else that—"

"I am not uncaring! I did not mean to hurt that man. And I am not a child. Ask Wilkes! He didn't think so!"

They were going about in circles, he realized. Accomplishing nothing, Resolving nothing. But he simply felt too overwhelmed and too furious with her to continue. What he wanted was to thrash some sense into her.

Jules felt his eyes on her, brooding, questioning, grim now with determination.

"What are you going to do?" she asked, hating herself for her high, thin voice.

"I'm going to do something I should have done

months ago," he said, straightening to his full height. "Since there is no reasoning with you, since I can't be certain you won't continue to lie to me with great regularity, I shall just have to do something much more basic."

He strode toward her.

"What?" she said, automatically backing away from him.

"Since there's no one here, I don't have to haul you upstairs," he said more to himself than to her.

"Why do you want to 'haul' me?"

He didn't answer her, merely grasped her wrist and pulled her against him. For a brief moment Jules believed he would comfort her, tell her that everything was all right, that he understood.

In the next moment he'd sat down in his chair and pulled her over his legs.

"No!" she yelled, twisting on his lap, trying desperately to lurch away from him.

She felt his hands pulling up her gown, jerking away her underthings. She felt the cool air on her bare bottom.

"Very nice," Saint said, and slammed down his palm.

Jules yelled, and arched wildly. His hand came down again, harder this time. She felt pain, but her humiliation was greater, and she yelled all the bad names she could think of at him.

He laughed.

Saint lifted his hand to smack her bottom again, then drew up short. Her white buttocks were now slashed with red, and he could feel her quivering with pain. He laid his open palm on her, his fingers, of their own accord, gently kneading her stinging flesh. He felt a surge of desire, and quickly raised his hand.

"If ever," he said, "you lie to me again, or do something so stupid, I'll use a whip on you. Do you understand me?"

"I hate you!"

He brought his hand down again, not as hard this time, but dammit, he had to gain her compliance, and, for that matter, her attention.

"Do you understand?" He punctuated each word with a smack.

"Yes," she said, her voice breaking.

"Excellent." He simply pushed her off his lap, and she landed in a welter of skirts on the floor at his feet, her underclothes about her ankles. He rose quickly, forcing himself not to look at her, for if he did, he knew he'd probably beg her forgiveness, hold her, and . . . Damnation!

He didn't bother with a coat. He left, slamming the front door after him.

Jules gingerly touched her hand to her burning bottom. She struggling to get her underclothes back into a semblance of order, then straightened her gown. But didn't rise—she couldn't manage to do that just yet.

She leaned down, pillowed her head on her arms, and breathed in the dust from the carpet.

22

Saint sat by himself at a table at the Wild Star. His friends and acquaintances now kept to themselves, leaving him in solitary splendor, nursing his whiskey.

"Hisself is takin' things too serious," said Dancer Drake, the local boxer.

To Bear Paw Ryan, Saint had been just plain rude. "He musta lost somebody important," Bear Paw said by way of excuse for one of the most popular men in San Francisco.

Saint stared down at his whiskey, unaware that his very unsaintlike behavior was leading to wild speculation. *What am I going to do now?* he was asking himself. It was a refrain that had no more acceptable answer now than when he'd first asked it months before. Jules's shocked white face kept swimming before his eyes. And her beautiful bottom, red-streaked from his smacks. He winced, hearing the sound of his hand striking her. *You damned brute,* he said to himself, and downed the remainder of his whiskey.

I hate you.

"Well," he said to his empty glass, "what the hell did you expect? You were beating her. Did you think she'd tell you how wonderful you were?"

He yelled for another whiskey.

Saint had never before raised his hand to a woman. His great size and strength discouraged men from trying to prove their manhood and courage by baiting him. All it had taken was one small woman who had finally driven him over the edge. What had she done, anyway? *She lied to you, she went tracking Wilkes, and she shot a man.* That was a start, he thought, grunting at Nero when he slapped his whiskey shot onto the table.

Nero backed away from the table, saw Brent Hammond, and waved frantically toward his boss.

"Mind if I join you, Saint?" Brent asked. "Excellent, don't mind if I do. Godawful weather we're having, isn't it? I imagine that Jules is having a problem with all the drizzle and fog, her being from Maui and all, huh?"

"Go away, Brent," Saint said, not looking up.

Brent sat down and leaned back in his chair. He studied his friend's face.

"Leave me alone, Brent," Saint said, his voice as rude as he could make it.

"I think I'll take my chances and bear you company for a bit longer. Thackery wanted me to find out what you'd done to your wife, actually. He's very worried about her." If the truth be known, Brent thought, Thackery was just as worried about Dr. Saint. "She pushed him too far this time," Thackery had said, shaking his head.

"I should have used a whip," Saint said suddenly, renewed fury gripping him. "And I will next time, damn her stupidity!"

"Thackery feels guilty, feels he should have prevented what happened. He tells me that your little one, as he calls her—"

"Would you just shut up?" Saint sent Brent the meanest look he could manage, but it wasn't as effective as he'd hoped. Brent laughed.

"Why don't you go upstairs, Saint? Any of Maggie's girls would be delighted to bring you some temporary . . . relief."

Brent waited for the explosion, but it didn't come. He watched in astonishment as Saint appeared to consider his suggestion. "I probably should," Saint said at last. "It would at least protect her from me."

For a long moment Brent simply stared at his friend. He didn't know what to do or what to say. Finally he said very quietly, "Can I tell you a story, Saint?" He continued without pause, "When Byrony and I were first married, we didn't get along—my fault of course. She followed me to Celeste's house, thinking I was going to my mistress to sleep with her. Odd. In fact, I wanted to ask Celeste about preventing conception. Do you know that she faced me down? Yelled at me like a fishwife. I was so mad I was ready to strangle her."

"Your point, Hammond?" Saint asked almost savagely.

"Hmm, well, I guess it's that Byrony showed a lot of courage to do that. It wasn't quite the same thing, but just maybe Jules wants and needs your attention, and you've frozen her out. Neither Thackery nor I, I might add, can understand why you don't appear to give a good damn about your wife."

Saint scraped his chair back and rose. He wasn't aware that a goodly number of men were regarding him intently. "It's gotta be a woman," Bear Paw said. Limpin' Willie nodded sage agreement.

"You want to borrow a whip, Saint?" Brent asked with interest, not at all intimidated by his friend's menacing size or mean stare. "Really bring the little fool to her knees? Or you could send her back East with Thomas. And if Thomas isn't going back East, hell, send her there by herself. Get rid of the thorn in your side once and for all."

Brent's mockery seared him. It's time to end it, Saint realized, staring blankly through Brent. "Yes," he said, "it is time to get rid of the thorn."

Brent felt a moment of fear at what his words had wrought. He wondered if he should cosh Saint over the head, if he should . . . No, he decided, violence was abhorrent to Saint. If he had indeed thrashed her, he wouldn't again. He watched Saint throw down several dollar bills and stride out of the Wild Star.

"You calm him down, Brent?" Nero asked.

"God only knows," Brent said. He rose and heaved a mighty sigh. "I think," he said, a crooked grin on his face, "that I shall go upstairs and tell my wife how much I love her."

Saint had sobered up dramatically by the time he reached his house. It was completely dark. What did you expect, you fool? It was, after all, well after midnight. He banged about loudly, wanting her to wake up.

Jules was awake. After Saint lit the lamp in the spare bedroom, she was sitting up in bed, regarding him warily.

"How's your bottom?" he asked, sitting down beside her on the bed. Her hair was in wild disarray about her shoulders, her eyes vivid and large in the spidery light.

She looked thoughtful a moment, as if considering his question. "I am fine," she said finally. "Are you drunk?"

"I was, but not much now. I guess that's one benefit to being a large man."

"Did you come to hurt me again?"

"No," he said, wincing inwardly at her words. "At least I hope I won't hurt you. I've come to end it all, Jules."

"Jules," not "Juliana."

"What do you mean, Michael?"

He gave her a crooked grin. "Well, first I want to have a look at your bottom. I was pretty heavy-handed with you, I'm afraid."

She flushed, and drew back a bit. "My bottom is fine, I told you."

"After I look at your bottom, I want to toss that nightgown of yours into the corner. Then I want to carry you to my—our—bedroom."

Jules couldn't believe his words, and gaped at him. She began nervously to pleat the sheet between her fingers. "Why?" she blurted out.

"It's got to stop," Saint said. "I've been a bloody fool. I want you, Jules. I want you so badly I hurt most of the time." He paused a moment, looking at her searchingly. Her expression was unreadable, but of course he hadn't tried all that hard to read her expressions. "First, I want to see your bottom."

Jules felt a surge of pure happiness flow through her. She knew that if she showed the slightest hesitancy, the slightest fear, he wouldn't touch her. She clamped down on the silly feelings of embarrassment. He was her husband.

She smiled up at him. "All right," she said.

Saint hadn't expected such a ready compliance— she saw it from the shocked expression on his face. Had he believed she would fly at him and try to scratch his eyes out for spanking her? He looked suddenly uncertain. Maybe it would be easier if he had drunk a bit more. Well, it was too late to give him more now.

Slowly Jules pulled open the three pink ribbons that fastened the front of her nightgown.

He watched every movement of her fingers.

"I would appreciate you looking at my bottom," she said, peering at him from beneath her lashes. "I guess I do hurt. Maybe you broke something."

"No, there's nothing to break in your bottom," he said, his eyes on a white breast newly revealed by the parting material.

"Still . . ." Jules temporized. She came up onto her knees and pulled her nightgown over her head. She balled it up and tossed it toward the corner. She placed her hands flat on her thighs, and didn't move.

Saint stared at her, not speaking.

Jules tossed her head a bit, thrusting her breasts outward. She felt foolish for her exhibition, and at the same time, hopefully excited.

As if in a dream, Saint stretched out his hand and gently touched his fingers to her breasts. He felt her quiver, and quickly drew back his hand.

"You aren't frightening me, Michael," she said. She didn't want to fling herself at him, but neither did she wish to be covered with gooseflesh sitting here watching him watch her. "My bottom," she said, and slowly stretched out on her stomach over his legs.

Saint looked down at the white expanse of back, to her very perfect bottom, down her slender legs. "Your bottom . . ." he said, and laid the flat of his hand over a buttock.

She felt his strong fingers begin to caress her, and inadvertently she moved her hips. She heard him suck in his breath.

She smiled, and placed her own hand on his thigh. "Is my bottom all right?" she asked, feeling his muscles tighten and move beneath her fingers.

"Perfect," Saint said with great sincerity. "All of you is . . . well, white and soft and sweet."

That was the nicest compliment he'd ever given her. Jules turned over, and clasping his shoulders, pulled herself onto his lap. "You said you were going to carry me into your—our—bedroom," she said.

"Yes," he agreed, "yes, that's what I said."

For an instant he simply couldn't believe this was happening. She was offering herself to him. After he'd been a nasty bastard to her, after . . . But what if he hurt her again? What if . . . ?

"I'm getting cold, Michael," Jules said, lightly kissing his jaw.

He rose, clutching her tightly against him, and strode to their bedroom. He wanted to see her, every inch of her, but would the light frighten . . . ? No, she had pulled off her nightgown, and there'd been a light on.

He laid her on the bed and pulled a thick blanket over her. "Now you won't be cold," he said. He moved quickly, lighting a lamp, then stripped off his clothes. Still, he was worried, even as he slipped in beside her, beneath the blanket.

"Jules," he said, looking down into her face, not touching her yet, "the first time we made love, I did hurt you, badly. I'm very sorry for that. I know that you must have thought me an animal, a brute, as bad as Wilkes . . ." He broke off a moment, but Jules didn't interrupt him. Let him get it all out, she thought. "I didn't mean to hurt you . . . it was your maidenhead . . . the first time is tough for a woman . . . and I couldn't stop myself. If you could trust me now, I think it could be better between us."

"I don't know," Jules said, managing a very serious frown. "It was truly awful that first time. You were a complete brute and used me so roughly. I didn't think you cared at all about me, and I thought I was going to die with the awful pain and—"

"Are you mocking me?"

She gave him a dazzling smile. "Me? Mock you?" She turned onto her side facing him, and her hand roved quickly over his chest to his belly.

"Jules!"

"All you have to tell me is that I won't bleed this time. Is that true?"

He closed his eyes a moment and remembered that wretched trip to Sausalito. He had imagined her waking up alone, but he hadn't thought about her bleeding. God, she must have been terrified. "There won't be any more blood," he said.

"Good," Jules said with satisfaction, and gently clasped him in her hand. He was quivering, swelling at a very excellent rate, and she loved it. "I want to kiss every inch of you," she said outrageously.

"Seduced by—"

"Your wife, Michael. Now, would you please kiss me, and touch me, and love me?"

"I've been a bloody fool, haven't I?" he said, and kissed her deeply.

"Yes," she said, "yes, you have. I could never, ever be afraid of you."

He knew he had to go slowly, despite her display of enthusiasm. And he did, until Jules was driven to distraction.

He said against her parted lips, "Remember how I fondled you that first night, when you were drugged, and crazy?"

"Yes, I remember," she said, and felt his manhood, swollen and throbbing against her thighs.

"I used my hand, my fingers, that night, Jules. Now I want to caress you with my mouth."

"Oh dear," she gasped, truly shocked. "I don't know, it seems so very . . ."

"Just trust me," he said. "It's the most natural thing in the world, I promise. It's something that a man loves to do."

When she felt his warm mouth against her, felt him lift her hips in his large hands, she felt only a brief instant of shock. She'd never imagined that he would . . . Her thoughts broke off and she felt a sudden tension building, felt her legs stiffening.

"Michael!" she cried, and arched upward, offering herself to him fully.

"That's it, love," Saint said, dazed by her response to him. "God, the sweet taste of you, the softness . . ."

Her body began to convulse even as he spoke, and he felt the shuddering pleasure consume her. He felt powerful, and tender, and so pleased that his own need was temporarily held in check. He caressed her until she quieted. He wanted her to experience every pleasurable feeling, he wanted . . . Again, he thought. Yes, again. He caressed her until she quivered, then cried out. He thought his own world complete at that moment. So much passion in her, he thought, so very much passion.

"Now, don't be afraid," he said, and very gently he came down over her.

"Yes," Jules said, dazed, her body still awash with the marvelous sensations. "I'm not afraid. Not of you."

"I'll go slowly, Jules, very slowly." She watched his face as he guided himself into her. He closed his eyes a moment when he entered her, felt her stretching for him, and stopped.

"It's all right," Jules said, seeing his concern for her. "You are so beautiful, Michael, like a god. Please, please, come into me." And he *was* like a god, she thought. A pagan god. She watched him, his powerful body poised over her, the muscles rippling in his arms, his strong legs tensed. She gasped in wonder as he thrust forward, deeply into her, and she held his shuddering body tightly. "Oh," she whispered. "You are part of me."

Her simple words wrought a dramatic change. She heard him curse, watched him arch his back and throw his head back, felt the surge of his seed, and softly cried out at his joy.

"Thank you, Michael," she said softly, her hands stroking down his smooth back.

Saint felt shattered, then laughed at his nonsensical thought. He knew he was too heavy for her, but when he made to move, she tightened her hold around his back.

"I love you, you know," she said. "I've loved you since I was twelve years old. Or was it thirteen?"

His entire body quivered at her words, and to his chagrin, he felt himself harden inside her. "No," he said, more to himself than to her, "I don't want to hurt you." He pulled out of her, rolled to his side, bringing her with him, and clasped her full length against him.

"You were twelve," he said, tangling his finger in her wild, soft hair.

"It seems forever. I'm sticky," she added, kissing his shoulder and weaving her fingers though the hair on his chest.

"Yes, I imagine so," he said tenderly. "Will you forgive me, Jules?"

"I will if you promise never to call me Juliana again."

"No, I shouldn't do that. I can just imagine some of our future arguments. 'Juliana' comes trippingly off the tongue when I'm angry with you."

"All right," she said agreeably. She sighed and nestled closer. "That was nice, very nice. You can thrash me if you promise to end it like that."

"You didn't think at all about Wilkes, or about John—"

"No, not for a moment. My weak woman's mind has quite recovered. After all, Michael, I did take off my own nightgown and toss it into the corner, with no help from you."

"No more derringers?"

She hesitated, but just a moment. "No," she said, shuddering a bit from reaction. "That was awful. I think I must have been somewhat deranged."

"No," he laughed, "just starved for your husband."

"You do have a lot to make up for," she said, slipping her hand between their bodies.

"Jules, you're probably sore. You are quite small, you know, and I felt you stretching to hold me, to take me into you."

"You don't know," she said, "you can't imagine what it feels like, Michael. I think it's much nicer to be a woman. You become part of me, you know. I possess you."

"Possess me?" he said, grinning as he kissed her temple. "I've never heard a woman say that before."

"You, inside of me, filling me. I like it very much."

He groaned, and she simply smiled up at him as he became a wild man. Until she became as wild as he. Her last thought before her body exploded into almost painful pleasure was that, at last, she was a woman, a wife, Michael's wife.

"Have I just been branded?" she asked after he'd calmed her and settled her against his body for sleep.

"Twice, branded twice. But," he added, his voice deep with satisfaction, "you've been pleasured three times."

"Such possessiveness," she said. I will make him love me, she thought, oh yes, I will.

"Michael?"

"Hmm?"

"Did you enjoy making love to me?"

He was silent for a moment, and she could practically see the devilish grin on his lips. "It was all right, I suppose," he said blandly. "You could have shown a bit more enthusiasm, of course. But all in all, I didn't fall asleep from boredom, did I?"

"You're impossible!"

She felt the deep rumbling laughter in his chest

before it erupted from his throat. "You're hairy." She slid her hand over his belly.

"Dangerous, Jules, very dangerous. Have pity, sweetheart, I'm an old man." But not that old, he thought ruefully; he wanted her again, powerfully.

"Do you know what I was thinking when you were over me, inside of me?"

He groaned. "I'm scared to know."

"How powerful you are, how beautiful, and your legs, so strong and—"

He slipped his hand between them to cup her breast, and she made a sweet, mewling sigh. He said, "Would you like to know what I was thinking when I was covering you, inside of you?"

"You weren't thinking a single thing!"

"Shut up. I looked at you, so small, so delicate, so very female, and—"

He felt her punch his ribs, and he laughed, a deep, satisfied laugh. "Don't try to outdo the master, Jules, else I'll continue with how I felt when you wrapped your beautiful legs around me, drawing me deeper—"

"Michael!"

He eased her onto her back, kissed her breast, then said with all the triumph of a sated man who held a sated woman, "You're mine, Mrs. Saint, and don't you ever forget it."

"No," she said, so happy that she thought she would die from it. "No, Dr. Saint, I won't ever forget."

23

Lydia paused a moment in front of the closed bedroom door, started to turn the knob, then slowly drew back her hand. She walked to the smaller bedroom down the hall, saw that the door was open, and peered in. "Ah," she said, her eyes glittering as she took in the mussed bed and Jules's nightgown, a rumpled heap on the floor. "It's about time, Saint Morris. Yes indeed, about time."

She decided to take her leave thirty minutes later, a pleased smile on her face.

Upstairs, Saint, who usually woke quickly with his full faculties, slowly opened his eyes, My God, he thought, aware of the soft body curled against his, Sunlight poured through the windows, splashing across his face, and he smiled, a besotted smile he imagined, and tightened his arm about his wife's back.

Jules mumbled something in her sleep and obligingly nestled her cheek against his throat. She's mine, he thought. He didn't wake her just yet, content to think about the pleasant turn the world had taken. He couldn't quite understand how she could still love him, but she'd said she did. Had loved him since she was twelve. A heady thought.

"You're a lucky bastard," he said quietly to the bedroom. He'd prayed he could give her pleasure, but her naturalness had surprised him as much as it had excited him. He remembered so clearly the older woman who had taught him about women. Her name was Lottie. Older, ha! She'd been about the same age as he was now. She had seduced him, very gently, after he'd gotten word that Kathleen had died in Ireland. She had given him renewed life, then shown him how to satisfy a woman. He'd failed Kathleen, of course, but had been too ignorant to realize that she could and should enjoy sex as much as he. He'd learned since that most men considered it nearly a perversion if their wives enjoyed the marriage bed. More fools they.

Saint smiled, remembering Lottie's exact words. "You've quite an aptitude for this, dear boy. Yes, indeed, I truly admire a man who enjoys his work."

He slipped his hand between them very gently, again splaying his fingers to feel the width of Jules's pelvis. She would have his children, but not more than two or three, he amended to himself. He would take no chance with her health, nor did he want her to bear a child every year until she was thirty. He wanted her to himself—himself and two daughters and a son. He was blissfully picturing a daughter, red-haired, vibrant, and loving, just like her mother, when he felt a smooth hand glide down his belly.

"Jules?"

"Good morning, husband," she said, and continued the journey with his inquisitive hand. "Goodness," she said as her fingers closed around him.

"What do you expect?" he asked, nibbling at her

ear. "I've been thinking about you for the past five minutes."

"I think, Michael," she said impishly, "that I have great power over you."

"At least part of me."

"Michael?"

"Yes, sweetheart?"

"Will you teach me . . . things?"

"I'll teach you everything you want to know," he said with great conviction, and rolled her onto her back.

"Lydia!"

Saint frowned. "Damn, I'd forgotten all about her."

"Oh dear, this is dreadfully embarrassing. Do you think she saw us?"

He laughed and kissed her deeply. "We're married, Jules. And no, I sincerely doubt that Lydia, once she'd been in the other bedroom, would dare open the door to this one."

Jules pressed her face against his throat. "I'll never be able to face her!"

He breathed in the sweet scent of her hair and also the smell of sex. This bedroom, he thought, grinning, has never been so appealing before. "Tell you what, Jules," he said, his hand closing over her breast. "Ouch! Not quite so much enthusiasm, sweetheart."

She released him, and giggled. "Shall I kiss it and make it well?"

He gave her a wicked grin. "What a lucky man I am, married to a thoroughly lascivious woman."

"I think I like the sound of that," she said.

"I do too. Tell you what, Jules, let me give you some instruction first, all right?"

"What kind of instruction?"

"Just lie still and attend to what I'm doing."

When he lifted her hips in his hands and gazed intently down at her, Jules found herself trying to squirm away. "It's daylight," she managed. "You're looking at me!"

"Yes," he said, his voice sounding hoarse in his own ears. "I'm not only looking, but I'm offering up thanksgiving to heaven. Now, you just be quiet, and don't interfere with a man's pleasure."

She decided she had no choice, and he thought he would yell with pleasure when he felt her ease and relax, offering herself to him.

"Now I can look at you," Jules said many minutes later. He was deep inside her, moving gently, rhythmically, and she watched every expression on his face.

"Oh no," he said after a while, and slipped his hand between their bodies and found her. It was he who watched her face at the moment of her climax, allowing himself his own release after she'd gained hers.

"The world is a very nice place," he said, squeezing her so tightly that she yelped.

When they ventured downstairs close to noon, Lydia was nowhere to be seen.

"Smart woman," Saint said, eyeing the food she'd left out on the table.

He'd wanted to spend the entire day in bed with Jules, but realized he'd been quite fortunate not to have already been rousted by a patient. It was Avery who showed up, the man Jules had shot.

Jules, who had scampered upstairs at the rapping

on the front door, heard him say to Michael, "It hurts, Doc. Bad."

"Come in here, Avery," Saint said, "and let's have a look."

When he joined Jules sometime later, he saw that she was pale and looked very guilty. He took her in his arms and hugged her. "No, sweetheart, it's all right. The man is just fine. No infection. I gave him some laudanum."

"I feel so bad!"

"I didn't charge him, not even for the laudanum, and you know how much I pay for that. How's that for salving your conscience?"

She nodded—reluctantly, he thought—then said unexpectedly, "Do all men consider a woman to be a whore if she's alone?"

"Of course not. Well, not always. It's San Francisco, sweetheart. So many of our females are prostitutes. Poor old Avery probably took one look at you and didn't give a damn about what you said to him. In the future—"

"I know, I know, Michael. Behold a docile creature!"

"I should live so long," Saint said, and kissed her. "What about Thackery?" he asked her sometime later.

Jules was thoughtfully silent for a long while. "I don't know," she said at last. "I do know that Wilkes is out there somewhere. I feel it, as odd as that sounds. I don't understand why he would still want me, but I know that he does. It really makes no sense, does it?"

It made no sense to Saint either, but he privately agreed with her. He said nothing, however, for it would only add to her fear. He said instead, "How about we find Thomas and invite him over for dinner this evening."

She brightened immediately. "Yes," she said, "I should like that, if . . ."

"If what?"

"If he leaves early!"

"Greedy woman," he said fondly.

Thomas was aware of the change the moment he saw his sister's face. "Well," he said, "how are you?"

"Wonderful!" Jules hugged him close. "Lydia made your favorite dish—roast sweet potatoes and pork chops."

"Lead on," said Thomas.

They had no sooner got settled at the dining-room table than Saint said, "Why don't you move back here, Thomas?"

"But—"

"No, no, please, brother," Jules said.

"I really don't think it would be wise, Jules," Thomas finally forced himself to say. "Just as for Saint, the sofa's a bit on the short side for me."

Jules flushed just a bit, then levered her chin upward. "You may have the spare bedroom. Michael has decided that he misses his old room, his old bed—"

"—and his young wife," said Saint. "I've finally tamed the little twit, Thomas."

"So I see," Thomas said, "so I see. It's about time. Did you beat her, Saint?"

"Not really," Saint said, frowning a bit at himself as he remembered her reddened bottom. "Well, not much, in any case. Just enough to get her attention."

"Ha!" Jules said. "He's a brute, Thomas."

"I don't suppose I'm going to hear this story?" Thomas asked somewhat pensively.

Saint sent a wicked glance toward his wife. "You mean the story of my pulling down her drawers and beating her—"

"Michael!"

"If you could bear all the laughter and the giggling, we would enjoy having you back."

"Michael!"

"Very well, Jules, I'll do all the giggling. Thomas," Saint continued, "have you decided anything yet? Is the world to have another doctor?"

Thomas played with the mashed sweet potato on his plate for a bit. "I have decided that I can't go back East, Saint," he said at last. "I have no money and I can't drag Penelope with me."

"So," Jules said, "you've decided to marry her?"

Thomas nodded, a crooked grin on his lips. "The problem is, of course, that she's never known a day's want in her life. And I refuse to take money from her father."

"You might have to," Saint said bluntly. He raised his hand to stem Thomas' protest. "No, listen to me. You've some years of study ahead of you, with no income. Either you negotiate a ... loan from Bunker, or you don't get married."

"But you did," Jules said.

"Only at the very end," Saint said, "and it wasn't easy for a while. Incidentally, Thomas, I was speaking to Dr. Samuel Pickett at the Seamen's Hospital about you. He needs good men, and at least he's an excellent doctor. You'd get good training there. Not as extensive as in New York or Boston, but adequate."

Thomas brightened considerably. "He'd take me on, really?"

"Yes," Saint said. He didn't add that he himself would provide funds during Thomas' instruction period.

"You could live here, Thomas."

But Thomas was frowning. "What about Penelope?"

"You're having problems fighting her off?" Saint asked, his wide grin revealing his white teeth.

"Yes, I am." Thomas sighed. "And myself as well," he added.

"You could marry and live at the Stevenson mansion," Jules said.

"Damn," Thomas said. "I don't know." He smiled suddenly. "Do you know what Bunker Stevenson offered me? He's willing to give me the foundry as a sort of wedding present. Penelope's dowry, I suppose."

"That sounds like a financially wise solution," said Saint.

"He wants me to run the place. I told him I wanted to be a doctor, and he stared at me like I was one of Jules's arc-eye ravenfish."

"If I were you, Thomas," Jules said, "I think I'd let Penelope convince her father that you'd be the greatest doctor in San Francisco, after Michael, of course. And it's an arc-eye hawkfish, Thomas."

"I'm glad to see you happy, Jules," Thomas said to his sister later that evening when they were alone for a few minutes. "It's about time. Saint's a fine man, and for a woman, and my little sister, you're not so bad either."

"Yes," said Jules, "yes, he is." She heard Michael's booted step upstairs and smiled wistfully.

"My little virgin sister is no more," Thomas said, grinning at her lecherously.

She poked him in the stomach.

"You sure you want me to move back in? I don't want to find myself lying in my bed at night listening to your . . . well, your devotion to your husband."

"He is equally devoted," said Jules, refusing to let him bait her into blushing.

"I'll just bet he is! Good night, love. I'll bring my meager belongings back tomorrow."

"I'll knit you something to cover your ears at night, brother!"

"I simply don't understand how we fit so well," Jules said, her eyes resting on her husband's swollen manhood. "You are so large."

"Fate," Saint managed.

"And so different from me. Now, my love, I want you to relax so I can begin my lessons."

Jules delighted in the results of her handiwork, and Saint thought he'd die from the pleasure of it. "No," he gasped, pulling her away, "no more."

She gave him a slightly dazed, very pleased smile. "I don't pull you away," she said in a voice of reproach.

"It's not quite the same thing," he said. "Now, my beautiful, greedy, wife, it's my turn."

"Oh dear," she gasped. "Thomas—"

"I'll put my hand over your mouth," said Saint. "Just promise not to bite me inadvertently, all right?"

The first explosion rocked the house and the bed. Saint, instantly alert, leapt out of bed and rushed to the window. He could see nothing.

"What was that?" Jules asked, sitting up.

"God only knows. Whatever and wherever it was, I'll be needed, Thomas too."

He began to pull on his clothes.

"I'll come too," said Jules.

He started to tell her no, but saw that she would argue tooth and nail with him. And there wasn't time. "All right. Hurry."

When Saint opened the bedroom door, he saw Thomas in the hallway struggling into his shirt.

"I don't know," Saint answered the unasked question. "Jules, wear a cloak! It'll be chilly."

They found Thackery downstairs, dressed, and leading two horses. "It's the Stevensons' foundry, Dr. Saint," he said. "Gawd, you can see the flames from here!" Thackery was right. To the south, the sky was streaked with bright crimson and orange.

Damn Bunker, Saint was thinking. Normally at this time of night there shouldn't be anyone around. But Bunker liked to have night shifts at the foundry. He prayed there were no fatalities.

He lifted Jules in front of him, and Thomas mounted the other horse.

"I'll follow as soon as I can," Thackery called.

When they arrived at the foundry, or what remained of it, there were already a good thirty men there, passing buckets of water with incredible speed.

"Anyone hurt?" Saint asked Morley Crocker, the foreman.

"Thank God, Saint! Yeah, we've still two men unaccounted for, and a half-dozen wounded over there."

Jules ran to keep pace with her husband and Thomas. Flames leapt into the air, and cinders flew about them. Her cloak felt suddenly stifling in the intense heat. She heard men yelling, saw the devastation.

"Your foundry," she said blankly to Thomas.

"I think my decision has just been rendered much simpler," he said.

Saint was bandaging a burned arm when Dr. Samuel Pickett came. "No fatalities, thank God," Saint said. "The burns aren't all that serious, but we've got one man unconscious, shock probably. My wife is watching him and keeping him warm."

Jules stared down at the man's still face. His clothes were tattered with burn holes and there were black smudges on his face and hands. She took off her own cloak and covered him. She heard Saint telling Thomas what to do, and saw Dr. Pickett hovering over a man who was moaning pitifully. It started to rain, and Jules lifted her face to the cooling water. The drops thickened and soon it was a deluge. Thank God, Jules thought. That should put out the bloody fire. Thackery appeared beside her.

"What happened? Do you know?" she asked.

Thackery shook his head. Suddenly he straightened and yelled, "Dr. Saint, no!"

Jules whirled about to see Michael running toward the still-flaming ruins. She could barely make out the form of a man stumbling out, clutching his stomach.

She felt her heart plummet to her toes. She rose jerkily to her feet and ran toward her husband.

Saint had almost reached the man when there was another loud explosion. Gashes of fire rent the sky, and debris hurled outward. My God, Saint thought blankly, it's hell and I've arrived! He felt his body hurled into the air from the force of the explosion and thrown backward. Then he felt no more.

Jules knelt beside her husband, her hand pressed against his chest. His heartbeat was strong, steady. She swallowed, swearing at herself that she wouldn't succumb to the awful tears and sobs she felt building inside her. No, she thought, I won't be a fool, not now. She eased down beside him and held his head in her lap. In the next moment Dr. Pickett was on his knees beside Saint.

"His heartbeat is steady," Jules said, blinking away the rain so she could see him clearly.

Dr. Pickett looked at her briefly. "You're Mrs. Morris?"

"Yes."

"You're doing just fine, ma'am. You just stay as you are and let me examine him . . . Nothing appears to be broken," he said after some minutes had passed.

"He's very pale," Jules said, watching the rain wash away the black streaks from his face.

"No wonder. He probably struck his head. You won't faint on me, will you, ma'am?"

"Of course not," Jules said, her voice suddenly stronger and more forceful.

"Stay with him, ma'am. I'll be back shortly."

Saint moaned.

"Hush, love," Jules said. "It's all right now."

He opened his eyes, felt a deep, searing pain, and closed them.

"Jules?"

"Yes. Do you hurt anywhere, Michael?" She leaned over him, protecting his face from the driving rain.

"Jules," he said very calmly, "cup the rain in your hands and wash out my eyes. Quickly."

She froze, but just for an instant. She lifted her

hands, cupping them as he'd said, and soon they were filled with water. Very gently she splashed the rain into his open eyes. He winced, and she saw him biting his lower lip.

"Michael—"

"Again, Jules. Keep doing it."

She continued, becoming more adept each time. Finally he said, "That's fine, Jules. Now, there's a clean handkerchief in my pocket. Fold it and tie it around my head over my eyes."

"Saint, you're back to the world again, dear boy?"

"Samuel?"

"Yes, what's this, ma'am?" He wondered briefly if the young woman had finally cracked as he watched her tie the handkerchief around Saint's head. She smoothed it firmly over his eyes, then sat back on her heels.

"Thank you, Jules," Saint said. "You did fine, just fine."

Suddenly Samuel Pickett closed his own eyes, feeling sickness rise in his stomach.

"Michael," Jules whispered.

"Help me up," Saint said. "Now, Jules, I know you're looking at me as if I'm on the brink of dying. But I'm not, I'm all right. Come."

Both Jules and Dr. Pickett helped him to his feet. He swayed a moment, then stood firmly.

Slowly he raised his hands and pressed the handkerchief more firmly against his eyes. "I think, Sam, that my usefulness here is over."

"Is there much pain, my boy?" Sam Pickett asked quietly.

"It's lessening . . . a bit. Jules probably got most of the fragments, but . . ."

Jules stared at him, hugging his side. "You're soaking wet," she said, her mind refusing to accept what she knew to be true. "We'll go home, Michael, and you can have a hot bath and—"

Saint knew she was trying to keep a firm hold on herself, and he admired her vastly at that moment. "Jules," he interrupted her quietly, "get Thackery and Thomas—"

"Not Thomas," Samuel said. "He accompanied some of the wounded men to the hospital after I assured him you were all right. The black man, is that Thackery?"

"Yes, it is. We're not going to lose anybody, are we, Samuel?"

"Perhaps the one man you did your damnedest to save. I'm not certain yet. Maybe old Bunker will escape with a clear conscience after all, but the foundry's gone. Now, Saint, let's get you home."

"Michael," Jules said, her voice high and taut. "Yes, we must go. You're going to catch a chill."

He turned at the sound of her voice and said very quietly, "Hush, sweetheart. Everything will be fine."

He paused a moment, squeezed his wife's hand, heard her gulp down a sob.

Dr. Samuel Pickett said quietly, "I've got my buggy. Mrs. Morris, stay with him until I bring it around."

24

Jules was squeezing his hand so hard it hurt. If Saint had been able, he would have tried to reassure her. He said nothing. He was scared. The searing pain was lessening in his eyes, but he knew as well as Sam Pickett that even those pale flashes of white he'd seen briefly could fade forever, leaving him completely and forever blind. Dear God, a blind doctor would be good for absolutely nothing.

The buggy lurched into a muddy rut, and he groaned, unable to keep it inside. He felt Jules lightly stroke her fingertips over his forehead and gently ease him a bit so that his head was firmly pillowed in her lap. He heard her say gently, "Everything will be fine, love, I promise."

He would have smiled, but it required all his concentration to control the damnable pain. She was sounding like him. Soothing and in control.

The buggy finally came to a halt, and Sam's voice said, "Mrs. Morris and I are going to help you down now, Saint. Just hang on a bit longer."

He said nothing, allowed them to assist him into the house. It seemed odd in the extreme to be stretched out on his own examining table.

"Now, my boy, I'm going to take off the bandages.

It's likely that you've still got some fragments in your eyes, and I've got to get them out. Then . . ." Sam paused.

"Then," Saint finished, "we'll bandage me back up and pray."

"Yes," said Sam.

Saint listened to Sam give Jules instructions, and forced himself to lie quietly. When Sam unwound the handkerchief about his eyes, he blinked and opened them.

"Anything, Saint?"

"Same as before. Pale white, like hoary ghosts from my boyhood, and that's it."

"That's as much as we can expect and you know it. You've got to hold very still now, as I'm certain you well know. Mrs. Morris, please hold his head very steady for me, and move that light closer."

Saint didn't move, didn't utter a sound when Sam, with a light touch he appreciated, removed more fragments from his eyes. "It looks to me like the cornea is cut, but of course that's to be expected. As for retina damage, impossible to tell. Now, Saint, I'm going to wash out your eyes again."

"You didn't tell me one damned story to keep my mind occupied," Saint said when his eyes were firmly bandaged again.

"I should have, I'm sorry," Jules said, her voice stricken.

"Don't be a fool, Jules," Saint said, turning toward the sound of her voice. "It was Sam's duty, not yours."

"Mrs. Morris," Sam Pickett said, "would you please fetch your husband some tea?"

Saint frowned at that, but bided his time, hearing Jules's skirt swish against a chair as she left the room.

Strange, he thought, he'd never noticed that sound before.

"How much pain, Saint?" Sam asked immediately.

"Enough. A bit of laudanum in the tea, Sam?"

"Yes. I didn't want to worry your wife. She's being a big help, Saint. Does she assist you with your patients?"

"No," Saint said slowly. "At least she hasn't in the past. We haven't been married all that long."

"I see. Do you agree that the bandage should stay in place for three days?"

"Sounds reasonable. Then we'll see, won't we?" Saint sighed, grinning crookedly at his words. "At least I hope I'll see."

"If not then," Sam said, "we'll keep your eyes bandaged another four or five days."

They were talking about canes when Jules came into the surgery, balancing a tray on her arms.

"Just a bit, Saint," Sam said, pouring laudanum into the teacup.

Jules watched him silently. She knew Michael would never tell her if he were in pain. He was a man, and for some reason unknown and not understood by her, men thought it weak to admit to anything less than perfection. She desperately wanted to talk to Dr. Pickett about his eyes, and she suspected that they'd had a frank discussion while she, weak woman, had been in the kitchen.

She would ask Michael.

"Now, Mrs. Morris," Sam said to her with a kindly smile, "why don't you help me get this giant upstairs to his bed. He needs a lot of rest, and after working with you, ma'am, I think you can handle him quite well."

Saint frowned at that, but said nothing. The moment he began walking, the pain seared his eyes. He knew they were red and puffy.

Sam helped Jules undress him. He was nearly asleep by the time he was on his back in bed. "Thanks, Sam," he said.

"See you in the morning, Saint," Sam said, nodded to Jules, and took his leave.

Even with his senses dulled, Saint heard Jules undressing. He wanted to tell her that he would be all right, but the words faded from his mind. He was asleep when she leaned over him and gently kissed him.

Jules sighed at the sound of knocking on the front door, and trotted down the stairs. The stream of visitors, all of them worried about her husband, had been steady, giving her little time to brood, which was probably just as well. Lydia was baking in the kitchen, for each guest must be offered food and drink.

Jules opened the door.

"Hello. I'm Jane Branigan. I heard about Saint. You are Mrs. Morris?"

She's lovely, Jules thought. Jane Branigan, tall, voluptuous, glossy black hair. "Yes," she said. "Please call me Jules. Come in, ma'am. Saint is awake. A lot of friends have been here."

Jane had managed to quash the jealousy in her worry about Saint. But now, faced by this vibrant girl, she felt herself grow cold. She told herself yet again that it was over, had been over for quite some time. She was now a friend, no more, no less.

"If I could see him for just a few minutes," she said.

"Certainly," Jules said, stepping back.

She wanted to dog Mrs. Branigan's heels, but held herself back. No, the woman wanted to see her husband alone. So be it.

Saint felt a cool, soft hand on his forehead.

"Jules?"

"No, Saint, me, Jane Branigan. Your . . . wife is downstairs. The boys send their love, of course. I just wanted to assure myself that you would be all right."

Because it was Jane, because he'd forced himself to provide optimism to all his friends during the day, because he was scared and angry and trusted her, he said bluntly, "I don't know, Jane. My poor wife just might find herself saddled with a damned cripple. God, I could become some sort of institution. People could say, 'Yes, there's poor old Saint, blind as a bat, you know, but tells great stories. Give him a few pennies and he'll talk as long as you want.' Shit!"

Jane understood, but she refused to pity him, at least not now. She said, her voice laced with humor, "Don't forget that those people could also demand medical advice. I can just hear old Limpin' Willie saying, 'Saint, bless him! Told me to lance the boil on my leg, and I did, and my leg rotted off!' "

"Damn you, Jane!"

Jane felt tears sting her eyes, and leaned over without thought and hugged him close. "You'll be all right, my dear, you'll see. I mean that literally."

Jules stood in the doorway, a surge of evil jealousy washing through her. Slowly she backed up, and returned downstairs to the kitchen.

Saint hugged Jane, a reluctant laugh emerging from his throat. "As I said, damn you, Jane. You don't let a fellow bitch at all, do you?"

"You complain all you like, but you know very well that pity is the last thing you need."

"Jane, be kind to Jules. I think she's very afraid, but of course she's a chattering, optimistic little bird around me."

Jane was silent for a long moment. In truth, though, it was a brief war. She said, "I suggest you give her a bit more credit, Saint. She is your wife. Now I must go. I will come back, tomorrow perhaps."

"Jane?"

"Yes?"

"Thanks."

Jane was relieved that he couldn't see the tears in her eyes. She met Jules in the downstairs entrance-way. "Thank you, my dear," she said. "I'll leave you now. You must be exhausted."

"Yes," Jules said in a rush, unable to hate this woman, "it has been mad all day, and Michael needs to rest. I don't know what to do!"

"You give the orders, that's what you do," said Jane. "Let him complain and snap, but you do know what's best for him. Good luck."

And she was gone, leaving Jules to stare thoughtfully at the closed front door. She's right, Jules thought, perfectly right!

"Lydia!" she called, her shoulders back, her chin up.

Saint heard her light footfall on the stairs. "Jules," he said. "Wasn't that the front door? Who's here?"

"Who *was* here. It was Horace and Agatha Newton. They'll return tomorrow."

"Why?"

"I told them you needed rest. They understood and send their love."

"I'm the doctor," he said, stiffening. "I think I'm well able to decide when I need rest and when I don't!"

"I brought you some tea and fresh sponge cake Lydia just baked," Jules said, her voice calm, soothing.

He wanted to strike out. "Dammit, Jules! Don't you dare treat me like a mewling child!"

"Here, love. Drink this."

He did, with ill grace. Jules sat on the side of the bed, studying his face. "I'll shave you, if you like," she said, gently stroking her fingers over the stubble on his cheeks.

He grunted.

She leaned down and kissed him. "I love you, Michael. After you've rested, I'll give you a bath. That you should like," she added, her voice as wicked as she could manage.

"You want to beautify me so you can have your way with me," he grumbled.

"Yes," she said. "And I can do whatever I wish to you, and you'll not gainsay me."

"Dear God, a blind man dying from overexertion. Wife takes revenge on blind husband. I think I'll give Tony Dawson some headlines for the *Alta* for when I expire."

Jules smiled down at him, noticing the slurring of his words as the laudanum took effect. He would sleep a good four hours, Sam had assured her. And he needed the rest. The best thing for him, she knew. His eyes would heal. She would make them heal.

* * *

Jules held his hand as Sam unwound the bandages. "Keep your eyes closed, Saint, until I tell you otherwise."

"Doctors," Saint said in disgust.

"Now, very slowly, open your eyes."

He did. He was praying, hard. Nothing but the same shadowy pale white light. He wanted to curse and cry. He swallowed, knowing Jules and Sam both were holding their breath.

"Just the lights," he said. "I guess I need more time to heal. Another week, Sam?"

Sam was bitterly disappointed, but not overly surprised. He'd seen quite a bit of damage in the cornea. He couldn't bring himself to look at Jules, as he now called her. She was a strong girl, and he knew she was silent because she would refuse to cry.

"Yes," he said calmly, "let's give it another seven days. Is the light any clearer?"

"No, just pale and hazy."

"Hold very still. I want to take another look to make sure all the fragments are out."

Jules was fighting the lump in her throat. He doesn't need you to burst into tears like a silly ninny, she told herself firmly. Don't you dare!

"Looks good to me," Sam said. "Any pain?"

"No."

"Back on with the bandage." Sam looked at Jules. He stretched out his hand and took hers, squeezing it hard. "Why don't you put it on, Jules? You've a light, sure touch."

It gave her mind direction, focus. She smiled at Sam, looking up for his approval as she fastened the bandage. He nodded.

"We've seen little of Thomas," Saint said, then laughed roughly at his choice of verbs.

"I've got the boy working hard, as you can well imagine. He'll be a fine doctor someday, Saint, a fine doctor." He added a moment later, after sending an assessing look toward Jules, "He's got grit, just like your wife here. Yes, indeed. Seems to me, Saint, that not all your patients need to come to me. Lord knows I'm old and tired! Perhaps Jules here could examine some of them, and you could tell her what to do. What do you think, Jules?"

"I think that's a fine idea."

"Good, I'll spread the word."

When Jules returned to the surgery, she stopped cold in the doorway. Saint had gotten off the examining table and was feeling his way toward her. He bumped his leg against a chair and cursed.

"To your right, about a foot away," she said in a calm, clear voice, "is your drug cabinet. If you walk straight, you'll come right to me."

He wanted to yell at her that she was a stupid twit and that every goddamned thing in the world was nothing but black, impenetrable black. He said instead, "Keep talking. Balance is still difficult."

"I shouldn't wonder," Jules said. "You're doing fine, Michael." She swallowed convulsively, and forced some wickedness into her voice. "As you come straight at me, stretch out your hands. But not too far apart, mind!"

That did make him smile, a bit.

"Now, lower your arms, Michael."

He did, and encountered her breasts. He stood quietly a moment, concentrating on the shape of her. "You're beautiful," he said, and Jules moved quickly into his arms.

He felt her cheek nuzzling his shoulder, felt her slender arms tighten about his back.

"I'm glad you're my wife, Jules, but dammit, it's not fair to you and—"

She clasped her hands behind his back and squeezed as hard as she could. "If you finish that thought, you will make me very angry. Now, do you promise?"

"Promise what?" he asked, resting his chin on the top of her head.

"Are you truly glad I'm your wife?"

Her voice was muffled, and he wished more than anything that he could see her face at that moment. Her expressions were so open, at least to him. Now, he thought, he had to rely on the nuances in her speech. "Yes," he said.

"And can we work together with patients?"

Pleading, he thought. It was important to her, and, he realized, it wasn't such a bad idea for him. It would certainly keep his mind occupied.

"We'll try," he said.

But it wasn't Dr. Pickett who sent them their first patient, it was Limpin' Willie.

"Me name's Ryan," the huge, shaggy man said, standing in the doorway, his black felt hat in his hands.

"Do come in, Mr. Ryan," Jules said. "Come into the surgery. I'll fetch my husband.

"Limpin' Willie told me he'd rather come to you, no matter you can't see nothing."

Saint smiled. "Tell me what's wrong, Ryan."

"I got meself pounded on the back of the head a couple of hours ago."

Saint wasn't about to ask how the pounding had come about. Ryan sounded every bit as much of a villain as any other Sydney Duck. He asked instead, "Any dizziness?"

"Yep, a bit. When I walk."

"Any blurred vision?"

Ryan thought about this for a while, then nodded.

"Yes, Michael," Jules said for him.

"All right. Sit still now, Ryan. Mrs. Morris is going to hold up a finger. First follow it to the right, then to the left . . ."

Jules was scared to death that she wasn't following Michael's instructions exactly right. After each test, Jules told him the result.

Saint said finally, "Sounds to me like you got yourself a concussion, Ryan. Now, here's what you're to do. I don't want you to be alone for another twenty-four hours. When you sleep, have someone with you, have them wake you every four hours and ask you who you are and where you are. That's just to make sure that your brains aren't addled. Then . . ."

After the grateful Ryan had taken his leave, pressing money into Jules's hand, she returned to the surgery, a wide smile on her face. The smile dropped away when she realized Saint couldn't see it.

"This," she announced, "is the first money I've ever earned in my entire life. Fifty dollars, Michael!"

He heard the excitement in her voice and said, "Come here so I can congratulate you."

He drew her down onto his lap. "Well done, sweetheart."

"We're a good team, aren't we?"

"Yes," he said slowly, "I think we are."

"Michael?"

"Yes?"

"I don't know if I can stitch somebody. I think I'd throw up all over them, and that wouldn't be very reassuring for the patient, would it?"

"We'll see," he said. "And now, wife, I think what I would like to do is spend the next hours upstairs studying your body with my hands."

"Oh," Jules said.

"Do you know," Saint said a few minutes later in their bedroom, "I can hear you take off each item. You're only in your chemise now, aren't you?"

He heard a whisper of a sound, and grinned. "Lord, now my imagination is becoming overworked. Come here, Jules."

He was still completely dressed, but Jules didn't hesitate. She felt an odd kind of excitement as he lightly began to touch her.

"Your nipples," he said, his voice deep, "I can't feel their exact color. Pale pink?"

"Yes," she whispered.

"And soft as velvet. Now, let me see if they taste pink and velvet."

It had been too long, she thought, as his mouth caressed her. She felt the familiar stirrings deep within her, and arched upward to give herself more fully to him.

She was responding to him, he thought, pleased, and so very quickly. He let his right hand journey slowly downward, pausing to trace her ribs, feel the small contour of her navel. He sucked in his breath, wishing desperately that he could see her face at that moment. His fingers were gently probing, caressing, and she was very warm to his touch, her woman's flesh swollen and moist. "Jules," he said, "does that please you?"

"It pleases me so much that I'll scream if you stop."

"The feel of you," he said, his fingers exploring her, "it's almost more than this simple male mind can handle."

"If you don't stop a moment, husband, I shall . . . Please . . . Oh, Michael!"

She pushed his hand away, her breath coming in hoarse little gasps that made him smile.

"Now for you, arrogant man!"

With his enthusiastic cooperation, Saint was naked in minutes. He knew she was looking at him, and since he could hear her breathing, knew she was very interested. She thought him beautiful, and that pleased him inordinately.

Her hands and mouth were a torture. "You are very methodical," he moaned when at last her fingers were weaving in the thick bush of hair at his groin.

"Oh yes," Jules said, her fingers lightly closing around him. "And you are most appreciative."

He nearly leapt off the bed when she took him into her mouth, her tongue teasing and light, driving him nearly beyond control.

He felt her hand pressing his chest. "No, Michael, you must do what the doctor's very excellent assistant wants you to. It's all for your own good, so you hold still."

When he could stand it no longer, he grabbed her beneath her arms and hauled her over him. He felt incredible need, incredible pressure, and he wanted to thrust inside her and . . .

She guided him into her at that moment and he thought he would die from the nearly painful sensations swamping him. "Jules," he said, "you . . . Sweetheart, I've got to . . ." She took him deep inside her, and he couldn't begin to think straight now, much less talk. But as she moved over him, her hands splayed on his chest, he pressed his own palm against her belly, feeling the motion of her body as she moved over him.

"Can you feel yourself inside me?" she asked, closing her hand over his and pressing it inward against her.

He wanted to laugh at that, but couldn't. "Very nearly," he said, and pulled his hand loose from hers. His fingers roved downward, purposeful now, to find her.

"Dammit, I want to see you!"

Jules was nearly frantic, her body taut, her legs locked against his flanks, but she heard the anger, the sense of betrayal in his voice. She took his hand and raised it to her face. When her body exploded into pleasure, his fingers traced her open lips, felt the warmth of her cries.

She was kissing him deeply when he gained his own release. He gasped into her warm mouth, "God, I want you, Jules."

Jules was relieved he couldn't see the tears shimmering in her eyes. He wanted her, he'd said so. Soon, she thought, trying desperately not to sniff, he would feel more for her than just want.

She smiled down at his face. He was lying quietly now, still deep inside her, his breathing even and slow.

Very gently she eased off him and rose. She thought

he was asleep, and started when he said in a deep, satisfied voice, "I feel like I really am a saint at this moment. Nearly dead and gone to heaven. Lord, woman, you've worn me to the bone."

She dashed her hand across her eyes and smiled. "I will let you rest awhile now, husband. Then we will see about this bone business."

There was no thought of seeing about bones or anything else. An hour later Thomas came dashing into the house, his face white and drawn.

Jules jumped out of her chair, her face paling at the sight of her brother. "Thomas! What is wrong?"

"It's Bunker Stevenson," Thomas said. "The bloody damned man has had a stroke!"

25

"I'll be right along," Saint said without thinking. He pushed back his chair, kicked his foot into one leg and sent the chair sprawling. To keep his balance, he grabbed at the table, knocking his plate to the floor. He stood perfectly still, his hands braced against the table.

"Shit," he said very softly.

Thomas jumped forward. "I didn't mean . . . That is . . . Oh hell, Saint! I shouldn't have blurted it out like that. Dr. Pickett's with him, but it doesn't look good. Mrs. Stevenson, as you can imagine, is in hysterics."

"And Penelope?" Jules asked, her eyes on her husband's rigid body. She saw that his knuckles were white from clutching the edge of the table so fiercely.

"She's all right. Hell, she can't collapse, not with her mother carrying on like a Bedlamite."

Jules didn't really hear her brother's words, for she was too worried about Michael. What could she say? It seemed to her at that awful moment that anything to come out of her mouth would but hurt him more. Merciful heavens, he was hurting enough now.

"Thomas," she said very calmly, breaking the tense

silence, "why don't you sit down a moment? I'll get you something to eat. You too, Michael. Would you care for some wine, perhaps?"

Saint wanted to lash out. Hell, if there were a full moon, which he couldn't see in any case, he'd howl like a crazed animal. He got a grip on himself, turning toward his wife. "Yes, thank you, Jules. A glass of wine would be just fine."

"Excellent. Why don't you sit here, Michael?"

He allowed her to take his arm and lead him to another chair at the table. His mouth was drawn in a thin line. When he heard her pick up his plate, he couldn't help himself, and shouted, "Damn you, leave it! I made the mess, and I'll bloody well clean it up!"

Jules slowly straightened. She saw Thomas' startled look, and silently shook her head at him. No excuses, no pity. He wasn't a hurt child, to be soothed. He was a man and he was proud. And he was frustrated and angry. She supposed she would be also.

"No, I will clean it up," she said, forcing a bit of humor into her voice. "Since for the time being you can't see a thing, I will be your eyes. Besides, Michael, the peas scattered all over the carpet. I don't want you to squish them with your big feet."

"Jules—" he began, then broke off abruptly.

She continued smoothly, "Thomas, tell Michael exactly what happened and what Dr. Pickett is doing for Bunker."

Jules listened with only half an ear to Thomas as she cleaned up the mess on the carpet. Then she poured each man a glass of wine. She said nothing, merely took Michael's hand and placed his fingers about the glass stem.

"Thank you" was his stiff reply.

"So," Thomas concluded a moment later, "Dr. Pickett thinks that the shock of the explosion at the foundry probably triggered the stroke. What do you think, Saint?"

"Perhaps," Saint said, well under control again. "That and the fact that Bunker is fat as a stuffed turkey, something I've spoken to him about many times, to no good effect. You say his entire left side is paralyzed?"

Thomas nodded, then quickly added, "Yes."

"But his speech isn't terribly impaired?"

"Only a bit. That surprised Dr. Pickett."

Saint said thoughtfully, "I've been Bunker's doctor for over two years now. I tend to think that he'll make it mainly because he's so damned stubborn. But then again, helplessness and dependence tend to change one."

Jules shot her husband a pained look, but his expression was unreadable, at least to her it was. It was difficult to know what he was thinking with his eyes bandaged. Talk about looking helpless, she thought, staring at her brother. Thomas looked drawn and worried and scared.

Thomas said, "The question is, what am I going to do now?"

"I think, Thomas," Jules said, smiling at him reassuringly, "that it might be the best thing if you married Penelope now and moved into the Stevenson house. You aren't needed here, my dear, merely appreciated."

Thomas would have protested, but Saint said quickly, "Jules is right, Thomas. Penelope and her mother are used to having a strong man about to take care of them. The two of you should probably marry immediately."

Thomas and Penelope were married one day before Saint's bandage was to be removed. It was a private ceremony at the Stevenson house, and Bunker was carried down by a servant and his driver to give his daughter away.

"I have never seen her so subdued," Chauncey Saxton said to Jules. "I'm beginning to agree with Del that this is probably all for the best."

"I certainly hope so," Jules said. "Thomas is my brother, after all." Penelope looked lovely, Jules thought objectively, and then realized: *She's now my sister!*

It was a rather unsettling thought, given the fact that Jules's only sister, Sarah, hadn't played that role with much warmth or caring. Please, she prayed as the two solemnized their vows over the loud sniffling of Mrs. Stevenson, let it work out properly. Let Thomas be happy.

There was, of course, champagne, and heavier drinks for the men. Chauncey had helped with the buffet, and it was impressive. Jules was slowly eating a lobster canapé when she heard Bunker say in his loud, carrying voice to Michael, his speech only slightly slurred, "Well, my boy, here we are, two war horses, shot down! But Dr. Pickett tells me you'll be eyeing that lovely wife of yours again in no time at all now."

Sally Stevenson, her mother's duty accomplished, was smiling now, accepting congratulations. But, Jules thought, she looked ill, her jowls noticeably sagging, as if the shock had aged her five years. She wondered if the shock was about her husband or her new son-in-law. Thomas had never said if his mother-in-law approved or disapproved of her daughter's marriage to him, a penniless young man. I must tell Mrs. Stevenson how very lucky she is.

Thomas didn't let his bride out of his sight, his hand always either under her elbow or around her waist. Jules knew about desire and passion and she saw both in her brother's eyes when they rested on Penelope. As for Penelope, she looked somewhat dazed, her voice and movements mechanical.

Jules couldn't get near her husband. Friends surrounded him, unwilling to leave him alone. Some were studiously careful to avoid any reference to his blindness; others, like Bunker, spoke freely, then went on to other matters.

She moved closer, hearing Brent Hammond say to Michael, "You'll not believe how Wakeville is shaping up, Saint."

"Thackery gives me progress reports. And how is your pregnant wife, Brent?"

Brent grinned. "My own little fat spider," he said, winking toward his wife. "She says she feels fine and for me to stop driving her crazy, but—"

"I know, the first child and all that."

"Well, by the time the first perfect child makes his or her appearance, you should be back on your feet and back into your eyes, old man."

Byrony joined the group. "He is driving me utterly mad, Saint. Would you please tell him that his part in this entire affair is well over?"

"Hell no," said Saint. He stretched out his hand toward Byrony, and clasped her fingers in his large hand. It took Jules a moment to realize that it was a thoroughly doctorly thing he was doing. She heard him say after a moment, "No swelling. Good, Byrony. How about your ankles?"

"Here I thought you were getting forward with my wife," Brent said on a chuckle. "Her ankles swell if she doesn't lie down every couple of hours," he added.

"Just see, Brent, that she does lie down, then," Saint said, patting Byrony's hand. "Alone."

Brent moaned, and if it was possible for a woman to guffaw, Byrony did.

"It was well carried off," Jules said to her husband as Thackery drove them back home.

"Yes," Saint said.

"Do you think Thomas will continue wanting to be a doctor?"

"I don't know," came the clipped reply. Oddly enough, Saint was thinking about his rearranged closet. He'd always been neat and orderly with his belongings, but not sufficiently for a blind man. It had galled him to have Jules hand him each item of clothing in the morning. Usually she'd have to rebutton his shirt, for he always seemed to mismatch buttons and holes. He'd said nothing to her, but that morning she'd led him to the closet and had him run his hands over the array of shirts, then trousers, vests, and coats. All in magnificent order now, all arranged with darkest coats first, then the blues and grays. He'd managed to dress himself for the wedding, and he supposed he should feel good about it. But he didn't.

Jules eyed him with mounting frustration, but said nothing more. When she helped him into bed an hour later, she smiled into the darkness, slipped off her nightgown, and snuggled next to him.

He said nothing, nor did he move to touch her or kiss her.

Jules swallowed her disappointment and leaned down to kiss him lightly on his closed mouth. "I love you, Michael," she said, kissed him again, and settled beside him to sleep.

She awoke suddenly at the sound of an anguished moan. She blinked, and saw that it was still quite dark.

"No, dammit, no! Oh God, no!"

Saint lurched sideways, tangling himself in the covers, crying out.

Oh God, she thought, and began shaking him. "Michael, wake up! It's a nightmare, love. Wake up!"

She felt the beads of perspiration on his forehead, felt the pounding of his heart beneath her hand. "Michael!"

"What?" Saint came awake with a shudder. For a moment he held himself utterly still. Then very softly he whispered, "God, Jules, I'm so bloody scared."

She straightened the tangled covers with trembling hands, then pulled him close. "I know," she said against his temple. "I would be too. But, Michael, listen to me . . ." For a moment she could think of nothing to say, for this large, proud man was shuddering against her, and she couldn't bear it. "Listen to me," she repeated, stroking his thick hair, hugging him. "If you don't see tomorrow, then you will see next week. Your eyes will heal, I swear it to you."

And if they didn't? If he became completely blind? No, she couldn't, wouldn't, accept that, at least not yet, and she couldn't allow him to give up.

"I dreamed that you needed me," he said, his voice low and taut. "You were hurt, I guess. I told you I would help you, and I smiled at you and began to tell you a stupid story. And then suddenly I couldn't see, and you were begging me to help you. I couldn't see!"

He was clutching at her, his face buried against her breasts. He was shuddering as if he were freezing to death. "I was useless," he said.

"Michael," she said softly, "it was a dream, that's all, just a dream. I would have been scared silly if I'd dreamed it was you who were in trouble. You know something else? I can prove that it was stupid, ridiculous."

She felt him listening to her now, and she smiled, kissing his ear. "Yes indeed. You are incapable of telling a stupid story. You would have had me laughing and cursing you. If I had been doing any begging, it would have been to make you stop because I was giggling so hard." It wasn't good enough, she knew, not nearly. Jokes and humor were all right in their place, but not in the dead of night when monsters roamed freely through the mind.

"I will tell you something else, husband. I know you married me because you are an honorable man. That, and you did care for me, or at least you cared for that child you'd known." She felt him tense, but continued inexorably, "No, it's all right. But the fact is that we are married. We are a partnership. We are to share in everything. And we will. You said something about helplessness and dependence changing one. Well, if it does happen, if you don't regain your sight, we will both of us change, and adapt and adjust. You would never be useless, and I think if you say that again, I'll cosh you on your hard head."

Saint felt her words seep into mind like soothing balm. The fear, the ghastly pain of the dream, were fading, leaving his mind free and alert.

"Do you believe that I could ever love you any less if you were blind for the rest of your life? Have you no idea of what I feel for you? How much I admire and respect you?"

"Jules, I . . . Oh, dammit!"

Suddenly it was too much. Jules burst into tears, scalding, burning tears, and she hated herself, but she couldn't stem their flow. The dam had burst.

"Ah, sweetheart, no," he said, moving against the pillows so he could take her into his arms, protect her, soothe her. He realized that they'd just reversed roles, and he smiled a bit. "Jules, don't let me hurt you . . . my anger and bitterness, well, it's all within me, and I've heard it said that the loved one gets all the misery. Hush, don't cry so, you'll make yourself hoarse." He stroked her hair, kissed her, caressed her bare back. "I don't know how a bastard like me could ever attract a beautiful creature like you, much less have her care about me."

Her sobs lessened and soon she was hiccuping against his throat. "I'm sorry," she managed after a few more minutes.

"About what?"

"You need me to be strong, and I just became what I despise—a weak, silly woman. I'm sorry, Michael, please forgive me."

"No."

It was as unexpected as it was angering. She reared up and stared down at him. She could see the outline of his bandage, the planes of his face, but she couldn't see the smile on his lips. "Just what the hell does that mean?" she demanded.

He laughed, and she pounded his chest with her fists.

"Some weak woman," he said, grabbed her arms, and tossed her onto her back. "Will I have to tie you down so I can have my way with you?"

"No, but only because I don't think you can manage it!"

He moved on top of her, his knee pressing against her closed thighs. "Open your legs, Jules," he said, his mouth against her throat.

The feel of him naked, covering her . . . "What will you do if I do?" she whispered, moving restlessly beneath him.

"I'll caress you with my mouth until you yell and then I'll come inside you, so deep that neither of us will know where the other begins or ends. And I'll fill you with my seed, and you'll feel it, and know that you are part of me."

"All right," she whispered, her body already quivering from his words.

When at last he teased her with his mouth, to caress her as he'd said he would, she couldn't bear it. The pleasure that convulsed her body was nearly painful in its intensity, a pleasure that held all their shared pain, and she cried out again and again. And when he thrust into her, a long, deep thrust, she clutched him, arching upward, yielding to him, opening to him, wanting him to become a part of her.

"My God, woman," he said many moments later when he could finally speak, "I never envisioned doing that to that scruffy little girl in Lahaina, at least not consciously," he added, and laughed.

"No," she said, clutching her arms about his back, "don't leave me, Michael."

"I won't," he said softly, his fingertips stroking her face. Her teeth nipped his fingertips and he kissed her again. He felt the sweet, smiling curve of her lips as his tongue traced over her. Her eyes would be smiling too, he thought. At least, he wanted to tell her, at least I have seen you in the moments of your pleasure. He felt her legs tighten about his flanks, felt her smooth hands stroking down his back to his buttocks, and his body responded. He moaned softly at the sensations as he filled her again.

"You are the most exquisite lover in the world," Jules said just before she fell asleep.

"Yes," he said, his voice deep with satisfaction. "I guess I am."

"No," Saint said very carefully, "it is still the same, Sam."

Jules wanted to moan like a wounded animal, but she didn't. She said nothing.

"Still the white?"

"Yes."

Sam laughed. "Excellent, Saint. You're healing." He clapped Saint on the back. "All you need now is rest, lots of it. No worrying, now, and no fighting with your wife."

"I don't understand," Jules said.

Saint reached out his hand and she quickly took it. "What Sam means, Jules, is that since what vision I have hasn't faded, it's hopeful, very hopeful." He drew her against his side and hugged her. "I do promise not to *fight* with her, Sam."

Dr. Pickett smiled and in that smile was a prayer. He patted Saint's shoulder. "Well, you don't need me anymore. We'll try again in another week, Saint. Another thing, no more than two, three patients a day." He turned to Jules, his voice more serious now. "Rest, Jules. He must have rest. I count on you to handle him."

"I shall, Dr. Pickett," she said, "indeed I shall."

After Jules had shown Samuel Pickett out, she returned to the surgery. "Here is your cane, Michael. Let's have some lunch and tell Lydia the good news."

She watched him like a hawk, of course, but bit down on her tongue when he bumped into a chair. To her great relief, he laughed. He listened to her right the chair, and said, "Tell me how romantic I look with this cane, Jules."

He did, she thought. It was ebony, with a carved lion's head. She'd said nothing about the cane before, uncertain as to his reaction. "Well, Michael," she said, slipping her arm through his, "if you looked any more romantic, I would insist that you rest now, without your lunch."

Jules insisted that both Lydia and Thackery join them in the dining room. At first Thackery looked at her as if she were speaking gibberish.

"For heaven's sake, Thackery," Lydia finally said, "would you please cease acting like a slave!"

"But—" Thackery said.

"No, no more," Jules said. "Come to the dining room. Saint will tell you about Mr. Leidesdorff, the first black man in San Francisco."

That got him, Jules saw, winking at Lydia.

Saint, when applied to for the story, sat back in his chair and smiled in Thackery's general direction. "His name was William, and unfortunately, I didn't have the pleasure of meeting him. He died a young man, only thirty-eight, in 1848, and what with the inflation brought by the gold rush, his estate was worth over a million dollars. Just six months ago, as a matter of fact, our own John Folsom"—this said in a sarcastic voice—"hauled himself to Jamaica and bought interests from possible claimants to the estate, for, you see, William Leidesdorff left no kin. Lord only knows what will happen now."

Jules tapped her fork impatiently. "But the point is, Thackery, this is California, and everyone is free to do as he wishes here." It was on the tip of her tongue to have Michael relate Leidesdorff's tragic love affair, but she realized in time that it had been tragic simply because the man had been a mulatto, and therefore unacceptable to the white family.

"If you ate with your fingers," said the irrepressible Lydia, "that would be another matter entirely. And that's why Saint here doesn't invite all those Sydney Ducks to dine with him!"

Saint chuckled, and Jules wanted to shout with the pleasure of the sound. She looked at Lydia, then at Thackery. We're becoming a family, she thought.

Two days later, in the early afternoon, Jules, with smiling firmness, helped her husband upstairs to rest. Lydia had gone to do some marketing, claiming she'd best get out now before the rains started again. As for Thackery, he'd left to go to the Wild Star to see Brent Hammond.

When there was a knock on the front door, Jules

sent a worried glance upward, praying it wasn't a patient. She hated to turn anyone away, but Michael was more important.

It wasn't a patient, however. It was a young boy.

"Miz Morris?" he asked, his voice a lisp through the gap in his front teeth.

"Yes," Jules said.

"This is for you, ma'am," the boy said, thrust an envelope into her hand, and scurried away before Jules could say anything else.

She frowned at the envelope, for there was no name or direction written on it. There was one sheet of paper inside. She read:

My dearest Juliana,
   I trust you haven't forgotten me. I wished to send my condolences about your poor husband's blindness. I am near to you, my dear, very near. Do think about me, Juliana, and know that soon I will have you again.

It was signed with a bold J.W., nothing more. Jules dropped the paper as if it were a snake to bite her. She felt the familiar fear building, and wrapped her arms about herself, as if for protection. Her eyes went toward the windows, but the streaking rain prevented seeing outside. She thought vaguely that Lydia hadn't missed the rain after all. Slowly she walked to the sofa and sank to the floor beside it. She heard a small, broken sound, and realized that it was from her own mouth.

26

Thomas sat behind Bunker's large, ornate mahogany desk, a medical book propped open in front of him. He realized that he'd read the same paragraph at least three times and hadn't taken in a single word.

He looked up with a snort of disgust and eyed the opulent library. Three walls were lined with bookshelves, filled with impressive tomes that nobody read. A thick bright red Aubusson carpet covered the floor, a lovely carpet, he thought, if one could but see more of it. His mother-in-law had covered it with heavy, clumsy furniture that depressed him. He wondered for a moment how his wife would have decorated the library.

Penelope. His wife. She was upstairs with her mother. My beautiful bride of three days, he thought, and sighed. It had never occurred to him that Penelope wouldn't enjoy the marriage bed as much as he. His only experience with women had been with native girls on Maui. They had been loving, giving, and not at all reticent of telling him how to pleasure them. He'd learned a great deal, particularly from Kani, and when he'd finally gotten his new bride to bed, he was confident and anxious to begin his pleasure, and hers. She'd allowed him to kiss her and fondle her breasts, but when his hand moved downward, she'd acted as if he were insane—no, worse, he amended bitterly to himself: as if he were a disgusting animal. He'd breached her maidenhead finally, his teeth gritted at hearing her sobs of pain. And afterward, as he'd held her and stroked her and told her how much he loved her, she whimpered against his shoulder. Still, Thomas was optimistic. The first time couldn't be very nice for the woman, but surely when he made love to her again, she would welcome his caresses. She hadn't.

He realized, sighing more deeply, that he hadn't even seen her naked. Her modesty dictated that the room be utterly dark. How could she love him, he wondered, and not want to see him or enjoy him physically?

He forced his attention back to his medical book. Surprisingly enough, it had been his father-in-law who, only three days after his stroke, had presented Thomas with the needed medical books, mumbling that if Thomas wanted to be a damned sawbones, he might as well get started, since Bunker fancied he'd need him.

"Not exactly yet, boy," Bunker said. "Maybe later, when I really get ill."

"Mr. Thomas."

Thomas started at the sound of Ezra's deep voice coming from the library doorway. The man walked as softly as a prowling cat, he thought. "Yes," he said, but moved a bit in his chair, uncomfortable with a bloody butler.

"It's your sister, sir, Mrs. Morris."

Thomas rose quickly, undefined fears churning in

him. "For God's sake, man, show her in!" Was Saint blind permanently? No, that couldn't be it. He'd spoken to Dr. Pickett and knew that Saint was healing.

When he saw her pale face, he rushed to her, every positive thought plummeting to his toes.

"What's wrong, Jules? It isn't Saint, is it?"

She shook her head. "No, he is resting at home," she said. "He must rest, you know, Thomas."

Thomas cocked his head at her. "Then you've come to see how your newly married brother is faring?"

"Not really," she said. "Here, Thomas, read this."

She thrust the paper into his hands. Frowning, Thomas unfolded the paper and read.

"That damnable bastard!" he said, his face darkening with fear and sharp anger. "Jules, when did you get this? Was it Wilkes himself?"

"No, a boy delivered it to me about an hour ago. I couldn't worry Michael with it. All he could do is rant and rave and worry, and I can't allow that. Thomas, why is Wilkes doing this? What am I going to do?"

Thomas was silent for a long moment. "Have you shown this to Thackery?"

"Not yet. I wanted to speak to you first, but Thackery suspects something is wrong. And no, I didn't come here alone, Thackery is outside."

"Wilkes is insane, he has to be to keep after you like this."

"Thomas, I'm afraid."

"Come, love, and sit down. Let me think about this. Would you like a cup of tea?"

She agreed, not really caring.

Ezra brought in a silver tray some while later, his disappointment evident when Thomas dismissed him.

"How is Bunker?" she asked as she stirred a bit of milk into her tea.

"Much better," Thomas said absently, then smiled. "In fact, he's a terror. He'll be back to his old self in no time, I think. Saint was right about his constitution. I begin to believe he'll outlive us all."

"And Penelope?"

"She is fine," he said abruptly.

Jules frowned a bit at this most unloverlike reply, but didn't dwell on it. She was too frightened.

"You were right not to tell Saint about this," Thomas said.

"Yes, I know, but I also realize that if he ever finds out, he'll be furious with me. He's so proud, you know, but—"

"Yes, but," Thomas said, interrupting her. "Thackery is your only protection. It is not enough, not with Saint helpless as a baby."

"Michael smashed my derringer," Jules said, wishing now that she'd bought a dozen of the deadly small guns. She saw the look of bewildered astonishment on her brother's face, and added quickly, "No, I refuse to explain. It doesn't matter now in any case." To her relief, Thomas let it pass. She watched him rise and begin to pace the library. He came to an abrupt halt, whirled to face her, a wide grin on his face.

"Here's what we're going to do, little sister. My new wife and I will move into your house until Wilkes is out of your life once and for all."

Jules's mouth dropped open. She waved a helpless hand at the opulent room. "Thomas, you can't take

Penelope away from this! Our house is small, and the spare bedroom would seem to her like a servant's room!"

"She is my wife," Thomas said in a very stern voice, "and she will do as I bid her."

"But your father-in-law—"

"Bunker is just fine and he's surrounded by servants. I am no longer needed here. Now, Jules, no more arguments from you. My wife and I will arrive this evening. All right?"

She gave him a dazed nod, and he walked her to the front door. "Jules, you will tell Thackery."

"Yes, of course," she said. "Thomas, it just occurred to me that Michael will wonder why you and Penelope are moving in with us. What should I tell him?"

Thomas grew thoughtful. "Tell him that Pen needs to get away from her parents for a while, more specifically, her mother. Tell him that if he doesn't mind, we'll continue our honeymoon with Dr. Saint on Clay Street."

It had begun to rain harder, and Thomas fetched her an umbrella. After he had handed her into the carriage, he saw that Ezra was regarding him with a great deal of interest.

"You'll take care of Bunker, won't you, Ezra?"

"Certainly, Mr. Thomas," Ezra said. "And you will take care of your sister, sir."

Thomas nodded, not bothering to ask him what and how much he knew, and headed up the stairs. For all Thomas knew, Ezra might have eavesdropped on their conversation. He paused a moment in front of his and Penelope's bedroom, squared his shoulders, and strode in. He might as well face the unpleasantness now and get it over with.

* * *

Saint cursed his blindness, for Jules's face always gave her away. He sighed. "That sounds pretty weak to me, Jules. Won't you tell me the truth?"

"You don't mind their coming here for a while, do you?"

"Stop dodging, sweetheart."

"Michael, please."

He heard the pleading in her voice, and said finally, "All right. If you and Thomas wish to keep your secrets, very well." He shook his head. "The thought of Penelope sleeping in our house is unnerving. I wonder if we'll survive it."

Penelope was wondering the same thing that evening. She'd said not two words to her new sister- and brother-in-law. She regarded Thomas from beneath her lashes in animated conversation with Saint. My husband, she thought, a trifle bitter. And I am to obey him. And that's what he'd told her that afternoon when she'd simply stared at him.

"You won't, of course, haul your entire wardrobe there, Pen, there's not enough room."

"How much room is that?" she'd asked him.

Thomas had looked about the enormous bedroom, dripping with opulent furnishings, and smiled. "The bedroom is, as I recall, about a third this size. You'll like the bed, though," he'd added, giving her *that* look.

"I don't want to go," she said, digging in her heels. "I must stay here, Thomas. My parents need me."

"No they don't. I've already spoken to your father. He's as worried as I am. Our reason for going is valid. I assume that you don't want my sister to be kidnapped again."

"No, of course not, it's just—"

"Enough, Pen. Pack your things. We'll leave after dinner."

"But—"

"You are my wife and you will obey me. Now, do as I tell you. Another thing, Pen, you won't say anything about Wilkes's threat to Saint. He is not to know."

And that, Penelope thought now, had been that. She'd seen the small bedroom and shuddered. And the bed, it was so small. She sipped at her tea and tried to think of something to say to her sister-in-law. But it was Jules who spoke first.

"You are very lucky, Penelope," Jules said, smiling toward her brother. "Thomas is a fine man. I was his slave when we were children."

"Such an odd life you had," Penelope said.

"Yes, it was like a Garden of Eden. Despite our father's rigidity, we managed to run wild most of the time and enjoy ourselves immensely."

"I don't have my maid," Penelope said abruptly.

What do I say to that? Jules wondered. She mustered a smile and some warmth in her voice and said, "It is very kind of you to come, Penelope. I realize that this is not exactly what you're used to, but I don't think you'll be unhappy here, especially since Thomas is here also."

Penelope merely nodded, and Jules felt a wave of frustration. This, my dear brother, she thought, isn't a very good idea.

The following morning, Thomas left to see Del Saxton, his explanation to Jules being, "Saint's Sydney Ducks need to be alerted, and I hope Mr. Saxton will know how to round them up." He'd kissed her cheek and left. Saint was with a patient, a man with a private problem, so her husband had told her, and thus her presence wasn't needed, or desired for that matter.

Jules wandered back upstairs, planning to see if Penelope had everything she needed. She paused outside the closed bedroom door, aware that Penelope was crying.

Oh dear, she thought. Had she and Thomas had a fight? What should she do?

She knocked softly, then entered. Penelope was still in bed, huddled under the covers.

"Penelope! What's the matter? Do you feel ill?"

Penelope froze, humiliation washing over her. "What do you want?" she asked, not looking at her sister-in-law.

"What's wrong, Penelope?" Jules asked, quashing the flash of anger she felt at the cold words. "Come, we are sisters now."

"It's your damned brother!" Penelope shouted, her cup filled to overflowing. "He's an animal, a brute, and—"

"*What?*"

"He forces me to do . . . things, and I hate it and it's awful and my mother told me it would be thus, but I didn't believe her!"

The light dawned. Jules regarded Penelope's flushed face. "What did your mother tell you?" she asked calmly.

"That men are animals, that they do unspeakable things to their wives, and we have to be brave and . . . bear it."

"And you believed her? By all that's rich, that is ridiculous! Don't you love my brother?"

Penelope stared at Jules. "Of course I love him. I shouldn't have married him otherwise."

"But you only wanted him to kiss your hand?"

Penelope drew back at the sarcasm. "I . . . I didn't know what it was all about. I don't like it, it's degrading."

"It? I assume we're talking about lovemaking."

Penelope shuddered at what she thought a most inappropriate term, invented doubtless by men to lull ladies' suspicions.

Jules felt an odd mixture of pity and anger. Poor Thomas! And, she amended to herself silently, poor Penelope. "I think," Jules said, moving to sit on the side of the bed, "that you need to think of me as your mother for a while. Now, I want you to listen very carefully, Penelope, because I will not lie to you."

Penelope gave Jules her full attention.

". . . and I told her that making love was more fun than anything else in the whole world," Jules told her husband smugly that night in bed. "I explained things to her." She added in some disgust, "I simply can't understand why mothers frighten the wits out of their daughters with such awful rubbish!"

"Your mother didn't tell you frightening things about filthy men?" Saint asked, pulling her closer to him.

"No, she never told me anything at all. I think complete and utter ignorance is better."

Saint kissed her nose, then nibbled on her ear. "I hate to tell you, sweetheart, but unfortunately many men believe that their wives should endure their base needs. It's only whores who are supposed to enjoy lovemaking. Men are fools."

"You don't think Thomas is a fool, do you?"

"He is young," Saint said thoughtfully, "but no, I shouldn't think that he'd be inept. But I suppose you want me to speak to him? Just to make certain, you understand?"

"Explain things to my brother?"

Saint's hand cupped her breast. "In delightful detail," he said, and began to knead the soft flesh. "Did you tell Penelope how much you adored my touching you?" His hand slipped down between her thighs. "And kissing you?"

Jules giggled, then sucked in her breath when his fingers found her. "Oh dear," she said, her voice breathless, "do you think I should have been that specific?"

Saint felt filled with warmth and deep swirling feelings that so stunned him with their force and their unexpectedness that he couldn't speak for a moment. "Jules," he said finally, "I don't want to think about Penelope any more tonight. All right?"

"Yes," she said, "yes, all right."

Jules managed to find her brother alone the following morning. "What did Del say?" she asked without preamble.

"Not to worry," Thomas said, hugging her. "He said they'd start the search again for that miserable bastard. It shouldn't be long now, love."

She felt great relief, and to her chagrin, tears stung her eyes. "I am so lucky," she said, and flung her arms around her brother. "Thank you, Thomas."

"Perhaps," he said quietly, a bit of humor in his voice, "it is I who should thank you, my dear."

She gulped, not pretending to misunderstand him. "Penelope told you that we had a little . . . talk?"

"Yes, though it took me a while to pry it out of her."

"You're not angry at me for meddling, are you?"

"No, little idiot." He gave her a wicked grin. "Actually, it pleases me mightily to know that Saint is such a . . . caring husband."

"Oh!" She pummeled his chest, her cheeks flushed.

"As for my wife, let us say that her attitude is changing. It's now up to me, I suppose, to be patient as a saint."

"My husband could give you advice about that," she said, grinning up at him.

Penelope came into the dining room at that moment, Saint beside her. "Good morning," she said, and when her eyes met her husband's, she blushed faintly.

"Michael," Jules said as she ate her scrambled eggs, "would you like me to change the bandage this morning?"

"All right," he said. "Then, sweetheart, it's off for good in three days. It's time I saw my beautiful wife again, as well as my complaining patients."

Jules was silent a moment; she was praying.

"I'll provide the champagne," Penelope said, surprising everyone.

Saint chuckled. "Your father does have the best wine cellar in San Francisco. Think you can sneak some out of there, Penelope?"

Penelope felt herself smiling. Indeed, she realized, she felt comfortable and . . . wanted. It was a heady feeling. "Yes," she said, joining in the laughter. "I shall lock Ezra in the cellar if he gives me any trouble."

"Or, love," Thomas said, leaning closer to her, "if you prefer, I could be convinced to have Ezra lock us in the cellar with the champagne. I can just see you now, Pen, your petticoats in wild disarray and a half-empty bottle in your hand."

To Thomas' utter delight, his wife giggled.

How could I have forgotten even for a moment? Jules thought blankly that afternoon as she stood in the entranceway, another letter from Wilkes clutched in her hand. It read simply:

> *My dear Juliana,*
> *You force me yet again to withdraw. It is not over.*
> *Pray do not forget me.*

It was Penelope who found her, white-faced, rigid, and alone, huddled next to the sofa on the floor.

She took the crushed paper from her sister-in-law's nerveless hand, smoothed it out, and read it. She said nothing, merely helped Jules to her feet and drew her against her, hugging her.

Jules said, "God I wish I had my derringer."

Penelope gently patted her back. "Why don't I purchase one for each of us?"

Jules could only stare at her.

"Yes," Penelope said again. "I believe I shall go out now."

And she did.

27

There was not a sound that morning in Saint's surgery. The small room was crowded. Thomas, Penelope, Jules, and Dr. Pickett all stood as still as stones, waiting. Thackery and Lydia were outside the open doorway in the entrance hall.

Jules could hear everyone else breathing. She was holding her own breath.

Dr. Pickett cleared his throat. "Saint?"

Saint said nothing for many moments. "Jules," he said finally, "is that a freckle I see on your nose?"

Jules stared at him, for the moment unable to accept his words. Then, at his slow smile, she flung herself into his arms, nearly knocking him backward. "Yes," she said against his shoulder, "it's a freckle. I don't know where it came from. I suppose I could use some lemon juice or something . . ." She finally broke off, knowing she was babbling.

"Or some cucumber lotion," Penelope said.

"Or just let me kiss that very cute freckle," Saint said. He drew her back, stared down into the dearest face he'd ever seen, and lightly kissed the tip of her nose. "Hello, wife," he said, stroking his fingertips over her face. "It's quite nice to see you again."

Thomas gave a loud shout and wrung Dr. Pickett's hand.

"It seems to me," Saint said after a moment, a mock frown furrowing his brow, "that a doctor's surgery is the last place to expect such an excess of spirits."

But nobody paid him any mind. He accepted handshakes, back slaps, with a big smile and his deep laugh. Jules saw his eyes glitter with pleasure, and she didn't believe she'd ever seen him so happy. She sent a prayer of thanks heavenward, and eyed him hungrily.

"Pen," Thomas said after a moment, "it's time to get on with the excess of spirits. And Saint's right—this surgery is too small for us."

"Actually," Penelope said a few minutes later when they were all in the dining room, "my father insisted I bring over six bottles of his best champagne."

"Drunk as loons by noon," Dr. Pickett said, raising his filled glass a few minutes later in the dining room. "To the return of the most saintly man in San Francisco."

"And the biggest tale-bearer," Lydia said.

"Could you rephrase that a bit, Lydia?" Saint said. He looked around the table at all his friends. It was a heady thing, this looking and seeing, he thought. "Lord," he said, his voice deep with his feelings, "it's good to see all of you again. Allow me to refill everyone's glass. If I spill any, it won't be because I'm not seeing straight."

Jules looked at Thackery and was surprised to see tears in the black man's eyes. He met her gaze and said with a crooked smile, "I never drank champagne before."

"Your wife, Thomas," Saint said as he refilled Penelope's glass, "looks as content as a spring rose, and just as pretty. Is he a good husband to you, my dear?"

Penelope gulped, her cheeks flushing with Thomas' laughing eyes on her. "He will improve," she said finally.

"Every day," Thomas said, "yes, indeed."

"Saint," Lydia said, "I've baked you your favorite apple tarts. If we're all not to be drunk under the table, I'd best serve them now."

Three hours later, Saint, a bit tottery himself, was giving out advice for hangovers.

But it was only the beginning. By evening it seemed to Jules that everyone in San Francisco knew that Saint had regained his sight. The stream of visitors was continuous. The women brought food, the men liquor.

At midnight Jules was so tipsy that Saint half-carried her upstairs to their bedroom. He called over his shoulder, "Good luck to you, Thomas." He grinned at the sound of Penelope's giggle.

"I don't believe I've ever seen you quite so sodden," he said to his wife as he undressed her. Jules looked at him owlishly and grinned. He kissed her freckle again. "Do you think if we listen we'll hear some marvelous lewd sounds coming from the other bedroom?"

"What if they listen, Michael?" she asked, her eyes nearly crossing in her effort to focus on his face.

"I fear," he said with a disappointed sigh, "that all they would hear would be the sound of your unladylike snoring."

She tried to punch him in the stomach, but missed.

Her head spinning, she fell onto her back on the bed.

Saint grinned down at her, and quickly pulled off the rest of her clothes. For a moment he was on the sober edge. "God," he whispered, looking down at her. "I prayed I would see again. Do you know how beautiful you are, Jules?"

Jules was too giddy to care that she was sprawled on her back, her legs parted.

"That flame-colored hair, very delightful, sweetheart." She realized vaguely that he wasn't looking at her head.

"Michael," she said, and tried to cover herself, only to feel his strong hands pulling hers away.

"Oh no, you are mine, all mine."

She swallowed at the richness of his deep voice, then felt a wave of dizziness and giggled. "You have your clothes on," she said.

"Not for much longer."

To his chagrin, Jules was sound asleep when he turned back to her. He kissed her lightly, drawing her slender body against him. She'd lost weight, he thought vaguely, his eyes studying her. He looked a moment toward the lamp by the bed. I can see you, he silently told the light. I can see everything. I am the luckiest man on earth. He was loath to plunge the room into darkness. I will see the sun in the morning, he thought. He grinned crookedly. And I will feel like the very devil and probably curse it.

The following afternoon, Saint *was* cursing, but not from a hangover. He was standing by the dresser in their bedroom, two pieces of paper in his hand.

He closed his eyes a moment, utter fury washing through him.

He strode to the top of the stairs and bellowed at the top of his lungs, "Jules! Come here, now!"

Jules, who was feeling a bit tentative, excused herself from her company and slowly, with great care, mounted the stairs. She heard Agatha Newton, Tony Dawson, and Chauncey Saxton laughing in the parlor, and wished they wouldn't be quite so loud.

"Yes, Michael?" she said, coming into the bedroom.

She stopped cold in her tracks, seeing him waving two sheets of paper at her.

"I was looking for a handkerchief," he said with great calm, "and I just chanced to come across these."

She looked at him helplessly.

"It is not that I haven't enjoyed having Thomas and Penelope staying with us," he continued, his voice becoming harder, "but this, Juliana! Damn you, how dare you?"

Juliana. She'd just regressed again. "Michael," she began, sliding her tongue over her lips, "you don't understand . . ." Her mouth felt like dry cotton.

"Yes?" he said, his voice silky. "You can, I am certain, manage a marvelously competent explanation. You're rarely at a loss for glib words, are you? . . . Well?"

"I don't know why I didn't throw them away," she said, cursing herself silently, her eyes, as if mesmerized, on those wretched sheets of paper.

"Juliana! Damn you, answer me!"

She raised pleading eyes to his face, and he cursed crudely.

"Do you have any idea how this makes me feel?" He waved the papers in front of her nose. "Less than a man—in fact, something far less than a tinker's damn! How dare you keep this from me?"

He grabbed her shoulders and shook her. The papers made a loud crumpling noise as they wrinkled between his hand and her shoulder.

"If I recall correctly, I said very nearly the same things to you before, didn't I? Did my feelings then mean nothing to you?"

How dare he treat her to this ridiculous tirade, she thought suddenly. She jerked away from him. "All right," she said, glaring at him. "I was protecting you, dammit! I love you and I couldn't allow you to be worried!"

"I had every right to know that this . . . vermin was threatening you again!"

"No," she said, stiffening her backbone, "no, you didn't." She added, "And stop cursing me. There was nothing you could have done in any case. If you don't remember, you were blind! Helpless!"

He realized the justice of her reasoning, but was not ready to release the meaty bone of contention. "So," he sneered, "you, my little wife, made the decision that I was to be left ignorant. Is there anything else I should know? Did it not occur to you to tell me yesterday, when, if you will remember, I saw the light of day again?"

"I was too drunk and too happy," she said. "I forgot to tell you." She thrust up her chin. "Even if I had thought of it, I wouldn't have said anything. We were celebrating, remember?"

That halted him in his tracks, but for just a moment. "Then you should have told me this morning."

Jules eyed him with growing anger. "You are acting ridiculously," she said. "I will have no more of your silly shouting and wounded male vanity. I would do the same thing again, do you hear? Now, we have company downstairs."

"I happen to be nine years older than you and twice your size," he said. "I refuse to be ordered about by a little twit now or ever. Do you understand me?"

"Damned arrogant man," Jules muttered. "If you wish to nurse your grievances, do so, Michael. I'm leaving!"

He stared at her a moment. " 'Damned arrogant man,' " he repeated, as if disbelieving of the words until they'd come from his own mouth. "That's what you think I am?"

"I do," she said firmly, "if you continue to call me Juliana."

"Oh shit," he said, and thrashed his fingers through his hair. "Come here, you idiot."

She gave him a hopeful, tentative smile, and at the answering tenderness in his eyes, she threw herself into his arms. "I'm sorry," she whispered against his shoulder. "I did what I thought I had to do, what I thought was best."

"I know," he said, "I know."

He began kissing her, and her response was immediate and most gratifying.

"Oh God," he said, reluctantly releasing her, "company downstairs, did you say?"

"You've a lot of friends, Michael," she said.

"Any chance of sending the whole bloody lot of them to the devil right now?"

"Probably not," she said, a wealth of disappointment in her voice.

He hugged her to his side. "Onward, love. Charm and all that."

He called me "love," she thought, dazed and so happy she wanted to yell. She paused. Perhaps it had just been another endearment, like "sweetheart."

At dinner that evening, Saint merely asked Thomas what he'd heard about Wilkes. Thomas drew a relieved breath, shot his sister a smile, and told his brother-in-law what they were doing.

As for Jules, she sent a conspiratorial smile toward Penelope. Both women now owned a derringer. When Jules had shown her how to fire it, she'd said, "Men aren't altogether reasonable. I am continually amazed that they actually believe that women are helpless creatures with even less sense. Here, Pen, you load it now."

Jules said nothing at all while Thomas and Saint discussed Wilkes. She watched her husband as he used his large hands to make a point, watched his beautiful hazel eyes change in intensity as he spoke. His white teeth gleamed with a wide smile. Her eyes drifted slowly over his body. She imagined him naked, and felt a spurt of warmth deep in her belly. At that moment, Saint met her eyes. A brow arched upward, and his eyes darkened.

Jules laughed, a nervous, silly sound that made Saint grin at her wickedly. "I don't think," he said to Thomas, "that I will ask your sister what she's thinking right now."

"Why not?" Penelope demanded. "Jules has very good ideas."

"Too true," Saint said blandly. "Too true."

"I will tell you later, Michael, exactly what I'm thinking," Jules said, trying to frown him down.

"Or you could simply show me," Saint said.

"But Jules," Penelope protested, "why don't you tell him now? This does concern you."

Thomas broke into merry laughter. He leaned over and clasped his wife's slender hand. "She can't, love, it would be too . . . embarrassing."

"Oh! You mean that . . . You are a wretched tease, Thomas DuPres!"

"Tease? Really, Pen, you know better than that!"

Saint didn't believe that he would ever tire of watching his wife brush her hair. She was wearing the dark blue velvet dressing gown he'd given her at Christmas, and her thick beautiful hair rippled down her back. He was lying on the bed, his head pillowed on his arms. He said idly, "I explained things to Thomas, just as you asked."

Jules looked at him in the mirror, a grin on her face. "And what did my brother have to say?"

"Well, he looked very surprised, really. Astonished, I suppose you could say. As I recall, he said, 'Saint, are you certain that is how it's done? I thought the ear—'."

Jules threw her hairbrush at him.

He let it bounce off his chest, then tossed it back to her. "To be serious about it, I simply asked him how things were going with his bride. He looked greatly pleased. Of course, sweetheart, two gentlemen wouldn't discuss techniques or exact approaches, not like you ladies appear to do."

Jules rose from her chair and slipped off her dressing gown. She enjoyed the feel of it and stood quietly a moment, stroking her hand over the velvet.

"Why don't you consider putting me around you? I imagine I'm much warmer than that dressing gown."

Jules looked uncertain, then, as her eyes began to twinkle, nodded. "Hairy velvet. It's certainly a thought."

"Come here, wench," he said, pulling back the covers.

She felt herself grow warm at the sight of him. "Have you never worn a nightshirt?" she asked, standing over him, her gaze going slowly down his body.

Just those few times when I was afraid I would ravish you if I didn't.

"No," he said, his voice growing thick as her eyes rested on his groin.

"You are so beautiful, Michael," she said, and slipped into bed beside him. "And much warmer than my dressing gown."

Saint did his best to slow her down, but it was impossible. She wanted him, and quickly. It was the first time they'd made love since he'd gotten his vision back, and he thought he would yell with pleasure as he watched her face at the moment of her climax.

Then he was deep inside her, thrusting frantically, beyond himself. He heard her moan softly when his seed burst from his body into her, and he knew that she was filled with him and that she was happy to be so. He pulled her onto her side, stroking his large hands down her back. "You are perfect," he said, kissing her temple. "And I love you, Jules. With all my heart."

She raised her face to look at him, and he said softly, "Don't cry, love."

She felt his fingertip wipe away the single tear that coursed down her cheek. "I'm not," she sniffed.

"I was just thinking that perhaps I didn't hear exactly what you said."

He squeezed her, feeling himself growing hard within her again. "Woman, you heard me right, and you know it. As you can feel, my body agrees with me. Will you rush me this time, Jules? Or will you let a simple man give you everything he can, and very slowly?"

Jules felt dazzling sensations, and her muscles convulsed, making him moan. "I don't know, Michael," she said. She came on top of him, and he helped her straddle him. He was very deep inside her. His large hands covered her breasts, and she arched her back, her hair streaming over her shoulders and over his hands. When his fingers stroked downward to find her, she gasped. "I don't think I can, Michael."

"Dear heavens," he gasped, arching up to fill her completely with himself, "I can feel your womb."

He felt her hands close over his wrists, felt her thighs tighten about his flanks. He thought he would never see anything so beautiful as the dazed sheen in her eyes. "Yes, love," he said, "come with me, now."

Her response was a shuddering groan.

Saint lay awake after Jules was sleeping like a sated little animal in the crook of his arm. His eyes traced the shadowy patterns cast in the far reaches of the bedroom by the moonlight silvering through the window. Life, he thought, would be perfect if it weren't for that bastard Wilkes. During his several years at Massachusetts General Hospital, he'd dealt with the insane, people who were mindless yet utterly harmless, people who were mindless and violent, people who believed they were someone else, usually long dead, and people, he realized, who were obsessed with an object, an idea, or another person. His reason rebelled against the notion, but faced with Wilkes's actions, he could not deny it.

He'd assumed in the beginning that Wilkes wanted this lovely girl because she was a virgin and would bring him a great sum of money. But her marriage should have made him realize the futility of his wish. Unless all he wanted was revenge. But no, Saint's thinking continued, that didn't make sense either. His arms tightened about his wife. There was no choice now, not really. He would have to kill Wilkes.

He would find Limpin' Willie in the morning. Perhaps Willie's criminal mind could aid him in finding Wilkes. Jules muttered something incomprehensible in her sleep and Saint smiled. He hoped she was dreaming of him and enjoying every bit of it.

He had helped her cleanse herself, Jules too exhausted to protest, and he wondered now how long it would be before she became pregnant with his child. His body stirred at the powerful thought, a useless action, he told himself, grinning. He began to breathe deeply and slowly, a habit he had learned early in medical school, and one that put him to sleep within minutes.

The following morning, Jules and Saint helped Thomas and Penelope move back to the Stevenson mansion. Bunker, Saint thought, after he'd examined him briefly, would live to be ninety.

"Well, my boy," Bunker said, "it's good to have you back again. Not that I don't like Pickett, mind you, but—"

"Thank you," Saint said quickly, cutting him off. "Now, what you need are more rest and a daily dose of fresh air. Have your man Ezra drive you out every afternoon."

Mrs. Stevenson was a different matter, and Saint felt a stab of pity for Penelope when her mother fell on her, weeping.

"Leave go, Sally," Bunker told his wife sharply. "The girl's a married woman now and has lots of new responsibilities. And she looks happy as a tack." He turned back to Saint. "A good man, my son-in-law," he said, not bothering to lower his voice even though Thomas was within hearing distance. "He'll make a fine doctor, I don't doubt. Ah, yes, Saint, I'll help him right enough. Next time I have one of these damned fool attacks, he'll be here to get me over it."

"I will miss Penelope," Jules said to her husband as they got into the carriage. "She has changed so much. Even Chauncey said she was having to revise her opinions. Del just shook his head and said something about every woman being tractable if handled properly."

"And what did Chauncey say to that?"

"Something about she would take care of him later."

"I'm certain that she did," Saint said.

"I'll miss Thomas too," said Jules.

"At least I won't have to worry about clamping my hand over your mouth every night, love."

She poked him in the ribs. "Do you never think serious thoughts? Elevating thoughts?"

"Maybe they'll return in, say, five years."

"Or so," Jules said, tucking her hand through his arm. She gave him a sunny smile even as she felt a sudden surge of guilt over her new derringer. No, she told herself firmly, I shall be very careful this time. She wondered what Penelope would do with hers, and had the inescapable feeling that her sister-in-law would keep it safe, and a secret from Thomas.

She was not at all surprised to see three patients waiting for Saint when they returned home. She was surprised, however, and delighted, when Saint asked her to assist him.

28

It was the middle of the afternoon. Patches of sun came through the bedroom windows, unnoticed by either Saint or Jules.

"That," Saint said many minutes later when his heart slowed a bit, "should probably be against the law. Debauchery, pure and simple." Her muscles tightened at his words, and he groaned, kissing her.

Jules wanted to moan and laugh at the sound of the knock downstairs on the front door. "I should be a banker, like Del Saxton," he said, slowly and very reluctantly pulling away from her. "Given the satisfied smile on Chauncey's face, I wager they spend many afternoons like this." He sighed. "I suppose I should count my lucky stars. That knock could have come ten minutes earlier."

He rose and quickly dressed. "You, love, are in no shape to be my assistant this time. Just lie there and think about me."

Before he left the bedroom, he leaned down and kissed her again, his hand gliding over her breasts. "You look utterly wanton," he said on a strained laugh. He gently touched his fingers to the damp curls, then forced himself to straighten. "Don't move," he told her. "Perhaps I'll be lucky and the patient downstairs only has a cold or a sprained thumb."

But the patient, a Chinese worker, had been beaten and robbed. Saint was with him for hours.

"Will he be all right?" Jules asked him over dinner that evening.

"It depends, dammit! There might very well be internal damages, something we great doctors know next to nothing about and could do nothing about in any case. If he lives the night, he has a good chance. And no, the men who did this to him weren't any of Limpin' Willie's friends. Strangers, his friends told me."

He was perturbed, and Jules noticed he'd eaten next to nothing. To distract him, she began to talk about the time he'd saved her from a jellyfish when she was thirteen years old. Soon he was laughing, remembering how she'd yelped and how he'd had to straddle her to keep her foot steady.

It was over a cup of Lydia's delicious coffee that Saint sat back in his chair and said, "Byrony is due to deliver in a week or so. I received a brief note from Brent today. Would you like to visit the new town of Wakeville?"

She nodded enthusiastically. "Oh yes, I should love it. I was hoping we'd be going soon. I can't wait to see what they've done."

Saint nodded, then shrugged with a show of elaborate indifference, saying, "We'll leave first thing in the morning, then, before it's light."

Jules wasn't fooled for a minute. "You believe Wilkes has someone watching the house?"

"I doubt it," Saint said, lowering his lashes so she wouldn't see the gnawing worry in his eyes, "but I won't take any chances." He saw that she would protest and said quickly, "Jules, I don't like sneaking about like thieves in the night, but dammit, I won't take any risks with your safety. Now, I need to make arrangements with Dr. Pickett to take over my patients, and you, my dear, need to write notes to Thomas and your friends. Lydia will continue as if we were here." But Saint was thinking to himself: Please show yourself, you vermin bastard! I want to put my hands around your damned neck. I want to destroy you as I would a mad dog.

"Thackery will accompany us?" Jules asked, pulling him from his violent but very satisfying thoughts.

He nodded. "Now, why don't you pack for us and I'll be off for a couple of hours."

It was drizzling before dawn the following morning, the fog thick and heavy. Ranger Tyson from Hobson's Stables had provided a carriage and two horses. "He still owes me" was all Saint said.

Jules felt the chill seep through her thick cloak and moved closer to her husband in the dark carriage. The seats smelled of old leather and tobacco smoke. And, she thought, her nose twitching, the carriage smelled of sex. It was a rather large one, she mentally added to herself, and grinned.

She heard Saint speak in a low voice to Thackery, and soon the carriage jolted forward.

They were nearly ten miles south of San Francisco when the sun came up. The air was clear and there wasn't a hint of rain.

"This is lovely," Jules said, staring out at the rolling green hills. "I can smell the ocean. I wish we could see it."

"The land was too rugged to build a road closer," Saint said. "Perhaps someday."

"We'll stop for breakfast soon. Lydia packed us a hamper."

They stopped on a rise that gave a view of the ocean to the west and rolling hills to the east. The sun was warm and there was a crisp early-morning breeze. Jules stood for a moment near the edge of the rise, breathing in the clear air. Saint watched her a moment after spreading out one of Lydia's checkered cotton tablecloths. He loved the way the breeze caught tendrils of her hair, lifting them, and the shine of the sun through the flame strands.

"Beautiful," he said quietly, lightly closing his hands over her shoulders.

"Yes," she said, leaning her head back against his shoulder.

She felt his hands ease beneath her cloak and cup her breasts. She shivered slightly and pressed herself more tightly against him. "Shall I tell Thackery to go find the Northwest Passage or something?" Saint asked, kissing her ear.

Jules's stomach growled and Saint laughed. "I suppose that's my answer," he said, turned her around, and kissed her mouth.

They breakfasted on fresh, still-warm bread, butter, and jam, and coffee in one of Lydia's jars, wrapped in heavy cloths to keep it hot.

"This is decadent," Saint said, leaning back a moment on his elbows. "How far to go now, Thackery?"

"Not more than another hour, Dr. Saint," Thackery said, and both Jules and Saint could hear the excitement in his voice. "The rains haven't been so bad so far, and the building never stops. Mrs. Byrony never stops either, and you should hear Mr. Brent yell at her."

The horses seemed to feel the excitement and quickened their pace. The first view of Wakeville came less than an hour later, and Jules sucked in her breath. "I don't know what I was expecting," she said, tugging at Saint's sleeve, "but this is incredible!"

It looked to Saint as if Brent Hammond had managed to buy the most fertile acres in the area. And the activity was astounding. There was even a Village Street, wide enough for two carriages side by side, with new buildings with sidewalks lining it. Nine out of ten faces in the new town were black.

"All this in six months," Saint said. Thackery turned the carriage off Village Street and pulled to a stop in front of a two-story white house with a wide veranda across the entire front. There were trees and flowers everywhere.

Brent Hammond came out of the front door at that moment, a very pregnant Byrony on his heels. An ancient black woman followed closely behind Byrony as if she expected her to keel over like a small ship.

"Ah," Brent said, grinning as he shook Saint's hand, "we've got the greenhorns from the big city."

"I'm afraid you can't get any closer," Byrony said, laughing as she tried to hug Jules. "This child is going to be born declaiming lines from a play! He certainly is dramatic enough in his movements."

Byrony saw Jules's eyes move behind her and said on a mock sigh, "This is my keeper, Mammy Bath. Mammy, this is Mrs. Morris."

"Just look at that hair, little missis," Mammy said, reaching out gnarled fingers to touch Jules's hair.

"And all that pretty white skin. Now, you two little ladies come inside and rest."

Byrony said behind her hand to Jules, "And the big strong men will ensure the running of the world. Don't argue, Jules, it's no use."

Soon the little ladies and the strong men were seated at a huge dining table, plates of sausage, eggs, and toast piled in front of them.

"This isn't nirvana by a long shot," Brent was saying, "but we're working through the problems as they arise. We have few fights, fortunately, and no thievery except for a month ago when some drifters came into town. They saw all our black people and decided to help themselves." Brent shook his head, grinning.

"He enjoyed himself immensely, Saint," Byrony said. "He was itching to bang some heads together and got his wish."

Saint watched Byrony with a professional eye. The child was large and it worried him. And Byrony, despite her smiles, looked tired. He heard her speak to Jules about their school.

"Little Tony, bless his heart, practically taught himself how to read and do figures. He's now in charge of deeds, births, deaths, and all the rest of the record-keeping."

"Yes," Brent said with a wry grin. "Little Tony—the fellow's nearly as big as you are, Saint."

It wasn't until that afternoon that Brent managed to get Saint alone. They were walking in the garden behind the house, Brent explaining what crops they were planting and how it was decided who did what. He broke off suddenly. "Well, what do you think, Saint?"

Saint didn't pretend to misunderstand. "She needs to be tied down," he said.

Brent cursed softly. "Lord knows I yell at her enough, but she'll turn those big eyes on me and say, 'But there's so much to be done,' and I always fold. Some gambler I am."

"Tie her down," Saint repeated. "The child has dropped, Brent, which means that she'll go into labor in, say, three or four days. She needs to stay in bed now. I won't lie to you. The child is large, even larger than I'd expected it would be. She needs to have all her strength because her labor will probably be long."

Brent turned white.

Saint put his hand on Brent's shoulder. "I don't mean to scare you. Byrony will be all right, I swear it. But I don't like to tempt fate."

"I'll tie her down," Brent said. "Excuse me a moment, Saint, and I'll do it right now."

"Better yet," Saint said, "let me examine her now. I'll give her the orders. You're only her husband, Brent, I'm her doctor." Saint paused a moment, then said, "You haven't seen any strangers about, have you, Brent?"

"As in Wilkes, you mean, Saint?"

"Yes, as in Jameson Wilkes. I really don't know just how extensive his spy system is, but—"

"Yes, *but*," said Brent. "Try not to worry. I'll ask about."

Saint said nothing more, but Brent knew he was worried. Hell, all his friends were worried and would be until the vermin was destroyed.

They found Jules and Byrony in the parlor laughing and drinking tea. Byrony was busily sewing something. Brent said firmly, "Hello, Jules. Byrony, come along now, Saint's going to take care of you." He held out his hand to his wife.

Byrony grumbled a bit, but allowed her husband to help her out of the chair.

"Jules," Saint said, "would you please see to Brent here? Byrony, at last I've got you to myself. Let's go upstairs, Mrs. Hammond."

Brent looked as if he would follow, but instead sighed and flung himself down in the chair Byrony had just vacated. "Damn," he said. "Excuse me, Jules," he added.

"You're worried, Brent. I don't blame you, but Michael is the best doctor in the whole world."

He gave her a crooked smile. "He's also going to be the busiest doctor in the whole world. Everyone in town knows he's here by now. A goodly number have aches and pains. There'll be a line two deep tomorrow."

Upstairs, Saint helped Byrony sit down in a chair, then sat down on the edge of the bed. He said very gently, "Tell me how you feel."

"I've had pains already, Saint. Then they go away. I do try to rest, but—"

"Yes, I know. These pains, Byrony, tell me about them."

She told him of the sharp, low pains, finishing with, "I thank my lucky stars I didn't tell Brent. He would have gone crazy."

"Yes, it's just as well. Now, I'd like to feel this child of yours."

Byrony undressed while Saint waited outside in the hallway. She was swathed in a long white cotton nightgown when he came back into the room. He helped her lie on the bed, then very gently slipped his hands beneath the gown to feel her belly.

"No, Byrony," he said, looking at her tightly closed eyes, "please, just relax." His knowledgeable hands lightly roved over her belly. "That's better." He decided to wait to examine her internally. Best to let her accustom herself to him first. He straightened her nightgown and took her hand. "Now, Mrs. Hammond, let's chat a bit."

Byrony was in bed by nine o'clock that evening. Saint looked at his wife and decided bed was the best place for her too. He felt a surge of desire for her, and frowned at himself. His hand, though, went around her waist, and she leaned into him, smiling up at him.

"You know something, Saint?" Brent asked.

Saint turned toward him.

"Never play poker, my friend. You'd lose." Brent chuckled, patted Jules's arm, and took himself off.

"What was that all about?" Jules asked.

"Brent saw the lustful look in my eyes, I think. He's right, I'd never win at poker."

"Would you care to play something else, Dr. Saint?"

"What a wanton woman you are, Jules," he said. "I suppose I have no choice?"

"None at all," she said, and dragged him upstairs.

29

The child screamed at the top of his lungs, so loud Jules wanted to clap her hands over her ears. Instead she held the wriggling little boy down while Saint vaccinated him.

"There," Saint said. "Stop your caterwaulin', boy. You'll live, I promise." He patted the boy's woolly head and helped him up. "Now, you're going to live forever—"

"Yessir," the boy gulped. "Ma name's Jonah."

"That chile need a whippin', Docta," the mother said, shaking her head fondly. "No guts atall. Yer little missis here is a real sweetie pie, yessir, she shoh is."

"Hi, sweetie pie," Saint said, kissing her the moment they were alone. "I'm about ready to drop, love. How about you?"

"A nice strong cup of tea would put me to rights, I think," Jules sighed. She shook her head. "I think I'm temporarily deaf."

"Did I ever tell you that Napoleon had all his troops vaccinated if they had not already had smallpox?"

She blinked up at him and he grinned, adding, "I've done about eighty-five vaccinations today, and not a soul would have known who Napoleon even was. I had to tell that interesting fact to someone, just to keep my hand in."

Jules clasped his hand in hers, silently studying the long, blunt-tipped fingers, the sprinkling of chestnut hair.

"Now, I wonder where you think my hand should be in next?"

She kissed each finger. "This is a start," she said. "Now, you need to tell me how you managed to get enough supplies to vaccinate all the children."

"A mistake, Jules, a simple mistake, at least that's what Sam Pickett told me. Some government fellow showed up at the hospital wanting to get rid of cases of what he believed were useless medical supplies. Needless to say, Sam nearly did a jig for joy, kept a straight face, and called me. And here we are and all the children are now protected, thank the Lord."

"You're a perfect man, you know that?"

"That's what my mother told me," Saint said, "but it was a number of years ago."

He stopped a moment, and straightened her bonnet. "The sun is strong, love. I do love that one freckle on your nose, but I don't know as I'd like to see more of the little fellows."

She poked him in his ribs, laughing. "You know that isn't a freckle on my nose—it's a liver spot."

"I've aged you so quickly, hmm? I think I'd best do a thorough examination. If you have any more of these liver spots, I'll just have to do something about it."

"What?" Jules asked, taking a skipping step to keep pace with her husband.

He leaned down and whispered in her ear.

"Michael!"

* * *

Jameson Wilkes stared at her from his post in the narrow alley. He was dressed roughly, a felt hat pulled low over his forehead. The scratchy wool pants increased his anger at Saint Morris. He hated having to appear like one of the black beggars in Brent Hammond's town.

He leaned forward and watched the breeze lift a waving curl off her forehead, watched her husband straighten her bonnet, and stiffened when the huge man who was her husband leaned down to whisper something to her.

Don't touch her, you damned bastard! He could barely keep the words from spurting from his mouth.

He'd lived with the dream of her, the fantasies of her that he'd woven over the months, and knew that he would have her, have her lying beneath him, helpless, yet wanting him as he did her. The reality of her shook him, as did her bright laugh. Reality, he thought, an odd word, something to avoid, to escape. He'd never heard her laugh before. He'd cursed himself again and again for ever taking her to the auction. He should have kept her with him, sailed from San Francisco and taken her to the far reaches of the earth. But for what reason? He shook his head, his thoughts tangled. His hand roved over his belly, rubbing frantically, and the pain made him think clearly.

Now she was married to that damned do-gooding bastard Saint Morris. He closed his eyes a moment against his anger. If only he'd kept her with him, if only he'd managed to take her the night of the Stevensons' ball, if only . . .

He wanted her. And he was here, and he was

going to take her, had to take her, and her husband, Dr. Morris. Oh yes, he had to see Saint Morris, had to . . . He winced at the increasing pain, but forced his mind away from it, forced his mind to plot, to come up with strategies. He had to have focus. No, he wouldn't dig into his opium supply until the pain made him want to howl.

Your last grand gesture, he thought suddenly. Your last gesture to affirm that you are alive, that you managed to win one last time. And he knew it was true. Juliana now represented both life and death to him. He smiled a bit, remembering how Hawkins had come to him, a huge grin splitting his ugly face. "Yessiree, they're off early, bound for the nigger town."

So easy, Wilkes thought. He wondered if Juliana now believed herself safe from him.

Saint Morris was here to deliver the Hammonds' child. Wilkes had only to remain out of sight and wait for his opportunity.

It would come, oh yes. He knew suddenly, at that precise moment, with the bright sun overhead, exactly when and how he would strike.

Jules was striding down the street beside Thackery and Little Tony, a black man who would intimidate the bravest of men. His size was formidable, his body hard with muscle, and he had the gentlest eyes Jules had ever seen.

She was listening to the two men talk. Although Thackery had never said anything to her, she realized now that he missed being here, missed being part of the town's growth. She silently cursed Wilkes.

"I must get back to work now, Miz Morris," Little

Tony said, pausing a moment before a freshly painted wooden building. "This is where we keep all our records," he added, pride in his voice.

"Please call me Jules," she said, but knew that he wouldn't. Old habits were hard to break.

Little Tony nodded to her from his great height.

"Thank you for the tour," Jules said. "Now," she continued to Thackery, "why don't we go for a ride? I should love to see the land around the town and all the planting and all the new building."

Thackery agreed and they walked to the livery stable. "Little Tony was telling me how much trouble they're having with names."

Jules cocked a questioning brow.

"Slaves have only one name," he said tersely. "Outlandish names, given by white owners."

"What are you doing about it?" Jules asked, fascinated.

"Mr. Hammond, he's made lists of names—real names—his missis too. All of us choose what name we want, then Little Tony writes out certificates."

"What name have you chosen?"

"Me? I was lucky. I just chose John. John Thackery."

Jules stopped and thrust out her hand. "A pleasure to meet you, John."

He gave her a crooked grin and enfolded her small hand in his large one. "As for Little Tony, he's now Mr. Anthony Washington."

"That's some name to live up to," Jules said.

They rented two horses and rode out. Jules was wearing her new blue velvet riding habit and a jaunty little hat. She felt happy and content. The morning was sunny and warm. The rolling hills surrounding the wide valley were green from the winter rains.

They reined in occasionally, Thackery showing her how the plots of land had been divided up, pointing out the constant building of small houses.

"I think Mr. Hammond has every banker in San Francisco involved," he said. "The amount of lumber we need is incredible. Just look over there—"

There was a loud cracking sound. Jules whipped about to see Thackery grab his chest.

"Thackery!"

She tried desperately to keep him upright on his horse, but his weight was too great and he slid to the rocky ground. Jules dismounted quickly, rushing to him.

"Leave him be, Juliana."

Jules knew that voice—it had played in her dreams countless times. Now it was hard and cajoling at the same time. And filled with triumph and satisfaction.

"I must help him," she said, her voice blank from shock, still disbelieving. She felt Wilkes's hand on her arm, felt him pull her about to face him.

"Look at me, Juliana."

She couldn't. She wouldn't.

She felt his long fingers grasp her chin and force her face upward. "You're insane," she said. "I am nothing, nothing at all to you. Why?"

Jameson Wilkes sought the depths of her eyes. He laughed. "If I could answer that, my dear, in a fashion you could understand, I shouldn't have lived in hell for so long a time. Come now, Juliana. We have a goodly distance to go."

"No," she said, her voice so calm it surprised her. "I must help Thackery."

"You touch him, my dear, and I'll put another bullet through his black hide." He saw the flaring of fear in her eyes, and knew he had found his lever. "However, if you come with me, I'll leave him as he is." He didn't want her fighting him, didn't want her struggling until she hurt herself. He saw the growing stain of red on the black man's chest and knew he would die in any case. But the man was tough, and Wilkes hoped he would make it back to tell Saint Morris. He was counting on it; that was why he hadn't put a bullet through the man's heart.

"You will die for this," Jules said as she walked to her horse. "My husband will kill you for this."

"Actually, my dear," Wilkes said easily, "your husband is at this moment helping Byrony Hammond. From what I could tell with all the excitement, she is now birthing her child."

Jules shut her eyes. When would she be missed? Would she be missed at all?

"Now, I believe I shall take your reins. Unfortunately, I cannot trust you to do as I bid you once we are away from your bodyguard." He grasped her horse's reins, pulling himself closer to her.

"Behave, Juliana, else I'll tie you up. Remember how I tied you up before? There is much we will do together."

Jules thought of her derringer, so safe and distant in the bottom of her valise. It was the oddest thing, but she wasn't particularly afraid, for the fear of the reality was much less than the fear of his shadow and his threats. The fear would come, though, she knew it. But before it numbed her mind, she knew she had to think clearly. She had only herself to rely upon. As Wilkes nudged their horses forward, she turned in the saddle to see Thackery. Pain seared through her. He was lying utterly motionless on his side.

"You are a filthy man," she said.

"Nothing a bath won't cure," Wilkes said. His eyes darkened, and she flinched. "Ah, you're remembering those baths aboard my ship, aren't you? And how I watched you and admired you."

"No, I am remembering how I coshed you on the head. I wish only that I'd hit you harder."

"Such a pity," Wilkes said before turning his attention to the trail in front of them.

"What is?" Jules demanded.

"That you are married, my dear. I wanted to marry you, but now you'll just have to be my mistress. Please me, and I will keep you with me."

"I won't please you, I'll kill you."

He threw back his head and laughed. "You've lost your girl's terror, haven't you? Now that you know about plowing, I fancy you will certainly please me in bed."

She shuddered, and she knew he saw it. She closed her eyes, but just for a moment. She had to keep alert, try to remember the way they were traveling.

Wilkes grew silent. He was thinking about his two men—Grabbler and Hawkins—scum, both of them. He didn't doubt for a moment that they'd want to share her. He considered not going to the caves where they awaited him.

When Jules suddenly dug her heels into her horse's belly, causing the mare to snort and rear back, tearing the reins from his hands, he knew he would need them. He caught the flying reins before Jules could grab them, and brought the frantic mare back down.

He crowded his horse next to the mare. He saw Jules breathing heavily, her eyes dilated. Without warning, he grabbed her about the waist and pulled her before him.

"How very stupid of you, my dear," he said softly.

Jules felt fear and rage flow through her. She began to struggle, striking at his face, her nails scoring his cheek.

He cursed, and dragged her off the horse. She fell onto her back, but the sharp stones digging into her body made no impression. She watched him pull off his belt.

She came up on her knees, and nearly fell back again, dizziness from the fall making her shaky.

Wilkes grabbed her wrists, forcing them together, and bound them with the belt. He saw her flinch, and loosened the binding leather just a bit.

"There," he said. He clasped her beneath her armpits and pulled her to her feet. For a moment he brought her against him, and Jules went rigid.

"No," she gasped. "No!"

"Well, not yet, at any rate," Wilkes said. He grabbed her chin to hold her still, and kissed her deeply. Jules felt his tongue probing against her tightly pursed lips. She opened her mouth and felt him slip in. She bit him, hard.

His yelp of pain brought her but a moment's pleasure. Her head reeled back at the hard slap on her cheek. She would have fallen had he not held her.

"If ever you do that again," he said, his face so close to hers that she could feel his breath fanning against her skin, "I will make you regret it. I might consider sharing you with Grabbler and Hawkins. I promise you, Juliana, you wouldn't like that. They are not . . . gentle men."

She stood rigid, saying nothing. Wilkes studied

her face for a long moment; then, satisfied that she understood him, he kissed her again. This time when his tongue probed between her lips, he felt her shudder. With distaste. That would change, he thought. Yes, she would change.

He hauled her in front of him on his horse again. He left her mare, knowing the animal would straggle back to the nigger town eventually. He hoped it would. If her bodyguard didn't make it, the mare would. *I want that husband of yours to come after you. I want to kill that bastard, kill him slow.* He looked back to see the mare already trotting back toward the town, and smiled.

They rode for several more hours, southward, hugging the cliffs overlooking the ocean. He allowed his hand to move upward to cup her breast. He felt her suck in her breath and shudder. He only smiled.

Jules closed her eyes against his hated hand. He's going to rape me, she thought. All the old terrors, the old nightmares, rose to choke her. She trembled, hating herself for showing him any reaction at all. Her only relief was that Michael was safe. With Byrony. But Thackery . . . She felt tears burn her eyes. Please, she prayed, let him be all right.

"Time to let Mammy Bath help you out of those clothes," Saint said, smiling at Byrony. "Call me when you're in bed."

Byrony's lips tightened as a contraction grabbed her belly. She saw Brent's white face, and tried to smile at him. It was she who said, "I'm just fine, love. You mustn't worry."

"Let's get this chile into the world, little missis," Mammy Bath said, and tugged at Byrony's arm.

Saint watched until Byrony disappeared from view at the top of the stairs. He turned to Brent. "If you like, you can stay with her for a while. Talk to her, distract her. First, though, let me examine her."

Brent nodded, his throat too tight from fear to let words out.

"That's right," Saint said on a grin, and clapped Brent's back. "You think celibate thoughts."

"Just wait until Jules is pregnant," Brent managed.

Saint was silent a moment. "It's a sobering thought."

This would be a long labor, he thought a few minutes later, gently easing his fingers from Byrony's body. Dammit! He forced a smile. "Just continue breathing easy, Byrony. That's it. Now, let me get your husband for you."

The pains were coming more quickly some three hours later, but still she was long from delivery. Brent was talking at his wife nonstop, nonsense, really, but it did distract her a bit.

Byrony gasped suddenly, a small cry tearing from her throat. Her body arched upward.

Brent sent Saint an agonized, helpless look, and Saint said quickly, "Breathe slowly, that's it. Now, Byrony, did I tell you about what was done to the expectant fathers in a long-ago civilization? No, I guess I didn't. You listen to me now, and you too, Brent. You see, these folk were very advanced. For every hour the woman was in labor, her husband was hung upside down by his heels beside her bed. Even after the baby was born, the father had to look at his son or daughter upside down and nod in approval before he was released."

"Talk about celibate thoughts," Brent said.

"You made that up, Saint!" Byrony gasped, her laugh cut off by another contraction.

"Nope, I swear. Now, the Siamese had an interesting method. After the birth of a woman's first child, she continued in her bed, exposing her abdomen and her back to the heat of a blazing fire not two feet distant from her. It was kept going night and day for an entire month, the husband in charge. The practice had at least one virtue—it allowed the woman all the rest she needed. What do you think of that?"

"I prefer Brent hanging by his heels," Byrony said.

"I'll hang myself by anything you want," Brent said as he gently wiped the perspiration from her forehead. "Well, not anything," he added.

Saint rose and stretched. He was racking his brain for more stories when he heard a shout from downstairs. "Stay put, Brent," he said. "I'll see what's going on."

He bounded down the stairs. Just inside the door lay Thackery at Mammy Bath's feet. His shirt was soaked with blood. Saint felt himself go cold.

He lifted the man in his arms and carried him to the dining table. "Mammy, get me hot water and my bag from upstairs. Quick!"

He cut away Thackery's shirt and saw the bullet wound in his chest.

"Dr. Saint."

"You just lie still, Thackery, just lie still."

"He got Mrs. Saint, he shot me and left me for dead, I guess. God, I let you down."

"It's all right—" Saint began, only to watch Thackery slump again into unconsciousness at the same time a piercing scream came from upstairs.

Brent appeared in the doorway a few moments later, his face white. "Saint, what the hell . . . !"

"Wilkes has Jules. He shot Thackery."

"Damnation! Oh God, no!"

Saint closed his eyes a moment, trying to think clearly, calmly. "Brent," he said at last, "listen to me. Byrony's hurting, but the baby won't be here for a while yet. I want you to stay with her . . . hell, man, make up stories, anything. I'll patch up Thackery."

"Then what will we do?"

Saint knew he couldn't leave Byrony. Yet that bastard Wilkes had his wife. "I don't know," he said. "Go to your wife now."

Alone with Thackery, Saint quickly dug out the bullet. He wanted Thackery conscious to tell him where Wilkes had captured her, but not before he'd gotten the bullet out. He was a strong man, a healthy man. He would live. Mammy Bath stood at his elbow, handing him instruments, cloths as he asked for them. Within minutes Thackery's shoulder was bound firmly.

"Now the smelling salts, Mammy," Saint said. He waved them under Thackery's nose. "Thackery," he said, leaning over the man. "I know you hurt and I'll give you some laudanum in just a moment. Tell me where you were when Wilkes shot you."

"Better yet, let him tell me. You wouldn't know, Saint, even if he told you."

Saint moved aside and let Brent lean over Thackery.

For a moment the pain was so great that Thackery couldn't breathe.

"It's all right, John," Brent said. "Take your time."

"At the northeast edge of the valley near MacGiver's place. I saw him heading south with her, and west, toward the ocean. He knew, Dr. Saint, oh yes, he knew that Miz Hammond was going to have the baby. He timed it that way."

Saint gently patted Thackery's shoulder to calm him.

There was another piercing scream from upstairs, and both men froze.

30

Brent felt fear crawl through him.

"You've got to go, love," Byrony whispered. "You've got to bring her back safely. I have a saint to look after me. A real-live saint. Go, love."

Then she was lost to him and to reason, her eyes glazing with pain.

A man shouldn't have to make such a choice, Saint thought, even as he gently rubbed Byrony's back to ease the contraction. He met Brent's eyes.

"Take care of my wife, Saint," Brent said. "I'll get Jules, I swear it. And I'll kill the bastard, you can count on that."

But *I* want to kill him, Saint thought, exhilarated by the rage that filled him.

He nodded then, unable to find words.

He watched Brent lean down and kiss his wife's pale lips.

Then he was gone. Saint listened to his purposeful stride down the front stairs.

Saint walked to the window that faced the front of the house. He saw Brent tie a rifle to his saddle, saw him thrust two guns into his belt. A half-dozen men, all of them black, waited for him to mount.

The horses whinnied and reared. Then they were

gone, leaving only the thick welter of dust kicked up from the horses' hooves.

It's just as well I didn't tell him, Saint thought, walking back to the bed. He sat down beside Byrony and gently took her limp hand into his. "Listen to me, Byrony," he said, his voice low and insistent, pitched to cut through her pain. "The baby's turned wrong and I've got to straighten him. Byrony, do you understand me?"

He realized that she didn't. He called to Mammy Bath. "Come here and hold her. You heard what I told her?"

"Yes, Docta Saint, I heard."

It wasn't the first time Saint had wished his hands were smaller. There was no help for it, of course. He had to try to turn the baby. If he failed, he knew Byrony Hammond would die. *And what of Jules? What of his beautiful, sweet wife? What was Wilkes saying to her, doing to her?*

Saint shook himself and forced his mind to the matter at hand.

"It is quite odd, I'll admit that," Jameson Wilkes said, and unconsciously tightened his arm around Jules's waist. But he'd wanted her too long, so long in fact that he could no longer remember when she wasn't in his thoughts. And in his opium dreams.

He sounds so reasonable, so *reasoning*, Jules thought, a stirring of hope going through her. "I can be nothing to you," she continued, her voice as persuasive as she could make it. "You've only imagined that you want me. But I am a married woman. I am not a virgin any longer. Didn't you tell me that my virginity was my only value?"

"Yes," Wilkes said. "That's what I told you."

"Then why?"

He felt the agony in his belly growing more insistent, more unrestrained, and was unable for the moment to answer her. The pain was the reality.

Her voice thin and high, Jules said, "You're old enough to be my father! Do you want a daughter? Are you so twisted that—?"

He tightened his arm about her waist, cutting off her breath. "Shut up," he said. He laughed humorlessly and said to himself, "Hell, what I need is your damned husband." His laughter trickled away. No one could help him, cure him. He was tired now, and worried. And he felt so old, so damnably used up, so finished. No! He shook his head and forced his mind into clear channels. He would handle Hawkins and Grabbler. The scum wanted the money he'd promised them more than a woman.

He watched the sun disappear in a ball of vivid red. He'd always been in awe of sunsets over the ocean. They were like a short burst of the most awesome Chinese fireworks. Never to see them again . . . He felt Juliana sag against him and breathed a sigh of relief.

"It's almost as if he wants us to track him," said Josh, a black man Brent had grown up with at his father's plantation, Wakehurst. He straightened, his eyes on Brent. "We saw Miz Saint's mare—"

"Which means he's carrying her on his horse and that will slow him down," Brent finished, shading his eyes toward the sun that was glowing fiercely over the ocean.

"That's not the point," Josh said.

"No, it isn't. I'm afraid I do know what the point is. Not only does he want Jules, he also wants Saint. Revenge, I suppose, since Saint saved her from him. Stole her, I guess, is Wilkes's reasoning."

But why did he wait until Byrony had gone into labor to take her? Did he believe Saint would leave her and come after his wife? No, he added mentally, Wilkes just wanted enough time. And, it seemed, he wanted Saint to be in a damnable position. The cruel bastard. "We've only got another hour of light," he said abruptly, and dug his heels into his stallion's sides.

But they hadn't found her when night hit. It was dark as pitch, only a sliver of moon, clouds obscuring the stars. They couldn't track any more until morning.

Brent didn't know what to do. He was faced with the most painful decision of his life.

"I'm sorry, Brent," Josh said, laying his huge black hand on his friend's arm. "Real sorry. But you can't go back, now now. Four hours there, four hours back. You'd be exhausted, and Missis Saint needs a functioning man, not a piece of dead meat."

Brent gave Josh a twisted smile. Then he closed his eyes, praying toward the cloud-strewn heavens, praying that his wife was all right, that Jules wasn't being savaged at this moment, praying that life would somehow become normal again.

"We need to build a fire," Brent said. "It'll be colder than a dead stone before long."

The cave was damp and chill despite the smoking fire in front of her. Jules drew her legs closer, kept her head down.

"She's a purty little thing," said Hawkins. "Lookee there, she knows I'm talkin' about her. She quivered all over."

Hawkins chuckled and emptied his tin cup of the remains of his coffee.

"It's time for you to spell Grabbler," said Wilkes. "Take him something to eat while you're at it."

He felt better. The opium always dulled the pain, for a while at least. He'd not taken too much to dull his mind.

"You gonna fuck the little gal while we're gone?"

"Get out, Hawkins," Wilkes said.

"Looks awful cold, she does," Hawkins said. "A nice big man atween her legs would warm her up."

Jameson Wilkes looked Hawkins square in the face. God, he was a villainous-looking creature, his gaunt face covered with a thick black beard, hiding, Wilkes knew, a puckered, ugly scar that ran the full length of his cheek. "You want her or the money?" He forced himself to shrug. "It's up to you. You don't get both. And you know, don't you, my friend, that the money isn't with me."

Jules felt her blood run cold at Wilkes's emotionless voice. She kept her eyes on the cave floor. The dirt was soft and very black, she thought vaguely. She tried not to think of Byrony in agony, tried not to think of Michael and Brent.

"Hell," Hawkins muttered finally, the toe of his dirty boot kicking at the fire's embers, "a man can always get hisself some tail."

"Tell Grabbler the same thing," Wilkes said coldly. "With what you two will earn, you'll be able to buy all the whores you want."

There was no more talk until Hawkins had left the

cave. Wilkes said calmly to Jules, "A pity, my dear, that I can't offer you a bath—or a bed, for that matter. I do apologize. I don't believe, however, that we will have to remain here much longer. Since it's dark, we'll be staying here the night. I suggest you get some sleep."

Spend the long night with this man and those other two villains? "Why are we remaining here at all?"

Wilkes studied her pale face in the soft glow of the fire. Her riding hat was long gone, and her beautiful hair was in riotous curls and tangles over her shoulders and down her back. There was a smudge of dirt on her cheek.

He was proud of her cold voice because he knew how afraid she was.

"I don't think you need to know that just yet," he said. No, he thought, if he told her, she'd become a wild thing, he knew.

"What are you going to do to me?"

He laughed softly. "Not fuck you, my dear, as Hawkins so crudely phrased it. Not yet, in any case. Not until we're away from here and safe."

Safe! "Not ever," Jules said. "No, not ever."

"I know," he said easily. "Your huge husband would kill me, is that right?"

"No," Jules said, "*I* would kill you."

He swooped down and kissed her hard on the mouth, then moved before she could react. "Get some sleep, Juliana." He gave her a smile that made her shudder. "If you need to relieve yourself, I suggest you ask me to be your companion."

Saint sat beside Byrony, his chin resting on his folded hands. The bedroom was in darkness save for the one lamp that cast dim shadows on Byrony's pale face. He'd finally given her some chloroform and she was in a stuporous sleep. He prayed she would regain some strength, because there were still hours before the child would birth itself.

At least he'd managed to turn the baby. He could still feel Byrony's pain, the dreadful stretching of her small body as he'd eased his hand into her. But the child was now head-down, as it should be.

He finally slept himself, fitfully, his thoughts of his wife. What had happened to her? It was twelve o'clock, midnight.

When Byrony awoke she lay for a moment in a painless, vague realm. She saw Saint's face above her, gentle, kind, yes, so very kind. She ran her tongue over her dry lips.

"Some water, Byrony," he said, and helped her sip from the glass.

The pain was nearer now, bringing her to full awareness.

"Chauncey told me you'd tell me where you got your nickname, Saint," she said, striving desperately for reason, for control over her pain-racked body.

"Yes," he said, "I'll tell you. You breathe deeply now, and when that contraction builds, I want you to push with all your strength."

"I don't think I have much more strength," Byrony said.

"Don't you talk like that," Saint said, his voice hard and cold. "You're young and strong. You're going to birth that baby soon, yes, very soon. Do you hear me, Byrony?"

"I hear you," she said, her voice so hoarse and raw that she wondered he could even understand her.

The contraction built, and she wanted to die, to do anything to escape the pain. But she heard his voice telling her to push, and she did, with all her might.

"Now," Saint said when the pain eased a bit, "let me tell you about my nickname. Look at my face, Byrony. Don't fight the pain. You know what you have to do and you will do it. Now, it was when I was a young man, at Harvard Medical School. Various folk would provide the students with corpses to dissect. Breathe sharp, shallow breaths, Byrony! Yes, that's it."

"I don't know if I want to hear any more of this story, Saint."

"It ends well, I promise."

He waited, hearing her scream, softer now because her throat was raw from her cries, saw her arch, and said, "Push, Byrony!" He knew she was trying, but she was weakening.

Jules, where are you?

It was four o'clock in the morning. Nearing dawn. When most deaths and most births occurred. He shook himself.

Byrony struggled to hold to something real, not to be dragged into the endless pit. "Tell me, Saint!"

"Yes, well, one day they wheeled in the body of a man who'd just expired at the hospital. The professor, Old Hook Nose, we young men called him, was waving his scalpel about, on the point of demonstrating to us stupid students how one was to proceed. But you see, Byrony, the man wasn't dead. I grabbed Old Hook Nose's wrist just as it was descending. There was a lot of shouting and cursing that I, a wretched student, would dare attack such a venerable man. But I'd seen the eyelids of the 'dead man' flicker. I thank the good Lord to this day that I'm a large man. I had to fight off a good ten men, Old Hook Nose included. Then, my dear, the supposed dead man opened his eyes. It was he, Robert Gallagher, who named me Saint."

"Saint, make it stop!"

He wondered briefly if she'd even understood him. He held her, felt the awful wrenching pain, and knew he must do something or she would be too weak to birth the child. She would die, and the child with her.

"Byrony, listen to me!" He clasped her face between his large hands, shaking her until her eyes focused on his face. "I'm going to help you, do you hear me? No, don't close your eyes. Look at me, Byrony! Here's what you'll do."

He felt her tears wet his hands and wanted to weep himself. For her, for Jules. For poor Robert Gallagher, who'd been run down by a carriage six months after Saint had saved him from being cut open by Old Hook Nose.

Dear God, what was happening? Sunlight poured through the bedroom windows. He glanced a moment toward the clock.

"We got company, Mr. Wilkes," Hawkins said, poking his head into the cave. "Six, seven men, riding slow, tracking."

"Ah," Wilkes said, his eyes turning toward Jules. He saw the wild hope in her eyes. "No, my dear, it won't be your husband, at least it shouldn't be. He wouldn't leave a woman in labor, now, would he?"

"I bet it's that gambler Hammond, the man who started the nigger town."

"Yes, I suppose so. They're all so honorable, aren't they?"

"They aren't scum like you," Jules said.

"Now, little girlie—" Hawkins began.

"Shut up, both of you," Wilkes said, and got to his feet. He cursed the damned pain, but managed to keep his expression impassive. He wanted more opium, needed it desperately, but he couldn't allow himself to escape, not yet. He said to Jules, "You will stay put, my dear, or I will kill Mr. Hammond. Hawkins, you come with me."

Jules watched the two men leave. She scrambled to her feet, looking about frantically for a weapon, any kind of weapon. She feverishly clawed through the bedrolls. Nothing. She felt dirty, her bones ached from sleeping on the dirt cave floor, and she was more afraid than she had ever been in her life. Before, it had been just her. Now it was Brent.

She crept toward the cave opening and peered out. She could see Wilkes's back, Hawkins just behind him, and Grabbler off to her left in the notch of a pine tree. She saw the ocean beyond, calm, gray like a whitetip reef shark.

"This is it," Josh said, his voice low, nearly a whisper.

"Yes," Brent said, nodding. He looked up at the cliff above them and scanned the wall. He heard a horse nicker. He held up his hand for silence, then rode forward a bit.

He called out, "All right, Wilkes. We are here. What the hell do you want?"

"Hammond?"

"Yes, of course. You know that Jules's husband is with my wife. What do you want?"

Jules, Wilkes thought blankly. How odd. It sounded ridiculous. He much preferred "Juliana." Had her damned husband given her that nickname? He wanted to kill him.

"You may be certain I don't want you," Wilkes shouted. "I want you and your niggers to take a message back to Saint Morris. He'll come here alone, or he will never see her again."

"Why didn't you just wait until he would track his wife?"

"Very simple, Hammond," Wilkes called out. "She wasn't out of his sight and wouldn't be until your dear wife started her birthing pains. He would not allow his innocent wife to be present, of that I was certain."

Brent cursed softly. Why had he imagined all sorts of wily, bizarre plots on Wilkes's part? It was all so simple really. And Wilkes was right, completely right. It was the first time Saint had let Jules out of his sight. Saint and Thackery had dogged her every step.

"Now, as I figure it, Hammond, by the time you get back to that town of yours, your baby will be born, that or your precious wife will be dead. In any case, Saint Morris will be free to come after his wife. Give him my message."

Brent felt his jaw tighten until pain seared his face. What the hell could he do? *Byrony, no! You won't die. Saint promised.*

Jules felt her blood run cold. Wilkes not only wanted her, he also wanted to kill Michael. She couldn't, wouldn't allow it. She didn't know what to do. Suddenly she yelled at the top of her lungs, "Brent, don't get Michael! He wants to kill him. Don't let him leave Byrony!"

"Jules, are you all right?" Brent yelled back. His horse shied sideways, and it took a moment of his concentration to get him back under control.

"I'm all right," Jules shouted back. "Don't let Michael come here!"

Wilkes was beside her, pulling her roughly back into the cave. He flung her to the dirt floor. "You keep your mouth shut, Juliana, or I'll kill Hammond, and his niggers can deliver my message to your precious husband."

She stared at him, hatred for him filling her. She wanted to spew her hatred out to him, but at that moment she saw his face pale, saw him clutch at his belly. My God, she thought, he's ill!

"You stay put," Wilkes said again, his voice low, his teeth gritted, "or I'll plow your belly in front of your precious husband. You understand me?"

"I understand," Jules said. She was silent a moment, then said very quietly, "Do you want my husband for revenge or do you want a doctor?"

"Interesting question," Wilkes said, and laughed. "Don't move, Juliana!" He walked from the cave, not looking back, for there was nothing she could do. Nothing.

Saint ripped off the sheet that covered Byrony. He couldn't allow it to go on any longer. He had to do it. "Mammy," he said curtly, "take her hands and hold her steady. Byrony, you're not going to give up, you're going to push with all your strength."

She made a soft mewling sound. "No, I can't," she whispered.

"Damn you, Byrony, do as I tell you!"

He thought he saw a ghost of a smile on her white lips. He saw the contraction and splayed his hands over her belly. "Push!" he shouted at her, and bore down with his hands. Almost, he thought, hope welling up in him. "Again, Byrony!" This time he slipped his hand inside her. He felt the baby's head, gently found the tiny shoulders and pulled. He shut his mind to Byrony's screams and eased the baby from the birth canal. Damn him for a fool, he should have given her more chloroform, but there hadn't been time.

"My God," he said, cuddling the slippery little body against his chest, fierce joy filling him, "it's a boy you've got, Byrony. A beautiful boy."

Byrony was unconscious.

"Mammy, bathe our little fellow here. Ah, that's it. A lusty cry. He's ready for the world. Then wrap him in a warm blanket."

"I know," Mammy said, affronted, and Saint smiled. The old woman was as exhausted as he was, but still feisty as hell.

He worked over Byrony, more mechanically now, because she would be all right. He'd taken the risk and she'd survived. It was Jules who filled his thoughts. Had Brent found her? What had happened? "Damn," he said softly. So many questions and no answers. He realized his hands were shaking, fear washing through him in great relentless waves.

Mammy Bath handed him the baby some minutes later. The child was a carbon copy of Byrony, not Brent. Honey-colored hair, fair-complexioned. Perhaps there was divine justice, he thought. Byrony had done all the work, suffered more than a human being should ever have to, so it was only fair that her child look like her.

He smiled down at the wizened little face, his finger under the tiny chin.

"I'll brings a sugar tit for that little man," said Mammy Bath. "His mama won't have no milk for a while yet."

"Good idea," Saint said. And he began to pace the bedroom. He was still pacing when Brent Hammond burst through the door two hours later, his face drawn and tense, his eyes going immediately to his wife.

Saint said quickly, "She's all right. You have a son and he looks like Byrony."

"She's all right?" Brent repeated slowly. His throat felt suddenly very scratchy, and tears burned his eyes. He gulped. "She's not moving."

"You wouldn't be either. She's asleep. Your son is in the next room with Mammy Bath."

Brent dragged his fingers through his hair. "We've got trouble, Saint, dammit."

"Tell me while you look at your son," Saint said, forcing himself to remain calm.

31

The men rode steadily south, high on the cliffs above the ocean, Brent beside Saint at their head.

"Have you any ideas, Saint?" Brent asked.

Saint shook his head, his eyes straight between his horse's ears. "None other than getting my hands around that bastard's neck." Why, Saint continued to wonder, did Wilkes want him? If it were revenge in the man's mind, it was chilling. He had Jules, why him? Why the elaborate ruse?

Brent well understood his feelings, and merely nodded. They had plenty of time to devise some sort of plan. He said finally, "I thank you for saving Byrony."

"She did all the work," Saint said, drawing himself from his thoughts. He quirked an eyebrow at Brent. "She was pleased that the baby looks like her and not you, a swarthy pirate."

"Gambler, not pirate. Hell, I wouldn't have cared if the baby looked like you, Saint!"

"The perfect child indeed. Incidentally, Brent, go see Maggie before you begin relations again with your wife. I suggest contraception. Another child in perhaps three years, then I'd be satisfied and call a halt."

"I don't want her to go through that ever again," Brent said, his face growing pale with remembered anxiety.

"That's up to the both of you." Saint fell silent, and Brent knew his thoughts had returned to his wife.

It was early afternoon when they reached the cliff.

"You can't just go up there, Saint," Brent said again. "He wants to kill you."

"He won't," Saint said. For a moment he wondered why he'd said it with such confidence. Hell, he had no reason to be confident. It was just that he had this feeling . . . So many things about Wilkes didn't make sense.

Brent sighed. "The two men he's got, we'll try to pick them off. Josh is the best shot I know, after Thackery."

"Thackery can give him lessons in another week or so. That man's as strong as an ox, thank God."

"I still don't like this," Brent said.

Saint shrugged, his thoughts moving ahead to his confrontation with Jameson Wilkes.

Jules felt numb. She'd spent the entire morning hating herself for her wretched helplessness. Hawkins had eyed her again, but she realized she wasn't afraid of him, nor was she afraid of Wilkes, not anymore.

She was afraid for Michael. He would come, she knew he would come. She didn't know what to do.

"Ah," Wilkes said, an odd relieved tone in his voice, "I do believe your precious husband has arrived."

Jules bounded to her feet and rushed toward the cave entrance, screaming, "Michael! No! Go away!"

Wilkes jerked her backward and she landed in the dirt on her bottom. She scrambled to her feet.

"You stay put or I'll put a bullet through him before you can even see him."

Jules believed him. Oh, Michael, she thought, closing her eyes a moment, why did you come? Why do you have to be so noble?

She prayed that Byrony was all right.

Then she heard his voice, strong and deep, coming from below.

"Wilkes! Can you hear me?"

"Good afternoon, Dr. Morris," Wilkes shouted down. "I see you brought your friends. Leave them down there and come up alone!"

I've got to do something! Without conscious thought, Jules rushed at Wilkes, clutching at the gun in his belt. He whirled about, caught her hand, and struck her with the flat of his palm.

She staggered back, and he came toward her, drawing his gun as he stalked her.

Saint felt the barrel of the gun in the small of his back. He didn't pause, but continued walking until he came into the cave entrance.

"Here he is, Mr. Wilkes," Hawkins said, and gave Saint a shove.

Saint blinked rapidly to adjust his eyes to the dim interior of the cave. Wilkes was holding Jules in front of him, one arm across her breasts, the gun in his other hand.

"Hello, Dr. Morris," Wilkes said. "I have wanted to meet you, indeed I have. I believe it was you who clipped my jaw."

"I was hoping," Saint said calmly, his eyes boring into Wilkes's face, "that I'd broken your jaw that night at the Crooked House. Did I?"

"No, no, you didn't. Of course, I have heard that you aren't a violent man," he added, his eyes boring into Saint's.

"I'm not. But I realized months ago that I should have killed you." He shrugged, his eyes roving over his wife's strained face. "Then again, I'm supposed to save lives. You have always posed me a difficult problem, philosophically, at least."

"Stay where you are, Dr. Morris!" Wilkes pressed the gun against Jules's left breast.

Saint didn't move. He met Jules's wildly frightened eyes. "Are you all right, love?" he asked quietly.

"Yes, yes, of course. You shouldn't have come, Michael," she said, her voice an agonized whisper.

"I'm your husband, little fool." He met Wilkes's eyes. "I *am* her husband, you know, in all ways. Now, what do you want, Wilkes?"

The gun jerked and Saint froze.

"You took her from me," Wilkes said in a low, hoarse voice, the pain in his belly nearly bending him double. God, he'd just had as much opium as he could take and still be coherent. "I wanted her and you stole her from me!"

"That isn't how I seem to remember it," Saint said slowly. "You were selling her. Hardly the same thing. All you lost was money."

"I would have gotten her back."

"Would you have? Really? After she'd been raped and abused? And what would you have done with her, Wilkes? Raped and abused her more?"

"Shut up, damn you! You know nothing about it, nothing!"

"I know that you are not . . . thinking straight." *His eyes look odd. His flesh is gray. The flesh around his eyes and mouth is scored with pain.* "Let her go, Wilkes. If you kill me, she will kill you. Perhaps not today, but tomorrow or the next day."

"She is mine!"

"Like hell she is."

Jules could bear it no longer. "Michael, I'll go with him, please, just leave. I don't want you hurt . . . please leave."

He merely smiled at her, shaking his head. "He wouldn't let me leave even if he trusted your promise, sweetheart."

"No," Wilkes said, the pain so bad now that he spoke through gritted teeth. "No, Doctor, you aren't leaving."

Jules felt him jerk behind her.

It was then Saint saw the spasm of pain on Wilkes's face. It was fearful, his mouth working like a death rictus. "Has she already tried to kill you?" he said.

"No, damn you! Oh, my God! My belly . . ."

Jules felt him ease his hold on her as his body bent forward with pain. She didn't think, merely acted. She sent her elbow into his stomach, and he yowled with agony. Jules grabbed at the gun. In the next instant, Saint jerked away her hand, pulled the gun from Wilkes's unresisting fingers. He met Wilkes's glazed eyes. He felt a spasm of pity.

"You're dying, aren't you?" he said very softly, knowing that only Wilkes could hear him.

"I didn't need you to tell me, damn you!" Wilkes

was panting, his breathing an agony. He staggered backward.

"No," Saint said, "no, you didn't. How long have you lived on opium? How long have you had none to ease the pain?"

But Jameson Wilkes couldn't answer. His mind was clouded with agony, with strange broken images of the ravaged face of his wife, long dead.

Then Saint knew. He was on opium, to his limit.

"Michael!"

Saint whirled about at Jules's shout, saw Hawkins looming in the mouth of the cave. He fired. There was another shot, and Jules saw a bullet slam into the wall of the cave. She watched, frozen, as Hawkins, a bewildered look on his face, stumbled forward, then fell on his face.

There was a loud shout from outside the cave. Then a rapid staccato, at least six more shots.

Suddenly Saint felt Wilkes's hands clutching at his wrist, bearing downward. Again he looked into Wilkes's eyes, and saw madness and more pain than a human being should have to suffer. Stomach cancer, he thought, a slow, agonizing death. He saw something else in his eyes, something he couldn't yet understand. Then he did. He realized, deep in his soul, that Wilkes could have shot him in the confusion. He saw another pistol lying in the dust very close to Wilkes and knew Wilkes could easily have grabbed it. He knew that Wilkes had made a decision. For a split second Saint wavered. He closed his eyes, knowing what was to happen, what the dying man wanted to happen. He let him bring the gun between them.

Jules was weeping softly. "No, please, no."

There was a muffled shot.

Jules screamed.

Neither man moved. Then Saint very gently eased Wilkes's limp body down to the cave floor.

Jules backed away, turning her head, unable to bear the fixed gaze in Jameson Wilkes's eyes.

Brent burst into the cave, drew up short, and slowly slipped his gun back into its holster. "He's dead?" He nodded toward Wilkes's body.

"Yes," Saint said. *Just as he wanted to be. Thank God, he didn't linger, even for a moment. Jules couldn't have borne that.*

"Josh shot the other man. I see you got this scum," he added, nodding toward Hawkins' body.

Saint nodded. He looked one last time at the man who had caused so such suffering, lived with such suffering, then walked slowly over to his wife. "Love," he said, taking her into his arms. "It's all over now."

Jules leaned against him, beyond tears now. She wrapped her arms around his back, burrowing her face into his shoulder, feeling his strong heartbeat against her. He rocked her, gently stroking his hand through her tangled hair. He looked over at Wilkes again, a strange sadness filling him. Had Jules somehow become twisted in his opium dreams into a fantasy to save him from himself? Or had he wanted her with him when he died, to complete some eerie ritual, some twisted dream? Saint shook his head. He doubted he would ever understand. He certainly wouldn't speak to Jules about it. She'd suffered too much already. And most of it had been for him.

"You're a godmother, Jules," Saint said. "Come, let's go admire Byrony's perfect child."

"I'm a godmother?" she repeated blankly, and he knew she was striving desperately for something real to grasp.

"Yes, and I'll wager Brent will even let you suggest names for the little fellow."

"Yes," Brent said, "I will, Jules."

"I want to see my godson," she said.

"I'm proud as hell of you," Saint said, kissing her, and led her from the cave.

He became aware of Wilkes's blood on the front of his shirt.

There was so much hell on earth. But then, there were also other people who made life bearable, people who made meaning of things, who gave joy and love. And he had his wife, he had his Jules. He realized something then that would be with him throughout his life: he loved someone more than his own life. God, he was lucky. The fragility of life, the preciousness of life . . .

He clutched her against his side. And that's where she would be, always. Beside him, part of him.

Jules stared around the Hammonds' parlor, feeling disoriented for a moment, until Michael said gently to her, "You think we can make as cute a little boy as Byrony did?"

"What about me?" Brent said, grinning down at his wife. She was still dreadfully pale, but the sparkle was back in her eyes. Their child, Damon Michael, was sleeping in a crib beside her chair.

"What about you?" Saint said, his voice sardonic. "All you did was enjoy yourself, repeatedly."

"So true," Byrony said, giving her husband a radiant smile. "Jules, if ever you tire of that husband of yours, I will gladly take him. A most useful man. A most caring man, and he told me the most unusual story about how saints are created."

Saint cocked a brow at her but said nothing. He was, quite frankly, surprised that she remembered.

"I should offer the same for Brent," Jules said. "If it weren't for him, I should be on board a ship sailing for China."

No, Saint wanted to tell her, there would have been no ship. There would have been naught but an ending—and Wilkes had known it. Poor bloody bastard.

"I believe we should drink to how great we all are," Brent said. "Can Thackery have a glass of champagne, Saint?"

"Mr. John Thackery," Saint said, giving a heartfelt smile to the grinning black man, "has my thanks and good wishes for all eternity, not to mention free medical care."

"Excellent." Brent shouted. "Mammy! Champagne for everyone!"

"As for you, little one," Saint said to his wife, "I fully intend to cosset you and love you until I'm too old to move."

"In that case," said Jules, squeezing her husband's hand, her eyes twinkling, "I shall just have to give you my derringer."

"*Derringer?*"

"Yes, and you can stomp on it. Again."

"Jules, if ever I—"

"Perhaps Penelope will give hers to Thomas."

"What the hell are you talking about? Penelope? Don't tell me that the two of you—"

Saint broke off at Brent's shout of laughter.

"So much for cosseting," Byrony said. "Ah, the champagne."

"We'll give Saint the bottle," Brent said. "He looks like he needs it."

About the Author

When best-selling historical romance writer Catherine Coulter is not at work on her latest novel, she spends her time sailing, playing the piano, or enjoying Mill Valley, California with her husband, Anton.

Catherine Coulter is the author of historical romances—*Devil's Embrace, Chandra, Devil's Daughter, Sweet Surrender, Fire Song, Midnight Star,* and *Wild Star* as well as of a number of Regency romances—*The Autumn Countess, The Rebel Bride, Lord Deverill's Heir, Lord Harry's Folly, The Generous Earl, An Honorable Offer, An Intimate Deception*—all available in Signet editions.

Visit
ReaderService.com
Today!

**As a valued member of the
Harlequin Reader Service,
you'll find these benefits and more at
ReaderService.com:**

- Try 2 free books from any series
- Access risk-free special offers
- View your account history & manage payments
- Browse the latest Bonus Bucks catalog

Don't miss out!

If you want to stay up-to-date on the latest at the Harlequin Reader Service and enjoy more content, make sure you've signed up for our monthly News & Notes email newsletter. Sign up online at ReaderService.com or by calling Customer Service at 1-800-873-8635.

COMING NEXT MONTH FROM
Love Inspired

THE AMISH MATCHMAKER'S CHOICE
Redemption's Amish Legacies • by Patricia Johns
Newly returned to the Amish community, Jake Knussli must find a wife in six months or lose his uncle's farm. Can matchmaker Adel Draschel secure a *frau* for him—before losing her own heart to the handsome farmer?

THEIR PRETEND COURTSHIP
The Amish of New Hope • by Carrie Lighte
Pressured by her stepfather to court, Eliza Keim begrudgingly walks out with blueberry farmer Jonas Kanagy—except Jonas is only trying to protect his brother from what he thinks are Eliza's heartbreaker ways. When the two are forced to make their courtship in name only look real, they may discover more than they bargained for...

GUARDING HIS SECRET
K-9 Companions • by Jill Kemerer
When Wyoming rancher Randy Watkins finds himself caring for his surprise baby nephew, he seeks the help of longtime friend Hannah Carr. But when her retired service dog seems to sense all is not right with Randy's health, will he trust Hannah with the truth?

THE RANCHER'S FAMILY LEGACY
The Ranchers of Gabriel Bend • by Myra Johnson
Building contractor Mark Caldwell is ready to inherit his grandfather's horse ranch and put his traumatic past behind him—if he can survive working in Texas Hill Country for a year. But when his dog bonds with local caterer Holly Elliot's son, can they put aside their differences and open their hearts?

HER MOUNTAIN REFUGE
by Laurel Blount
Widowed, pregnant and under the thumb of her controlling mother-in-law, Charlotte Tremaine needs help—but she doesn't expect it to come from her estranged childhood best friend. Yet letting Sheriff Logan Carter whisk her away to his foster mother's remote mountain home might be her best chance at a fresh start...

A MOTHER FOR HIS SON
by Betty Woods
In town to help her grandmother, chef Rachel Landry plans to use the time to heal her broken heart—not help Mac Greer with his guest ranch. But her growing affection for his little boy could be just the push she needs to once again see the possibility of something more...

LOOK FOR THESE AND OTHER LOVE INSPIRED BOOKS WHEREVER BOOKS ARE SOLD, INCLUDING MOST BOOKSTORES, SUPERMARKETS, DISCOUNT STORES AND DRUGSTORES.

LICNM0422

COUNTRY LEGACY COLLECTION

19 FREE BOOKS IN ALL!

Cowboys, adventure and romance await you in this new collection! Enjoy superb reading all year long with books by bestselling authors like Diana Palmer, Sasha Summers and Marie Ferrarella!

YES! Please send me the **Country Legacy Collection!** This collection begins with 3 FREE books and 2 FREE gifts in the first shipment. Along with my 3 free books, I'll also get 3 more books from the **Country Legacy Collection**, which I may either return and owe nothing or keep for the low price of $24.60 U.S./$28.12 CDN each plus $2.99 U.S./$7.49 CDN for shipping and handling per shipment*. If I decide to continue, about once a month for 8 months, I will get 6 or 7 more books but will only pay for 4. That means 2 or 3 books in every shipment will be FREE! If I decide to keep the entire collection, I'll have paid for only 32 books because 19 are FREE! I understand that accepting the 3 free books and gifts places me under no obligation to buy anything. I can always return a shipment and cancel at any time. My free books and gifts are mine to keep no matter what I decide.

☐ 275 HCK 1939   ☐ 475 HCK 1939

Name (please print)

Address   Apt. #

City   State/Province   Zip/Postal Code

Mail to the **Harlequin Reader Service:**
IN U.S.A.: P.O. Box 1341, Buffalo, NY 14240-8571
IN CANADA: P.O. Box 603, Fort Erie, Ontario L2A 5X3

"This community could be your home…"

"I'm going to stay," Jeb said, meaning it. "I'm Amish. I've been an Amish man lost in the world."

"You're not lost anymore," Rebecca replied, her eyes telling him the secrets she couldn't voice.

"No, I'm not alone, but I still have many roads to walk before I can be completely at peace."

"You did talk to the bishop. That is a start."

"It is. I have to let him know if I'm committed. Now, after your words to me, I am committed more than ever."

"I'm glad," she said, her hands clutched over her apron. "I like having you around."

He smiled. "I like being around you, but, Becca, we have to accept that before I can be true, I need to find God again. Then I'll work my way toward the other part of why I'm staying."

"And what would that be?" she asked, her breath held on the air.

"You, Becca," he whispered. "You make me feel this peace inside my soul."

With over seventy books published and millions in print, **Lenora Worth** writes award-winning romance and romantic suspense. Three of her books finaled in the ACFW Carol Awards, and her Love Inspired Suspense novel *Body of Evidence* became a *New York Times* bestseller. Her novella in *Mistletoe Kisses* made her a *USA TODAY* bestselling author. Lenora goes on adventures with her retired husband, Don, and enjoys reading, baking and shopping…especially shoe shopping.

Books by Lenora Worth

Love Inspired

Amish Seasons

Their Amish Reunion
Seeking Refuge
Secrets in an Amish Garden

Men of Millbrook Lake

Lakeside Hero
Lakeside Sweetheart
Her Lakeside Family

Texas Hearts

A Certain Hope
A Perfect Love
A Leap of Faith

Sunset Island

The Carpenter's Wife
Heart of Stone
A Tender Touch

Visit the Author Profile page at LoveInspired.com for more titles.

Secrets in an Amish Garden

Lenora Worth

LOVE INSPIRED

INSPIRATIONAL ROMANCE

LOVE INSPIRED®
INSPIRATIONAL ROMANCE

Recycling programs
for this product may
not exist in your area.

ISBN-13: 978-1-335-56767-3

Secrets in an Amish Garden

For questions and comments about the quality of this book, please contact us
at CustomerService@Harlequin.com.

Love Inspired
22 Adelaide St. West, 41st Floor
Toronto, Ontario M5H 4E3, Canada
www.LoveInspired.com

Printed in U.S.A.

Consider the lilies how they grow:
they toil not, they spin not; and yet I say
unto you, that Solomon in all his glory was
not arrayed like one of these. If then God so
clothe the grass, which is to day in the field,
and to morrow is cast into the oven; how much
more will he clothe you, O ye of little faith?
—*Luke* 12:27–28

To my dear editor Patience Bloom
for always helping me through the writing life.
You are the best!

Chapter One

❧

"April showers bring May flowers."

Rebecca Eicher smiled at her seven-year-old niece's solemn statement. "And who told you that, wise little Katie?"

"Daed," Katie said with a snaggle-toothed grin. "He's always telling me things."

"That's what makes *daeds* so special," Rebecca replied. She sure missed her parents, especially during spring. Glancing at the old clock on the kitchen wall, she said, "And it's time for you to run home. Your *mamm* will be wondering if Aunt Becca hid you under a honeysuckle bush."

"I won't fit under a bush," Katie said with her elbows out and her hands on her blue dress. "I'm getting taller every day."

"You for certain sure are," Rebecca replied as she took Katie's hand and guided her and the

bag of snickerdoodle cookies they'd just finished baking toward the front door. "Now, don't run or you'll break all the cookies and then the chickens will peck at them."

"I'll walk really slow," Katie retorted, walking like a creature from the forest, her steps wide and exaggerated.

"Perfect," Rebecca said. "I'll watch you across the road."

"And I'll watch for cars or buggies," Katie said, knowing the rules. "I promise."

Rebecca walked out to the end of the lane with Katie and gave her a kiss. "Okay, run along now, *liebling.*"

She loved her freckle-faced golden-haired niece as well as Katie's three older brothers, Michael, Elijah and Adam. Blessed that her own older brother, Noah, and his wife, Franny, lived across from her place, Rebecca turned back to her yard, the sign Noah had made for her a few years ago now showing a fresh coat of paint:

The Lily Lady.

The sign stated that in big black letters, with a variety of painted daylilies underneath and an arrow pointing to her home and the colorful fields beyond.

Ja, she was the lily lady all right. And right now, she needed what the other sign by her driveway asked for:

Help Wanted.

Dear Lord, send someone soon. Rebecca was having a hard time finding a permanent handyman to help her with not only the lilies but also everything else her parents' small farm required. Her helper of the last few years, Moses Yoder, had decided to move to a community in Ohio to be near his ailing sister. He'd left a month ago and she still hadn't found anyone to replace him.

Most men around here had to work their own land or had a regular job. And the young folks didn't want to work in a hot field most of the summer. They found summer work elsewhere or had to help their own families get through the crops.

She looked toward the sky, expecting more dark clouds full of rain, but the sun shone brightly in the midmorning sky. What a wet week it had been. Hoping her bulbs wouldn't rot away instead of blooming, she made it back to the front porch and turned to see Katie waving to her from Noah's porch.

Rebecca waved back. Then she noticed something else.

A man walking along the road.

People walked by here all the time. Rebecca loved to walk and often did that since she didn't like horses.

But this man looked different.

When he turned toward her house, she gasped and went inside. She had a phone she used for business. She'd use it to call the police, too, if need be.

The man kept walking, his dark hair shaggy around his face, his jeans worn and tattered. He carried an aged olive-colored pack on his back. He wasn't Amish.

Rebecca watched from the kitchen window. He came up onto the porch and stood at the unlocked screen door. One knock. Then another.

"Hello, anyone home? I came about the help-wanted ad." He stopped and Rebecca heard a distinctive sigh. "I need a job."

Rebecca had hoped someone Amish would take the job. She needed a handyman who liked working with the earth, someone who understood the art of growing lilies.

This man didn't look like that type.

More like a beggar wanting a *gut* meal.

"Hello? I have references. Mr. Hartford from the general store showed me your ad," he called again.

References. She'd verify that. And Mr. Hartford wouldn't send someone he didn't trust.

Yet, Rebecca hesitated. She wasn't sure what to do. She needed help now, and here he stood,

asking for a job. She watched him turn, his shoulders hunched in dejection, his head down as he eased off the porch.

Her spring season was here. She needed someone, had just prayed about it, and so far, this was the only person who'd shown any real interest. Well, the only person who looked strong enough for what the work demanded. She'd turned down two scrawny teens because she knew them to be troublemakers, and a *grossdaddi* who only wanted to get out of his rocking chair. But he could barely get up the porch steps. No one else had even tried to apply.

What should she do?

Rebecca stilled for two heartbeats, then hurried to the door.

"Wait."

The man turned around and looked up at her, his expression raw and edgy, dangerous. But his eyes—they held a world of hurt and pain. He looked broken. Completely broken.

She let out a little breath. He reminded her of someone—her deceased fiancé, John Kemp. Her heartbeat lifting to a new height, she blinked back tears. John had died when he was eighteen. Fifteen years ago. This stranger looked *Englisch*. He also looked lost.

"What's your name?" Rebecca asked, motioning him onto the porch while she gathered

her composure. His features only reminded her of John, but then she thought every day of the man she'd loved and planned to marry. She had to be imagining things. No amount of longing could bring John back.

Jebediah," he said, his voice like splintered wood. "Jebediah Martin."

That name didn't ring a bell with her, so she tried to relax. Pointing him to a rocking chair, she sat down on a nearby bench. "And why do you need this job?"

He glanced out at the yard and then back to her. "Because I need work. I need…money. I've been traveling and I wound up here."

"You have references?"

"Yes, a couple from other jobs."

"Do you know anyone here?"

"No."

"How do I know I can trust you?"

"You don't know, but you can trust me. I need a job."

"What can you tell me that would make me trust you?"

"Nothing. You *can* trust me."

Rebecca tried again. "Do you like working outside, with flowers and gardens? Do you know how to plow—with a horse pulling the plows?"

"I know horses, but as for gardening, I've

never done it before, but I can learn." He looked down at his old boots. "I know the earth, the seasons, the crops."

Rebecca lifted her hands, palms up, and let out an aggravated breath. "You're not impressing me."

The man finally looked directly into her eyes. "I told you I need a job. It's that simple."

Then he reached into the battered backpack and pulled out an envelope filled with folded papers. "Here."

He handed her two references—one from a restaurant owner in Indiana and one from a hotel where he'd cleaned rooms in Kentucky.

"These folks seem to think you're a *gut* worker."

"I am."

Trying hard to ignore the deep blue of his gaze, she said, "I grow lilies, you understand? I need someone with a strong back who can work long hours. I need someone to look after the horses—two of them. Red is the roan mare, and Silver is the draft horse. I have a small barn and stable. I have greenhouses and a vegetable garden and soon, my backyard and the lily field and the plant nursery will all be full of people buying lilies, other plants, and fresh vegetables. A lot of them *Englisch*."

"I can handle that."

"Horses?"

"I said I can handle horses. I grew up around horses."

She wondered if he could truly handle anything. With each question she asked, his eyes went dull and then lit up as if he'd just thought of that idea.

"What other jobs have you had besides the restaurant and cleaning hotels?"

He rubbed the dark stubble on his chin. "Let's see. Janitor. Bartender. Dog walker. Apartment cleaner. Trash man. Lumber company. Painter. Construction. Rented beach chairs to tourists in Florida."

Disbelief warred with curiosity. He'd been all around, it seemed. "But never gardening?"

"No. But… I like flowers. My mom used to grow a lot of flowers."

The way he said that coupled with the longing in his blue eyes told her what she needed to know. He was a black sheep, an outsider, a wayfarer. A man in need of something to cling to—in need of the earth and the wind, the sun and the rain. What should she do?

"Are you hungry?"

"Yes. And thirsty."

Rebecca made her decision, based on entertaining angels unaware. This man did not look like an angel, but he sure needed one. "Meet me

around back and I'll bring you some lemonade and a sandwich. Do you like cookies?"

His eyes stayed bright on that question. "Yes."

Jeb walked around the neat, compact white farmhouse, noticing all the colorful flowers in the yard. This place was so pretty and prim, it almost hurt his eyes to take it all in.

But then, he'd seen the ugly side of life for so long now, he'd forgotten that the earth was still beautiful.

He'd wound up here by sheer fate. Or God's will. After not finding work in another Pennsylvania community, Jeb had worked a few weeks with a building crew. But the whole operation got shut down due to outstanding permits. One night in his hotel room, he'd remembered some letters he'd kept through the years. Letters from his cousin who used to live here.

Campton Creek, Pennsylvania. He hopped on the next bus out and planned to find kinfolk here. Only, no one related to him still lived here. He'd gone into the local general store to buy some supplies, and while there he'd heard someone mention a local Amish woman was looking for help. Mr. Hartford had immediately told Jeb he should find out more.

The Lily Lady, they'd called her.

This little bit of earth was nice. This woman

was nice, too, despite her many questions. Legitimate questions, but pushy, all the same. She had pretty freckles and sun-streaked dark blond hair covered with a white *kapp*—a prayer bonnet. That *kapp* reminded him of his *mamm*.

He was a long way from home, but this town had sounded so peaceful and serene in his cousin's letters.

This place—the Lily Lady's place—certainly brought that feeling to his soul. But he wasn't sure she'd hire him, and he wouldn't blame her if she didn't.

He came around the house and stopped to take it all in. Daylilies, rows and rows, some with hardy blossoms ready to pop open, some just about ready to grow and bloom. He could smell the mixtures of a thousand scents. Lilies of the field.

He did not want to leave.

"Here you go."

He turned to find her with a wooden tray full of food and a tall glass of lemonade, the condensation on the side of the glass shimmering like teardrops.

Jeb hurried to take the tray.

"Denke," she said, pointing to a table on the porch. "Sit and eat and I'll talk."

He smiled at that, his brain rattled at find-

ing something to smile about. "Thank you for the food."

She nodded and tugged at a rebel strand of hair, tucking it behind her ear. "I live here alone, so I have plenty of leftovers."

After she said that, a wary glaze darkened her eyes. "My *bruder* and his family live across the road."

"So you're not too alone," he replied, hoping to reassure her. Then he decided to be honest. "I don't bite, and I'm not going to rob you or hurt you. As I said—"

"—you need a job," she interrupted, a soft smile on her face. "Let me see a few more reference letters."

Handing her the whole pack, he said, "Read whatever you want."

Jeb bit into the roast beef sandwich with fresh tomatoes. Then he took a swig of the freshly squeezed lemonade. "This is good," he said between mouthfuls.

She leafed through the references. "Don't forget the cookie."

He nodded and finished off the sandwich. "We can walk and talk if you'd like. I'll take the cookie with me."

"Bring your lemonade, too, then."

He got up and followed her. "This is all yours."

"Yes. I inherited it after my *mamm* passed

on. We lost my *daed* five years ago, and Mamm and I lived here together until she had a heart attack two years ago. She loved helping me with the lilies."

"How did this come about?"

She laughed at that. "I love daylilies. I started planting ditch lilies, and then I planted more and learned how to cultivate them since they like to spread. At first, we gave them away but after Daed died, we needed money—an income—so we planted different varieties and put a sign on the road. People started coming to buy them. I added different varieties and learned which worked best. With my *bruder*'s help, we planted a small field and he put up the sign. And now, this is my life." She stopped and took a breath. "I'm known as the *alte maidal* lily lady."

"You are not old," he said. And regretted it when her eyes went wide.

"You can interpret *Deutsch*?"

He had to think quickly. "Only a few terms. I've worked with Amish on construction sites."

She didn't look convinced, but she nodded and started back walking. "The creek is back there." She pointed to the right. "We use irrigation from the creek on a limited basis."

"Pretty spot, there by the creek."

"Yes, it is." Her green eyes seemed to lose some of their shimmer. "You'd need to plow—

that's where the horses come in. I don't like horses, so I usually have someone else handle them."

"I can do that. Me and Silver will get to know each other. And Red sounds like a nice lady."

"You'd also need to weed, fertilize with natural materials."

"You mean manure?"

"Ja." She laughed and it seemed the sun got brighter.

"I don't mind manure. Been in it a few times here and there."

She shook her head. "You do have a sense of humor."

"Yes." He rarely smiled this much in one day.

"We plant seedlings, we dig up bulbs and fans—the stems. We pamper the lilies, and we are open Monday to Thursday from nine to four. Friday is maintenance day. We open until noon on Saturday and never on Sunday."

"I don't mind the work," he said. "I like it here."

"You might change your mind during peak season when cars are parked all over the yard and children are running through the fields." She lifted her hand. "There are also the spring mud sales and festivals. I have a booth at all festivals, and we bring in a lot of income that way."

"I won't mind that either," he replied. "I'll do any work and I'll find solutions."

She stopped their stroll between the field and the barn. "Well, then, Jebediah Martin, I'm going to go on faith and trust you." She named his salary. "Is that fair?"

"More than fair," he replied, relief and gratitude moving through his frazzled system. "I can start Monday. I just need to find a place to live."

"I might be able to help with that, too," she said. "My *bruder* has an empty *grossdaddi haus*. He rents it out."

Surprised yet again, Jeb was beginning to think God had brought him to this place. "That might work."

"We can walk over to see him now if you'd like."

"Sure."

He put down his empty lemonade glass and hurried with her around the house. "I'm sorry," he said. "I never got your name."

"Oh, that's my fault. You surprised me and I forgot. I'm Rebecca. Rebecca Eicher."

Jeb's heart dropped to his feet.

Rebecca.

Could this be possible? Was this the woman his cousin John Kemp had planned on marrying so long ago?

Chapter Two

 $\sim$

There were a lot of women named Rebecca in the world, especially in an Amish community. He'd ask around to be sure, but while she chatted about rain and pests and pollen, he studied her with covert glances. Older, yes, but John had described a girl with dark blond hair and pretty green eyes.

This couldn't be possible, but the more he glanced at her, the more he became sure this was John's Rebecca.

Becca, John had said in his letters.

But John was no longer alive. Add to that, John and Jeb had kept their correspondence a secret, since Jeb's *daed* had been a Mennonite. His mother hadn't been shunned after she'd married Calvin Martin, but she'd faced an uphill battle between her faith and the man she loved. And so had her two sons. While she'd raised Jeb

and his brother as Amish, Calvin Martin had made their lives hard on all accounts. The man might have grown up in a Mennonite home, but he'd had no scruples and no faith in God.

Jebediah had to sneak John's letters into the house, and he'd also had to be careful when replying with his own. While his *mamm* knew how close the cousins had become, she never mentioned the letters to her husband. But she sure enjoyed reading them in private after Jeb had read them, and she made sure it was his job to collect the mail. John's letters were the only way she got news from her sister, who sometimes tucked in her own messages.

Now here he stood, about to go to work for John's once-fiancée, Rebecca.

Should he ask her outright? No, not yet. He needed to work, to get his life back on track, to find himself and God again.

He couldn't hurt her by blurting out something that might *not* be true, or that *could* be true. Either way, he'd bring pain to her. She'd never married, obviously. The timing and her age added up, but he kept denying what he saw with his own eyes.

When they reached her brother's house, a little girl ran out onto the porch and giggled. "Aenti Becca, I got home all by myself. Why are you here?"

Becca.

The woman standing by him said, "I have a visitor. Tell your *daed* to please come out here."

A woman with dark hair appeared at the door. "Becca, so *gut* to see you. Did Katie forget to tell me something?"

Rebecca shook her head, while the other woman stared at Jeb, making him want to turn and walk away. "*Neh*, I need to talk to Noah about renting the *grossdaddi haus* to my new worker. Jebediah Martin, this is my sister-in-law, Franny."

Franny came out onto the porch. "I see." She kept her eyes on Jeb. "Nice to meet you."

He knew she didn't feel that way. The woman was petrified and curious about him being here. "Same here," he said, not knowing what else to do.

"Franny?" Rebecca's amused smile sprouted a dimple on her left cheek. "Where is Noah?"

"Oh, look at me not minding my manners. He's out back near the barn. Pulling weeds."

"I'll go and find him," Rebecca replied. *"Denke."*

Franny nodded. "Do you want something to drink?"

Jeb shook his head. At least he'd never go hungry here.

"*Neh*, but *denke*," Rebecca said, motioning him around.

"Can I come?" the little girl named Katie asked.

Her mother grabbed her by the sleeve of her dress. "I need you in the kitchen with me."

Katie's bottom lip protruded in a pout, but she followed her mother all the same.

After they were around the corner of this bigger house, Rebecca whispered, "My *bruder* is the protective sort. He'll question my decision, but he will give in."

"If you say so," Jeb replied, thinking he should just walk away. He had no right to be here and if his guesses were true, his presence could bring pain to this kind woman. She might think he'd purposely come here to find her. He didn't know whether to let what he'd discovered stay unsaid, or just blurt out the truth.

Maybe if he got through the first week or so, then he could explain to her.

"There he is," she said, pointing to where a big man moved a hoe through some tall grass. "Noah?"

The man turned, his long beard holding a hint of gray, his straw hat low over his brow. "Sister, what brings you over? And who do you have with you?"

Rebecca walked closer to her brother. "This

is Jebediah Martin, my new helper. I just hired him, and he needs a place to live while he's working for me."

Noah's brown-eyed gaze moved over Jeb like a hawk searching for a ground mole. "Is that right, now?"

"*Ja*, right as rain," Rebecca replied, her hands held together over her apron. "He needs a job and I need a helper."

Noah placed the hoe next to the barn. "And where are you from, Jebediah?"

Jeb had not thought about people knowing of him, but John had promised to keep their correspondence a secret to protect Jeb's mom. He'd be vague on the details, just in case. "Ohio."

"You have people here?"

"Not that I know of."

"But you are *Englisch*?"

"Yes." For now, anyway.

"He starts Monday," Rebecca went on. "Can he rent the *grossdaddi haus*?"

Noah's frown made him look like a hawk waiting for a mouse. "What do we know of this man, Becca?"

She shoved several of his references into her brother's hands. "He comes highly recommended."

Noah read over the short references. Jeb had been meticulous about getting references. They

helped him find a lot of jobs. He hoped they'd work on this one.

"How do we know he didn't write these himself?"

Becca gave him a light shoulder tap. "Noah, these are handwritten, and some typed out. They have phone numbers to verify."

Jeb nodded. "They're real. I always ask for references before…before I move on."

"*Ja*, moving on. That concerns me," Noah replied. "Becca, you can't trust how long someone like this man will stay."

"I trust him for now," she said. "I need help. I prayed for help. He came walking up."

Noah handed the references back to her and dropped his hands to his side, eyeing Jeb with that intense frown again.

Jeb held his breath. If he lost this offer, he'd be at the end of the road. No hope left. He was tired of roaming.

Her brother glanced from Rebecca back to Jeb. "Could I have a word with my sister, alone?"

Rebecca stepped toward Noah. "I know what you're going to say. He's *Englisch*. He looks like a criminal. We don't know him. You don't want him hanging around me. Did I miss anything?"

Jeb held his lips tightly together to keep from laughing. But the serious look in Noah Eicher's eyes told him that would be a big mistake.

"That covers most of it," Noah said, his eyes on Jeb. "We can find someone within the community."

"I've tried that for a month now."

"Try harder. I don't like the looks of him."

Jeb held up his hand. "Whoa, I'm right here. I can see you don't want me here. But your sister and I talked all that out. I look this way because I don't have a home and I've been traveling around. But I work when I can find work, just to get back to the place where I need to be. Right now, this is the place I'd like to stay in for a while. I can do this work. I won't hurt your sister or do any damage to her property. I only want a good day's work for a good pay. She has offered me that."

Noah's dark expression softened. Then he shook his head. "You two should work well together. All that stubborn is burning a hole in the grass."

"Is that a yes?" Rebecca asked, her hands on her hips.

Her brother didn't seem so sure. "*Ja*, I reckon it is at that."

"*Gut*, because he's ready to move in on Monday."

Noah opened his mouth to speak, then shut it while he pondered this situation. "I'll have the place cleaned up and ready."

He named the rent price, and Jeb agreed.

Jeb extended his hand. "Thank you."

Noah took it, reluctantly, but held it in a firm warning of a grip. "Don't make me regret this."

Rebecca got up bright and early Monday morning and headed up the hallway toward the kitchen. After setting the kettle on for tea, she stood and looked out the kitchen window, marveling at the sunrise lifting out over the foothills and valleys. Her kitchen had windows on each side, front and back. Her *daed* had built it that way for her *mamm*.

"So you can see the day coming and see it ending," he'd told Mamm. Her mother had loved telling that sweet story.

Rebecca was sure glad he'd been so thoughtful. Because while the sun did remain in one spot, the earth revolved around it, and her world revolved around her morning prayers by this window and her evening prayers at the one across the way by the old dining table and buffet. She was allowed the afterglow of dawn and dusk, almost every day, and the full sun on special days. This helped her remember the afterglow of her parents' abiding love. She might not ever have that, but she had her windows.

After she'd stood silent, her prayers a mixed bag of hope tempered with a lonely grief that

never ended, she moved to the dining room and checked the fields. The buds just peeking out of the green field would open all the way in a few weeks. They'd bloom mostly from May through October, and some would keep blooming. The variations of her lilies, especially the hybrids, always amazed her. So much color, so much beauty. Some were more fragrant than others, but they were all perfect.

"*Denke*, Father."

She turned to make her tea and toast and brought her meal to the table. But something out the window caught her eye.

Jebediah Martin stood, dressed in Amish clothes, staring out over her lily field, his hands down by his side, his back to her.

Rebecca's breath caught in her throat and a swift piercing shot through her heart. She couldn't stop staring at the man she'd hired, but she wished with all her heart that her John was standing there, ready to start his day.

Before she could turn away, he pivoted and glanced toward the house, his gaze meeting hers. Rebecca stepped back from that intense glance. This man made her remember she was alone and lonely. She reminded herself that she had family to love, and she had a busy, blessed life.

Why should that change now?

She left the window and tried to eat her breakfast.

But she couldn't finish, so she took her tea and walked out to where he waited. "Have you eaten?"

He nodded. "Yes. I found food on the counter when I got to the house. You have a kind family."

"We like to feed people. Let me finish up inside and I'll be out to get you started."

He nodded. "Mind if I go to the barn? I'd like to learn my way around."

"Go," she said, relieved that he'd found something to occupy him. Also relieved that she didn't have to give him a tour.

All weekend long, she'd wondered about hiring this man. She knew nothing about him, and he knew nothing about daylilies. They made a strange pair. The whole community would be gossiping, but Rebecca had learned to let gossip run its course. How was she supposed to do all this by herself? It was hard enough with someone helping her. She hired local youths during the summer months, but right now she needed a capable adult who didn't mind the work involved in preparing before her loyal customers came from all over to buy their lilies.

Did I do wrong?

She watched Jebediah go into the barn, her

heart always escalating with fear when anyone got close to the horses. Sad, since she used to love the horses. But not now. Not after she'd witnessed John being thrown from an excited roan.

Thrown and killed.

Even though John's own horse had thrown him when a vehicle backfired on the road near his house, she had not been in the barn near her family's horses since then. Her brother and others kept up the stables for her. Relieved, she was glad this man didn't seem to mind dealing with that part of his job.

Rebecca turned toward the fields. She had two small ones, but between them, they yielded about two thousand rooted stems with fans per year. She'd try more if she had help.

Maybe this season.

Grabbing a hoe and basket, she hurried to the field, intent on getting rid of weeds before the day became warm. She loved late spring into early summer. The smell of lilies would wake her each morning and send her to sleep at the end of her day.

Lilies of the field, morning and night. She'd been content with that for so long.

But today, her contentment wasn't as serene as it had been last week, before he'd shown up. What an irony, that the Lord would send her someone to help, but that someone, that stranger,

only reminded her of the life she'd lost the day she'd lost her John.

What kind of summer did she have ahead of her with this mystery man? She'd hired him on an impulse and out of a fear of failure. Those traits could do her in one day, but Rebecca remembered that *Gott*'s will would keep her steady. She also tried to convince herself that she didn't hire him on the spot because he resembled her deceased fiancé. That would make her truly pathetic.

She tore into her pruning and hoeing—sending weeds and trimmings flying into her basket, her mind recoiling from the longing in her heart.

Until a bronzed hand touched her aching shoulder. "Let me."

Jebediah knelt beside her at the end of a row.

She'd been so lost in her musings, she hadn't even noticed him or the time of day. "What?"

"It's noon and you've been at this all morning. Rest. I can finish these rows."

She stood, her hands automatically reaching for her tired back. "I'm sorry. I left you in the barn too long."

"It's okay. I introduced myself to the horses, put them out in the corral, cleaned the stalls and freshened the hay. I'll get back in there later at feeding time. I want to organize everything."

Rebecca glanced at the barn and then back to him. "You've for certain sure been busy, ain't so?"

He gave her a direct gaze, his blue eyes battling with the sky. "I like staying busy."

She blinked, thinking too much sun had gone to her head. "*Denke.* I'll make dinner."

"Rest first. And, Rebecca, you don't have to feed me."

"Part of your pay," she said, glad to have someone *to* feed. Glancing around, she smiled. "Besides, I have a vegetable garden behind the barn. I'll need help with that, too. We get to eat the fruits of our labor."

"I like that idea. Do you have fruit trees, too?"

"Apples, blueberries, blackberries, cantaloupe late in the summer, pumpkins, turnips. I grow lots of vegetables. Beets—"

"I hate beets."

"I'll try to remember that," she said with a grin. "Do you like cranberries?"

"I do."

"I don't grow those."

"Too bad."

Rebecca motioned to him. "Before you finish what I started, *kumm* to the house and let's eat. I have cold chicken to make chicken salad. With sweet pickles and my secret ingredient."

"Not beets?" he asked, following her toward the house.

"No. Just a dash of paprika. Another sandwich on fresh sourdough. With chips."

"Chips?"

"I love potato chips," she said with a shrug.

"You are a woman full of surprises, Rebecca."

"We have that in common, then," she said on a saucy note. Maybe this would work out, after all. Jebediah seemed to like keeping to himself, same as her. But she hoped he'd open up about his own life and why he'd chosen to wander the earth, rather than plants roots in it.

Chapter Three

Day's end.

Jeb took a long breath. He'd sure enjoyed working again. He'd only been here a week, but this might be the best job he'd ever had—considering he got fed by everyone. He walked out of the barn and shut the big doors.

He'd taken care of the two horses. The roan, Red, was docile and sweet and the big draft, Silver, had a gray coat and white mane. Silver seemed spirited but dependable.

"Why don't you like horses?" he'd asked, curiosity getting the best of him.

Her pretty eyes had gone dark, a shutter falling across her smile. She'd glanced out at the barn. "They frighten me."

He'd left it at that, but he knew something bad happening usually caused people to fear animals. "I'll take care of them," he'd said. "You

don't have to worry about that anymore. I've cleaned and rearranged all the bridles and harnesses and mended some of the reins that are worn. Saddles look good, but I polished them. And I washed the summer buggy and checked the wheels."

"You have been busy," she'd replied, a faraway look in her eyes. "I've neglected the barn for a long time."

Now, he turned away from the brilliant sunset that had become a mixture of clouds warring with color just over the tree line. Puffy gray had turned to muted yellows and pinks. The prettiest sunsets usually came with low-hanging clouds, because the clouds and clear, clean air reflected the sun in those brilliant hues.

He could spend the rest of his days here, watching the sun rise and set. This was a peaceful, beautiful place. But he'd only been here a few days. He and Becca were getting along. Each morning, she'd give him coffee and food if he hadn't eaten, then tell him what needed to be done. They worked together at times and alone at other times. She was a gentle boss. Things could change. He knew that.

Rebecca came down the back steps with a basket in her hand.

"What's that?" he asked, liking the easy way they could talk to each other.

"Your supper," she said with a soft smile. "Beef stew and potatoes with string beans. No beets."

He laughed. She made him laugh. "I have to remember that with the Amish, lunch is dinner, and dinner is supper."

"*Ja*, we like to eat, same as most."

"Now, I like to eat," he said. "But you don't have to feed me supper all the time. I can cook."

"Was that one of your jobs?"

"Yes, I've worked in a few restaurants and cafés." He shook his head. "I'm a wanderer."

"A wayfaring stranger?"

"Yes."

"Do you want to tell me a little about how you wound up here?"

"No. Not yet."

She looked away, as if she already knew she'd find him going up the lane to the road one day. "As long as I have you through the summer."

"I think I'll be here a good long while," he said, realizing that he meant it. "Especially for the meals."

She giggled. "Take your supper and go get cleaned up. You had a long first week."

"I liked my first week," he replied. "I'll see you tomorrow, early. More weeding?"

She nodded and lifted her arms. "Always weeding and pruning, sorting bulbs, planting

bulbs and watering everything. But only a half day." Then she pointed to the basket she'd just handed him. "I know we've talked, and I've tried to explain everything to you, but I put some papers in there, about lilies and our schedule. That might help or you might leave in the middle of the night."

"I won't do that," he said. "Thank you."

She nodded and walked with him toward the front yard. "My *bruder*'s been busy with crops this week, but he will probably pay you a visit soon. He's protective." She waved her hand in the air. "I'm sure he managed to get in touch with some of those names on your reference papers."

"I'd expect that, having met him."

"He means well, but we have different mind-sets regarding outsiders. He will worry that you and I work here alone together. But I think I'm far past needing a chaperone."

"And I was taught how to respect women."

She smiled at that, her eyes full of questions he wasn't ready to answer.

Jeb wanted to tell her he wasn't really an outsider. He'd left the Amish close to twenty years ago after a horrible accident and a disagreement with his rigid father, and he'd never dreamed he'd want to return. But would she understand and accept that, or that he was her John's long-

lost cousin? He'd find the right time to tell her all of this, all about his life. But not yet. This would be a long summer, with plenty of daylight left to talk about the past.

They made it to the front and he turned to her. "I'll see you tomorrow, Rebecca."

"I'll be here, Jebediah."

"You can call me Jeb," he said, again not really thinking.

"Oh." Her eyes filled with shock and the darkness fell across her expression again. "Jeb. Only if you call me Becca."

"I can do that."

He turned, realizing his cousin John had called him Jeb. Had John mentioned that to her before?

Jeb Martin.

That nagging wonder she'd felt when this man first walked up the lane made Rebecca stop and stare out toward the orange-tinged afterglow of the sunset. Why did he have to remind her of John? Why did Jeb seem so familiar to her?

You are imagining what you can't have.

She'd had men court her since John died, but she'd never gotten past a first outing or two. Telling herself she'd rather be alone, Rebecca had been so adamant on that, her friends and

family had finally given up on trying to find her a husband.

Some frowned on her running a business on her own. But when she pointed out she was capable of taking care of herself, they usually quieted. She refused to live on handouts or the kindness of friends. She and her mother had made a nice enough living selling lilies. What was so wrong with her continuing to do that on her own?

This was what was wrong—this knowing she'd be alone for the rest of the day. With the sunlight, she had her work to keep her busy. But nighttime was lonely. She read by the propane lamp, mostly the Bible, a few novels and bulb catalogs, *The Budget* newspaper, and other weekly papers.

Boring. She had a boring, but peaceful existence. Now that existence had been shifted and rearranged by this man showing up out of the blue to ask for work.

Shaking her head, Rebecca went about getting her supper on a plate. She glanced at the calendar she kept on a small desk in the living room and saw that tomorrow, her sister, Hannah, was coming by to help with canning some early vegetables. They always had fun together with their Saturday frolics. Hannah was younger and newly married to Samuel.

That usually didn't bother Rebecca, but all the longing she'd managed to hide so well for the past fifteen years came back full force. She'd never be married. She'd missed her time for marriage and a family.

Gott's will.

She shouldn't question the Lord's plans for her, but today she'd certainly been near to doing that. She took her plate out onto the back porch to enjoy the last of dusk while she nibbled at the food. At least she had someone who seemed capable to help her through the summer. Would Jebediah—Jeb—decide to stay longer?

Did she want that?

You don't know this man.

No, she didn't know him. But she felt she should know him. He'd done all the work she'd heaped on him and done it without complaint. They worked together, but he left her alone once she issued him a task. She'd had a few early customers this week and he'd stayed in the background, absorbing and learning, then offering to load up the purchased plants.

He learned quickly and seemed to be well educated.

He'd made it clear he might wander off again. She needed to remember that and maybe start looking for a permanent solution while he was

still available. Surely someone in the small community of Campton Creek needed a steady job.

She wanted to ask him more about what had made him become a nomad, a wanderer, a loner. But that was none of her business.

She'd ask around in a discreet manner. Well, as small communities went, she'd try.

She wondered if people passed on her job offer because no one wanted to work with the old maid lily lady. Why did marriage have to define a woman's status? She knew her faith demanded certain things and she understood that but being alone wasn't much fun at the end of the day. Was it prideful to want to be strong and self-sufficient so she wouldn't need to rely on the kindness of others?

The food tasted *gut*, but like most things, food was better when shared with company. Rebecca thought about the few meals she'd had with Jeb. He made her laugh and challenged her with his worldly talk and all the occupations he'd tried.

She needed to know why he liked to roam around. She wanted to understand why he made her think of John.

She set her plate down and put her hands in her lap, her unfinished food on the table beside her, her head down in silent prayers.

Then she heard a voice. "Rebecca?"

Looking up, she saw Jeb standing there.

Startled, she stood. "What is it?"

"Nothing," he said, his hair clean and combed back off his face, a new shirt smelling of her sister-in-law's detergent. "I… I need a haircut and… I thought maybe you could help me with that?" Shrugging, he went on. "I meant to ask earlier and well, I forgot."

Rebecca bobbed her head, while her heart came to a skidding halt. The man needed a haircut, so why was she being a ninny. "I have scissors. We can set a chair in the grass, and I'll give you a trim."

"I'd appreciate that," he said. "Will you be able to see?"

"I think we have a few minutes before full dark," she replied. "If not—we'll see how I do when daylight returns tomorrow."

He grinned. "Okay, then."

Rebecca rushed inside to get a towel and her scissors.

She prayed her shaking hands didn't give Jeb the worst haircut ever.

Jeb sat in the high-backed chair and waited. He should have put this off until later, but after he'd cleaned up for the day, he realized his hair was too shaggy. Since he had no way into town to find a barber, he'd thought of Rebecca.

Dumb idea.

Now the pretty woman who was his boss would be running her hands through his hair. At least it was clean and smelled like some sort of flower garden, thanks to the goat's milk soap Franny had left for him by the kitchen sink in his tiny house.

Rebecca came back out of her house with a towel and scissors. "Do you want me to take off a lot or a little?"

He grinned. "I don't want a shaved head. Maybe just an inch or so and trim my bangs."

"I promise I won't put a bowl over your head," she teased, her laughter like wind chimes in his head. "Sit up straight and don't move."

"Yes, ma'am."

She shook her head at that, then started combing his hair. "You have a lot of hair."

"I know. Do you see that little bit of gray?"

"I think we all have that."

He thought about her hair and wondered how pretty it would look if she could wear it down. Which was forbidden, of course. Only her husband could see that. And obviously, she didn't have a husband.

As a teenager, he'd chafed under the Amish tenets, but after some of the things he'd witnessed through the years out there in the world, he didn't find it so bad now. Maybe, like his

strict *daed* had suggested he should do long ago, he'd finally become a mature adult.

"Okay, here I go."

He felt her hands on his neck, a little jolt of awareness going down his spine. Jeb blinked and refocused, his eyes on the rows and rows of green lily leaves across from them. He'd read over her reports while he'd enjoyed the home-cooked meal she'd given him. Growing lilies required nature's blessings and a human's hard work. But he thought it might be the best work for him, since he could gather his thoughts and process what he wanted to do next, while he gathered lilies and pulled up weeds. His mother used to say God was in all gardens.

He prayed God would touch his heart in this garden and show him the way when he reached the end of the row.

Rebecca's nearness brought him back to the gloaming. The sun shimmered over the trees, hovering in regret, not wanting to slip away. The air was soft and silent, as if a lightweight blanket had come down to comfort the world. Peace. He felt an intense peace sitting here.

Rebecca snipped and brushed his damp hair while he tried to ignore the feeling of her fingers against his skin, her touch as soft and quiet as the very air they were breathing. Maybe this had been a bad idea, after all.

She came around front. "Now your bangs. They like to curl, *ja*?"

"Uh-huh." He pretended to be looking out beyond her, but she was so close he could smell lavender and a hint of jasmine.

More of that homemade soap, he figured.

She'd just finished trimming his bangs, her comb flying through his new cut, when someone came stomping across the yard.

"Becca, what do you think you're doing?" Her brother Noah came charging toward them, a mad rage in his dark eyes. "This is not acceptable behavior. You need to stop right this minute."

Becca stood back, her eyes going wide. "Noah, calm down. He needed a haircut."

"He could have let me do that," Noah said, his hands on his hips. "You know this is not right."

"I'm all done," Rebecca replied, her blush showing even in the waning light. "And I dare say, I think I've done better than you would have."

"I don't like this at all," Noah said. "I'm going to ask around to find you more suitable help."

"Neh," she replied, her scissors clutched in one hand. "I have hired someone, and Jeb has proved he's capable of taking care of things for me."

"He might be capable of a lot more," Noah

said, his words thrown out like rocks. "And that will not go over well with me, and probably not with the bishop."

Jeb stood and moved away from Rebecca. "It's my fault. I asked her to trim my hair. I didn't think it would cause any trouble."

"You are trouble," Noah said. "I don't like this."

Rebecca moved to stand between Jeb and her brother. "Noah, do you think I'd do anything to dishonor myself or you, or anyone who knows us? I certainly won't stray from our ways. Jeb knows that. I was only cutting his hair and no harm came to anyone. I didn't even nick his skin."

"I'm not worried about his skin," Noah replied, his tone firm. "You mark my word, no good will come of this."

Jeb held up a hand. He had to stop this, or he'd be out of a job. But he wouldn't let Rebecca's brother make her feel bad on his account.

"Understood," he replied to Noah's heated words. Then he turned to her. "Rebecca, thank you. Noah, I get that you don't trust me but there's something you both need to know about me. Something that might help in relieving your concerns."

"What's that?" Noah asked, his eyes still blazing with distrust.

Rebecca shot Jeb a confused glance. "What is it, Jeb?"

Jeb took a deep breath and prayed he was doing the right thing. "I...know your ways, I know all the rules, I have read the *Ordnung*. I used to be Amish."

Chapter Four

Rebecca couldn't speak. All the signs were there, but she'd somehow ignored or missed them. He could understand some *Deutsch*, he knew his way around a barn and a farm, and he was humble and worked hard. Could those traits and mannerisms be the reason he reminded her of John?

She cleared her throat and looked at Jeb. "Why didn't you tell me that sooner?"

Noah held his hands on his hips. "*Ja*, that would have been a *gut* starting point."

Jeb sank down on the porch steps. "I've been away from the Amish for twenty years. I left my community in Ohio during my *Rumspringa*." He shrugged. "My *daed* and I didn't see eye to eye on anything. I left after we had an argument, and I never went back." He wouldn't tell

them the rest now. They'd probably ask him to leave if he became completely honest.

Noah's anger moved from boiling to a simmer. "Why did you come here? Why not go back to Ohio?"

"I have no one in Ohio," Jeb said, his eyes dark, a forlorn expression on his face. "My *mamm* passed when I was a teenager, and I lost my only brother. He was thirteen when he died."

"Oh, Jeb, I'm so sorry." Rebecca knew his pain, had seen it in his eyes. It reflected her own torment. "That must have been so hard on your parents and you."

"It was, for me and my dad. My mom had passed already." He stopped and shook his head. "After Pauly died, things got worse between my dad and me. So… I left. I regret that now. Leaving my *daed* alone like that—it was wrong."

"You could still go to him," Noah suggested, his tone full of understanding. "My *daed* and I had fights, but we forgave each other. That is the Amish way."

"I tried that," Jeb said. "He became ill about five years ago, but he died before I could get home. The farm went into foreclosure and was sold at auction. I have no home now."

This explained some of his sadness and why he roamed around so much. He must blame himself terribly for losing his father and the

farm, and after he'd lost his mother and brother, too. What a heavy burden for a person to carry.

"*Ja*, you do have a home," Rebecca said. "You have a home here in Campton Creek. We will make sure of that, won't we, *bruder*?"

Noah looked doubtful. "Do you want to return to the Amish for *gut*?"

Jeb nodded. "That is why I came here."

"Why here?" Noah asked, still being stubborn.

Jeb sat silent for a moment, then pushed at his new haircut. "I've been all over this country and a…friend told me about Campton Creek and the small community here. I don't know why I came, but I'm glad I found my way to this place."

He glanced at Rebecca, his gaze moving over her with renewed hope. "I like the work, and I can be good at it once I learn what I need to know."

Noah grunted. "We still have to consider you working here with Becca, day in and day out. Staying at my place means when the day's work is done, you do not return to visit my sister."

Rebecca tried not to roll her eyes. "Noah, I don't turn away visitors. And I don't mind feeding someone who works hard all day. Or cutting their hair."

Noah huffed and nodded. "Then it's settled.

I'll be sending Adam over to work for you—as long as needed. That is the only way I'll agree to Jeb's staying. Adam and he will return to my side of the road at sunset every day, or I'll *kumm* checking."

Rebecca wanted to stomp her foot in frustration. "You need the boys to help you."

"I can spare one. Adam is the youngest at twelve. But he has *gut* eyes and *gut* ears. He will report back to me."

"I will not have you forcing your son to spy on me," Rebecca said, her hands now on her hips.

Jeb stood and held up both hands as if to separate them. "Enough. Noah, I've tried to tell you I will not dishonor your sister or my job. She would fire me on the spot if I tried anything *dumm*. Since I like this job and want to work, I will not be stupid. Either you accept that now, or *I* will have to walk away."

Rebecca gave him an imploring glance. "I haven't fired you, Jeb. You can't leave in the middle of my busiest season. Noah has no say on that regard."

Noah glanced from Jeb to Rebecca. "I should make you do just that. But Rebecca is of her own mind on these matters. Probably why no man will come near her."

Rebecca let out a shocked gasp, then whirled

and headed for the house. "So, what are you fussing about? No man wants me, ain't so. I should be completely safe with Jeb."

She grabbed up her unfinished meal and held her scissors up with her free hand. "I'm surprised Jeb hasn't already left."

Then she went inside, the door slamming on her discontent.

Noah gave Jeb a long stare. "Well, that went as expected. She is easy to anger sometimes. Most times."

"You hurt her feelings," Jeb replied, angry on Becca's behalf. "You should know not to speak like that to a woman."

"I should, but I guess I'll never learn," Noah said. "Women have unpredictable ways, and I don't need unsolicited advice from a stranger. You're the reason she's angry."

Jeb bristled. "I'm not the one who made a rude remark about her. We've been getting along fine." He shook his head. "Go ahead and tell me I'm fired. See how she reacts to that."

Shrugging, Noah glanced toward the house. "You don't need to quit. She does need someone, and you seem willing to return to the brethren." Then he reached out his hand to Jeb. "I'm still sending Adam over to help out."

Jeb shook Noah's hand, silent. He worried

about Rebecca more than he worried that Noah would send him packing. "I don't mind having a youngie to help out here and there, and Rebecca will be glad for it, too, I'm thinking."

Noah let go of his hand and smiled, surprising Jeb. "I'm beginning to think this situation will take care of itself. If you mean to stay here, you'll need to see the bishop and brush up on our ways. You'll have to go before the church and ask forgiveness." Then he leaned in. "And you will surely have to follow our tenets. If you show me how badly you want that," he said, glancing toward the house, "I might begin to believe you could be one of us. And that it will do my sister some *gut* to have a strong, purposeful man around."

Jeb got the message, but he would not be bossing Rebecca around. She seemed to have her confidence under control. "I'll show you more than that. I'll work hard on all fronts. This is the most beautiful spot I've seen in a long time."

He didn't tell Noah, but he also thought Rebecca was the most beautiful woman he'd seen in a long time.

But Jeb would keep that particular observance to himself.

Rebecca hadn't slept well. Finding out Jeb was Amish had been both a blessing and a

shock. While she celebrated his return to the fold, she had to wonder why he'd withheld that from her when she'd hired him.

After she slammed into the house, he and Noah had walked home. She'd watched them out the window, her mind reeling with all that Jeb had told her. He'd never opened up before, so she knew his admission had been hard on him. He'd been forced, since her brother wouldn't stop pestering them.

Jeb had confessed as a last resort so he wouldn't be fired, but if he'd been honest up front, she would not have held that against him. Maybe the shame of being away so long had kept him from explaining. Or was there more to his story?

Her brother had taken the news much better than Rebecca, but as was the case with Noah, he had stipulations. She knew Adam needed work to keep the boy calm but sending him to her seemed like a punishment and a shout of mistrust from her well-meaning brother.

After finishing the cup of tea she'd made to eat with the slice of apple pie she'd decided to have for breakfast, Rebecca gathered her garden tools and headed to the herb bed she'd started in a raised box near the back door. She loved cooking with fresh herbs, so she'd planted basil, oregano, mint and parsley, along with rosemary,

dill and thyme, and a few sweet peppers. Sometimes, she'd take a bit of bread dough and make her own pizza, covered with her own fresh sauce, goat cheese, vegetables, and herbs. Her treat to herself.

She wondered if Jeb liked pizza.

Why did that matter? Her brother would make sure he was fed at the house, just to keep Jeb from hanging around to have supper with her after the workday had ended. Noah's words to her last night still hurt. Why did people judge her for not having a husband? And why would they judge her for finding a strong, hardworking man to help her?

It didn't matter. She'd have to stay professional with Jeb, so her brother would stop having tantrums about her being alone with a man. Now that Jeb had admitted he was once Amish, maybe Noah would back off a bit. Or that could make matters worse.

Her mind whirling with that predicament, Rebecca didn't hear Jeb approaching until he was right up on her.

"Oh," she said, putting a hand to her chest. "You scared the daylight out of me."

He backed away, a frown darkening his face. "I didn't mean to startle you. Just reporting for work."

"Grumpy this morning?" she asked as she

put down her trowel and took off her gardening gloves. "My brother does that to people."

Jeb's smile held a bit of understanding. "He's only trying to protect you. And you did warn me about that."

Rebecca crossed her hands over her stomach. "Jeb, why didn't you tell me right away?"

He looked down at his brogans. "I wanted to say a lot of things to you, but I wasn't sure how to go about it. I decided if you gave me this work, I'd keep quiet and do my job. And I hoped I could ease my way into my past."

"I don't think that worked for you," she replied, turning back to the tiny buds of green covering the foot-square sections of the long garden box. "Honesty is important in any relationship. We work together, so if there is anything else that I need to know about you, tell me now. I want the truth. That's all I ask of you."

Jeb couldn't look at her. He wanted to explain everything, but he'd jumped one hurdle by telling Becca and her overbearing brother that he was Amish. Or had been Amish at one time.

Did he really want to do this? Return to this world and make a life for himself here among strangers?

So far, the answer was yes, but the confrontation last night only reminded him of all he was

hiding. Not just that he was related to Rebecca's beloved John, but all the secrets Jeb held closely to his heart. Would she want him to stay if she knew everything about him?

He couldn't risk that, not yet.

He lifted his gaze to Becca. "I have nothing much left to reveal. I have no money, no family, and no future unless I start right here and now. I want to make enough money to get me started, then I hope to find a place of my own."

He wanted to add that he could be happy working here the rest of his days, but that would only make things worse at this point. He'd work the summer and then leave. She'd never need to know he was related to the man she'd loved and lost. "I don't want to jeopardize my job, Becca."

"Your job is safe," she said after a moment of eyeing him. "I'll handle my *bruder* and his concerns."

"I think he'll be better now," Jeb said. "We had a good talk when we walked home together. I think he now regrets what he said to you."

"That's fine," she said. "He was so kind to point out that I'm blessed to have you, since I'm such a bitter old maid."

"You are not old," he reminded her. "We're practically the same age."

She gave him a confused, questioning glance, as if she wanted to ask him more questions.

Then she looked out over the lily field. "Some days, I feel old," she admitted. "My brother has a point. I've missed my prime. He knows I'm bitter. I was about to be married, long ago. But one horrible accident ended that."

Jeb wanted to take her in his arms and tell her to stop listening to her brother. Instead, he grabbed a hand tiller and started helping her weed the herb box. "You are only as old as you feel inside," he told her. "Let's pretend we're young again. It's a pretty spring day and we have the afternoon off. I'd like to go fishing."

She looked up at him, then glanced out toward the creek. "I have poles and you'll have to dig for bait but do whatever you wish."

"I was hoping you'd come with me."

Rebecca pushed at her *kapp*. "Oh, I have things to do. All day."

Disappointed, Jeb thought it was for the best. Noah wouldn't like seeing them fishing together. "Okay. I'm sure I'll catch the biggest fish you could imagine and then you'll be sorry you missed it."

"You can brag about it all you want," she retorted, her tone firm. "But I can cook whatever you catch. Hope you like frog legs."

"Oh, you think I'll only catch frogs?"

"I don't know yet, but maybe."

They both worked their way around the long

rectangular garden box, clearing weeds and pruning heavy plants so the herbs could grow better. The scents of the tiny buds and unfurling greenery made Jeb think of home cooking and Sunday dinners. He'd had a lot of meals in greasy-spoon diners and fast-food places, so all the fresh, organic food here tasted even better than he remembered from his *mamm*'s cooking.

"I can't wait to use some of these," Becca said. "I'll sneak you meals when my brother isn't looking."

"That's a great idea."

Jeb went to grab a trowel at the same time she leaned over to get the watering jar.

They bumped heads.

"Ouch," she said, lifting up to rub her forehead.

He held her arm with one hand and his head with the other. "We both have hard heads. That hit me on my temple."

"Ja." She started laughing, her eyes prettier than the green grass and trees. "I've been called hardheaded at times."

"Me, too."

Jeb laughed with her, his hand still on her arm. Giving her a careful once-over, he asked, "Are you okay?"

Becca nodded. "I think we'll both have a knot."

He leaned close, studying her forehead. "Red right now."

She did the same with him. "Yours, too."

Then their eyes met, and Jeb's heart stilled for a moment.

Becca's eyes widened, a soft gasp escaping her mouth.

A current sizzled like a sweet longing in the air between them. He'd never felt anything like it, and he didn't want this moment to end.

Then a female voice called out, "Sister, what are you doing?"

Becca whirled so quickly, she almost hit Jeb again.

"Hannah, I thought you weren't coming until later."

"It is later," the woman said with a wide grin. "And not a minute too soon, from the look of things."

Chapter Five

"So this is the hired help," Hannah said with a grin while she watched Rebecca run around the kitchen to fix their noonday meal. "I had heard a lot about him already. Noah is fussing and stomping like an old bull."

Rebecca shoved a glass of iced tea toward where Hannah sat in a high-backed chair at the dining table. She'd planned to feed Jeb, too, but he'd taken off to his place to "eat a sandwich."

"Noah stomps around fussing about everything I do," she retorted. "Does he pester you about your choices and your household?"

Hannah nibbled on a sliced carrot. "*Neh*, but I'm married. I have a husband to do that."

Rebecca let out a sigh as she sliced cold chicken to go with the potato salad she'd made last night. "So that's the reason Noah watches me like a hawk?"

"I think so," Hannah said, her hazel eyes wide with understanding. "He means well, but he worries."

"I'm fine," Rebecca said, "but he upset me last night. Jeb asked me to cut his hair and I did so, out in the backyard. You'd think I was walking out with him without a chaperone or something." She told Hannah what Noah had said. "He's never talked like that to me before."

Hannah waited for Rebecca to join her for their light meal. "Sister, we both worry about you. I know you're independent and capable, but don't you want someone in your life?"

Rebecca looked at her plate. "Of course, I'd like that. But I haven't found that someone. I fear I might not ever find anyone, and I have to be okay with that. I have family. You and Noah, Franny and the *kinder*, and our community. I love my work here. I'm content."

"Content is one thing," Hannah replied. "Being happy is another."

"I was happy once," Rebecca said. "I'm as happy as I can be these days."

"Jeb makes you smile," Hannah said before she scooped up a spoonful of chicken salad and chewed, her eyes bright with mischief.

"We get along," Rebecca replied, shocked at her sister's antics. "He works hard and he's easy to be around."

"And not bad on the eye."

"You are a married woman," Rebecca admonished. "Don't let Andrew hear you talking like that."

"You know I love Andy. But I wish the same for you."

Rebecca ate some of the potato salad. "Are you suggesting Jeb would be a *gut* match?"

"From what Noah told me this morning, he was once Amish," her sister replied. "He could be again with a little coaching."

"So, you're suggesting that I coach Jeb into becoming Amish and then becoming my husband?"

"I might be…"

Rebecca put down her fork. "Did Noah put you up to this? Did he hurry to your house early this morning to ask your help in planning out my life for me?"

"You're angry," Hannah said.

"You haven't answered my question."

"He might have mentioned that Jeb seems to be a *gut*, strong man. And that there's really only one tiny problem."

"Jeb is not Amish anymore."

"Yes, that is the concern, but he has indicated he'd like to come home to his roots, to become one of us again. You could help in that area."

Rebecca shook her head and laid her hands on

the table to keep her temper from erupting. "Let me get this straight. The *bruder* who fussed at me and told me no man would want me anyway has decided that the very man he's so worried about being around me is now the perfect man to be my husband?"

Hannah bobbed her head. "*Ja*, that sums things up. What do you think?"

"I think you are both *lecherich*."

"I'm not being ridiculous, Becca," Hannah replied. "This could be a *gut* solution for both you and Jeb."

Matchmaking seemed to be the pastime around here, especially when a new man came to town. Was she that pathetic?

"Not if Jeb and I don't want it." Rebecca gave up on finishing her meal. "I can't believe you let Noah talk you into such a foolish task. Jeb has been here a little over a week and has just now admitted what he hopes for his future, and you two already have our lives planned."

"Noah feels better knowing Jeb wants to make amends and come back to the Amish way of life."

"*Ja*, I'm sure he does. He's found a man to pass off his lonely, bitter sister to." She wanted to scream, but she refused to upset her sister. Hannah had been a pawn in Noah's persuasive hands. "I will discuss this with my *bruder* as

soon as I see him again. If I ever speak to him again."

"You don't mean that." Hannah shook her head. "He lives right across the way. That would be hard to do since you see him almost every day."

"I can avoid him, but you are right. That would be hard to do since I love Franny and the *kinder.*"

"You love Noah, too," Hannah said, giving Rebecca a wry smile. "He loves us even when he oversteps. Remember how he followed Andrew around, telling him exactly what he could and could not do around me?"

Rebecca had to laugh at those memories. "He didn't want Andrew to even look at you or hold your hand. Makes courting a bit difficult, ain't so?"

Hannah giggled. "Imagine if you and Jeb were truly serious about courting. Noah would sit between you in every buggy ride."

They started laughing, both of them wiping at their eyes.

When they heard a knock at the back screen door, Hannah actually snorted. "Probably Noah wanting to know when the wedding is."

Jeb stood there, staring at them with an inquisitive glance. Rebecca looked up and saw him, her laughter ending as she poked her sister.

"Jeb, *kumm* in," she managed to sputter.

He looked so distraught, she feared something had happened.

"Are you planning on getting married?" he asked, glancing from her to her sister.

Hannah burst out laughing again.

While Rebecca blushed, her face going hot.

"Not anytime soon," she replied. Then she gave her sister a warning glance. "My sister was telling me a bad joke, that's all."

Jeb looked confused and maybe a little curious. Or she could be imagining things since her sister had planted that seed in her head. Jeb wasn't ready for marriage. First, he needed to find himself again and return to his faith. That could take a while. And second, she was in no hurry to marry just to please her siblings and this community.

But Hannah still had a big smile on her face.

Jeb had never understood women. Laughing one minute, in tears the next. They scared him with all the drama and emotions. His own *mamm* had been kind and quiet, following his *daed*'s every word or order. For a long time Jeb thought all women acted that way, but when he realized his mother was not happy, but just pretended to be, his heart hurt for her. His *daed*

had not been a kind man. Not even before his brother, Paul, had died. Even more so after.

After his *mamm* passed away, Jeb tried to so hard to take care of Paul. Pauly, as they nicknamed him, had some issues. Slow, his *daed* called the boy. Mamm always said Pauly was a true blessing from *Gott*. After she passed from a rare disease, Pauly got even worse with tantrums and outbursts. Daed didn't like that. Then as Pauly grew older, things escalated. Jeb had to work to keep his family together. Pauly would run away and show up at Jeb's workplace, a buggy repair shop down the road.

Then one day he came to the shop and Jeb had been busy. He was harsh to his brother and Pauly ran toward home…didn't show up. Pauly didn't come back home. He'd been hit by a vehicle—ran right out in front of it. The driver kept telling everyone that the kid just came running across the road.

Jeb stopped remembering. He couldn't go back and change things. His family was gone. With God now.

But he could work on the weeds in the yard, and he could get a head start on pruning the lilies. Rebecca had told him they'd start potting the healthier plants to sell on the road and at festivals.

He'd gulped down a thrown-together sand-

wich with some tea for his noon meal. Now he hoped the sisters were over whatever they'd been discussing earlier. He couldn't figure why the thought of Rebecca possibly being engaged had taken him so by surprise. She would have mentioned that to him. But then, they'd been wary of each other from the beginning, and he still held his secrets close. Why would he expect her to share the details of her life?

Maybe they *had* been telling a bad joke and he'd come in on the punch line. He'd see how Rebecca acted when her sister left.

He only had to work till noon, but he'd stayed to get some things done and he had to check on the animals anyway.

And maybe, just maybe, he wanted to see how Rebecca was doing since they'd bumped heads. Then he smiled.

Probably wouldn't be the last time that happened.

Rebecca waved to her sister, then turned to head to the back of the house. With an afternoon off from work, she felt at odds. She had some mending to do, and she'd promised Katie a new summer dress for church. She and Hannah had cut out the pattern and she'd sew the dress together. That task could wait. She'd walk the perimeters of the lily field and see if anything

needed her attention. The next few weeks would become busy. Locals and tourists alike would show up for lilies. Some wanted several to plant beds in their gardens. Others just wanted one to put in a pot or a special corner. She loved seeing people smile when they found the perfect hybrid. She had a special garden for shows, as many of her returning customers liked to display their plants in the local garden shows.

When she reached the back porch, she stretched and glanced around the property. Then she saw Jeb down at the creek with a fishing pole. He had invited her to go with him earlier, but she'd declined.

Should she at least walk down there now? Would that only add fuel to her brother's wishes for her?

Deciding to defy Noah and just be a friend to Jeb, Rebecca grabbed two glasses of lemonade and two oatmeal cookies from the batch she and Hannah had baked, and slowly made her way to where he stood by the bench she'd had the local furniture maker, Tobias Mast, build for her. She loved to watch the sunset from there. The wooden bench had a lily carved on the high back.

Maybe Noah wouldn't come running around the house, demanding a wedding, if she sat on the bench while Jeb fished.

"Hello," she called as she neared where he stood near a short pier. "I thought you might be thirsty."

He held his pole but turned to smile at her. "I am at that. I did some weeding and walked the field. I like walking through the lilies." He glanced back at the grid of rows, all with a different variety of lily. "I'm learning to identify the names, based on the charts you gave me. Some are really fragrant, and others hold a faint scent. *Hemerocallis*, day beauty. That's the technical name from the Greek." Then he added, "But daylilies are different from lilies, right? They got that name because they only bloom for a day or so."

"You have been studying," she said, impressed. "And yes, you are correct. Most lilies started in Asia, but the *Englisch* especially loved them—the Eng*lish* in England that is. America got a late start, but now they are highly popular. Obviously, or I wouldn't be in business." She glanced back at the field. "That's why I have two fields. One is purely daylilies, and the other is more exotic lilies that need pampering and watching closely. I've come up with some unusual hybrids."

"I hope I can learn all the varieties," he said. "We could do hybrids this summer—come up with our own lily."

"What would we call it?" she asked, her heart thumping against her apron. Their own lily?

"The JeBecca," he teased.

"Or the Beccediah," she shot back.

"Or just the Becca," he replied, his tone soft and low.

"I never thought of naming one after myself."

"I'll name it—that way I get all the credit."

She pushed at his shoulder, noting how firm his muscles were. Quickly pulling back her hand, she grinned at him. "We'll see about that."

"But we can call them *Tetraploids*, too." He laughed. "It's confusing when they are really just beautiful flowers."

Rebecca nodded in agreement, gathering her scattered emotions. "You didn't have to work overtime."

"I didn't mind. You needed the time with your sister."

"I did," she admitted, trying to put what he'd suggested out of her head. Hybrids with their names joined. A wild suggestion. Naming a lily after her, even more so. Getting back to earth, she said, "Normally, Hannah comes by on Saturdays since I sometimes get last-minute guests who can't wait to buy lilies. She helps me with the money and such."

"She seems like a nice girl."

"*Ja*, wait until you get to know her. *Mischief*

is her middle name." Rebecca laughed again. "She's married to Samuel Yoder. He's related to Moses Yoder, the man who used to work here."

Jeb nodded at that. "She surely had you laughing this morning."

How much had he heard? Rebecca didn't dare tell him what they'd discussed. Noah sending Hannah to push Rebecca onto Jeb. It was *baremlich*—terrible.

"We like to tease each other, and we compare notes on our overbearing brother. She's married now, so I'm the one he finds fault with most. I'm surprised he hasn't *kumm* running to fuss at us for fishing."

"Noah?" Jeb grinned. "I saw him leaving with his family a little while ago. I reckon they have plans for the day."

She wanted to say that was *gut* to hear.

Instead, she replied, "They go to the Hartford General Store to buy supplies. It's a perfect day for a buggy ride."

"A perfect day for fishing, too," he said. "I've caught two nice bream and I have a frying pan waiting for them."

She sat on the bench and offered him a glass of lemonade. "Sounds like a *gut* supper to me. You can take some tomatoes to add. Do you have potatoes?"

He put down his pole and took the lemonade

and a cookie. "I don't have any potatoes. I could stir-fry them and slice the tomatoes."

"I'll gather them when you're finished fishing."

"Denke." He glimpsed back toward the house and then looked at her. "May I sit here with you for a moment or two?"

She nodded. "Longer than that, Jeb, if you'd like."

He slid onto the bench, leaving a measure of space between them. "So if you were engaged, you'd have mentioned that, right?"

She decided to tease him a bit. *"Ja,* in the same way you mentioned you were once Amish." Then she smiled. "Gotcha."

Jeb shook his head and bit into his cookie. "I can see your sister is not the only one who has mischief on her mind."

Rebecca laughed and ate her cookie. "You'd better keep an eye on your pole. I've heard there is a big bass roaming this creek."

"He might already be in my fishing net, floating just beneath the surface."

"Ah, so you can make jokes, too."

"Every now and then," he admitted.

She laughed and wished this kind of day could last forever. The buzz of bees, the wind singing through the trees, the scents of spring.

For the first time in a long time, Rebecca felt hope in her heart.

Then she looked into Jeb's eyes and saw John there.

John should be here on her bench, not a stranger who was lost like a prodigal. Jeb was a kind person, and a handsome man. But could anyone ever measure up to her John?

Her laughter died down and she looked out over the water, no words forming on her lips. Tears formed in her eyes while she remembered how happy she'd once been. Why did this man have to remind her of all she'd lost?

"What's wrong?" Jeb asked, a frown on his face, questions in his eyes.

"I was engaged once," she admitted, the streaming water blurring as her eyes misted over. "But that was a long time ago."

Chapter Six

Jeb wanted to tell her he knew all about that engagement. But he couldn't find the words. He'd bring hurt to her either way. If he brought up John, and told her he was his kin, it would hurt. If he sat here and stayed silent and she found out later, it would still hurt.

"Do you want to talk about it?" he asked, deciding that staying neutral might be the best plan for now. He might not be here long anyway, and once he was gone, she'd never need to know.

Rebecca gave him a quick glance, then looked at the gurgling water that flowed through this small community. "What is there to say? We were engaged and about to be married. He was riding a horse, one his *daed* had just purchased and brought home. The horse was fidgety and skittish and a vehicle on the road backfired near where they were riding."

"It scared the animal," Jeb said, closing his eyes to the worst, and quickly opening them to see the horror in her expression She'd gone pale, her lips trembling.

She nodded, her hands held tightly together in her lap, her knuckles white against her blue dress. "I was there. I'd been watching him, my arms dangling over the fence rail." She shook her head, as if to get the memories out of her mind. "The horse lifted up and took off so fast, John lost the reins and... He was thrown. He landed too hard and hit his head against a fallen limb." She stood and stared at the water. "He... didn't wake up. I ran to him, and he wouldn't wake up. He was already gone."

Jeb tried to find air. He knew his cousin had died young, but he'd never heard the details. Her description was so close to what had happened to Pauly. "I'm so sorry you had to witness that, Rebecca. This is why you're afraid of horses?"

She bobbed her head. He stood up and moved close. "And this is why you never married?"

She whirled then. "*Ja*, how could I ever marry anyone when the man I loved so much died before we ever had a chance to be happy together?"

Jeb realized two things standing there, the scent of her milk-and-honey soap wafting out

around him. She would never get over losing John, and Jeb could never reveal that he was John's cousin. He couldn't bring her any more pain when he wasn't even sure if he belonged here.

Father, what should I do? How do I pray for this woman? Help me see the way.

It had been a while since Jeb had turned to God. He'd cried out to God a lot, blaming the world for his problems, and railing at God for creating them. But he'd learned his problems were because of his own doings and the consequences of his choices.

But Rebecca, what had she done to deserve such a cruel turn of events? She'd say this had been God's will.

Why would God do that to her?

You're here now.

Jeb took in a breath. He *was* here now. When he'd seen the sign on the road and walked up that lane, weary and drained, he'd immediately felt a sense of home.

I am here now.

"Rebecca," he said, wanting to say so many things, "I'm sorry for that horrible loss. Sorry that you had to witness the death of the man you loved. You've done something remarkable, though. You've created a thriving busi-

ness and made a life for yourself. A good life. You managed, even with tremendous grief, and you should be proud of that."

She wiped at her eyes. "*Ja*, I am content most days. But… Remembering is never easy. Remembering what might have been, that gnaws at me and stays with me every day of my life. I know John is with *Gott* now, and that there has to be a reason why this happened. I will find out that reason one day."

Jeb almost reached for her but drew his hand back. He had no right to let her think they could be anything but friends. He was drifter, a wanderer, a lonesome soul. Lost.

And she was a beautiful soul. Lost.

Would it be so wrong to think they could be together?

Maybe not wrong, but first he'd have to find a way to help her forget the man she truly wanted to be with. John, the man who'd left her all alone.

And Jeb would have to make some life-changing decisions. Did he want to stay here? In his heart, he did. But his head didn't think he could ever be worthy of a woman like Rebecca. He should pour out his heart to her, tell her everything. But then she'd never trust him again. It might be too late for the truth between them.

Jeb decided he'd leave all of it in the Lord's hands.

He'd do the work, be a friend to Rebecca and try to show the world he could be more if she ever hinted as such.

But would she ever see beyond her grief? And could he be more to her, as damaged and doubtful as he was?

He glanced back at her. "Do you want me to catch that big bass?"

She laughed at that. "*Neh*, let him be. He's been around a long time." Then she looked into Jeb's eyes, her heart showing in that beautiful gaze. "But I will be happy to fry the fish you did catch."

"You mean, for supper?"

She nodded. "With me. I'm inviting you to supper with me. Would that be okay?"

Jeb thought that would be wonderful. "Yes, that would be great. I hate eating alone."

"So do I," she said. "Fish a bit more and we'll go get things started. We'll have a feast out on the old picnic table under the oak."

"I'll try to catch another big one, but not Old Man Bass."

Smiling, she said, "I'm hungry. You might need to catch two." Then she headed back to-

ward the house. "We can talk about our lilies. Next week, we start transferring them to pots."

Jeb could think of nothing better than a good meal with a pretty woman who loved to talk about lilies.

"This is so good," Jeb said after he'd eaten his fish. "Crispy and perfect."

"I'm glad you caught several," Rebecca replied. She poured more tea into his ice-filled glass. They'd fried potatoes with sweet onions and sliced the tomatoes. She had apple pie that Hannah had brought.

"It's a nice night," Jeb said when she passed him his slice of pie. "You have good spot to watch the sunset."

"I do." She told him the story of the two windows in the kitchen. "My *daed* was always so proud he could do that for my *mamm*. She was able to see most of the sunrises and sunsets, depending on the season."

"That was thoughtful," Jeb said. "So your parents were happy here."

"They were. We all were. They loved each other so much, and they loved us." Curiosity made her bold. "How about your family?"

Jeb put down his fork and looked out at the glow of pink and purple over the water. "My

folks pretended to be happy, but they had a hard time of it."

Rebecca could see the deep pain and regret in his eyes. "I'm sorry, Jeb. Is that why you left?"

"I left for all the wrong reasons," he said. "I felt guilty after my brother died."

"Why?" she asked, figuring it had been hard for him to admit that.

He had to trust her. He knew he could, but he wasn't ready to let go of his shame. "It was my fault."

"How can that be?"

He sighed and gave her a look of resolve, as if he knew she'd keep asking. "He looked up to me. Paul—we called him Pauly—had issues. I didn't understand at the time, and neither did my parents. But now, having been out in the world, I found some answers. He had a birth defect that left him with the mind of a four-year-old. He was sweet one moment and angry the next."

He stopped, his eyes on the flowing water off in the distant. "My *daed* would beat him."

Rebecca put her hand over her mouth. *"Neh."*

Jeb shook his head. "It's hard to understand. Mamm loved Pauly so much. She always said he was a special gift. He'd be young forever. Only after she died, he changed even more. We all did. Daed got worse. He stopped with the ver-

bal abuse, but he shunned Pauly. It was up to me to take care of him."

"And you tried?"

"I did, but I was a teen. I had a job—we needed the money. Daed wasn't the best farmer." He took a sip of tea. "I worked at a buggy-repair shop not far from our house. I usually walked to work. Pauly didn't like being with Daed, so he'd sneak out and run away. Usually, he'd come straight to the buggy shop."

Rebecca put a hand on his arm. "You don't need to tell me the rest." She could imagine what had happened and she didn't want the details. Not yet. Not until he was ready to tell her everything.

Jeb let out a sigh. "Good, because I usually don't go further, even when I relive that horrible day in my nightmares."

She glanced at the creek and then back to him. "We share similar grief, ain't so?"

He nodded. "Becca, as Amish we learn that everything is *Gott*'s will, right?"

She nodded. "Correct."

"Do you ever question that?"

"I have, especially after I lost John."

"I did the same after Pauly's death. My *daed* and I never got along and being just the two of us—well—he used that to pick on me and blame

me and tell me how worthless I was. So, I left. I've been running ever since."

Rebecca's heart caved in. What this man had suffered—no surprise why he had been roaming the earth in search of peace. "You find it hard to believe that could possibly be *Gott*'s will?"

He nodded, his eyes full of torment. "I've been wandering for twenty years. My entire family is gone now. Did God put me through all of that, knowing I'd wind up here one day?"

Rebecca wasn't sure how to answer that. Had the Lord let John die, so she'd be sitting here with this man one day?

Anger pieced through her heart. She wanted to get up and go into her house and shut all the curtains. Why did Jeb bring this out in her, this need to let go of her bitterness and sorrow and find joy again? She wasn't ready for joy again. Not the kind between a man and a woman.

She'd had enough joy living here alone.

Hadn't she?

"Why do you think he brought you here, Jeb?" she asked on a sharp shrill.

"I've upset you," he said, standing. "And it's getting late. I should go."

"Neh," she said, her hand in the air. "Sit back down. You can't ask me something like that and then just get up and leave."

Jeb put his hands on his hips. "I shouldn't have shared all that and I know I asked a stupid question. I wound up here out of desperation."

"Maybe," she said, calming a little. "Why did you come here?"

He stared out toward the waning sun. "I've been to so many different places, some Amish and some *Englisch*. I guess because I'm getting older and I no longer have a home in Ohio, I thought I'd cross to the other side of Lake Erie and see what Lancaster County had to offer."

"It is one of the biggest Amish settlements," she said. "At least that's what the tourists like to repeat."

"Yes, and Campton Creek sounded perfect. Not too big and not too small. Beautiful."

"You did your homework on that, too."

He hesitated, then looked down at the ground. "I asked around, yes."

"So why would you ask me if *Gott* brought you here?"

"Look, it was a dumb question," he said as he started gathering dishes. "I got too deep. Never mind."

Rebecca stood back. She shouldn't push him when he'd been asking an honest question. "Jeb, we can't outguess the Lord. If He brought you here, He had a *gut* reason. But we'll have to see

if that reason is ever revealed. Maybe He just wanted you to come home to your faith."

"Maybe," Jeb said. He went quiet as they gathered dishes and walked toward the house. "I enjoyed supper. I'll find my answer one day. I have to believe that."

After they'd placed their dishes on the old farm sink counter, Rebecca turned to him. "If you mean to stay in Campton Creek, I think it's time you go and talk to the bishop. He's a kind man who offers advice and wisdom. Were you baptized?"

"No. I left before I took that step."

"Then you'll need some preparation so you can go before the church and ask forgiveness."

"And then it will be over. I'll be a true Amish again."

"Ja," she said. "If that's what you really want."

"It is," he said. His eyes stayed on her for too long. "That and so much more."

Before she could ask any more questions, Jeb turned and headed out the front door. Rebecca walked around the kitchen, the last glow of the sunset glistening through the trees and beaming a good-night to the creek stream.

"Why did You send this man to me, Lord?" she asked before she turned out the lamps and went up to bed. That was the burning question now. A question she might not ever understand.

Jeb had shown up out of the blue, but he'd also picked this spot, out of all the Amish communities in this area.

Did he know more about Campton Creek than he'd told her? Would he stay and become strong in his faith again? He sure was the best worker she'd had, but then she'd only had an older man before. He had not been inclined to talk, and he'd stayed out of her way most days.

Jeb had stepped into her heart from the moment she'd seen him strolling up the lane. She told herself she was only caught up in offering a stranger help and getting help in return, and she had to admit, because he reminded her of John, she'd been intrigued by him.

She needed answers in the same way she tried to figure out growing lilies. She had to have proof of what worked.

"I will keep praying for those answers," she told the Lord before she drifted off to sleep. Just like her beautiful lilies, Jeb needed to be cultivated and pruned a bit so he could shine brightly and find his faith, and so he could put down roots.

Chapter Seven

Jeb woke up the next morning still wondering why he'd blurted out his past to Rebecca. She was just so easy to talk to. He'd never felt comfortable around women, maybe because his father had not been a good example of how to treat women. His mother had tried to teach him to be kind and respectful of women.

"You are not your *daed*," she'd whispered one late night after his father had been on a rant. "You are a kind boy and I know you'll grow up to be a *gut* man. Kindness and respect will take you a long way in this world."

Jeb wished that to be true, but it wasn't in all circumstances. He'd tried so hard to forgive his father and turn the other cheek, but after Pauly died that had been almost impossible. If only he'd done the right thing that day.

After they buried his little brother, Jeb gave up on forgiving his *daed*.

He'd left his home believing that kindness and respect didn't always win out. He'd met some wonderful people out there in the big world, but he'd also met some cruel ones who would do anything to make others suffer. He didn't want to be that kind of person. When he gave someone his word, he kept it.

At least now he was home, and he had a job he really enjoyed, even with the hard work it required.

Even with the woman he couldn't help but be attracted to—his boss. Rebecca was kindness personified. An amazing woman. And so pretty at that.

Stop it, he told himself. He hadn't finished his story and he never would. Rebecca wouldn't want him here if she knew the whole story. The saddest part of that day Pauly had died.

Besides, Jeb was John's cousin, and he couldn't even bring himself to tell her that. Maybe that made him selfish, because he wanted her to like him on his own merit, not because he was related to the man she'd loved and lost.

I loved him, too. I just don't know how he'd feel about this. And Jeb sure didn't know how Rebecca would feel about him withholding something so important.

Jeb finished dressing and went to make breakfast. A knock on the door of the *grossdaddi haus* brought him out of his thoughts. He went to see who had come to visit this early in the day.

Noah stood there, dressed for church. "Are you ready?"

"Ready for what?" Noah asked, squinting into the morning sun.

"Church," Noah said, bringing himself on into the room. "I'll wait while you change."

"I hadn't planned on going," Jeb admitted. Amish church started early, around eight thirty in the morning, and lasted till noon. Jeb didn't mind that, but he wasn't sure if he was ready for being exposed to the whole community. Most Amish didn't judge and forgave easily, but just like the world out there and his *daed*, some did not.

"Oh, you're going, and you'll meet the bishop," Noah replied. "I mean—if you're serious about returning to your faith, of course."

Jeb wanted to be angry, but he was so confused he decided talking to the bishop might be for the best. "Is everyone in your family this bossy?"

Noah laughed. "*Ja*, better get used to it." Then he tugged at his Sunday hat. "I'll be waiting by the family buggy."

"The whole family?" Jeb asked, wondering if that included Rebecca.

"Sure," Noah said with a glint in his dark eyes. "My wife and I and Katie. And Becca always rides with us to church. The boys follow on their bikes or horses. Don't worry, we've got room for you."

Jeb stood there after Noah shut the door. What was up? Noah forcing him to go to church and yet, knowing he'd have to sit in the buggy near Rebecca. Noah sure was in a hurry for Jeb to meet the bishop. Rebecca had mentioned that last night, too. While Jeb knew it had to be done, he'd rather meet and talk with Bishop King in private.

But Noah had not asked, he'd told. Jeb didn't want to start off on the wrong foot on a Sunday morning, so he changed into the black pants and white shirt Franny had given him, telling him he might want to go to church now and then.

"I guess it's now," he mumbled as he grabbed a dark hat, hoping it was the proper one for church.

He had not been to any church in a long time. He'd entered a few when they were empty, just to hear the silence. He loved the way a still, silent church felt, so safe and protective. He loved the scent of sweet flowers and burned candles, the perfume of a hundred blossoms left over

by women who wore hats and used fans and walked around in their dresses and suits. Then he'd found other churches where everyone wore flip-flops and T-shirts and smelled like coconuts and pineapples. Where the women wore shorts and not much more than bathing suit tops. Some of the worst bars in Florida held church on Sunday morning. What was that all about? Maybe a bit of forgiveness for Saturday night transgressions?

The Amish didn't consider church as a building but rather a state of mind. That was why they held the service from place to place, home to home, moving around the community in a time-honored rotation. Jeb had missed that steady routine, too. It would be good to sit and listen to the old hymns and get acclimated to the old language, too.

He finished dressing and walked out into the warm morning, the buzz of bees humming in his ears.

He didn't have to look up to know what Rebecca would be wearing to church. But he couldn't keep his head down, so he took time to smile at her when she approached the buggy. Her green dress smelled fresh like her fields, the scents of sun and wind mingling with a slightly fragrant something. Peach, maybe?

"Jeb?" she asked, her eyes bright as he walked toward her. "Are you going with us?"

"Yep," he replied. *"Ja."*

She gave him a once-over. "Did Noah make you *kumm*?"

Jeb grinned. "Kind of, but he also told me I had to sit by you in the buggy, so I agreed on that stipulation."

She hid a giggle with her hand. "My *bruder* is so...difficult."

"He wants me to talk to the bishop, same as you suggested last night."

He saw fear in her eyes and a hesitancy. "What's wrong?"

"My *bruder*, going all around *me* to find someone for *me*."

Jeb shook his head. "I don't understand."

Her smile turned into a feminine pout. "Noah has decided to make a match for me—with you."

Jeb couldn't believe what he was hearing. Jolted down to his feet, he shook his head. "But Noah doesn't like me."

"I know," she said, whispering as the family came out to the waiting horse and the big buggy. "But when you told him you used to be Amish and you wanted to return, he got it in his head you'd make a fine match for me—his poor unmarried sister. Now he's determined to make that happen."

She must have seen his shock on his face. "Jeb, think nothing of it. I…we…can't listen to my misguided *bruder*." Shrugging, she said, "I won't let him force us into something we'd regret, and you shouldn't either."

Noah and Franny came out the door with Katie on their heels. Rebecca shot Jeb a warning glance. "Don't mention this."

"Are you two through passing secrets?" Noah asked, grinning. "It's time to go."

Jeb took the covered basket Rebecca held and placed it in the storage area of the open buggy. Then he helped her up onto the wide back seat. Katie jumped in between them. "Daed said I could sit with you, Aenti. He said between. Between."

Rebecca shot Jeb a wry smile. "Your *daed* always thinks of me, ain't so?"

Jeb wasn't sure if he should get in the buggy.

Katie nodded and grinned at Jeb. "I always get to sit with Aenti Becca, but never between before."

The three boys came charging out. "Getting our bikes," Michael called.

Noah nodded. "Do not be late. Stay right behind us."

His sons elbowed each other, scrambling for their bicycles, and took off ahead of the buggy. "We'll get a head start," Elijah shouted.

Katie giggled. "Can Jeb sit with us? Does he get on the side of me?"

"I can," Jeb said, thinking he still had a brain in his head after all.

Rebecca shrugged and mouthed, "Sorry."

He gave her a returning, "It's okay."

At least he was sitting close to her, even if Noah had forced his young daughter to be a temporary chaperone by stuffing the sweet child between them.

Katie, blissful and full of life, pointed out flowers and trees as they went along. Her chatter kept him from being able to talk to Rebecca.

But he was confused. Did Noah want him to marry Rebecca, since he was available and about to return to the fold? Or did Noah want him to bolt and run like the coward he was, knowing he couldn't marry her. That would break her heart, even if she didn't want to marry Jeb. She'd think she wasn't worthy of any man. Jeb told himself he couldn't fall in love with Rebecca. That would never work. He'd brought too much of his past with him, and he was withholding an important part of that past—the letters from John and his relationship to John.

Noah had backed him into a tight corner. Either get on with being Amish or get going.

And now, Jeb wasn't exactly sure which of those two choices he should pick.

* * *

Rebecca placed the container of roast beef sandwiches she'd made for the church meal on one of the broad tables the men had set up under the old oaks of the Weaver place. Jeremiah and Ava Jane made such a sweet couple. They now had four children, Ava Jane's older boy and girl, and now a younger boy and a baby girl. Their house was a four-square nestled on the property by the creek that Jeremiah's family had owned for generations. Jeremiah kept the place spic-and-span, and Ava Jane had made a lovely home inside the house and out. They often bought lilies to plant along the well-tended beds Ava Jane worked on all year long.

While Rebecca held joy in her heart for her friend, her own heart ached like a festering wound. Her brother schemed to pass her off on her employee. Jeb had looked so shocked earlier, she wanted to go home and curl up in bed. But Rebecca had learned a lot, being on her own. She had to be tough and gentle, determined and flexible, and she had to take care of the things no one else could tackle. She'd explain to Noah that he needed to stay out of her love life, or lack thereof. Neither she nor Jeb would be pushed into something so ridiculous. She'd make that clear to Jeb, too, so he need not feel obligated.

"Hi, Rebecca," Ava Jane said in passing. As

the hostess, she had to be frazzled but Ava Jane handled it easily. "How are you these days?"

"I'm…all right," Rebecca replied. "My busy season is about to start, so I'm a bit preoccupied."

"I heard you found a helper," Ava Jane said, her blue eyes matching the perfect, cloudless sky. "And just in time, at that."

"I think everyone has heard about Jeb, both *gut* and bad." Rebecca placed napkins and utensils on the table. The men would eat first.

Ava Jane stopped bustling about and touched Rebecca's arm. "Jeb seems like a nice person. Jeremiah can sniff out anyone who's faking in the same way he can sniff out fresh cookies. He likes Jeb. And if you hired him, you must trust him, right?"

Rebecca nodded, thinking of how kind Ava Jane was. "You've heard the rumors?"

Ava Jane nodded, her golden hair peeking out from her *kapp*. Placing a plate full of peanut-butter-and-marshmallow sandwiches closer to the other trays, she said, "About him being Amish, even though he came here as *Englisch*, *ja*." She scanned the table, then, satisfied everything was in place, turned back to Rebecca. "There were many rumors when Jeremiah returned after being away for twelve years. You

can imagine how he was scorned and judged. I was the one who judged him the worst."

"And now you are happily married."

"*Ja*, over five years and still going." Ava Jane ran her hand over the tablecloth. "Just remember, *Gott* knows how things begin and he knows how they will end. I've always admired your courage and your wisdom, Becca. Stay the course and forget the *blabberwauls*." Then she leaned close, "And don't let those who think you should be married worry you. *Gott* has that figured out, too. Trust me on this—Jeremiah and I are living proof."

"*Denke*," Rebecca said, touched that Ava Jane had been so honest with her.

Ava Jane nodded and whirled when one of her youngies screamed too loud.

Rebecca finished helping get the food out, her thoughts streaming along like the gurgling creek. She'd felt Jeb's eyes on her during the short buggy ride to church and then later, across the aisle through the hymn singings and the ministers preaching. She'd tried to focus on the sermon, but it had been extremely hard, knowing her brother wanted her to make a match with the first man who'd shown up to work for her. She was surprised he hadn't tried to finagle old Mr. Yoder.

She wished she hadn't blurted out Noah's

grand plan for them, but she had to be honest. Now she'd probably frightened Jeb right out of being her friend.

Because she couldn't imagine him wanting to be anything more.

Chapter Eight

Jeb walked up to Bishop King and nodded. "I'm guessing you'd like to talk to me, sir."

The bishop smiled and shook his hand. "I'm guessing you are the one who needs to talk. And don't call me sir."

Jeb nodded. "When could we speak? In private?"

Bishop King chuckled. "Anxious?"

"I guess I am at that," Jeb admitted. "I had not planned to get going on this right away."

He didn't know how much the bishop knew about Noah's interference in this decision, but he did know that if he didn't do something to prove he was an honorable man, he'd have to quit his job and leave Campton Creek behind.

Leave Rebecca behind. Which he should probably do on his own. Just go back to wandering around like a nomad. Only he wasn't

ready to go back out into the world, so he had to do this.

Bishop King motioned for him to move over to where a giant oak shaded them and gave them some space as people began to leave for home. The familiar sounds of horses being hitched up and buggy wheels squeaking mingled with children laughing and mamas calling. The spring air held a hint of warmth, a promise of summer, hope for a new beginning.

Jeb wondered if Becca was looking for him so they could leave. He wondered when he'd become so indecisive.

The bishop waited until Jeb gave him his full attention. "Why are you holding back on returning to your faith, Jeb?"

Jeb hadn't realized he'd been holding back, even though he obviously had taken a long time to reach this decision. "I'm afraid," he admitted, glancing around to see if anyone was listening. He figured everyone still here after church knew to steer clear when a newcomer and the bishop were standing alone and in conversation.

He was right on that account.

The bishop's shrewd dark eyes pinned him to the spot. "What are you afraid of?"

Jeb tried not to squirm under that solemn stare. "I've been away for twenty years." He explained the situation. "I don't have anyone

left. I knew this place from a relative who is no longer with us, so I came here."

"And you like our community?"

"I do. I found work that I enjoy, and so far, everyone has been kind to me."

"That is our way," the bishop replied. "Are you willing to work on returning to *Gott*?"

"I never left God," Jeb said. "I thought at times He'd left me, but I can see now He was there, but He was waiting for me to do what I needed to do." He shrugged. "He led me here, I think."

Bishop King's dark eyebrows lifted like curling fence wire. "You need to be sure."

Jeb took in a breath. It was now or never. "What is required of me? I was never baptized."

The bishop's smile held wisdom and kindness. "You'll have to do a refresher course on our ways—read the *Ordnung*, study your Bible and mind your manners. Once you've completed your learning, you'll go before the church and confess and ask for forgiveness and a return to the way of life you left. Your past will not be mentioned again."

Jeb didn't want to ask how long all of that would take. What if he decided to leave at the end of summer?

The bishop sensed his trepidation. "This is a

firm commitment, Jeb. If you can't follow our ways, you won't be able to return. You will have to live in the *Englisch* world."

Jeb nodded. "I'm going to ponder what you told me. I knew as much but hearing it from you makes it real."

"Take time to think on this," Bishop King suggested. "*Kumm* and see me next week." He gave Jeb his address. "I have faith in you, Jeb Martin. I've already heard *gut* things about you."

"But if I go through with this, you might hear bad things."

The bishop touched a hand on his arm. "All the more reason to be reborn in your faith, ain't so?"

"Yes," Jeb said. "The very reason I've been roaming around. I didn't feel worthy of ever returning."

"*Gott* will be the decider of how worthy you are," the bishop replied. "I feel confident that he has deemed you so."

"I want that," Jeb said. He did want that. He turned and looked up for the first time. And saw Rebecca across the way.

She waved and he waved back.

Bishop King chuckled again. "I think you want a lot of things, young Jeb. God did bring you here. Now I have no doubt of that."

* * *

Rebecca didn't ask any questions on the way home, since Katie was back between them and chattering like a little magpie.

"Aenti, did you like the sandwiches? Peanut butter and marshmallow is my favorite. I could eat them all day long."

"I had a bite or two," Rebecca replied, giving Jeb a smile. "I enjoyed all of the food."

"I had peach cobbler," Jeb said to Katie. "It was sweet."

"My *daed* says I'm sweet," Katie replied.

"You are at that." Jeb looked over at Rebecca, making her wish she had children of her own.

Noah glanced back. "Katie, aren't you tired yet?"

"Neh," his daughter said. Then she yawned.

They all laughed at that, but Rebecca could see the tension in Jeb's face, even when he smiled. She'd have to talk to him about his meeting later.

Once they were home, Jeb and Noah went to take care of the buggy and horses, leaving her with Franny and Katie. "I'm going on home," she said, watching as the boys biked up to the house. After they hurried to do chores, she turned back to Franny. "I'm tired."

"I'm sure you're more than tired," Franny re-

plied, glancing toward the barn. "Noah should mind his own business."

"He told you of his wild scheme, then?"

"He told me of his *wunderbar gut* idea," Franny said on a snort. "In his mind, anyway."

Rebecca shook her head. "He's forcing Jeb into something he might not be ready for. Being Amish again is a big step and he's been away a long time. That's enough in itself, but now my bossy *bruder* throws me into the bargain, too."

"I tried to reason with him, but you know how he can be," Franny said. She stooped to deadhead a geranium. "I'll try again. Don't let him force you or Jeb into something you don't want, Becca."

"I don't plan on that." Becca thanked her for the ride and then started toward home. She'd have to talk to Jeb some more tomorrow. Today, she was too weary to think about her interfering brother. She'd make sure she talked to Noah, too, but in private. She needed him to understand she was happy with things the way they were.

She went inside the coolness of her empty house, then cleaned and put away the casserole dish, made herself a cup of mint tea and decided to walk out to check the fields. It was her daily habit, to go back out and just…be still.

Gott would want her to be still and think things through. Then she'd have to trust Him. Not anyone else.

Just as the gloaming came in a wave of burnished sunset, the air became cooler, and the wind died down to a sweet melody that played through the trees. She stood by the lily field, thanking the Lord for His provisions, for her love of flowers and for sending her a helper who could keep up with her.

Rebecca breathed deep and accepted that she had no control over any of this. She'd have to wait on the Lord to show her the way from here on out. Jeb had come into her life when she needed someone to help her with her work.

But she had to wonder if he was meant to be here. When she looked back on the last few months, and the day she'd heard that her long-time employee would have to move on, she'd felt a sense of panic. But she also trusted that she'd know when the right person came along to replace him.

She'd known that day she'd seen Jeb walking up the road. She couldn't send him away when he desperately needed to be needed.

And she had so desperately needed someone.

Not just for these beautiful budding lilies, but for her own peace of mind, too.

She sighed, turned around to go into the house and saw Jeb standing there in her yard.

She'd take that as a *gut* sign she'd made the right decision.

Jeb had waited until near dark to go for a walk. That walk had brought him to Rebecca's backyard. Afraid Noah would see him if he came up the front lane, he'd snuck out through the woods like a thief running from the law.

But this place calmed him and gave him time to stop and think of everything that had brought him here. He wished John could be here, married to Rebecca, with children running around. Then Jeb could feel right, more at home again.

But John wasn't here. He was with God now. Guilt filled Jeb's soul. He shouldn't have erratic feelings for his cousin's girl. But he also knew marrying again after becoming a widow was not frowned on in an Amish community. More like, it was expected so no woman had to go it alone. Would John approve of him now, however? Technically, John and Becca had never married. And yet, it felt as if they had. It felt wrong, even when it felt right.

He saw Rebecca on the edge of the lily field. She looked as if she belonged there, like one of the slender, elegant lily buds that would soon be

bursting with color. She was a burst of color, a taste of spring, a ray of hope.

Stop that mushy-head talk, he told himself. He cleared out his brain and walked toward her.

"What are you doing?" she asked, her voice breathless.

"I don't know," he admitted. "I needed some air, and this is the best place to find that and some space."

"So, you decided to claim my favorite spots as your own. First the bench by the creek, and now my lily field?"

"I can leave." When she didn't speak, he turned, feeling at a loss.

"Jeb."

Her voice carried over the wind like a prayer.

He whirled back around. "I can leave. I mean really leave. Pack up and move on. That might be for the best."

"Is that what you want?" she asked, her tone low and full of that small question.

"I don't know," he said again. "I've never been this confused in my life."

"Are you warring with *Gott*, then?"

"I could be. I want so much to just be at home again, but is this where I stop? Is this where I need to stay?"

She moved closer, the last of the sun's glow set behind her like a painting. "I think home

isn't a physical place. It's where you feel the most *at* home. It's a place inside your head, and your heart. But to be here, to be Amish, you will be making the most important decision of your life. I don't believe you left the Amish, Jeb. I believe you left a life that was not best for you. You couldn't save your *mamm* or your brother, Pauly, but you could save yourself in the only way you knew."

"To run."

"*Neh*, to walk away from everything and try to find some peace. And that action spanned twenty years and brought you here. This community could be your home, your place to live, your place that comes to mind when you think of home."

She was close now, so close he could reach out and touch her. He didn't. He stood a foot or so away, enjoying the lilt of her words, accepting the truth in those words, and accepting that he did feel at home standing here with her.

"I'm going to stay," he said, meaning it now, knowing it now. "I'm Amish. I've been an Amish man lost in the world."

"You're not lost anymore," she replied, her eyes telling him the secrets she couldn't voice. He believed she wanted him to stay, but maybe she also wanted to deny that.

"No, I'm not alone but I still have many roads to walk before I can be completely at peace."

"You did talk to the bishop. That is a start."

"It is. I have to let him know if I'm committed. Now, after your words to me, I am committed more than ever."

"I'm glad," she said, her hands clutched over her apron. "I like having you around."

He smiled. "I like being around you, but Becca, we have to accept that before I can be true, I need to find God again. Then I'll work my way toward the other part of why I'm staying."

"And what would that be?" she asked, her breath held on the air.

"You, Becca," he whispered. "You make me feel this peace inside my soul."

She gasped and put a hand to her mouth, tears forming in her eyes. "I have prayed for us, Jeb. Prayed for you to stay and find your faith again, prayed for myself to accept what comes, if it is *Gott*'s will. I don't want you to be forced into something you'd regret."

Jeb's heart opened at the agony in her words. She seemed sure about her feelings. They could only be friends. "And I don't want that for you either."

"We need to let things take a natural course. Nothing can be pushed or rushed."

"I have the rest of my life," he said with a smile, thinking being a friend of this woman would be an honor and a blessing.

"So do I."

He turned then and walked back toward his little house. But he pivoted at the corner of her porch. "I'll see you tomorrow."

"I'll be here," she replied with a wave.

The sun settled for the night and the sky turned to a deep blue shot through with creamy oranges and vivid pinks that made the whole horizon sparkle like a bright quilt over the trees.

Jeb walked home, a peace coming over him. He smiled and took another look at the beauty around him. He could almost hear a sigh going out over the land.

Chapter Nine

"I'm here, Aenti Becca."

Becca looked up from her *kaffe* and toast to find Adam standing at the screen door, grinning at her. "Daed told me I get to help you all summer."

Even though her brother wanted her to make a match with Jeb, provided Jeb followed through on becoming Amish, he'd still sent Adam as a chaperone of sorts to work with her and Jeb each day. Now that school was done for the year, Adam needed to stay busy. Amish children had plenty of free time during summer, but they were taught chores and work all year long.

"Kumm," she said, tugging at his hat. "Did you have breakfast?"

He nodded. "Jeb is on his way. I saw him before I ran over." Her nephew tucked his straw hat low. "I like Jeb and if I work with you in your big garden, I don't have to muck stalls."

"A *gut* trade-off, ain't so?" She ruffled his long bangs. "I'll feed you and Jeb lunch, too."

He bobbed his head, joy on his youthful face. "What are we doing today?"

"Ah, today we'll start moving the harvest into the pots and containers I ordered a month ago. They're in the barn. We'll set up a worktable and get going. I'll be selling them on the road and also here on-site." She pointed out the window. I usually set up the potted plants just on the outskirts of the field, so customers might ask me to dig up more."

"And you do *gut* at the mud sale," Adam reminded her. "Two weeks from now."

"*Ja*, and I need to prepare for that, too. You are a *gut* helper already, reminding me of that important event."

A knock at the back door brought her head up. "Jeb, *kumm* in."

Jeb nodded to her. "We have acquired a hard worker," he said, poking at Adam's arm. "Let's see how much we get done."

The twelve-year-old beamed. "I can outdo you."

"You think so, huh?"

Rebecca shook her head. "Don't make me regret hiring you two."

Jeb gave her a quiet smile, his eyes telling her nothing. Maybe it was a *gut* idea to have

Adam here to break the tension and force her to focus on work.

"First, I need the big long table in the barn to be brought close to the house. Then I need the wheelbarrow and a shovel. Adam, you can bring the compost to and from the compost bed behind the barn."

"That stuff smells," Adam said, twisting his nose.

"That's because it's a natural mixture of food scraps and—"

"—manure," Adam finished, giggling. "I'll have to wash *meine* boots for sure."

"And your clothes," she added. "This is what we do. I know you'll be fine."

Adam grabbed a biscuit and headed for the door. "I'm going to find the wheelbarrow."

Jeb smiled after him. "He's a good boy."

"The best of the three," she said. "He's kind and sweet, while his older *bruders* are at that age where they think they know better than anyone."

"I remember that age," Jeb said after taking the coffee she offered him. "I was trouble from the get-go."

She wanted to ask him more about those days, but decided he'd talk about it if he wanted to do so. "I think we all have times in our youth we'd rather forget. Being a teenager is hard—that

transition from child to adult comes with a lot of drama and doubt."

"Were you trouble, Becca?"

She gazed at him, wishing she could tell him how she'd felt when she was young. "I had my moments."

They finished their coffee, neither ready to give up any past indiscretions.

"Are you ready?" she asked.

"I am." He smiled and put on his straw hat. "Lily field, here we come."

They worked together in the morning sun, transplanting lilies from the ground to the pots. Jeb learned the names and varieties of each one. Becca showed him how a bigger bulb could produce a stronger plant and bring more blooms. She smiled each time she held a hardy bulb in her hands.

He smiled because she smiled. Adam worked back and forth bringing what they needed to get several different varieties potted.

"I pot a lot of what is called Asiatic lilies—Stargazers are one of our most popular ones. People can use them for cuttings, or they can take them from the pot and plant them in a cutting garden. A lot of hostesses like to have that as a separate garden, so they can have fresh-cut

lilies inside and not bother their blooming lilies, which can return next year."

"The best of both worlds," he replied. "How deep should I plant these, then?"

She held up a clay pot and gave him the measurements and depth that would be best for the bulbs. "This one will work well for the section we're potting today."

"And we leave them along the back of the house, in the pots, until we're ready to sell them?"

She nodded. "*Ja*, but we water them often and let them do what they do best. Grow and bloom." Then she grinned. "Sometimes, I talk to them."

Jeb shook his head. "You are a constant surprise."

"Then you don't find me *lecherich*?"

He had to stop and remember the translation of that word. "No, you are not ridiculous. You're smart and you're passionate about your work."

She blushed and went back to work. "That I am. Let's get back to it."

"They love the sunshine," she said later, right after they'd had lunch underneath the great oak by her back porch. She kept glancing at the three-row-deep cluster of potted lilies lining the area by the porch.

"I think you love sunshine, too," he told her

while they watched Adam playing with a stray dog that came to visit daily, but never stayed. Adam named the dog Lily since the little thing seemed to like catching varmints around the fields and in the barn.

"I do love being out in nature," she said, laughing at the tan-colored dog and Adam tugging at a thick string of old rope. "I especially love midsummer when the different varieties begin to fully bloom. It's like…a rainbow sent by the Lord. Heaven surely smells like this field in summer."

Jeb couldn't take his eyes away from her. She glowed with the kind of contentment and hope that he'd longed for all of his life. She glanced back at him, her eyes going wide, and then she started laughing.

"What's so funny?" he asked, the lump in his throat making his words husky.

"These days, Jeb. They are so beautiful and so rare. I haven't smiled so much in a long time. But watching Adam and that little dog and having a picnic under my favorite tree with you—it's a blessed day."

"The best day," he replied. "I will remember this for a while to come."

Lily ran right into their picnic, then skidded to a stop when she smelled ham. Then she be-

came pristine and sat to stare at them with begging brown eyes.

Rebecca threw a small piece of the meat out from where they sat. Lily took off and gulped it down in one bite.

"That's all you get until supper," Rebecca said.

Jeb was almost glad the dog had interrupted them before he said something he'd regret. Becca was a lot like her lilies. She needed to be cared for and she needed air and sunshine to keep her happy. Strong but delicate, she might crumble if he told all he already knew about her. He had envied his cousin back in the day. John's letters had held happiness, while Jeb's life had only held hopelessness. Now, the guilt of his feelings for Becca made Jeb draw back. It would be best if he never shared that time with her. John's letters would only bring her pain.

And Jeb's confession to her would surely do the same.

Adam finished watering the potted lilies and turned to Becca. "I only gave 'em a little water, just like you said."

"You've done a fine job today, Adam. Think you'll like doing this all summer?"

Adam bobbed his head. "*Ja*, for certain sure. I don't have to put up with my *bruders* nagging

me, and Katie wanting me to play dolls with her. I like being here on my own."

Rebecca laughed at that. "Sometimes, it's *gut* to have a little time to ourselves."

Adam grinned and ran a dirty hand over his face, leaving a black streak. "Jeb is smart. He's showing me how to care for the horses— I mean—Daed has taught me a lot, but Jeb lets me do things right off. And he doesn't stand there watching every move I make so he can correct me."

Becca hid her smile. Her brother had a way of micromanaging everyone. She only knew that word from hearing her *Englisch* customers complaining at each other. Husbands and wives didn't always agree on how many lilies they actually needed to plant, but one customer had told her his wife worked in finance, so she liked to micromanage both her employees and her family.

When Rebecca had obviously looked confused, he'd whispered, "She thinks she has to oversee the whole family, and check every little detail, or we'll mess things up. Her staff fears her, but they get frustrated with all her suggestions and abrupt decisions. Me, I just love her anyway. She means well, most of the time. You know anyone like that?"

Noah had come to mind that day, same as

right now. She'd only nodded to her customer and now she only smiled at Adam. "Your *daed* has a big heart and he loves you. Jeb has a big heart, too, and he likes having you around."

"I guess I am nice," Adam said so seriously, she did laugh then. "Jeb told me I'm *gut* with the horses."

Jeb might be training his replacement. That made her both happy and curious. Would he leave once he had Adam trained in all his duties? Had that also been part of her brother's plan if they refused to go along with his arranged marriage for them?

Maybe they were all micromanaging things around here.

"You are indeed nice and also kind," she replied. "Now, go wash up and we'll have cookies before you go home."

Adam took off toward the pump, little Lily trotting after him before she pounced at his feet, wanting him to play. He'd worked without complaining, so her brother had taught him some things about hard labor at least. Noah had never sent any of the boys over unless she really needed them. He had to depend on them to help with the milking and care of the livestock. Noah raised dairy cows and sold their milk. Franny and the older boys took care of the goats. Franny made goat milk soaps to sell. Rebecca

always received supplies of the good-smelling soaps and lotions on her birthday or Christmas.

Franny had a regular shelf in Raesha Fisher's Bawell Hat Shop. While a crew made hats in the small factory behind the storefront, Raesha's staff sold local products of all kinds—the kind of genuine Amish products tourists loved. The shop carried Franny's soaps and lotions and took a small commission right off the top, but Franny got most of the profits. Several of the retailers around the community took in Amish products on consignment. Hartford Hardware always carried local foods and produce and handmade items, and also provided a garden section where Rebecca's lilies took center stage.

When Jeb walked over to help her finish tidying up, she told him about Adam's compliments. "He really looks up to you."

"I think that's good," he replied, his eyes going dark. "My little brother looked up to me, but I let him down when he really needed me."

She saw pain in that darkness. Jeb's guilt weighed him down. "You couldn't help the accident, Jeb."

He heaved a breath and gave her a longing stare. "I wish I could go back and change that day."

"What really happened?" she asked, hoping he'd trust her enough to explain.

Jeb glanced at the lily field and then back to her, his expression full of regret and torment. "Rebecca—"

"Hey, me and Lily found a lizard." Adam came running up to show them the squirming prize before Jeb could speak, and the moment was lost.

What secrets did he hide behind those compelling eyes?

Chapter Ten

They soon had a routine going. Potting, pruning, weeding, fertilizing, watering. Jeb loved the ebb and flow of the days, even as spring turned to summer, and the days grew longer and hotter. Customers trickled in and out and some days got really busy, but Becca handled her clients like a pro, and let him stay in the background doing the physical work, while she chatted with her returning buyers.

He liked to eavesdrop on her conversations regarding the lilies. He learned a lot this way, and he got to hear her sweet voice lifting out over the countryside.

"*Ja*, that one's okay. That blue mold on the bulb won't hurt a thing. And this is a *gut*-size bulb to replant in your garden. It will produce a fine showoff as the years go by."

"If you want fragrance, try the Fragrant Re-

turns. It lives up to that name. Lemony and it reblooms."

"Now, Miss Amelia is a more creamy-yellow but with a nice mild fragrance, but one of my favorites is Lullaby Baby. It's a white-pink blushing lily with a sweet fragrance. It really adds to your garden."

She knew all the names, the history, the scientific names, the award winners, and the everyday ditch lilies that had started her on becoming a prominent master gardener.

Jeb thought of the blushing lily with the sweet fragrance. Did she think of holding babies when she sold that particular flower? It sure made him think of that—a surprise since he'd resigned himself to the fact that he might not ever be a father.

Pushing such thoughts away, he took a glance at the dark sky. Today, rain had kept the buyers away and forced her two bored employees inside.

On rainy days, he stayed in the barn, and Adam took to hanging alongside him. He showed the boy everything he knew about livestock, because Jeb wanted to earn his pay even if he didn't work much on bad days. Adam had a general knowledge since Amish youngies were trained from birth on how to care for their live-

stock. While Becca only had the two horses, they still required daily attention.

"We have goats," Adam said this morning. "But we have to watch them. Aenti Becca does not like them in her lilies. Besides, if they eat too many, they can get real sick, real quick."

"Huh, I thought goats were notorious for eating everything and anything they wanted."

Adam did a little head shake. "Most people think goats will eat anything. They might try everything, but they get picky when they want a real meal. Mostly they forage until they find something tasty. But they can destroy whole gardens before they decide. The deer love lilies, too. But Aenti only shoos them away. She loves the fawns and does, so she makes sure she leaves them some feed to keep 'em out of her plants. But the goats—she's not too fond of them."

"So no lilies for goats, and be kind to the deer," Jeb said, thinking he learned something new every day. "My folks never raised goats. Just a couple of cows and some pigs."

"Pigs are messy, and they slide right through your hands," Adam said, his tone one that showed he'd had firsthand experience with fleeing pigs.

Jeb liked to quiz Adam. The boy was smart. Plus, that took Jeb's mind off Becca and helped

Jeb get to know people around here without actually speaking to them. "So how do you protect your goats and keep them from straying toward those tempting lilies out there?"

"We have high wire fences—the kind they can't chew through—and we feed them hay and some feed first thing each morning, while they're still in the paddock. That way they're full enough to roam around the big pen. My *daed* had to cut down all kinds of trees and shrubs—pines, rhododendrons, rhubarb, sumac, honeysuckle, any blooming or ornamental plants—just so they'd have a clear paddock and pen. We let them out there and they can't reach anything beyond what's healthy for them."

"You sure know a lot about taking care of goats."

"We learned the hard way, as Daed says. Lost a few goats to ferns and such. That's why Aenti Becca doesn't want them in her garden. It's bad for her plants and bad for the goats." He shrugged. "She might not like the goats, but she'd cry if anything happened to them."

"I'll keep that in mind," Jeb replied. He never wanted to make Becca cry.

"Look, the rain's stopped," Adam replied, grabbing his hat. "I'm gonna see what else I need to get done today."

Adam nodded, smiling at Adam's work ethic.

"*Denke* for helping me clean the buggies." Then he said, "Hey, Adam, I have a project, but I want it to be a surprise for Becca. I want to build her a potting shed close to the fields. If I let you help, can you keep it a secret?"

Adam's brown eyes lit up. "*Ja*, I can keep a secret, even when my *bruders* do something I don't like. Course, they kind of make me promise to keep their secrets—or else. Just let me know when you're ready to get going." Then the boy pivoted around like a top. "Uh, how do you plan to keep something so big a secret?"

Smart. Jeb grinned. "I'm going to cut the boards and make the frames, piece by piece, here in the barn and maybe at your *daed*'s place if he'll let me. Then I'll ask your *mamm* and Hannah to take her somewhere—a frolic or a shopping trip to town for an afternoon."

Adam's eyes brightened. "And we'll haul it all to the spot, and have it together before they get back? Like a barn building, but smaller!"

Jeb nodded and put a finger to his lips. "Not a word."

Adam did a silent zip with his fingers. "This'll be so *gut*."

Jeb hoped so. He was anxious to start his secret project.

After all the hauling they'd done to pot several varieties of lilies, he wanted to save Becca

some steps by creating a work building closer to the field. He'd make it enclosed with a window on each side, and with lots of shelves for displays and storage. But he'd create two big doors that could be opened wide, so customers could walk right up to buy their lilies. Later, he hoped to build her a small shed out by the road where she could be available there to sell lilies, produce and other products. He'd already altered a hauling buggy to hold more plants. It'd be easy to load one up and hitch a horse to take everything to the road. Her old wheelbarrow was about out of steam.

Those projects should keep him busy all summer. The more he worked, the more tired he'd be each night. So instead of lying there thinking about Becca, hopefully, he could fall asleep.

Becca had mended everything she could find, but the rain kept up. Now she'd turned to baking. Four loaves of bread sat cooling on the table. Two schnitz pies rested on the old sideboard, the scent of orange juice, cinnamon and the dried apples she'd boiled earlier filling the damp air.

She took her tea and stood looking out toward the fields. This had been a gentle rain, the kind that begged for a book to read and a hot cup of tea to sip. The drip-drip of the rain falling off

the old roof soothed her soul, while the homey smells in her kitchen made her wish for a family of her own, so she could share the food.

She'd send some home with Adam if she could catch him. The boy shadowed Jeb like a young buck following a stag. As much as she'd objected to Noah sending Adam over so she and Jeb wouldn't be alone, she did appreciate Adam's willingness to work hard. Jeb could be a *gut* influence on the boy, considering Adam learned way too much of what not to do from his older brothers.

Jeb had been a great influence on her, too. He'd reminded her of John when she'd first seen him, but now, he was just Jeb. He still had the same build and the thick, dark hair that stayed unruly, but his features were harder, more jagged and craggy. Still handsome, but he wasn't John. Jeb Martin filled his own skin and his own personality very well. She could appreciate him for who he was, not because of the man he reminded her of.

She'd heard from Franny he'd had several visits with the bishop, but Rebecca hadn't pressed him for details. That was between him and the bishop. That meant, however, that he was serious about joining this community. She hoped and prayed for that, not because of her confused feelings for Jeb, but because he needed a

home, and this community could be the perfect place for him. This job could be his as long as he needed it, too.

She turned from the window, thinking she'd have a quiet supper and go to bed early. But a knock at the back door brought her around. Jeb and Adam stood there looking sheepish.

"Ask her," Adam said, poking Jeb's ribs.

"You ask her," Jeb replied, grinning. "She's your aunt."

"We smell pie," Adam blurted. "And we're hungry."

Becca couldn't hide her smile. She let them stew there on the covered porch for a while. Then she lifted one of the pies from the sideboard and deliberately let them see it. "You mean this pie?"

Adam bobbed his head. "Told you, Jeb. Schnitz." He touched a finger to his nose. "I have the gift of scent and I smelled cinnamon and orange, and a whole stew pot of apples."

Jeb rolled his eyes and glanced at Becca. "Well, I have the gift of a grumpy stomach. That looks and smells delicious, whatever you put in it."

She laughed and motioned them in. "Wash your hands and make sure your boots are passable."

"We checked our boots," Adam replied as he

almost knocked Jeb out of the way to get into the kitchen. "And Jeb makes me double-wash all over every day."

Becca sniffed. "You both smell clean enough. Have a seat and I'll pass the pie. Jeb, would you like *kaffe* or milk?"

Adam lifted a hand. "Milk is real *gut* with schnitz pie."

"Then milk it is," Jeb said, his gaze moving over Rebecca's face.

She blushed, thinking she'd missed him. This visit was a surprise and a joy. She didn't even mind that Adam was with him. She'd send pie home with her nephew. Really, she was almost glad Adam had come inside. She could be with Jeb, but not be alone with Jeb. Because her heart might do something stupid like make her flirt with the man if they were alone.

His eyes told her he might be thinking along the same lines. That, or he really just wanted some pie.

Jeb enjoyed every bite of the pie. He enjoyed watching Rebecca even more. She moved around her kitchen like a dancer doing a choreographed waltz. When she turned and saw him staring, he lowered his head. "This is really good. I haven't had schnitz pie in many years."

He glanced out the window. "I think this crust is even better than my mother's."

Adam's head shot up. "Jeb, why did you jump the fence?"

The question, asked with such earnest curiosity, threw Jeb, and surprised Rebecca.

"Adam, do not be so nosy."

"It's okay," Jeb said. He'd give the boy the honest truth. "I was mad at the world, and I think I was mad at God, too. I had a bad home life. Then I lost two people that I loved."

Rebecca shot her nephew a warning glance. Adam looked from her to Jeb. "I'm sorry, Jeb. I reckon that could make anybody mad."

Jeb fought against the lump in his throat and the hot mist forming in his eyes. "I shouldn't have blamed anyone," he said. "And I shouldn't have stayed gone for so long."

He pushed the pie plate away, leaving a big chunk of crust.

He didn't tell the boy that he blamed himself more than anyone for not taking care of the two most fragile people in his family—his mother and Pauly. He failed them…and his father, too, in every way.

"I'd better get home," Adam said, giving Rebecca a worried glance. "Did I ask too many questions? Mamm says I'm too chatty for my own good."

Jeb stopped the boy with a hand on his arm. "You did nothing wrong, Adam. I enjoy our conversations. It's just difficult to talk about those who've gone on before us. But take this as a lesson from me. Never abandon the people you love. Family is more important than anything. Remember that."

"I will." Adam swallowed, his eyes going wide. "I hope you can stay here and be part of our family, Jeb. I sure do like you. And… You make Aenti Becca smile."

Then he grabbed the extra pie Rebecca had cut and wrapped and turned to head out the door, leaving Jeb to stare over at Rebecca. "Is that true? Do I make you smile?"

She wiped at her eyes and sank down across from him. "Most of the time, *ja*, but right now I just want to cry. You've been carrying a heavy burden, Jeb. Don't you think it's time to let it go?"

Jeb stared over at her. He wanted to let it go, so much. He wanted to let it all go, tell her the truth, and then take her in his arms and hold her tight. He wanted to feel the goodness and pureness that flowed through her, needed it to cleanse his sins and his soul.

Instead, he stood. He had to get out of here before he made a big mistake. He couldn't blurt

out the truth. Not yet. "Thank you for the pie. I'll see you tomorrow."

Then he went out the door and walked home in the gentle rain, his sins still burning at his soul.

Chapter Eleven

Noah was home when Jeb got there. Normally, he'd dread seeing Rebecca's overbearing brother, but today he needed to talk to him.

"Noah," he called, thinking if he started his secret project as soon as possible, he'd feel better about everything. "I need to ask a favor."

Noah waved him into the barn since it was still sprinkling rain. Once Jeb was inside, Noah stood staring. "What do you need?"

Jeb explained what he wanted to do for Rebecca. "I thought I'd work on it here, mostly so Rebecca won't see it. Then we'll ask Hannah and Franny to get her out of the house for a few hours, so we can bring in people to help put it together while she's away."

Noah gave him a confused stare. "That's a mighty ambitious project, but she does have a

birthday coming up. Do you have enough lumber for such a project?"

"I found some in the barn and it's in good shape. I might have to add a few pieces, but it's not going to be a big shed. Just a place where she can work—like a greenhouse."

Noah's fierce stare didn't evaporate. "Why are you doing this?"

Jeb felt the fire of that stare. "Because she needs a shed close to the field. She wasted a lot of steps yesterday and today, going back and forth with plants and pots. I tried to fix the old wheelbarrow and it's not going to do. She shouldn't have to stoop and bend all day long when she can have a nice place with shelves and stools and a whole wall full of any kind of tools she might need."

Noah burst out laughing.

"Is this funny to you?" Jeb asked, anger and frustration mounting. Was he wrong to want to make Rebecca's whole operation more efficient?

Noah put a hand on his shoulder. "You really do care about her, ain't so?"

Jeb shifted on his work boots. He might have known Noah would get the wrong impression. He'd never understand the man. "Of course. She's my boss and she works hard. Adam has been a big help, but honestly I don't know how

she did this with the old man she told me about being her only helper most of the time."

"I've encouraged her to hire more help, even offered to help her pay for it, but my sister likes her solitude and the quiet," Noah replied, serious now. "I'm glad you want to do something nice for her. How are the lessons with the bishop going?"

And there it was—the reason Noah was so pleased with this idea.

"We aren't talking about me," Jeb replied, wishing everyone would stop trying to pair him with Rebecca. "I need your permission to use the barn and I'd like to borrow some of your tools to plan out the shed pieces and have them tagged and ready so we can get this built. Adam wants to help, and he's promised to keep it a secret."

Noah laughed again. "Did he, now?"

"He promised."

"I'll speak to him." Noah glanced around, then turned back to Jeb. "My sister lost the man she loved before they were married. Right before they were to be married. She's never quite recovered. I don't want her to get hurt again. Understand?"

"I do understand," Jeb replied. "More than you'll ever know." Then he got bold. "But explain to me, if you're so worried about her get-

ting hurt why are you insisting that I consider marrying her?"

Noah looked surprised and then he looked sheepish. "Well, she has a lot of love to give, and she needs someone who can match her, step by step. I keep my eye on her, as you well know, and it irritates her to no end, as you've probably noticed. I'd rest better knowing she has a *gut* man in her life. You fit the bill, except for you needing to reaffirm your faith, of course." Noah paused and let out a sigh. "I know I've been hard on you, but this is what I mean—if you and Becca become close and then you just up and leave, she'll be devastated all over again."

Jeb could see the love and concern in Noah's eyes.

He looked over at Rebecca's house. "I like the work, Noah. It's helping me in more than just financial ways. A good day's work makes a man feel worthy and hopeful. I won't mess that up by hurting the woman who was willing to give me a chance. The only person in the world, really, who was willing to give me a chance."

Noah stayed silent, his hands holding to his suspenders, his dark eyes solemn. "I will help you build the potting shed, as a gift to my sister. We will make sure it's a surprise." He shrugged. "And I have some lumber here in the barn that needs to be put to *gut* use. If you need more,

let me know. I'll buy some at the lumberyard in town."

Jeb breathed a sigh of relief. "I'll pay."

Noah gave him an appreciative stare. "No, you're doing enough. Sometimes, Jeb, the thought is worth much more than the cost."

This would cost Jeb a little bit more of his heart, which he was willing to give. But Noah's warnings still rang loudly inside his head. Could he follow through and stay the course?

He prayed he could, and he would talk to the bishop about his fears and concerns.

"Denke." Jeb nodded and shook Noah's hand. "I'm glad we've come to an understanding. I want this to be a work shed Rebecca can use every day. I believe she will find the shed efficient and accommodating."

Noah chuckled and hurried toward his house. Then he called back, "I have no doubt she will appreciate it."

The next week was a busy one as the whole community prepared for the upcoming mud sale. Jeb helped neighbors put finishing touches on the things they wanted to sell at auction and also helped set up the grid for the sale to run smoothly.

On Saturday, Jeb and Adam loaded up the hauling buggy with potted lilies and a few other

perennials and took off to the third sale of the season. Rebecca, Hannah and Franny had all kinds of foods and crafts to showcase, and Noah had some farm tools to be auctioned, so Noah packed the family buggy with their wares, including two quilts to be auctioned off, too.

Noah had told Jeb this particular sale went toward the volunteer fire department, and since several Amish men volunteered, the whole countryside came to show their appreciation. "It's like a big festival, with food and celebrations."

"I heard Becca and her sister talking about the quilts they'd made."

"Some of the quilts go for hundreds of dollars," he'd said. "The *Englisch* get intense about handmade Amish quilts."

Jeb had liked Campton Creek from the moment he set foot in the quaint little township. Everyone here from the *Englisch* to the Amish had been kind to him. He didn't mind helping to pay it back somehow. He might even volunteer himself.

Soon, the two buggies were heading into town, where the sale would be held in the big park by the creek, Jeb and Rebecca in front with Noah's family following.

While the horse trotted leisurely, Rebecca explained how the town came to be and pointed

out the Campton Center, which used to be a private home. Majestic and big, the brick house with the grand white columns took center stage on the main thoroughfare. The *Englisch* Camptons were the original founders of the town and still had relatives here. Judy Campton, the matriarch who had lived in the house, was now in an assisted living facility that she'd funded to be built not far from here. It served both *Englisch* and Amish. But her friend and assistant Bettye still lived in the carriage house apartment and often helped out in the offices.

The house and grounds were pretty, but he rather enjoyed looking at Rebecca. She wore a light green dress that matched her eyes, and her hair was perfectly parted down the middle, not a strand out of place underneath her shining white *kapp*.

"A lot of people have been helped there—with legal issues, heath issues and financial issues. They serve the Amish mostly, but anyone in need is welcome. You might see Jewel running around. She's the manager and… Well, she's a bit eccentric but she has a heart of gold."

"I take it this Jewel person is not Amish."

"Neh." Rebecca giggled. "She used to be a bouncer at a bar, and she went through a lot— drugs, assaults, depression. But she got herself well of all that and now she likes to say she's

high on Jesus." When he frowned, Rebecca added, "Jewel is one of those rare people who loves everyone, no matter their flaws. So, we in turn love her back."

Jeb listened in awe, wishing he had someone in his life to love him unconditionally. He had the Lord. He knew that and Bishop King had encouraged him to remember his faith, to breathe it and accept it, rather than trying to force himself onto it. "Let the faith grow from your heart, Jeb. Don't pretend. That won't work. You have the foundation, but you lost your way. You'll know it's in your heart the minute you accept *Gott*'s love fully back into your life. Your heart will burn with such joy." Then the bishop had smiled. "And you will be worthy of that joy."

Jeb could feel a burn right now. It happened each time he glanced at Rebecca. The day was beautiful and bright, with low humidity and the kind of spring breeze that made a man feel alive. And hopeful. A new life, a new beginning.

He felt it, all right. And he thanked the Lord for providing such moments. But how could he ever be worthy of such hopes, of a new beginning? He wanted so much, but he couldn't risk hurting Rebecca. She loved John, still loved John, or she would have married by now.

He'd not told her the truth—about John—and

about what had truly happened the day Pauly died. Jeb's hope sank. If he were to be honest with her, Rebecca would send him packing.

He'd have no new beginning. Just another tragic ending.

Rebecca wondered about Jeb. They'd been laughing and talking, then he'd gone quiet on her. She'd noticed that about him. Sometimes, he'd go to a place in his mind, a faraway place. The place where he kept his secrets and his pain.

She wished she could help him, but she had her own dark times, her lonely times full of regret.

She wished they could help each other.

Lord, I pray You will show us the way.

Her silent petition on their part would stay between *Gott* and Rebecca. As they pulled up the wagon full of plants, she turned and checked to see if Noah and Franny were behind them. Katie waved to her and smiled. Rebecca waved back, then she looked over at Jeb. "Are you ready for this?"

"As ready as can be. I'll do whatever is needed."

"Is something wrong?"

"No." He gave her a crooked smile. "I guess I'm feeling homesick and missing those I love."

Ah, that would explain his sudden quietness. "They are safe with *Gott* now. And you are here

on earth, on this fine day. I hope you have *gut* memories of today."

He gave her a soulful smile. "I think I will."

"Everyone is here and accounted for," she told Jeb. "The boys came early in the summer buggy to help set up. We hope. Those three manage to get right into trouble just standing still."

"Adam says his brothers keep him in trouble."

Rebecca couldn't argue with that. "I think that's part of why Noah sent him to help us. That and the poor youngie is a distraction for us."

"Oh," Jeb said, back to smiling. "Do I distract you from your work?"

She gave him a quick glance and caught the smile he tried to hide. "At times, yes."

After they found the big open booth where they'd set up their plant nursery, he laughed and hopped down to get the horse situated. Then he started helping her unload the plants. "So, I'm a distraction," he reminded her. "So are you at times."

Rebecca shook her head. "We are so concerned with distracting each other that it's becoming another distraction. Why don't we just accept that we are friends?"

Hiding his disappointment, he said, "I thought that was a given."

She pursed her lips in a teasing way. "I need something official."

He grinned. "I took this job because I needed money and a purpose. You've given me that and more. I'd like to be your friend."

"Then you are my new friend, Jeb."

"Ah, then call me Jeb, the way you've been doing."

"And you call me Becca, the way a friend should."

They stood with a white lily between them. An Easter lily.

"To new beginnings," Jeb said, watching how she held tight to the plant.

"To new sunrises and sunsets," she replied. Then she sniffed at the lily, her eyes closed in bliss, her smile shining a light on his heart.

Jeb had never wanted to kiss a woman so badly, but he stood and took in the lemony scent of the lily, along with the sweet perfume that seemed to surround Becca.

That joy burned another warm thread through his heart, a thread that warred with the secrets of his soul and bound him to this woman forever.

Chapter Twelve

Rebecca's nursery booth stayed busy all day long. She could hear the auctioneers calling out, their gavels hitting against the podium each time an item was sold. Hannah came to help and told her their quilts had sold quickly.

"Both went to sisters who live next to each other in Florida. They were so happy to get them and know that sisters had quilted them together. One loved the wedding ring quilt and the other had to have the tiger lily." She poked Rebecca's arm. "When I told her how you'd made it and also grow lilies, she said they'd come by here soon."

"The threads of life," Rebecca said with a smile. "They flow through all of us. It's nice to know what we created together might be shared with their daughters one day. Or that lilies I grew will grace their gardens."

Hannah glimpsed at her, then waved to an Amish couple as they strolled by. "You're sounding wise, sister, but I think I hear a bit of resolve in your observation."

"I'm not wise, just beginning to see more and more how we're all connected. But I am resolved. I have to remember I am content, and *Gott* knows my future."

Hannah moved some colorful pots of Gerber daisies closer to the front row so customers could see them better. "Does this resolve have to do with the man over there loading lilies into that tiny car?"

Rebecca glanced to where Jeb moved back and forth to help Jewel place several White Lemonades into the trunk of Jewel's vehicle. Jewel planted a new garden of lilies just about every year at the Campton Center. The ruffled, creamy lemonade flower would open early with lush, hardy blossoms, and it tolerated the winters.

"It might," she admitted, after considering her sister's question. Keeping her voice low, she watched Jewel and Jeb having a lively discussion. "Jeb and I had a *gut* talk on the way here. But I don't expect him to stick around, even if he does become Amish again."

"Where would he go?" Hannah asked. "He says he likes it here."

"Onward," Rebecca said while she fussed and plucked at her plants. "He's a wanderer."

"Might he settle one day, if he found the right place and the right person?"

"That's what I have to be practical about," Rebecca said. "I have to accept whatever *Gott* has planned for Jeb. But I'd like it if he stayed. He and I have reached an agreement. We will be friends."

Hannah almost snorted but held her hand over her mouth instead. "Friends? Well, that's so practical I can hardly stand it."

"Don't tease," Rebecca cautioned. "There can never be more between us, and I must accept that."

"Because you have feelings for him?" Hannah asked, surprised.

"Because he needs a community and *Gott* back in his life," Rebecca said. "That is his priority right now. But... I do like him. A lot."

"Does he know that you like him a lot?"

"Shh, he's coming back. Of course not. I can't tell him anything when I'm not even sure myself. Now, hush up and help me line up the Stargazers."

Hannah nodded. "*Ja*, while I try to ignore those stars in your eyes."

"Who has stars in their eyes?" Jeb asked from the corner.

Rebecca shot her sister a warning glance. "I do. We should make a fair amount of money and be able to contribute more this year to the Volunteer Firemen's Fund."

"A good cause," Jeb said. "I talked to Jeremiah Weaver about joining up."

Her sister smiled at Jeb. "You're settling in nicely, ain't so?" Hannah's voice held that mischievous tone Rebecca knew so well.

"For now, I'd say so," Jeb replied, his eyes on Rebecca. "I'll go find us a quick lunch. Anything in particular you'd like, ladies?"

"The roast beef hoagies are great," Hannah said. "I'll have one of those."

"I'll take a chicken salad sandwich," Rebecca told him.

"Okay, I'll be back soon with that and some drinks."

"I can give you some money," Rebecca offered, digging through her tote bag.

"No, my treat," Jeb replied. "My boss pays me well."

They all laughed at that, but after he strolled away, Rebecca gave her sister a playful slap on the arm. "You are so bad."

"I can ask a person a simple question," Hannah replied with a smirk.

"It is interesting that he's thinking about be-

coming a volunteer fireman," Rebecca said, her gaze following Jeb as he greeted people.

"So interesting," her sister teased. "I think Jeb's wandering days will soon come to end. Think about how many people come here, some to come home, some to hide away from the world, but most always stay."

Rebecca shook her head. "I have given this over to the Lord, sister. If Jeb stays here, it will be *Gott*'s will, and it will have to be Jeb's decision. We are friends, and that will have to suffice."

She wouldn't hold him back from moving on, because she wasn't sure she could give her heart to anyone again. No matter how much Jeb made her feel as if she'd already lost part of that heart.

"Aenti Becca, I bought a doll," Katie said as she rushed up to Becca's booth.

The little faceless doll wore a light blue dress and tiny apron. It had no face because the Amish believed everyone was alike in the eyes of God. They didn't believe in graven images of any kind.

"That is a pretty little doll, for certain sure."

Katie swayed and hummed. "I named her Becky after you. Mamm said that name is a lot like Becca."

"Well, that's mighty sweet of you," Becca

said, giving Katie a hug. "Where have you been all day?"

The crowd had dwindled to just a few strollers, and she only had a few potted lilies and plants left. It had been a nice day.

"I had to stay with Mamm," Katie said, shrugging. "She fretted about me getting lost. My *bruders* don't like me tagging along."

Her cute pout only reminded Rebecca of the days to come. Katie would be a heartbreaker one day. Rebecca wished she could prepare her sweet niece for the hard parts of growing up.

"Does your *mamm* know you're with me now?" she asked Katie.

Katie danced back and forth with her faceless doll. "Uh-huh. She watched me and said to *kumm* straight here and stay put, while she cleans up and gets ready to go home."

Becca glanced down the way and waved to Franny. Her sister-in-law nodded and waved back. Franny's thoughtfulness in allowing her children to spend time with Rebecca made her thankful, but also hit her with a bittersweet pain.

Thinking about John, she remembered how kind and sweet he'd been, always with a smile or a joke. He made her laugh. He made her want to be a better person. She'd dreamed of the day they'd have a child together. When she lost him, her world had gone dark and even now, she pre-

ferred being in the shadows. She craved a quiet life. But lately, she'd become restless, her heart yearning for something she might not ever have.

Jeb had changed her way of thinking and lightened her loneliness. He'd brought their lunch and sat to eat with them, in between customers. Hannah helped there while they finished their meal. The food fulfilled Rebecca's hunger, but each time she glanced at Jeb, she thought again of how much she'd lost. She could never forget John. But Jeb was different—world weary and aged, but still handsome. He'd brightened in both spirit and looks since the day he'd come walking up to her house.

Thank You, Father.

Now, she began to pack up her plants, handing them off to him one by one, so he could carry them to the waiting buggy. When he returned for another round, Katie showed him her doll.

"That's nice," he said, glancing from the *kinder* to Rebecca. "My *mamm* used to make those dolls. She only had boys, so she'd give them to her friends for their daughters."

"You didn't have a sister?" Katie asked, surprise shining in her eyes.

"No, just a brother."

"Where is your *bruder*?"

Jeb looked at Rebecca, helpless on how to answer.

"Katie, do not pester Jeb. He has to finish his work."

"Can I help?" Katie asked, on to another scattered thought.

"Why don't you put Becky here by my tote," Rebecca said, giving Jeb a quick glance. "Then you can carry the small herb pots back to the wagon."

"Okay." Katie carefully lifted one clay pot of mint. "I'll be so careful." Then she tiptoed her way to the buggy.

Jeb smiled, then let out a breath. *"Denke."*

Rebecca nodded. "She is inquisitive."

"As she should be at that age."

He grabbed more pots and hurried to the buggy. Soon, he and Katie were in a deep conversation about butterflies.

But Rebecca could see the darkness falling back over his features. He somehow blamed himself for his brother's death. She prayed he'd be able to talk to the bishop about that and hand it over to the Lord. Sometimes, forgiveness didn't *kumm* easy, especially if a person couldn't forgive himself.

She had a feeling Jeb would not quit wandering until he could do that very thing.

* * *

Katie managed to get permission to ride home with Rebecca and Jeb, but she didn't squeeze between them. She sat in the back with what was left of their supply of plants.

"I like lilies," she said in a singsong voice. "Consider the lilies of the field…" Katie went on humming and talking to her doll. "My *aenti* grows pretty flowers. She has a gift."

Rebecca shot a quick glimpse toward Jeb and smiled. "Her *mamm* teaches her Bible verses in both Deutsch and *Englisch*," Rebecca whispered. "She is a good learner."

"She is wise," Jeb replied, his gaze on Rebecca for a moment. "God takes care of the lilies of the field and all creatures."

"He does, indeed." She settled back, tired but content, the lingering scent of Easter lilies—*Lilium Longiflorum*—wafting out around them. "He gave us such a beautiful earth. I'm honored to be able to work with His world."

"We had a profitable day, didn't we?"

She nodded. "*Ja*, better than I'd expected." Then she added, "*Denke* for your help today."

"Just doing the work you pay me to do."

"You will receive extra for the overtime."

He took a glimpse at her as they turned the big buggy onto her lane. "Then I can buy you a meal again."

"Or I could cook us a meal, to celebrate."

"That would work."

They dropped Katie off and watched for traffic as she crossed the road and ran home, Noah waiting for her with a smile.

"Your brother didn't even fuss at me today," Jeb said after they'd unloaded the few remaining plants from the buggy. "He kept me busy, though, probably so I wouldn't spend too much time with you."

Rebecca had seen Jeb helping out wherever he was needed. Noah would call him to do a favor in his stall, then send him to take over for someone else so they could go on a break. Noah's way of getting Jeb involved in the community, and it seemed to have worked. People had commented to Jeb each time he helped load pots and flowers onto their cars or vehicles.

As they pulled the buggy up to the stables, Rebecca turned to face Jeb. "Well, my *bruder* isn't here now, is he?"

Jeb gave her a look that told her about many things without him saying a word. Then he leaned toward her. "Are you saying you want me to stay and visit for a while?"

She glanced at the dusk. "The sun is about to set. It would be a shame to watch it all by myself."

Jeb looked from her to the creek. "I wouldn't

mind seeing the sunset. Let me get the animals settled and I'll meet you back there."

Rebecca watched as he hurried to the barn.

Now, why did I do that?

She should have said good-night and sent Jeb on his way.

But as much as she loved watching the sunsets to the west, she hated sitting on that bench alone.

Would it hurt to enjoy just a few more minutes with a man who had become her friend?

Chapter Thirteen

Jeb hurried with taking care of the horses and made sure the chickens were fed. Since Rebecca had no other animals, he made quick work of his chores, then washed up at the pump near the barn. He was tired, but in a good way. He'd met a lot of nice people today. Some frowned at him, but the bishop had made a special visit to their booth to talk to Rebecca and him, probably to see how they acted around each other.

"You are a great help to our Rebecca, Jeb," Bishop King had told him after buying two bright yellow lilies.

Jeb thought about how this place settled him and kept him calm. It would be hard to leave if he did decide to do that. Rebecca made each day so easy, and he had meant what he told her. He wanted to stay in Campton Creek. But want-

ing and doing were two different things. And even the best plans could change in a heartbeat.

When he came out of the barn, he saw her sitting on the bench, the old oak nearby shading her from the last of the sun's rays. She held a small tray with lemonade and two small plates of what looked like cake.

"What do you have there?" he asked as he approached. She smiled and scooted over.

"I had one loaf of apple bread left. Thought we could have a bite."

"That's nice. I like apple bread. But then, I've never turned down any food you've offered, in case you haven't noticed."

"I have noticed. *Gut* thing I like to bake."

He took the glass of lemonade and a chunk of the moist cake. "You are a kind person, Becca."

"*Denke.* I could say the same about you."

He chewed another chunk of cake, wondering what she'd think if he blurted out all his secrets and fears. "I have not always been kind. Bishop King has helped me to find a way to let go of all of the things holding me from my faith."

"Such as?"

"Anger, bitterness, regret and my need to fight starting over in a new place."

"That's a lot to let go of and straighten out." Rebecca gave him an earnest appraisal. "Would you like to tell me why you're so angry?"

Here was his opportunity to come clean, but Jeb held back. They'd had such a nice day and he didn't want to ruin it now. "I guess I'm angry about my home life not being so good, and that I tried my best and still failed. I seem stuck in the past, but I can't go back to fix it."

"You can't blame yourself for everything, Jeb." She sat silent, her hands in her lap. "When you're ready, will you tell me more about Pauly and what happened to him?"

She wanted the truth. He needed to give her the truth. "I want to tell you everything, but could we just be friends while we sit here? Could we enjoy each other's company and this evening?"

"I did say whenever you are ready," she replied on a soft whisper. "I want you to know you can tell me anything and I won't judge you."

He nodded, his appetite gone, his fears like talons clawing at his skin. "I'll remember that."

They finished their apple bread, and she set the tray down on the grass. Then Rebecca did something that made him wish he could be honest with her.

She took his hand and held it in hers while the bright yellow orb of sunlight slipped over the trees and the whole sky glistened and shimmered in a cascade of pink and purple.

As the last of the sun's rays descended, Jeb

knew one thing for sure. They had gone past the friendship mark.

Something more was going on with them now.

The next week, Jeb started on cutting the boards to build the potting shed he'd planned out for Rebecca. She rarely came into the barn, so he managed to saw several boards and number them before he stacked them in a corner.

Adam ran back and forth to alert Jeb if Rebecca was nearby.

"She's hanging wash."

"She's hoeing the vegetable garden. I'll go help and distract her."

"She's playing with Lily. That dog likes the treats she bought for her at the general store."

"Aenti Becca walked over to see Mamm. We're in the clear."

Today Jeb stepped out of the barn with Adam, since he'd just reported Rebecca had gone with his *mamm* to see a sick neighbor.

"Okay, so we'll measure the square footage underneath that old live oak that borders the corner of the field closest to the house. I've already cleared the ground since she doesn't want weeds growing on the edge of her garden."

"She's mighty thankful for that," Adam told him.

"But you didn't let anything slip, right?"

"*Neh*, I'm not going to spill the beans. Mamm and Daed know, 'cause I heard them talking about it the other night. Daed told me if I ruin the surprise, I'll have to clean the chicken coop for a month."

Having cleaned a few chicken coops, Jeb could commiserate with the boy. "Try not to mention it when she's around," he said. "You've been a great help. On Saturday, after half day, we'll work in your *daed*'s barn to build the frame for the roof."

Adam bobbed his head. "Then we just tote it over here and frame it up. Only after Mamm and Hannah take her to town."

"That's the plan," Jeb said. "Now let's measure this ground to be precise."

They hurried and figured out the dimensions and Jeb wrote them on an old slab of wood he kept out of sight.

They finished and went to prune the herb box so Rebecca would have fresh herbs to dry and some to use in her cooking.

By the time she came home, they were done with work and fishing at the creek.

She marched out and did a quick inspection, glancing over the growing lilies, then back to the vegetable garden, then the herb box.

"We did it all," Adam called. "Everything on your list is finished, Aenti."

"That's *wunderbar gut*, Adam. You can go home early."

Adam shook his head. "I wanna catch some fish first."

Jeb sent Rebecca a big smile. "He's already caught two nice breams."

"Okay, then," Rebecca said. "I have things to do in the kitchen. I will talk to you later."

Jeb waved and watched her walking toward the house, Lily Dog at her feet. It was a beautiful picture to see her there beside the blooming lilies, a dog dancing at her feet. A homey, welcoming picture.

One he thought of every day.

Since she'd held his hand the other night, something had changed between them. They were shy at times and laughing at other times. He had to wonder if this was what it felt like to fall in love. He smiled more, had more patience, tried hard to please Rebecca, enjoyed his talks with the bishop and slept better every night.

It could be the work and the sunshine. Or it could be the food and fellowship. But Jeb knew in his heart, he was changing because of Rebecca's sweet disposition and her tolerance of a stranger showing up on her doorstep. Rebecca showed people grace and kindness, things he'd not always had at home or out in the world.

But this week, he'd felt a shift in her that

concerned him. Did she feel the tug and pull of feelings, just as he did? Was she fighting those feelings, too?

After Adam went home, Jeb lingered to water some plants and hopefully see Rebecca again.

She finally came out on the porch. "All done for the day?"

"I think so," he said, noting she looked tired. "How about you?"

"I'm done here. We had a good crowd this morning. Thank you for taking the buggy of plants up to the road. I sold all of them." She studied her blue sneakers. "I like the bench you fixed and placed up there. I can sit and read while I wait for any customers."

"Well, you are welcome, but you don't have to sit there in the sun all day."

"*Neh.* I only sell there during heavy traffic times—morning rush is a *gut* time to catch people."

"Is there such a thing as morning rush in Campton Creek?" he teased.

"*Ja,* it gets a little busy now and then," she retorted with a smile. "A lot of buggies heading out for the day."

They laughed together, then Jeb asked, "Rebecca, are we okay, you and me?"

"What do you mean?"

"Are we friends?"

"*Ja*, but why do you ask?"

He couldn't blurt out his feelings, so he said, "I would never do anything to upset you."

"You haven't."

He wasn't handling this right. He tried again. "You held my hand the other night. It was nice."

Realization colored her eyes. "Oh, I did, didn't I?"

Jeb waited.

"I enjoyed holding your hand, but Jeb, you know how it is. We have to be careful. Noah is always watching."

"Noah had nearly given us his blessings."

"But he has to be sure… And I have to be sure."

"I see. You're all waiting for me to fail?"

He turned to leave, but she ran down the steps. "That is not what I said. Noah might be waiting for that, but I'm not."

"But you still aren't sure about me?"

"I'm sure of you, Jeb. I'm just not so sure of myself."

"Well, the same goes for me," he retorted, holding his disappointment tight. "I reckon we can keep working on it."

Rebecca gave him one of her soft smiles. "We are like those lilies out there. Growing, changing, blossoming. A work in progress."

Jeb wasn't sure he liked being compared to a

flower, but he did see one correlation between himself and the lilies. "I aim to put down roots, Rebecca."

"*Ja*, and that's *wunderbar gut*," she replied. "But the question is—will you put down roots here or will you keep wandering and try again somewhere else?"

"I'm talking with the bishop weekly. Doesn't that prove something to you?"

She smiled again, which only made him more agitated. "It proves you are working hard to find your way home—to your faith. You can take that with you anywhere as long as you're truly back among us."

"Or I keep my faith right here in Campton Creek and be a content man."

Her next smile held a bit more mirth. "And that would make me a content woman, Jeb."

"Right now, you are a confusing woman," he retorted. But he said it with his own smile widening. "I'm going across the road now, Becca. See you tomorrow."

"Good night, Jeb."

He chuckled and waved as he walked away, the glow of their banter giving him new hope, even while the old fears pushed at his heart. He'd find a way, some way, to stay here and he'd also find a way to tell her what he'd held

on his heart since the day she'd let him into her kitchen.

He wanted to spend the rest of his life as near to Rebecca as he could be. If that meant just being her employee, he'd have to accept that and consider it a gift from God.

Chapter Fourteen

As summer progressed, Rebecca's field of lilies grew and developed, the scent of the blooms filling the air from dawn to dusk. She opened her bedroom window as night settled over the yard and gently sloping hills. The scent of the lilies, along with the magnolias her *mamm* had planted years ago, and a few gardenias she'd managed to keep in pots and bring in during the winter, surrounded her. Inhaling, she thanked God for his beautiful world.

But summer also brought tourists, and today had been a busy day. Some just stopped to take pictures of the symmetric rows of lilies covering the countryside in shades ranging from white to lemon and orange, followed by reds and burgundies and deep purples. She tried to plant her lilies so the lighter shades would show off and

lead to the deeper shade. It made for a beautiful field, almost like a colorful quilt.

She also mixed up a few in a special area, so they could hybridize and produce new variances. Most people came to buy but weren't sure where to begin or how. The mixed garden gave them an idea of which colors worked together. It had become a popular new addition to her garden.

Jeb had suggested she have pamphlets made up, explaining the basic steps of planting, growing and hybridizing the exquisite flowers. He'd helped her draft a sample, and he'd taken his design to the Campton Center where Jewel studied it and created a mockup on the fancy laptop that she used to keep the center running.

Jewel had delivered the big box of pamphlets this morning.

"See what you think, Rebecca," the sturdy woman with short, cropped hair and dangling red earrings had said, her smile shining bright with joy. "I had so much fun designing this for you. I found stock photos online and bought us a few. I even came to your field the other day when you'd gone visiting and snapped some photos. Jeb had a great idea with the handout information. That one, he's a keeper. Hardworking and easy on the eye."

Jewel had winked when she'd said that, caus-

ing Rebecca to blush. "He sure brags on you," the eccentric woman had whispered. "I think he's got a big old crush on you."

"We are friends," Rebecca tried to explain. "But I do appreciate his knowledge on such things. I never thought to create a pamphlet on growing lilies. I can hand them out, rather than repeating myself over and over. Progress."

Jewel, wearing a bright floral long tunic over blue jeans, had agreed. "Jeb is smart. You let me know when these run out. I'll order more."

"How much do I owe you?" Rebecca asked.

"It's paid," Jewel replied. "The man who has a crush on you covered the tab, but don't fret. I gave him a supergood deal." Another wink, which Rebecca interpreted to mean Jewel had saved Jeb from giving up too much of his pay.

Now as she stood looking out at the moonlit field, which showcased her moon garden lilies nicely, she felt a bittersweet ache in her soul. Her loving parents were gone to heaven, up there with her beloved John.

But she was still here on earth, and a new man had come into her life. A confusing, complex, tormented man who seemed to be running from himself more than from the world. Yet, he'd stopped here, had come to her door begging for work. And he'd done a lot of things to improve her little farm. He worked with the horses

and cleaned and polished everything from the bearing reins to the saddles and back straps and fixed up broken buggies and even the old wheelbarrow. He'd cleaned and organized the barn and he planned to repaint it when things settled down after the spring rush.

So many little tasks she'd neglected, Jeb had found and taken care of. He never complained and he loved having Adam around. Did Adam make him think of his own brother, Pauly?

Rebecca closed her eyes and prayed to the Lord to help her make her way through this maze of feelings that shifted and shined in the same way her lilies did. Why did she feel this pull toward Jeb? Her feelings had gone from a soft pastel to a deep burning fire red. What was she to do?

She had no answers. She'd have to wait on the Lord with this predicament. But it was hard to wait sometimes.

She was about to go to bed when she saw a white flash moving along the outer row of lilies.

A goat.

Rebecca grabbed a shawl and ran down the steps and out into the yard, her hands flapping, her shouts sounding over the night. The big billy goat ignored her as he sampled some of her prettiest Farmer's Daughter circular-shaped blooms.

Rebecca screamed and stomped her foot, but the old goat ignored her.

She went closer, hoping to scare him. "Get away. You'll be sick."

Then she heard footsteps running behind her. "Rebecca!"

Jeb. She whirled and motioned to him. "Old Billy's out and he's messing with my Farmer's Daughters."

Jeb went to work. He ran to the barn and came back with a broom and hurried to hit at the goat. The animal lifted his head and hurled his body toward Jeb, but Jeb was ready. He side-stepped and slapped the broom lightly on the goat's backside, causing the animal to career away and back toward the pen from where he'd obviously escaped.

Jeb ran up to Rebecca. "Are you all alright?"

"Ja," she said, out of breath, her braid of hair slipping over her shoulder. "I don't want him to be sick. He rules the roost over there."

Jeb glanced at the road, and then turned back to her, a smile cresting his face. "But he ruined the Farmer's Daughters."

Rebecca realized the implications of what she'd shouted out, then she smiled, too. Soon, they were both laughing so hard, he held her arms to steady her.

"I suppose that did sound strange," she man-

aged between giggles. "But he'll be the one to pay. He's going to be sick."

"I'll find him, and I'll let Noah know what happened," Jeb said, still snickering. "Do we need to check on the...uh... *Farmer's Daughters*?"

They started laughing again. Rebecca shifted to turn and hit a stump. She went right into Jeb's arms.

Jeb stopped laughing, his eyes on her, his breath coming in huffs. "Rebecca..."

Rebecca's heart burned for something she couldn't describe. A need, a longing, a wish.

He leaned in and pulled her head to his, his hand on the thickness of her braid. Then he put his lips on hers and kissed her in a slow, sweet, lingering way that had her sighing into the moonlight.

She didn't want to let go, but logic took over. She pulled away. "I... I should get inside. It's late."

And her hair was down, her head bare of her *kapp*. She still had on her old work dress, but her apron was in her room.

Jeb nodded, his eyes dark in the grayish-white light. "I'll go find Old Billy."

They both stood still.

"Rebecca?"

"Ja?"

"Do you regret me kissing you?"

"*Neh*. Because I kissed you back."

"I noticed that," he said, his smile showing.

She tugged her shawl around her. "I might just thank Old Billy on that account, but I won't forgive him for ruining, I mean, tearing up my lilies."

Jeb grinned again. "And I will always remember the name of that particular lily."

He walked her back to the porch. "I might want to kiss you again, just so you know."

Her heartbeat raced, her pulse hummed, her hope soared. "And I might let you, just so you know."

She went back inside and checked her field again. No more goats. If Old Billy had broken out, more might come.

But Jeb and Noah would take care of that.

She wondered if Jeb would mention he'd helped her scare the ornery goat off her property.

He surely wouldn't mention what else had happened.

Jeb had kissed her in the moonlight mist. And she'd liked kissing him back.

The next morning Noah showed up on her doorstep.

"I'm sorry about Old Billy getting out. The

fence near the edge of the goat pen has been damaged, probably from him trying to break out. It's fixed and he's gonna be okay, but he had a bad upset stomach. Doc King came to check on him this morning."

Samantha Leah King was the only female veterinarian in this part of the county, and she was also the only Amish vet available for miles around. She'd returned to the fold a year or so ago, after surviving a tornado and criminals trying to silence her, and married Micah King. They lived on the other side of Campton Creek on Micah's farm, where she had an office and kennels out back.

"I'm glad he's okay," Rebecca said as she guided Noah inside and gave him a cup of coffee. "I hurried the moment I saw him out there."

"Jeb told me."

"*Ach*, is that why you're here?" she asked, giving her brother a questioning glance.

"He told me he heard you screaming—that he was sitting on the stoop at the *grossdaddi haus*."

"Do you believe him?"

"I do," Noah admitted. "I'd seen him there when I was making my final rounds, but I didn't bother him. A little while later, I heard shouts and then I saw him sprinting across the yard. Before I could get to him, I saw one of the nannies trying to break through. I had to go and

fetch one back and get the others and the kids settled. I'm surprised they didn't all escape."

"Did he bring Billy back?"

"Ja," Noah said. "And told me what had happened."

"You didn't come to fuss at me, or warn me against him?"

Noah let out a sigh. *"Neh,* and I was wrong on that account. I can see he's a good, trustworthy worker, but he is still an outsider, sister."

"He's trying, Noah. At your request. Don't pressure him."

"Are you afraid he'll leave?"

"I'm not afraid. I know he'll leave if you keep pushing him. Let it be. *Gott* will show him the way. You move between forcing us together or wanting him to just go. None of this can be your doing, or mine. It's Jeb's decision." Then she touched Noah's arm. *"Gott's* will."

Noah's dark eyes softened. "I will stop, then. You need to understand, I only want the best for you."

Rebecca put her hand over his. "Then let me be, *bruder.* I'm content and I'm fine. Jeb is an honorable man who still knows our ways, even if he's been out there on his own for a long time."

"You'll wait to see if he follows through?"

"I know he's following through. He meets

with the bishop once or twice a week. He's learning and he's willing to return to us."

"To us?"

Leave it to her brother to misinterpret her words.

"To his Amish ways, and to *Gott*."

Noah finished his coffee. "He helped me last night and I will remember that. He's a big help to you—so I will consider that. I have no quarrel with Jeb if he does what he's saying he wants to do. Either staying or going, he'd best do right by you, too."

Rebecca stood and took their empty cups to the sink and pumped some water over them. "Then we both need to let him do his work and finish what he's started. I have faith that Jeb will make the right decision."

"We cannot make it for him, as you say," Noah replied, nodding, his hand tugging at his beard. "I'm sorry I've tried to arrange things to suit *mein* self. I had *gut* intentions."

"I know you had the best intentions," she told her brother as he stood and tugged at his straw hat. "Now let's find out Jeb's intentions and *Gott*'s intent."

After Noah left, Rebecca got ready for another busy day. When she heard Jeb and Adam laughing and talking, she watched them from

the kitchen window. Jeb carried a huge blue umbrella and a white chair, heading for the lane.

She moved from the back window to the front and watched, amazed, as he dug a small hole at the end of the lane, near her sign, and placed the umbrella's pole into the earth and secured it with some boards and big stones. Adam, grinning, then opened the bright blue umbrella wide.

Jeb had made her a better place to sit when she sold lilies and herbs on the side of the road. Adam put a small ice chest down beside the umbrella. She guessed it held water and other drinks.

Rebecca sat down and accepted the tears rolling down her face. A simple gesture, a thoughtful surprise, from a man who wanted so much to be seen, to be loved, to be a part of something.

"Please stay, Jeb," she whispered. "But not for me, *neh*. Stay for yourself, and for your faith."

She said a silent prayer to the Lord and asked Him to guide Jeb, and to help her. She wanted to be a friend to Jeb, but now she knew her feelings had changed to something more.

She wasn't ready to admit what that something was, but her heart burned like a field of dirt in the stark sunshine.

Rebecca remembered how she'd felt with John. This felt much the same, but different. Stronger, intense and overwhelming.

Did she ever really know this kind of love before, even with John? They'd been so young. Now, she was a mature woman who'd witnessed births, weddings, life and death.

Her feelings too overwhelming to think about, she wiped her eyes and went out to thank Jeb and Adam for this thoughtful gift. She could never tell Jeb whom he reminded her of. That would put a wedge between them and make him think she was only being kind because he seemed so familiar.

"What have you two been up to so early in the morning?"

Adam beamed. "For you, Aenti. Jeb says you don't need to sit in the hot sun. I'll sit here and help you sell your lilies while he takes care of anyone wanting to see the field. It's our new Saturday morning tradition, ain't so, Jeb?"

"That's right," Jeb said, nudging Adam with his elbow. "We'd better get started, huh?"

"*Ja*, I can't have any slackers around here," she teased to hide the tremendous emotions rushing over her like the creek's gurgling waters.

But when her gaze met Jeb's and he smiled his soft smile, her thoughts settled into one realization. She was beginning to care about him as more than just a friend. It might even be love.

Chapter Fifteen

❧

Jeb stood with the men at church the next Sunday, watching across the way for Rebecca to enter Noah's big barn. After the ministers had entered, the married men came next, then the married women. The single men filed in, so Jeb fell into place, being one of the older single men. He kept his eyes on the open doors. When Rebecca walked in with the other single women, she shot him a quick smile, then lowered her gaze. The younger girls and boys then entered. The men removed their hats and soon the service began.

As they sang the old hymns in High German and without music, Jeb thought about how he would eventually have to stand up in church and ask for forgiveness so he could return to the Amish way of life. Here in Campton Creek. He'd been happier here than he'd been in his

whole life. Rebecca was a big part of that happiness, but there was more. He felt at home here. This place seemed to bring people home, to reunite families and sweethearts, no matter their flaws, or the past, or their secrets. Maybe some of that goodness would rub off on him if he stayed. Being around Rebecca made him want to be more faithful, more truthful, more focused on community and Christ.

But before he could do any of that, he would have to tell Rebecca the truth about his relationship to John. Her John. Would she understand why he hadn't told her from the beginning?

He couldn't even understand it himself, so how could he make her see his reasons for keeping that from her? It had come time to reveal his secret to the bishop. He couldn't honestly confess without telling the bishop and Rebecca about the letters John had sent him, especially about the last letter he'd received from John telling Jeb he was to be married. It would look like he came here purposely to find Rebecca, but he'd come here because his cousin loved this place.

Then God had dropped him right into Rebecca's world.

Coincidence or God's—*Gott's*—will?

After the service, the men ate sitting on benches set up underneath the old oak trees

by Noah's barn, not far from where Jeb stayed in the smaller house. Jeb went to sit with Jeremiah and Micah, two men he'd already become friends with because Rebecca knew their wives, Ava Jane, and Samantha the vet, who some called Leah, the name her grandmother called her.

A couple of other men showed up, their gaze hitting on Jeb with curiosity.

"Where'd you come from?" an older man named Shem asked. "You remind me of someone."

Jeb lowered his head. He didn't want to lie. "I grew up in Ohio, but I moved around a lot, doing odds and ends."

"But you've been in the *Englisch* world, correct?" another man asked. "We don't get a lot of Martins around here."

"*Ja*, I've been moving around for a long time but I'm more Amish still than *Englisch*." Then he added, "My *daed* was a Mennonite. My *mamm* stayed Amish, and he... He tried to be Amish."

"There is no trying," Noah said as he settled next to Jeb. "Jeb here is going through the steps of returning to his faith—completely." He sent Jeb a determined smile.

Jeremiah laughed and looked at Noah. "I had to study with some youngies while working on

the process of getting back to my faith. If I can sit and take the teasing I had to endure, I'm sure Jeb will make it all the way through."

Micah nodded. "Leah, as most of you know, had to do the same. She had been out in the world for a long time. But she fell right back into her Amish ways, although she did have to get approval to continue her veterinarian practice."

"We are all thankful for that," Noah added with a chuckle. "She is really *gut* with the animals."

Jeb smiled as the stories were told. Then he leaned toward Jeremiah. "I'm thinking of volunteering as a firefighter."

"We can always use another hand," Jeremiah said. "Let me know and I'll give you a tour of the station *haus*."

The conversation moved on, but after they'd eaten and now stood mingling, the older man who'd questioned Jeb before came up beside him.

Shem Yoder grinned at him. "Minna Schlock married a Mennonite close to thirty-five years ago. I know 'cause I had a crush on her. That might be who you remind me of, except I can't remember the man's name."

Jeb's heartbeat danced out of control. This man remembered his mother. He was about to

come up with an answer when Noah called him to help with packing up the buggies.

"I must go," he said, nodding to Shem.

Shem stared after him for a moment and then turned and walked away. But Jeb had a feeling this was not over yet. He'd need to tell Rebecca the truth, and soon.

Two days later, Noah found Jeb inside the barn back at Noah's house. "Can I speak to you about something?"

Jeb lifted a long board and turned to Noah. "*Ja*, what is it?"

Noah let out a sigh. "Have you been completely honest with us about your reason for coming here?"

Jeb's heart accelerated into a high beat. "I believe I've told you all the important stuff."

"Shem Yoder thinks he knows you."

Jeb looked down at the board he'd been staining for Rebecca's potting shed. He worked here most afternoons when he got done with his paying work. Today, he'd loaded enough lily plants for the many buyers streaming in to make him never want to see a lily again.

But he did want to see those lilies, Rebecca's field of beautiful flowers, again. He wanted to finish this project and see how she'd react to it. He wanted so many things.

"He mentioned something about that to me Sunday," Jeb replied. "I'm not sure what's he's talking about. I could look like someone he knows."

Noah's shrewd gaze stayed on him. "Shem has a *gut* memory for his age. He says you remind him of a girl he walked out with, until a man named Calvin Martin, a Mennonite who was just passing through, took her away."

Apparently, Shem's memory had returned, or he'd done some asking around. Jeb couldn't lie. Noah had begun to trust him. "Calvin Martin was my *daed*, Noah."

Noah looked surprised, then he became angry. "So, you did *kumm* here for a reason. But you couldn't have lived here before."

Jeb stopped his work and laid the staining rag down, then wiped his hands. Turning back to face Noah, he heaved a great sigh. "I never lived here. My *mamm* did, but she left when she was nineteen. She and my *daed* got married and moved to Ohio. Her family was not pleased that she'd married a Mennonite."

Noah let that soak in. "You grew up in Ohio, so that much is true, at least."

"I did, but I did not have the best childhood. I had a brother named Pauly. I've told Rebecca most of this."

"Except the part about your *mamm* being from here," Noah retorted.

Jeb decided to come clean. "There's more, Noah."

"I was afraid of that. You'd better get to the truth, Jeb."

They leaned back against the work counter, the soft hot wind of summer washing over them, the sounds of animals snorting and birds chirping making this seem like an ordinary day.

Jeb felt anything but ordinary.

"My *mamm* had a sister," he began. "Aenti Moselle was a bit younger than my mother, but they were so close. Aenti Moselle visited Mamm a lot, but she married a man who lived here in a nearby community. Emmett Kemp. They settled here in Campton Creek and had two children, a boy named John and a girl named Sadie."

Noah frowned. "The Kemps. Moselle was your *aenti*?" Gasping, he stepped back. "John Kemp was your cousin?"

Jeb nodded, his eyes burning with a hot moisture. *"Ja."*

Noah got in his face. "What are you doing here, trying to take his place? If Becca finds this out—"

Jeb held up a hand. "I didn't know, Noah. I did not know who she was until she'd already hired me. Then she told me her full name."

"But you did recognize the name? How?" Noah's face reddened with anger. "You didn't live here, and your grandparents have passed on. John's parents took Sadie and left. So how did you know to find her?"

"I didn't come here to find her," Jeb replied, trying to make sense of it. "I came here because John and I were close, and we visited each other when we were boys. Mostly he and his *mamm* would come to Ohio to visit. My *daed* didn't like to travel." He took off his hat and ran a hand through his hair. "John and I wrote to each other secretly for several years—because my *daed* didn't like my *mamm* getting letters from home. The last letter I got from him came just a few weeks before he died. He told me about being engaged to the most beautiful girl in the world."

Noah gasped again. "Rebecca. She was so in love with him, and I don't think she's ever recovered from seeing him being thrown from that horse."

"She told me about it and her fear of horses," Jeb said. "She knows most of what I've told you. Seems we both are still grieving things."

"But you have not told her the truth of you being John's cousin. Now I know who you remind me of—John. Almost like twins. Your

mothers weren't twins, but they resembled each other, ain't so?"

Jeb nodded. "They were like twins and *ja*, they looked almost the same, but after a few years, my *mamm*'s health went down. They looked nothing alike by the time she died."

"I'm sorry for that," Noah said. "What happened in your home, Jeb?"

Jeb let out another sigh. "Alcohol. My *daed* drank too much and took his sorriness out on my mother, Pauly and me."

He explained his life to Noah. But still, he couldn't bring himself to talk much about the day Pauly died, or how he'd died.

When he finished, Noah stood staring at him, the sympathy in his eyes as clear as the anger he'd held earlier.

"And you say you've told Becca most of this?"

"I've told her everything but…me being John's cousin. I wanted to tell her a hundred different times, but Noah, I like my job and I mean Becca no harm. I was afraid I'd add to her pain and make things worse for her."

Noah studied him, shaking his head. "I don't see how she missed you looking so much like John. I'm surprised she's never mentioned that to you."

"It might be the same as me never bringing him up. Too painful."

"And she might have held back because she wouldn't want you to compare yourself to him," Noah replied.

"I'm nothing like him," Jeb admitted. "I left after Pauly died and I never looked back. I didn't make it home in time to make peace with my *daed*. I was too bitter and angry. I regret that, but I can't go back there. This was the place that stayed in my head. I still have some of John's letters. But I don't have much else."

Noah patted him on the shoulder. "First, you talk to the bishop, and then, Jeb, you talk to Rebecca. She believes in honesty above all else. You must tell her the rest of your story." Then he stood back. "Or I will."

Chapter Sixteen

Something was bothering Jeb.

Rebecca watched him now while he moved through the field alongside her, checking for spider mites and slugs. She had natural products to help combat pests, but it was a constant battle. Her lilies were hardy and resistant to most anything, but they had to be checked for every little thing. She liked pampering her crop. She'd explained this process to Jeb, and since he'd worked in fields before, he knew what needed to be done.

But he wasn't joking with her as he usually did or talking to Lily Dog in a low sweet voice, or mentioning Noah fussing at him about something, their usual workday banter.

Did he regret kissing her?

That thought popped into her head, coming from a place where she'd buried her own feel-

ings about their kiss. She'd loved kissing him, but she'd also accepted that it was wrong. He'd lived out in the world, and now he was forbidden until he'd finished his sessions with the bishop.

Jeb must have buried his own feelings deep, too.

He was pulling back, shutting down. The kiss had made him realize he couldn't stay here. He didn't want to give her the wrong impression. He didn't want to hurt her or bring shame on her. That was Jeb, always trying to do the right thing.

So noble. But neither of them could deny the intensity of being in each other's arms.

Those thoughts played through her head as swiftly as the wind played through the hundreds of blossoming lilies.

She was so lost in thought, her heart hurting while her head decided this was for the best, she didn't hear Jeb calling out to her.

"Becca?"

Rebecca stood and found him on the far side of the field by the woods. He motioned for her, so she started out at a trot to reach him.

He was in what she called the breeder plants section, seedlings that could be used to breed new plants even though the seedlings hadn't been given a name themselves. These were used to hybridize, and she usually suggested them

to customers who wanted to experiment with cross-pollination.

When she ran down the slope of the hill, she saw why Jeb had called her. Half of that row of plants and some nearby had been destroyed.

Jeb motioned to the woods. "I found animal tracks—most likely deer."

"Ach," she said, frustration coloring the one word. "I've been so distracted, I haven't had time to check down here. Deer do love daylilies."

"You mentioned this could happen," he said, staring down at the trampled, half-eaten plants. "But I didn't know to check here."

"It's not your fault, Jeb. I need to put up a fence or use some kind of deterrent, but I need money and time to do that."

She placed her hands on her hips, wondering what could happen next.

"I'll handle it," he said. "I can build a sturdy fence."

"But we can't fence the whole field."

He looked from the front of the field to the back, where the Green Mountain hills sat against the horizon. "No. We will take it one row at a time, if need be."

"That will take a long time, Jeb."

He stopped and stared over at her, realization making him frown. "Rebecca…"

"Don't," she said. "I know you might not be here forever, but for now, *ja*, I need some sort of fence. We'll clear this up and then I'll sit down and go over the budget."

She turned and hurried toward the house before he could tell her the truth. He had obviously decided to leave soon. Maybe sooner than he'd planned. She wished she'd never let him kiss her. And she wished she'd never kissed him back.

Jeb went into town and bought as much fence wire as he could find, then he loaded some fence posts onto the hauling buggy. He wouldn't have much time to work on the shed project. This new fence would take up most of the week and next week.

Mr. Hartford came out the back door of the general store. "Jeb, you got another project going on?"

"*Ja.* I'm going to try and fence up the back part of Becca's lily field—the section closest to the woods. The deer have found it."

"I see," Mr. Hartford said. "You'll need some help with that. It'll have to be a mighty tall fence to keep deer out."

"I can do it," Jeb replied, hoping that he wouldn't be proved wrong. "I'm buying tall posts and I'm going to wire it tight and high."

"All you have to do is put out the word," Mr. Hartford said. "You know your neighbors will show up."

Jeb finished loading the fence posts. "You are correct," he said with a grin. "I tend to forget that."

"Well, I hear you're back for good," the storeowner said. "Make the most of it and don't break your back. Then you won't be able to help anyone." After looking around, he added, "The Amish like to be helpful and since you're new around here, you'll become more endeared to them if you don't shun that help."

Jeb laughed and turned to his friend. "I'll do that. Thanks for the reminder. If I get a few able bodies, I can get this done much faster."

"Then you can return to your secret project," Mr. Hartford said with a wink. "And besides, anyone around here would want to help Rebecca. She's one of the kindest people I know."

"I cannot argue with that," Jeb said, wishing he could shout it to the rooftops. But other than anything work related, Rebecca had been avoiding him. She must have decided that kiss was a bad idea. Or... Noah had said something to her about Jeb being related to John.

Jeb left and headed home. He'd get the word out that Becca needed help. Her good name would bring people, but his hard work could

get the back fence in place. The deer would have to take a long detour if they wanted to nibble more lilies.

By the time he'd made it home, he had enough men to help. He'd first stopped at Micah's house. Micah had readily agreed.

Then Micah told him he'd help get the word out.

Noah showed up just as Jeb was unloading the fence posts.

"I heard Becca had deer trouble, and I'm not referring to you."

"Funny," Jeb said. Then he explained what he planned.

Noah listened, nodding. "I told her last time this happened I'd get her a fence up, but I got busy and neglected that. So, I'm here to help today."

Soon, buggies pulled up with more posts and fence wire.

Jeb saw Rebecca hurrying out of the house, her expression full of surprise. "What is all this?"

Noah chuckled. "Your worker here is going to fence up the back side of the property, to hopefully keep the deer away. Word got out that he might need some help."

Rebecca glanced from her bemused brother back to Jeb. "Is this true?" She looked out over

the field and then back. "That would mean from the road to the creek."

"Ja," he said, wondering if she'd get mad. "Now I can fence up almost half of the open field, and after we save up a bit more, I can finish fencing the whole field, almost up to the creek. I'll put a fence there with a gate but leave room to walk along the creek. Mr. Hartford suggested I find some help to get this first phase going, and, well, word got around pretty quickly."

"I can see how the word spread," she replied. "I'm amazed that you thought of everything— even leaving the creek walking trail open. You sure make a good assistant, Jeb. I'm not sure what I'll do when you're gone."

Then she turned to head to the house.

Jeb glanced at Noah. "Does that mean she approves or that she's mad?"

Noah shook his head. "I can't figure women, but I think she's grateful, and if I know my sister, she's getting a pitcher of water or lemonade for us and probably finding some snacks, too."

"You could be right," Jeb replied, still worried. "I haven't had a chance to talk to her, Noah."

Noah gave him a disappointed stare. "I can tell you've been busy. But soon, Jeb. Better make it soon because Shem is a *gut* man and a

gut friend, but he likes to stick his nose in everyone's business. Wouldn't you rather she hears this from you than from someone else?"

Jeb nodded, but the others were gathering, ready to work. "I promise, I'll tell her the truth, Noah. You have my word on that."

Noah gave him a slight nod. "Let's see what we can get done on this fence today. But I'll hold you to that promise."

Hannah showed up to help.

"How did you know?" Rebecca asked her sister when she met Hannah at the door to help her carry in some food.

"How does anyone know anything around here?" Hannah asked, laughing. "That grapevine keeps growing."

"*Denke* for coming over."

Hannah hugged her. "Of course. I brought some sandwiches and chips. Samuel will *kumm* later when he gets home from work."

Rebecca glanced out the back window. "I can't believe this is happening. I have to fight off deer every season."

"That's because you never asked for help," her sister said with a shrug. "Apparently, Jeb didn't either. But Mr. Hartford gave him a nudge since you never listen to his advice."

"I always thought Mr. Hartford was being

kind, and felt sorry for me because I'm all alone," she admitted.

Hannah made a face. "No one feels sorry for you. You're an established businesswoman and your business brings in tourists and locals alike. That benefits all of the companies around here, Becca. You need to see your own value to this community."

Rebecca sat down, shocked. "I've never thought of it that way. Mr. Hartford knows if I succeed and have an easier way of doing things, I'll benefit him and the entire town."

"You can't see the good you do," Hannah replied, her tone gentle. "But we can, and Jeb surely can. He's already improved things around here."

"He has done so much," she admitted. "But I still don't know if I can count on him to stay."

"He's doing everything he can to settle down, from what I hear," Hannah replied. "Everyone's talking about him getting ready to commit to his faith again. Why can't you believe that?"

Rebecca stood and went back to work. "I want to believe he means to stay, but I don't want to get my hopes up. Things can change in the blink of an eye."

She couldn't bring herself to tell Hannah that she and Jeb circled around each other—sometimes

talking and laughing, other times avoiding each other. They'd done that since that one kiss.

She didn't plan on sharing that information either. If Noah got word of that—he'd set the wedding date for certain sure.

Hannah came to stand by her. "I know you'll never get over losing John, but you can't base every decision on what might go wrong. Try trusting *Gott* and yourself, for a change. Try focusing on what could go right. And try focusing on Jeb doing the right thing instead of wondering when he might walk away."

"Are you through?" she asked her sister with a teasing smile.

"*Neh*, I'm just getting started," Hannah shot back. "You're too stubborn for your own good at times."

Rebecca nodded. "I suppose I am at that. I won't forget what Jeb—and all of you—are doing for me. I'll ask for help from now on. If I need it."

"We all need it," Hannah said. "Now, let's get this food in place out on the porch. You know those men will be hungry once they finish this task."

Rebecca gathered trays and drink cups. "What a *wunderbar* thing—no more deer, or maybe even no Old Billy breaking out to sample my lilies."

"And a new understanding about yourself," her sister added.

"I'm not sure how you became so wise," she told Hannah, "but I love you for it."

"I love you, too," Hannah said. "And I like that light that sparkles in your eyes when you're looking at Jeb."

"I do not have a light or a sparkle," she retorted. "Jeb and I are friends. He's a *gut* worker."

Hannah snickered. "Just keep telling yourself that."

"I will."

They both giggled like teenagers, making Rebecca remember the days when they were young.

"I miss Mamm and Daed," she said. "I could use their wisdom these days."

"They are always with us," Hannah reminded her. "They taught us well."

"*Ja*, they did at that."

Rebecca watched as Jeb and the other men dug holes and stretched fence wire. While she appreciated the help, she also realized she needed someone around here to help her all the time.

She needed Jeb, in more ways than just for work.

But she'd keep that secret to herself for now.

Chapter Seventeen

Two days later, the weather turned nasty. Thunderstorms shook the earth with lightning, and rain fell in heavy silver sheets of mist. Jeb had to shut down the fencing, but with the help of most of the men in the community, they'd managed to complete the high fence directly next to the woods. The deer gathered there most nights, so the fence had become a way to hinder them from eating the lilies. But he needed to get the rest of the fence up, and soon.

"Your fence helps with so many issues," Rebecca told him as they sat on the porch that afternoon, waiting for the rain to lift. "Now if we could find a way to keep the *kinder* from crashing through the rows, too. They are like little lambs after the pretty blooms."

He laughed at that image. Children running through the fields. Somehow, that made

his heart ache more than it made him mad. "You're right, there. Children are less inhibited than adults."

She glanced over at him. "Are you thinking about your brother?"

He nodded. "I guess I was. Pauly stayed childlike...up until he died at thirteen. Everything was a joy to him. Everything but our *daed*."

Shock darkened her eyes. "I can't imagine how that must have been. My parents were so gentle, so kind. I'd like to think I'd be the same if I ever had a child."

"You'd make a great mother, Becca."

She lifted her head, her gaze on him. "You did the best you could with Pauly, I'm sure."

Jeb stared out as the wind picked up and the trees swayed. "I tried, but I wasn't always patient with him."

He closed his eyes and asked God to help him. Then he looked over at Rebecca. "I'm the reason he's dead."

"What?" Yet another jolt of shock—because of him telling her the truth. But Jeb felt he had to tell her something about his past. Maybe he'd get up the nerve to tell her about John's letters, too.

"He'd run away when Daed got really mean, usually to where I worked in a buggy repair shop."

"What happened?" Rebecca said. "I won't judge you, Jeb. You've been punishing yourself enough for the both of us."

She saw so many things not spoken, he thought. "*Ja*, I have at that."

"Then let go of some of your pain. Tell me and it will stay here between us."

Jeb stared at his glass of tea. "I was busy when he came running in, crying. When Pauly got in that kind of frantic mood, he was hard to contain." He stopped, gathered his emotions. But the lump in his throat wouldn't go away. "He was crying and stomping. My boss had been kind about these episodes, but on that day, we had some important visitors from a furniture place in Pittsburgh. They were interested in having us do a huge order for wardrobes and rocking chairs."

"You needed to focus on work, and your upset *bruder* showed up?"

He nodded. "My boss wasn't happy. It was the worst possible time for Pauly to have a meltdown."

"What happened?"

"I excused myself and took him out back. I tried to get him to settle down and wait there at the picnic table. I promised I'd get him a hamburger—his favorite food."

Rebecca smiled at that. "I like hamburgers myself." Then she nudged Jeb. "Go on."

"I left him there, fuming and crying. He kept repeating, 'I don't like Daed. I don't like Daed.'" Jeb swallowed again, his heart burning with sorrow and guilt. "I hurried back inside to finish up with our customers and when I finally went back out, Pauly was gone."

Rebecca put a hand to her lips. "Oh, no."

Jeb studied her, looking for condemnation. When he saw none, he decided he needed to tell her the rest of the story. "I went searching for him along the roadside. After a few minutes, I spotted him up the way and ran toward him, calling to him."

Rebecca put a hand on his arm, her eyes meeting his.

"When he saw me, he ran toward me." Jeb gulped in air, his heart hammering. "But he didn't look both ways, Becca. He didn't look. He only wanted his brother. The pickup truck never saw him coming. It all happened in a few seconds and then... He was gone."

Rebecca stood and then kneeled in front of Jeb, her hands grasping his. "This is not your fault, Jeb. Pauly was a special child and *Gott* knew that."

He lifted away and stood. "Then why did *Gott* let that happen to him? He was upset and

he was innocent. Pauly didn't care if I had work to do. He needed me and I failed him."

Rebecca was there by him, the rain and wind slashing at their clothes, water falling off the eaves to wet them. She turned Jeb to face her, then she put a hand on his jaw. "Jeb, you did not cause this. It was a tragic accident, a horrible accident. You have to see that."

Jeb looked into her misty eyes and shook his head. "What I see every day and every night is my Pauly flying through the air and then landing on the asphalt road. Then he didn't move. He never moved. He never woke up."

"Jeb," she whispered. "Jeb." Then she tugged him into her arms and held him. "I'm here. *Gott* is here. You've found a home now, and you can seek forgiveness and comfort."

Jeb's emotions exploded with as much fire as the pounding rain. The wind washed at his tears while Rebecca held him and hugged him. He sobbed until he had no tears left.

But Rebecca didn't move. She didn't walk away. She didn't ask him to leave her property. Instead, she stayed with him.

Finally, he lifted his head and wiped at his eyes. "Rebecca?"

"Ja?"

"You are an amazing woman."

Her bashful expression showed she didn't believe that.

"I mean it," he said. "I've never told anyone about this—about my part in this. Daed, of course, blamed me and acted as if he really cared. After the way he'd treated Pauly, his reaction made me angry, and we had words—horrible words said to each other. Once I'd buried my brother next to my *mamm*, I left Ohio. I've been searching for something since then."

"You were searching for redemption, Jeb. And now you've found it."

Jeb saw by her earnest expression that she meant those words. He held her, their eyes meeting, and with a sigh Rebecca lifted up and pressed her lips on his. The kiss was soft and welcoming and full of that redemption he'd needed for so long.

When she pulled away, she studied his face and gave him a soft smile. "How do you feel now?"

Jeb touched her wet hair, one finger tracing a loose curl. "I feel as if I've been washed clean. I feel...hopeful." He was about to tell her the rest—about John.

But a clap of lightning filled the sky, and the world went dark.

Becca automatically tugged him close, more

from fright than anything else. Then they both stepped back and checked the clouds.

"This weather is about to get worse," he said. "Let's get inside."

Grabbing her hand, Jeb rushed Rebecca into the house and shut the door. The trees leaned sideways as walls of water and wind pushed over the land and lashed at the earth. Small limbs twisted from the trees and catapulted across the yard.

"My lilies," she said, her voice hollow with fear. "This could ruin my whole crop."

Jeb tugged her away from the window. "Let's pray that won't happen."

They sat on the stairs, holding tight to each other while the world outside screamed and thundered with a mighty rage.

Jeb could understand that kind of rage, but while the storm hissed and sneered, he managed to let go of some of his own rage. And he had Rebecca—and God—to thank for that.

After the storm ended, leaving a soft drizzle behind, they put on muck boots and rain capes and went to check on the crops. Sure enough, Rebecca found some damaged stems.

"If the blooms are broken past about two-thirds of the stem, that plant might not produce again. I need to check on the cutting plants.

Remember when I explained I have customers who want to have fresh-cut lilies in their homes. They come back each year to buy more just for cutting and displays, so those plants are considered annuals. Those might be damaged the worst since they're near a low spot that rushes with water in storms like this one. They won't like being too soggy either. That causes the bulbs to rot."

"Remind me the spot and I'll go check those," Jeb said, a new reassurance between them now.

She pointed to a corner near the barn. "I'll be there in a moment or two. I want to check my more-expensive plants, the ones people like to grow for shows. I have some beautiful Casablanca lilies that should bloom later in the year if they didn't get too damaged."

They parted, her going toward the best of her hybrids, and Jeb rushing toward the plot of lilies growing near the barn and the rushing creek.

Lily Dog came running from the barn, her yelps showing she didn't like storms either. The shaggy little mutt shivered in the cool air as she trotted along with Rebecca.

"It's okay," Rebecca said, bending to pat the wet dog on the head. "Just a big blow over, is all."

Rebecca hurried through the showstoppers, as she liked to call them. She got top dollar for

these cultivars. She'd lose a chunk of her profits if they'd been damaged. Such was the way of any farmer. The crops depended on the weather, but the weather could turn on the crops. Nature was always something awesome, and it required a lot of respect.

After walking the rows, she found a few spots where the early blooms had been snapped off, and several plants that had been bruised or crushed by the heavy wind and rain. Some of the taller stems had broken, so she would have that to deal with.

Finally, she emerged and looked toward where Jeb stood near the other plants. Lily Dog woofed and took off toward Jeb. Rebecca followed, too tired to hurry.

"These look bad," he said, nodding toward the short rows of lush plants. "Most are damaged or broken."

"We'll replant and hope for the best," she said. "It could have been a lot worse. We'll clean up, prune and get things going again."

"How can you be so calm?" Jeb asked, his eyes on her now.

"I'm used to this," she replied. "One year I had aphids so bad, I lost half my crop. Another, a tornado flattened everything in Campton Creek, and that's how Micah met Samantha, or Leah, as we all call her. The tornado lifted

her car and it landed in his wheat field. She has a little dog named Patch—reminds me of our Lily Dog."

"I've got a lot of catching up to do," Jeb said with a grin. The dog barked in agreement.

"*Kumm* inside," she said, her voice hollow and tired. "I'll fix us some *kaffe* and we'll make a quick dinner."

"Are you sure?" he asked, his gaze still on her.

Rebecca took his hand. "I'm sure, Jeb. You've done so much for me. I owe you more than I can say."

"What if I want more than gratitude?" he asked.

Rebecca's finger tightened over his. "We have all summer," she said. "Let's see how we feel when fall arrives."

Jeb squeezed her hand back. "I hope fall takes its dear sweet time getting here."

Chapter Eighteen

Jeb had the damaged part of the garden re-planted and reworked in a few days. He suggested they build up the soil there to keep that patch of lilies from being flooded with water after each rain. This project had kept him busy, and it had given him time to think hard on what he should do next. He'd shared the worst part of his past, and Rebecca had kissed him during the storm. His heart filled with joy in that moment, but he had tried since to avoid her as much as possible. He wouldn't let this go any further with his one last secret standing between them. It wouldn't be fair to her.

But he sure did like being with her, helping her, making her livelihood stronger and more secure. And he could tell she was beginning to feel the same. Would she forgive him after he told her the truth?

He prayed so and hoped to find the right time to come clean. It had been a few days since the storm, so he'd had limbs to clear away and lilies to pamper. They'd both been hard at work. Rebecca's garden was overflowing, so she'd been over at Franny's house most of the week, canning and freezing vegetables and making fruit preserves.

The day was coming to an end. He'd have to stop and go take care of the animals.

Now, he stood back and checked the new grid. He'd moved wheelbarrows of soil from the outskirts of the fields to this area, building it up until he'd managed to level it off. Then he'd made a dirt drain full of rocks beside the grid, so any rainwater should flow away from the lilies planted there. It looked different, but clean and ready to go. He'd taken the bulbs with stems Rebecca said they could transplant from the big garden and planted them deep into the soil. Rebecca said they should start producing in a few weeks.

"I see this project is done," Noah said as he strolled toward Jeb. "That's a much better layout than the original. This part of the garden was an afterthought that turned into a new responsibility for Becca."

"Well, now it's my responsibility," Jeb said,

wondering what Noah was doing here so late in the day.

"You are taking on a lot more of the everyday tasks," Noah replied, holding his suspenders.

"What's wrong?" Jeb finally asked, his instincts telling him he probably did know why Noah was here.

Noah looked him over. "You haven't told her yet, have you?"

"No," Jeb said, since he had no excuse except hard work and a deep dread holding him back. "I took some time earlier in the week to tell Bishop King and he agrees she should know. He thinks she'll appreciate my being kin to John once the dust settles."

"If the dust settles," Noah replied. "The longer you wait, the harder it will become."

Jeb nodded. "I know. But I'm finishing up her garden shed. I have all the boards marked so all we have to do is haul them to the spot I've measured and get going on putting the whole thing together. Are you still willing to help?"

"Are you still willing to be honest with her?" Noah shot back.

"I will tell her everything," Jeb replied, "after her birthday and after she sees the shed."

"And then what?"

"And then I'll either be a forgiven man, and I can stay. Or I'll be in a bad spot again, and

I'll leave." He stopped, took in a breath. "As a heartbroken man. Still."

Noah shook his head. "I can't be the one to tell her. And I cautioned Shem on passing what he'd figured out to anyone because he wasn't for certain sure, but we don't want Shem messing around and letting it slip if he runs into Rebecca."

"I know." Jeb took off his straw hat and swept a hand through his hair. "I know. I've made a mess of things, but, Noah, Becca and I are growing close. There will come the Sunday I'll go before the church and confess all."

"Even this last secret."

"Even that, but I want her to know before that happens."

"So do I," Noah replied. "She'd be mighty upset to hear this with all the brethren around her. She'd be humiliated."

Jeb didn't want that to happen. "I could go and talk to Shem. Would you go with me?"

"And aid you in keeping this a secret?" Noah asked. "I'm already doing that. I won't keep adding to the lie."

"It's not a lie. I'm only trying to protect your sister."

"Neh," Noah said. "You're only protecting yourself and that's the worst thing you can do at this point."

After Noah left, Jeb stood staring at the creek. Noah was right. He needed to get this one last hurdle out of the way and then he could truly feel free and clear—cleansed and complete. He had run out of excuses.

He prayed Rebecca's gracious heart and her promise of not judging him would still hold when he told her the truth.

"Noah, have you said something to Jeb again—about me?"

Rebecca knew something was wrong. She'd sensed a change in Jeb now that they were back to their routines and clearing away the storm damage. He and Adam stayed busy, of course. But Adam followed him into the barn in the late afternoon and then they walked home together. No more suppers alone with Jeb.

He'd kissed her there on the porch the other night, with the rain falling all around them. Rather, she'd kissed him. Why had she gone and done that? Now he'd shut down again and managed to avoid her at every turn. He stayed in the barn until late in the day, after they'd done their chores. Was he ashamed that he'd told her what had happened to Pauly? Or had her brother somehow seen them and told him to stop kissing Rebecca?

"Noah?"

Noah frowned, then he looked away. Then he frowned again. "What do you mean?"

"I mean, he is barely talking to me and after work, he heads to either my barn or yours. How many harnesses can a man mend?"

Noah almost smiled, then he shook his head. "I think, sister, Jeb is at a crossroads. He likes it here and he aims to stay, but whatever he's been through is causing him to doubt. He's afraid he'll be hurt again. Heartbroken even."

"Then you have been talking to him!" Had Jeb told her brother all that he'd shared with her about his past, his *daed* and Pauly?

Flustered, Noah tugged at his beard, a sure sign he had something on his mind. "We talk, *ja*. He's around a lot, so I talk to him. Surely you aren't upset about that. I thought you wanted me to be nice to him."

Rebecca started walking with Noah toward her house. She'd come over to visit with Katie and Franny and to help process some of the first crops of wild blueberries and blackberries, and the fresh vegetables from both of their thriving gardens.

Today, they'd blanched beans and peas, and shucked and cleaned fresh corn to store in the propane-operated refrigerator. Noah was helping her carry her baskets full of jars of jam and

vegetables back home to put in the storage room in the basement.

"I do want you to be nice to him," she said. "I don't want you pestering him or pushing him off on me."

Noah's thick eyebrows lifted like a set of wings. "Well, I thought you were beginning to like him, same as me."

She had to be careful what she told her brother. He'd get the wrong impression and meddle even more. "I do care about Jeb. He's one of us and he's been fighting a hard battle. He and I get along, but he's been acting strange lately. Not as friendly and talkative. Now I think I understand. He's still struggling, ain't so?"

"Struggling how?" Noah asked, surprised.

"You just said it yourself. He's reached a time of no return. He either comes back to the Amish life, or he has to move on. Is that what you've talked about?"

Her brother looked both ways when they reached the narrow ribbon of road. "*Ja*, sure. We've talked about that and a lot of things."

"So… This is why he's been so distant? He's still having doubts even though he says he's going to be okay?"

"*Ja*, that could be it."

Frustrated, Rebecca shifted her basket of blueberry preserves. Noah answered her in rid-

dles. He was either protecting her, or he was protecting Jeb. Maybe both of them.

"Well, thank you for making all this as clear as mud."

Noah carried the jars of beans and crushed tomatoes into the kitchen. "So now you're cross with me?"

"I'm not cross with anyone," she said. After placing her basket on the table, she turned to Noah. "I'm having doubts, too. I don't know how I feel about Jeb or anything else these days."

Noah's eyes widened, and he twitched like a newborn foal. "Has he done or said something to hurt you?"

"*Neh,* I'm fine. He's respectful in every way, he works hard, and your little chaperone hangs on his every word."

She hoped she wasn't blushing, but each time she thought of their kisses, she got all warm and dreamy. Her brother didn't need to know that. "I'm just used to having Moses Yoder following me around. He rarely talked, mostly grunted and nodded and mumbled."

Her brother grinned. "Jeb is quite different from Old Moses."

"*Ja*, and there's the problem. He is my friend, and he works for me. It's a lot different."

Concern rimmed Noah's face, causing her even more worry. "In a good way, or a bad way?"

Her brother's genuine sincerity touched Rebecca. "That's the confusing part. In a good way, and in a bad way. Jeb is a *gut* man and he's doing all he can to come back to his faith. But just like Jeb, I don't want to ever be heartbroken again either." Then she put her hands on her hips. "Which is why you need to stop playing matchmaker to us."

Noah nodded, his fingers moving down his beard. "And that means I must not worry about the both of you being here alone with each other so much. I miss Old Moses, for certain sure."

Rebecca patted her brother on the arm. "Noah, you do not need to worry on my account. I'm grown now, remember?"

"Every day, I remember this," he said. "I dread when Katie grows up and starts walking out with boys. I will not like it, not one bit."

"But you won't be able to hold her back either," Rebecca said. "I can figure out my life, and you go and take care of your *wunderbar* family. If I have doubts, I promise I will *kumm* to you. You are so much like our *daed*."

Noah's eyes misted. "I will take that as a compliment."

"You have been *gut* to me and you've watched

over me for a long time. I know I can depend on you."

"Even when I overstep?"

"Even so," she said with a smile.

Noah looked uncertain, making her suspicious all over again. But she knew him well enough to think she wouldn't get any information out of him unless he wanted her to know it.

"Now, go," she told him. "I'm tired and it's almost suppertime."

Noah nodded. Then he turned at the door. "I won't force you and Jeb together. I think this is something you two have to decide on your own, with prayer and consideration. If *Gott* wants you together, it will work itself out."

"Denke," Rebecca said. "I'm glad you've come to that conclusion."

Noah nodded, started to speak and then shook his head. With a sigh, he turned. "I'll see you later, then."

Rebecca watched her brother go, still not sure. Something was up. Noah knew more than he was letting on. She'd never seen her brother so befuddled or *verhuddelt*—confused. Noah always spoke his mind, and especially about Jeb. But he'd hesitated today.

She had to wonder what her brother and Jeb were hiding from her.

* * *

Jeb finished the fence, doing most of the last bits of work after he'd completed his other chores. Adam helped, talking away about fishing, riding his bike, milking cows and goats, and just about any subject. Jeb let the boy talk, and he answered when asked a question. That gave him time to his own thoughts, mostly about Rebecca and how much he appreciated this job.

"Hey, Jeb?"

He looked up to find Adam holding a hammer. *"Ja?"*

Adam scrunched his nose. "Are you mad at me?"

Jeb stopped tugging at the leftover fencing wire and turned to the boy. "What makes you think I'm mad at you?"

Adam put his hammer on the fence post next to him. "You ain't been talking much lately, is all."

Jeb had so much on his mind, he'd shut down a bit. His young helper must have picked up on that. "Well, I'm letting you do most of the talking. You entertain me and that keeps me from wanting to take a nap."

Adam grinned at that. "My *mamm* says my talking puts her to sleep."

"Well, it keeps me awake," Jeb replied, thinking the boy might splutter along, but he was

observant. "I do have a lot going on—things I have to fret about."

"So you're not mad, you're just stewing in your head?"

"Exactly. Stewing a lot."

"You're gonna stay here, right?"

Jeb took a sip of the big water jug Rebecca always provided. "I haven't decided, but I'm ninety percent sure that I will be staying past summer."

"I'm glad," Adam said. "You're like one of my best friends. I want you to be one hundred percent for certain sure."

Jeb was so touched, he had to blink and look away. He prayed for 100 percent. "I'm glad we're friends," he said, his voice husky because of the big lump stuck in his throat. "You know, I had a brother who followed me around all the time."

Adam's eyes got big with surprise. "You did? I didn't know that." Then his expression changed, and he hung his head. "You said once you'd lost two people you loved. Was your *bruder* one of them?"

"*Ja,*" Jeb said, his heart burning. "My *mamm* died when I was a teenager. My *daed* wasn't an easy man to live with, so I tried to take care of Pauly—my brother. I didn't do such a good job."

"Well, most kids need a *mamm*, ain't so?"

"You are right there, my friend. Pauly and I sure needed our *mamm*."

Adam stared over at him. "I'd be sad if my *mamm* passed. Is that why you don't tell about it much? Cause it might make you cry?"

Jeb loved this kid. "I don't talk about it much because it still hurts and because I've made a lot of mistakes in my time of grief. Pauly died when he was a bit older than you."

Adam leaned over the nearest fence post. "That's a shame. Terrible. My *bruders* get on my last nerve sometimes, but I'd be sad if something happened to either of 'em."

"It does make me sad," Jeb admitted. "I've been angry about it, so sometimes I get quiet and…moody. But you need to know I'd never be mad at you. You're right—we're best friends."

Adam's grin made all the bad thoughts go away. Jeb had to wonder what it would be like to have a son like Adam, so inquisitive, so full of life and promise.

Then he thought about Rebecca, could see her holding a baby. If they were to marry, could they have a child? Or had they already missed that time in their lives?

He didn't dare dream any further. There was still a lot he needed to work through before he

could even contemplate marriage and a family. But he already knew in his heart, he wanted to be with Rebecca, children or no children.

Chapter Nineteen

"You have a birthday soon."

Rebecca glanced at her sister. Hannah always showed up on Saturday to lend her a hand or help her with customers. Now that she had Jeb and Adam, Rebecca had more time to keep things organized. This morning, she and Hannah were watching over the gardens while Jeb and Adam sold plants and produce up on the road.

They'd pulled two lawn chairs out into the shade of the old oak near the field, with a small wooden table between them serving as Rebecca's desk. Rebecca let her customers roam on their own until they needed her help. Hannah had made a huge container of honey lemonade to offer their visitors, and she'd brought paper cups to serve the sweet, refreshing drink. Rebecca handed out the pamphlets Jeb and Jewel

had created, so customers could read her tips and pass that information on to others. That one gesture had brought her a lot more business.

"I'm trying to forget my birthday," she told her sister while she kept her eyes on the half-dozen people milling around her gardens. The fields were at their prime, so she expected a lot of business today. "I'm getting older by the minute."

"You still look young. Mamm always looked so young. You take after her." Then Hannah shrugged. "The *Englisch* don't think being in your thirties is old, you know."

"The *Englisch* are different from us, you know," Rebecca shot back with a smile.

"*Ja*, they just have fancy doctors to lift everything," Hannah said with a giggle.

"Hannah!" Rebecca never knew what would come out of her sister's mouth. But Hannah did make a valid point. "I'm past worrying about wrinkles and such. I'm thankful I've made it this far."

"You and Jeb are about the same age."

"Really, I hadn't noticed," she quipped. Did everyone around here want her to marry Jeb?

"Have you thought about him anymore?"

Rebecca wanted to say she thought about nothing else, but she wouldn't give anyone fodder or hope. "I work with him, so *ja*, I think

about him a lot when I'm planning out the daily tasks around here."

"That's not what I meant."

Rebecca gave her sister a frown. "I know what you meant, and I have no answers. I care about Jeb. We've grown close, but that information is between you and me. Noah has backed off, at least. He knows I like Jeb and that's all he needs to know."

"So if you and Jeb were to become really close, it won't be because our brother demanded it, ain't so?"

"That is correct. It will happen naturally and because it is the Lord's plan for our lives." Rebecca watched her customers and then she turned back to Hannah. "Have you heard Noah talking about Jeb? Our brother seemed skittish the other day when he came by to talk."

Hannah shook her head. "Noah doesn't confide in me. He thinks I can't keep a secret."

Rebecca raised her eyebrows and they both started laughing.

"Okay, so maybe I do find it hard to not repeat things," Hannah said, "but Noah won't tell me any gossip, so I can't repeat what I don't know."

"Noah likes Jeb now, same as me. I'm beginning to think those two are in cahoots about something."

"You know how men are—they hold everything in, trying to be all manly. Maybe Jeb shared something with Noah that he didn't want to talk about with anyone else."

Rebecca stood, her mind reeling with possibilities. "That is the best answer anyone could give me. Men do talk, but they speak differently than women."

"*Ja*, and we are all thankful for that," Hannah replied.

"So, if Noah and Jeb have been talking and passing secrets, that means our brother trusts Jeb, at least."

"And that also means Jeb must hold trust in our stubborn, well-meaning brother," Hannah said, proud of herself.

"This could be *gut*," Rebecca replied, relief washing over her. "Whatever those two have going on, I will stay out of it. Just to keep the peace around here."

A customer approached with a question, so she hurried off to help. Hannah poured more lemonade and then went to help another customer. Soon Rebecca got so busy, she didn't worry overmuch about how strange her brother had been acting. But if Noah and Jeb were growing closer, why did Jeb seem to be avoiding her at every turn? Noah might have befriended Jeb,

but he might also still be trying to push Jeb toward her.

Would she ever understand how Jeb really felt about her?

He'd tried.

Jeb let out a sigh as the last of the marked timber was put away. He could finally build the potting shed he'd imagined for Rebecca. Meantime, he'd tried every which way to find the courage to tell her about John. Her John, his cousin. He had letters written by the man she'd loved.

Why can't I just be honest with her?

He finished up in the barn, hiding the last of the wood he'd managed to saw and shape into a passable puzzle that had to be put together in a few hours while she was away.

Noah was in charge of making that happen. He'd explained to Franny that she should invite Hannah and Rebecca for a town day. They'd buy fabric for dresses and quilting, thread, anything they needed to make Franny's soap and candles and anything that could keep them away for a few hours. Next Saturday afternoon, after they'd done their half day of work.

Franny would use Rebecca's birthday as an excuse to get her away from the house. It just happened to fall on a Saturday this year.

Noah had given him a grace period.

"You don't want to upset her before or on her birthday. So get this done and then, Jeb, you have to be honest with her. Or I'll have to be the one to tell her, and that will make it twice as humiliating for her."

Jeb's head hurt from lack of sleep, trying to keep a secret surprise, and having a bombshell secret he'd kept from Rebecca.

"You look sad."

Surprised, he found Franny standing in the barn door with a glass heavy with sliced lemons and tea.

"I have a lot on my mind," he admitted. Noah's wife was quiet and steady, like the creek behind Rebecca's house. She didn't gossip and she kept her four children under control. But she rarely talked to Jeb. "Did you need something?"

She offered him the drink. "I need to speak to you."

Jeb got that feeling of dread in his stomach. "All right." He took a sip of lemony-sweet tea with mint. "This is *gut*."

"I'm trying new versions," Franny admitted. "I read about mixing tea and lemonade in a magazine at the doctor's office. Sounded refreshing, *ja*?"

"It is that."

Franny's shy smile changed to seriousness. "I know what you have planned for Rebecca. I

think this is truly kind of you, Jeb. She will be so touched."

"I hope so. I want to make her life easier."

Franny nodded. "I wanted to apologize for judging you when you first showed up here. I've heard nothing but the best about you from day one. Most of that coming from Adam, of course. He really looks up to you."

"Adam is a *gut* kid, and we're best friends."

"He has learned a lot from you," Franny said, smiling. "Noah is so busy, and he tries to take time with all the boys, so letting Adam work with you has also helped him become closer to his *daed*, too."

"How's that?" Jeb asked, wishing he could have discovered some way to help his *daed* and Pauly become closer.

"Adam is a talker, inquisitive and smart. Noah doesn't often have the patience to deal with that. But now that Adam has been around you, he has also learned to speak to Noah in a different way, with understanding and respect. I owe you for that, Jeb."

Jeb's heart swelled with pride for Adam. Not for himself. "It's easy being around Adam. We've had some great conversations."

"Maybe I should send the other two over to take lessons from you, *ja*?"

He laughed, afraid Franny might be serious. When she grinned, he breathed a sigh of relief. "You had me there for a minute."

She laughed again. Then she said, "Don't worry. I'll get Hannah and Rebecca away so you can build the shed. Hannah only knows I want to take them into town to celebrate a bit. As you know, we don't go all out for birthdays. But I can't wait to see Becca's reaction when she comes home to find it there."

"Let's hope she'll be pleased."

Franny gave him a knowing smile. "She will be pleased because you are a thoughtful person, someone she admires."

"*Denke*, Franny," he said, handing her back the almost empty glass. "I hope she'll like the new shed."

Franny left, and Jeb stood there taking in a breath. He'd won over so many doubters. But how could he win over the one person he wanted to believe in him and trust him? How could he win over Rebecca after being dishonest with her for weeks now?

One more week until her birthday and the shed being built. Could he wait another week? He had no choice. He wouldn't mess up her surprise. If she told him to leave later, at least she'd have that gift to use and maybe to remember he

did have a good, caring side to him. He wanted
her to remember the good in him, not his one
sin of omission.

The days seemed to flow for Rebecca. She
kept thinking about her birthday. She'd long ago
given up on a husband and children, letting her
niece and nephews give her the joy of what must
feel like mothering her own child. But each time
she glanced at Jeb, she wished she could be ten
years younger.

Silly, but he'd make a great father.

That could be the thing between them that no
one talked about—that she might be too old to
have children. Did he think about that? Just one
more reason for them to remain friends.

He'd been a bit more talkative lately, but she
felt as if they were walking a fine line. So she
decided to take matters into her own hands.
She'd learned long ago if you want something
done, do it yourself.

"Jeb," she said late on a Thursday after they'd
had a busy day in the heat of summer, "I'd like
you to stay for supper tonight."

Jeb had been gathering vegetables, as he liked
to do at the end of the day. The asparagus and
cabbage were both exploding, so they had to
constantly gather buckets full of both. She and
Franny would make sauerkraut with the cab-

bage, and they could eat the asparagus fresh and sell most of it. He glanced up in surprise, his cutting scissors in one hand. "Are you sure?"

"I wouldn't ask if I weren't sure," she retorted, the sting of his words hitting their mark. "Unless you have other plans."

"My only plan is to wash up, find food and collapse," he admitted. "I've cut a whole row of cabbage and cleared off the outside leaves. And this asparagus is ready to clip so I want to finish this row."

"*Denke* for doing that, but if you're tired, you might not want to linger or eat a real meal."

"I didn't say that."

She took one of the buckets and started clearing heavy green cabbage leaves from the sturdy stems. "Why are you avoiding me, Jeb? Is it because I was bold enough to kiss you? Did that make you think less of me?"

Jeb put his bucket down and stared at her. "Kissing you would never make me think less of you, Becca. It only made me want to kiss you more."

She blushed but blamed the heat rising up her face on the warm day. "I see."

"*Neh*, that is the problem," he said, his brow wet with sweat. "You do not see. You fight against what we are feeling because you are just as afraid as I am, aren't you?"

She set her bucket down with a thud. "What do I have to fear, Jeb?"

"Everything," he said, frustration echoing out behind that one word. "I'm a stranger. I need to confess everything to become Amish again. I'm a hard man to deal with, a man who has a past. That's a lot to have to accept."

"I have accepted you in every way," she replied, anger and frustration boiling over. "Is there anything else I need to know? Is it me? Because I'm old and I can't bear children? Is it because everyone wants you to marry me, so they can all stop feeling sorry for me?"

"Becca..." He started for her, but Lily Dog chose that moment to come running toward them from the creek.

Rebecca turned to keep the dog from shaking creek water all over her, but Lily Dog kept coming. Then next thing she knew, the dog ran around her leg and accidentally tripped her up, causing her to start a fast fall.

Right into Jeb's arms.

Cabbage and asparagus flew through the air.

Together, they stumbled and fell to the ground, Lily Dog dancing and barking all around them, enjoying this new game.

Becca hit his chest with a thump, her breath leaving her body. Then she glanced down at

him, saw the need in his eyes, and felt that same need inside her heart.

"Becca," he said again. "I need—"

Rebecca pushed away, not daring to kiss him, although she wanted that badly. She pushed against the ground and managed to stand. Grabbing enough fresh asparagus to feed two, she said, "I'm going to make supper. You can stay or not. It's up to you."

"I'm staying," he said. "And Becca, I'm not just talking about staying for supper. I'm going to find a way to stay here in Campton Creek for the rest of my life."

Rebecca's heart lifted at that passionate declaration, but it sank fast when she thought of all the things still between them. "Biscuits or corn bread?" she asked, thinking she sounded *dumm*.

He blinked, got up and wiped his hands down his pants. "Biscuits sound *gut*. And I do like asparagus."

Rebecca marched to the house, thinking between his mixed signals and her constant state of confusion, it would take something big to ever bring them together.

Or something big to destroy both of them all over again.

Chapter Twenty

Jeb thought this would be the time to come clean, except he and Noah had agreed to wait until after Becca's birthday.

So now here he sat, his hair still damp from sticking his head under the cool pump water, his skin smelling like lemongrass and heather soap, watching Becca move around her kitchen. She'd barely spoken to him, but he heard her humming as she worked. Somehow, this felt right. Better than any of the places he'd worked and lived before.

He wished with all his heart he could have supper with her for the rest of his life. Surely, God hadn't brought him here and let him fall for this woman, just to have him leave again. He'd tell the bishop he was ready to go before the church. He knew in his heart he needed to be right here.

"That sure smells good," he said. "Do you need any help?"

She whirled, her expression showing he'd insulted her in some way. "I don't mind cooking for you, Jeb."

"I didn't mean you're not capable," he said, his tongue becoming tied. "I love your cooking. I guess I'm used to batching it, is all."

She finished checking on the steamed asparagus and then checked the baked chicken and rice in the oven. Wiping her hands down her apron, she fixed tea for them and came to sit at the table. "It will be ready in a few minutes."

Jeb took a sip of tea. "Franny brought me some tea the other day—tea with lemons, mint and honey. It was good."

"Would you rather I added those items?"

"Neh," he said, getting more flustered by the minute. "Why are you so mad at me?"

Rebecca looked sheepish. "I don't know. I don't want to be mad, but… I can't name why I'm feeling this way. I wanted us to have a nice dinner. I made a cake—strawberries and white cake with whipped cream."

"I like that kind of cake."

"Gut."

"I don't think you're mad at me, really," he said. "I think we're trying hard to not like each other, but Becca I do like you. A lot."

She stared over at him, her hands in her lap, her eyes as pretty as any forest he'd ever seen. "What are we to do, then?"

"We can continue as we've planned, and let God show us the way," he said, meaning it. Wanting it.

"I like that plan, and I'm sorry I've been... mad."

"Does that mean you care about me?"

She nodded, looked down at her hands. "I don't want you to feel obligated, Jeb."

"Obligated?" He couldn't believe she didn't see how much he'd fallen for her. Yet, he couldn't tell her that. Not yet.

"I know Noah has been pushing you toward me. It's pathetic that my brother is constantly trying to match me with anyone who comes along." She twisted her apron in her hands. "I told myself I'd just ignore him, and I even warned him to stop. He did seem to stop, but now you're acting strange and he's acting strange, and I know something is going on with you two. Is my brother hounding you about me? You don't have to sacrifice yourself for me. I can take care of myself. I've learned that. I will be okay."

He saw the tears she'd tried so hard to hold back. Jeb got up and lifted her out of her chair. "Becca," he said, taking her hands in his, his

eyes on her, "no one is hounding me, and you are not pathetic. You are one of the strongest women I've ever met. I've had every opportunity to marry—either Amish, Mennonite or *Englisch*. But none of them have compared to you, do you understand me?"

She bobbed her head and wiped at her eyes. "But I kissed you and messed things up—I was too bold and reckless."

Jeb shook his head. "I told you I liked kissing you."

"But—"

He stopped her, his nose lifting in the air. "But… I think something is burning."

She whirled and ran to the stove. "Your biscuits."

"*My* biscuits?"

She grabbed a potholder and opened the oven to grab the pan of slightly singed biscuits. "And the chicken and rice will be dry now."

"My biscuits," he repeated, a smile cresting his face. "You have burned my biscuits."

"This is not funny," she said, fussing with getting the chicken and rice out. "I've ruined our meal."

He held a hand to his lip to keep from laughing.

"What is wrong with you?" she asked, glancing around.

"It's just between Old Billy ruining the Farmer's Daughters and you burning *my* biscuits, we seem to always be in trouble a lot, don't you think?"

Rebecca put her hands on her hips and tried to be mad. But instead of pouting, she started giggling. Then they both started laughing. Jeb came to her and grabbed her hands again, dancing her around the kitchen.

They stopped, both out of breath, and he looked into her eyes. "I like burned biscuits, Becca. I like the way you make me laugh. I haven't laughed this much in such a long time."

He held her there, savoring having her in his arms. Then he leaned over and whispered, "This is the part where you kiss me again."

She did kiss him again. When she finally pulled away, Jeb stepped back and smiled. "Don't ever think anyone feels sorry for you, Rebecca. I think everyone around here admires you. I know I do." Then he looked at the food. "And I can't wait to eat burned biscuits and dry chicken."

She slapped at his arm, but her smile countered that action. "Then help me get our food on the table and we will enjoy our messed-up meal."

Jeb smiled and helped her finish up. "Nothing with you is messed up," he said. "And just

so you know, Noah has not been after me about marrying you. Other things, yes. But not that."

She gave him a puzzled glance. "Then what's wrong with both of you lately? You've avoided me and he's acting like a cat in a roomful of rocking chairs. What is he after you about now, Jeb?"

Jeb seemed to like the cake. She sent some home with him, watching him out the front door. She half expected Noah to *kumm* running with either a knowing grin or a stern frown. But her brother seemed subdued these days.

Rebecca was more confused than ever.

Jeb hadn't really told her anything to ease the nagging dread she felt in her heart. After her question, he only said that Noah liked to pick at him about almost everything, but that lately they'd been getting along a lot better.

So why had Jeb avoided her so much before their supper together?

True, they had been busy, and they couldn't stand around flirting while customers kept coming on a daily basis. Today, a whole bus full of tourists had arrived and they'd asked a lot of questions. She and Jeb, and sometimes Adam, had done their best to answer all the questions.

Now as she looked out over the yard and fields, she could see all the improvements Jeb

had helped her with. The barn looked fresh from a new coat of red paint. She knew it was in tip-top condition inside, too, since Adam went on and on about helping Jeb fix it up. She'd peeked in once or twice, but she still couldn't bring herself to go near the horses. It wasn't that she was so terrified of them, but the trauma of seeing John go flying through the air and then never waking up was just too much to remember all over again.

John.

She felt the guilt of not remembering him as much now. It had been so long, and yet, she didn't want to forget him. Jeb reminded her so much of him at times, she had to turn away. But Jeb was different, more confident, and older, strong, and dependable. John would have been all those things if he'd lived.

She had to stop comparing the two of them. It wasn't fair to Jeb. Since their dinner the other night, he'd been kind and considerate and he found ways to make her smile. He and Adam were *gut* at doing silly things to get her attention. Lily Dog always went along with the fun, causing all of them to giggle.

But Rebecca still had that feeling that something wasn't right. Maybe it was because she'd forgotten how it felt to be in love. She had fallen for Jeb. It was an easy fall, a soft, delicate drift-

ing, as a leaf would let go of a tree and fall softly to earth. She couldn't come out and tell him, but he had to know. He had to feel her heart beating against his chest when he held her, he had to feel the warm intensity that flowed over her when he kissed her. He had to see it in her eyes each time he looked at her.

Especially after the burnt biscuits episode. She still giggled and got all dreamy—over biscuits! He'd eaten them with butter and declared they were the best biscuits ever.

That had to mean he loved her in some small way. He just had a lot to work through to come to his own conclusions. But the bishop had stopped her at church the other day.

"Jeb is a *gut* man, Rebecca. I hope whatever his future holds, that he will stay here among us. I'm praying for you, and your part in that decision."

Bishop King never pushed, and he never made demands. He usually laid out how things should be and the consequences of anyone's actions if they strayed. Then he guided that person into making the best decision. He wanted Jeb to stay.

And so did she.

But Jeb and *Gott* would have to have that discussion.

She stood on the porch now, taking in the

late afternoon sun that shifted in a golden glow across the trees and fields. Jeb had gone home, Adam trailing by his side, talking away about the snake they'd found and sent to the woods, and the big fish he'd seen jumping in the creek.

She loved hearing their conversations.

When she saw a shadow coming around the side of the house, her heart expected Jeb. But Franny waved to her and smiled.

"What brings you over?" Rebecca asked, thinking they'd done enough putting up and canning to last for years.

"I want to go into town Saturday afternoon," Franny said. "I thought you and Hannah might want to ride with me. It can be your birthday outing. Then when we get home, we can have a picnic supper out under the trees."

Surprised, Rebecca stared at her sister-in-law. "That's a lot for one day. We usually just have cake and punch."

"Oh, we'll have cake," Franny said. "I ordered one from Ava Jane Weaver."

"Oh, she makes the best cakes," Rebecca said, touched that Franny was being so kind. "You don't have to do this, you know."

Franny glanced around. "But I do. I mean I want to give you a special day. You've worked hard and helped me with getting all the jellies and jams made, and the produce put away. We

won't starve this winter. Let's have some fun, okay?"

"I really didn't want to dwell on my birthday."

"You won't dwell. You'll be having fun with your sisters."

Rebecca did consider Franny a sister, same as her real sister. "What does Hannah say?"

"She's excited to be included. We'll leave after you shut down for the day. I have meat for burgers and Noah said he'd help with preparations—something he rarely offers."

"A real picnic, for my birthday. I can bring a side dish."

"*Neh*, you are the birthday girl. You don't have to worry about anything."

Franny seemed so set on doing this, Rebecca couldn't refuse. "I will be ready after dinner hour," she said, smiling. "*Denke*, Franny. This is so thoughtful, and it sounds like fun."

"*Gut,*" Franny said. "No church on Sunday so we can rest up then."

Rebecca hugged her sister-in-law, then Franny took a glance at the lily field. "Oh, my, Rebecca. This looks so pretty with the late sun shining on it. You and Jeb have done wonders."

"Adam helped," she said, smiling. "This summer has been my best so far. I've had more customers than ever."

"You're so smart and I'm so happy for you,"

Franny replied. "You've helped me with the youngies so much. *Denke.*"

Rebecca smiled. "I'm thankful to have you and Noah so close."

"And now you have help, *ja*?"

Rebecca chuckled. "Jeb is certainly strong and hardworking. Moses Yoder reminded me of a tortoise, but he did try."

Franny chatted a little more and picked out a pretty apricot-colored lily with curly, plush blooms. "Take it," Rebecca said. "On the house."

She waved her sister-in-law home, smiling as she thought of the fun day they'd have on Saturday.

Her life was settling into a nice, pleasant routine.

And Jeb had become a part of that routine. She only hoped her peace could last past summer.

Chapter Twenty-One

Saturday turned out to be a beautiful day, warm with a gentle breeze and blue skies for miles. The kind of day with many possibilities.

Jeb went through the morning eagerly awaiting the time when he and his friends would meet in Noah's barn to move wood slats, and then do the same in Rebecca's barn. They'd piece together the numbered boards to quickly build Rebecca's shed.

Jeb had made a sign for it—Rebecca's Lily Garden—that he hoped she'd like. Franny had painted a bright burgundy lily with a yellow throat on the small piece of wood. He'd hang it over the double doors that he'd already had Tobias Mast smooth and polish at the furniture shop where he worked. Noah had kept them in his barn and Tobias had come there to finish up

his work. Just about everyone except Rebecca was in on this surprise.

He only hoped his grand plan wouldn't backfire on him.

The day passed with vehicles coming and going up and down the lane leading to the gardens and fields. Not only did they sell all the potted lilies, but Adam and Jeb had dug up a few and potted them on the spot. Rebecca patiently answered the many questions people asked, handing them one of the pamphlets Jeb and Jewel had created. They seemed to do the trick, especially since Jewel had added several good websites on growing lilies.

They needed to set up their own website, he thought as he hurried around to clean up everything and make sure the lilies hadn't been trampled by all the folks who'd been here.

A lot of their visitors only wanted pictures, so last week he and Adam had set out benches and made designated trails for the lookers to follow. He'd noticed several parents taking pictures of their children sitting on one of the benches, lilies blooming like a rainbow in every color behind them.

He thought of the bench by the creek, smiling when he remembered being there with Rebecca. Maybe after today, after they'd celebrated her

birthday, she'd see that he cared for her deeply. And she'd understand why he hadn't been honest with her.

He was headed toward the barn with the wheelbarrow when he heard her calling.

"Jeb?"

Jeb set down the wheelbarrow and turned to greet her. She'd changed her work dress for a mint green fresh frock and a crisp white apron. She looked so pretty as she walked toward him.

"Ja?"

"I'm about to leave with Franny and Hannah for our town trip." She gave him a shy smile. "Are you coming to the gathering later?"

"Oh, you mean, will I be at your birthday celebration?"

"It's not a celebration, just people getting together. Family."

He wondered if he would be part of her family one day.

"I plan to. I wouldn't miss it."

"You want cake, right?"

"Right. That's why I want to be there."

Her eyes lit up while her smile shot hope straight to his heart. "I'll be back in a few hours. Try to stay out of trouble."

"I will," he said, his heart beating so fast, he had to take a deep breath. "You do the same."

She laughed and waved, looking so young

and happy, his guilt kicked at him like an old mule. He would hate to destroy that happiness.

A few minutes later, Noah and the crew showed up. Adam came running toward the barn. "Are you ready, Jeb?"

"I'm so ready," Jeb said, waving to Jeremiah Weaver, Tobias Mast, Josiah Fisher and Micah King.

"We have others on the way," Jeremiah said, ready to get to work. "But we can get the framework set up."

Jeb nodded and showed them where the slats and boards had been hidden in the back of the barn. Noah and his sons went back to his place to load everything they had hidden there.

Soon the fields echoed with hammering and men shouting and talking. Jeb stopped and glanced around, making sure no women were approaching.

He wanted this to be the best surprise Rebecca had ever had. And the best birthday.

Franny held tightly to the buggy reins, occasionally turning to check on Rebecca in the back, while Hannah rode up front with her. "How ya doing back there?"

"I'm okay, Franny," Rebecca said. "I know you're a *wunderbar gut* driver."

"And I'm right here," Hannah said, smiling over her shoulder. "This was such a sweet idea, Franny. I haven't been on a girls' outing in so long."

"Noah suggested it," Franny said. "He's getting mellow in his old age."

"Wait," Rebecca said, leaning up. "Did you say my brother suggested this?"

Franny checked the reins, but she looked *ferhoodled*. "I mean, he asked if I'd like to take you both into town. Just a thought."

Rebecca smiled at her sister-in-law's confusion, but she got that feeling inside that something was off. Why would she think that just because her brother and his wife were thinking of her on a special day?

"That was thoughtful of our *bruder*," Hannah said.

At least she hadn't been acting strange. But then, no one told Hannah their secrets. Rebecca was surprised her sweet but talkative sister hadn't blabbed about Rebecca's feelings regarding Jeb.

"I thought we'd start with a quick bite at the Campton Creek Café," Franny said. "It's that new place that Jewel and some of our friends have opened. A lot of Amish are employed

there. Jewel helps when she can, but she has her hands full with the Campton Center."

"That would be nice," Rebecca said. "But I must save room for supper tonight, too."

Hannah grinned. "I'm hungry already." She looked so shy, Rebecca now had to worry about her, too. What was she hiding?

Franny parked the buggy across from the new café, secured the horses and marched them across the street. The café was in what used to be a small Victorian-style house. It was past lunch hour, so they found a nice table on the big porch where they could sit in the shade of an aged oak tree.

Once they were seated, Rebecca glanced at her sister. "Hannah, are you feeling poorly? You're pale today."

Hannah shook her head. "*Neh*, I mean… I'm feeling a little faint is all." She took a sip of the water a young Amish girl had brought them. "I'm feeling…different."

Franny stared at Hannah and then put a hand to her mouth. "Are you with child?"

Rebecca glanced at Hannah, and then she saw her sister's apologetic eyes. "You're expecting?"

Hannah nodded. "I didn't want to spoil your day, but I'm a little shaky. I need food."

Rebecca got up and came around the table

to hug her sister. "Why would you worry about me? You know I'm thrilled for you."

"Are you?" Hannah asked. "I was afraid…it would make you sad."

Rebecca touched a hand to Hannah's face. "Silly, I'm happy. I will be the first to spoil this child."

Hannah hugged her tight. "I'm so glad you're okay with this. I…miss Mamm so much right now."

Franny got up to hug her, too. "You have us, sister. We will pamper both you and the *bobbeli*."

The waitress came back, concern on her face. "Can I help?"

"We're fine," Franny said, a smile on her face as she wiped her eyes. "We are celebrating a newcomer to our family."

The girl clapped her hands together. "We have cupcakes. I'll bring a big one for dessert."

Rebecca laughed and nodded. "We'll let the expecting mother eat most of it."

They ordered salads and laughed and talked.

Rebecca kept smiling at her little sister. A new baby for her to spoil. She couldn't wait to tell Jeb.

That thought made her heart burn with a need she had tried to hide. She wished she could ex-

perience having a child of her own. But she prayed for God's guidance and wisdom.

Being married to Jeb would be more than enough.

Three hours later, Jeb stood back and smiled.

"We did it, Jeb," Adam said, slapping Jeb on the back. "It looks real pretty, too."

"It does look nice," Jeb replied, ruffling Adam's hair.

"I need some water and a snack," Adam said. "I'm tired."

The other men had left for home. Now Jeb had to get cleaned up for supper at Noah's house. But first, he wanted to finish cleaning up things around here. Becca should be home before sundown, so he wanted to be here when she spotted the fresh new shed near the old oak. He'd found an old wooden picnic table at a garage sale a couple of weeks ago and taken it to the Furniture Mart in town where Tobias worked. Together, they'd spruced it up and Tobias had brought it today.

Now, it was centered off to the side of the shed with a potted lily—a Farmer's Daughter— sitting on the table.

He finished up, pleased that everything was coming together. The minute he saw the buggy returning from town, he'd walk over and ask

Rebecca to come back here with him for just a few minutes.

He'd get through today, and his gift to her. Then tomorrow, he'd tell her the last of his secrets.

"We are running out of room."

Franny and Hannah laughed as Rebecca tried to find a spot for all the bags and boxes they'd loaded into the buggy.

"But we have so much—our fabrics for dresses and quilts, more jam jars for canning, some new books to read. Did I miss anything?" Franny asked, laughing.

"I need to run into the general store," Rebecca said. "I remembered I need some more pots. We've used so many more this season. I can buy up what is in stock and order a new shipment through Mr. Hartford and get a discount."

"Okay, I'll go in with you," Franny said. "I'm sure I can find something I need."

Hannah got out of the buggy and sat on a bench out front. She had grown tired. "I'll be here, napping like an old man."

Franny and Rebecca hurried in and headed back to the garden section. Franny went one way and Rebecca went the other.

Rebecca was trying to decide how many pots to order and which colors when she ran

into Shem Yoder. He and Moses were related in some way, but she rarely saw the reclusive widower.

Smiling, she said, "Hello, Shem. I haven't seen you in a while."

The older man stared at her. "Rebecca?"

"That's me," she said, thinking he'd aged a lot.

"I was just thinking about you the other day," he replied, his face squinting into a grimace. "You and John—so sad that."

She blinked, surprised to hear that coming out of his mouth. Nodding, she turned back to her pots. But Shem kept standing there. "Did you need something, Shem?"

He scratched his beard. "Minna had a sister, Moselle."

Confused, Rebecca nodded. "Yes, John's *mamm* had a sister named Minna, but she moved away before I ever met her."

"Minna married a Martin," Shem went on. "John's cousin sure looks just like him, ain't so?"

Rebecca thought she'd heard wrong. "What did you say?"

Shem's eyes widened and he turned so quickly, he almost knocked over a shelf full of gadgets.

"Shem, are you all right?"

Shem looked confused. "You know, the man who works for you." Then he put a hand to his mouth. "I'm sorry. I've said too much."

He lifted his hat and slowly walked away, leaving Rebecca so shocked, she dropped the plastic flowerpot she was holding.

John's cousin looks just like him, ain't so?

You know, the man who works for you.

Rebecca couldn't move. John's cousin? Martin. Minna Martin. Jeb Martin.

Franny came rushing toward her. "Becca, what happened?"

Rebecca grabbed her sister-in-law's hand. "I need to get home."

"Are you ill?" Franny asked as she reached down to pick up the cracked pot.

Rebecca held a hand to her head. "*Neh*, but I need to talk to Jeb. Right now."

Franny set the pot back on the table and took her toward the front door. "We'll pay for the busted flowerpot later, Mr. Hartford," she told the surprised owner. "Becca isn't feeling well right now."

Rebecca could barely get into the buggy. Her hands were shaking, and a cold sweat inched down her spine. Hannah kept asking what had happened, but Franny just shook her head.

Rebecca sank back on her seat, her stom-

ach roiling and lurching with each bump of the buggy.

Could it be true? Could Jeb be John's cousin?

And if so, why hadn't he told her that from the beginning?

Chapter Twenty-Two

Jeb saw the buggy coming up the lane, his emotions going from relief to gratitude to happiness and back to fear and doubt. What if Becca didn't like surprises? What if she hated the shed? Then, would she ever forgive him when he explained things to her?

As Franny trotted the horses to the barn, everyone waiting for them waved. Hannah's husband had arrived, and he was all grins. Noah and the boys tried to stand still, but Adam was hopping from foot to foot. And Katie, who'd pouted most of the day for not being able to go with the women, went running to the buggy.

"You're home," she shouted. "Did you bring me some candy, Mamm?"

Franny hopped down, her eyes on Noah. She motioned to him.

Jeb saw Rebecca and started heading toward

them, but she glanced up, got down from the buggy and took off toward her house.

"What's wrong?" Noah asked, while Hannah hurried Katie toward the house, her husband, Samuel, hurrying after her.

Franny glanced toward Rebecca's house. "I don't know. She was talking to Shem Yoder in the general store, and she looked so…shocked. She wanted to come home immediately."

Noah sent Jeb a knowing glare. "We knew this would happen. Now what are you going to do?"

Jeb knew what he had to do, and he also knew it was all over now. He'd have to leave. If Shem had told her the truth, Rebecca would never forgive him.

Franny's gaze moved from him to Jeb. "What are you talking about?"

Noah motioned to Jeb. "Go after her."

Then he took Franny by the arm. "I'll explain everything."

"*Ja*, you will," his wife said. "I've never seen Rebecca so shattered. At least not since John died."

Jeb took a deep breath, went inside the *grossdaddi haus* and found the letters from John. Then he walked up the lane to Rebecca's house. It was the hardest walk he'd ever made.

* * *

Rebecca made it as far as the kitchen, where she sank down on a chair and held a hand to her mouth. It all made sense now, of course. Jeb looked so much like John. She'd seen that, felt that in her heart. But she'd decided she just missed John and she'd imagined the rest. How silly, how naive she'd been.

When she heard a knock at the front door, that day she'd seen Jeb walking up the lane the first time came back to her. She wouldn't allow him into her house again, and she'd get him out of her heart. Somehow.

"Becca." He called her name like a plea. "I'm so sorry. I wanted to tell you a thousand times, but I had an excuse for not telling you—any excuse I could find. I didn't know, Becca. I didn't know until you told me your name. And by then, I didn't want to go. I wanted this job and later after we'd worked together and I got to know you and your family, and this community, I wanted to stay here with you forever."

Rebecca gulped a sob, her head falling into her hands. She'd never been betrayed in such a cruel way. Never. This hurt almost as much as losing John.

"Becca, please. I... I have letters from John. I'll let you see them. I wanted to tell you so many times."

Letters? He had letters from the man she was meant to be with, the man she'd longed for all these years. All this time, he'd had letters. Every time she'd mentioned John, Jeb had known. He'd known what he was doing.

She sat, her hands shaking, her lungs burning, her eyes streaming silent tears—tears of grief, anger, disbelief and heartache.

She was living it all over again because she'd trusted a man who reminded her so much of John.

John was in heaven.

Jeb was here on earth.

In her whole life, she'd only loved two men.

One she'd never forget, and one she'd never forgive.

She got up and went upstairs and fell across her bed.

Then she remembered it was her birthday, and the tears came all over again. Her heart hurt so badly, she felt the burn of it all the way to her soul.

There was no getting over this. Ever.

Jeb didn't know what to do. She wouldn't open the door, so he went around back. He didn't try to go up on the porch or into the house. Instead, he took the bundle of letters to the new shed, the smell of fresh wood and lil-

ies merging around him with what seemed like a taunting scent.

What have I done?

He stood in the shed, praying to the Lord. Asking for true forgiveness, from the Master. Asking for redemption from the One who could give it. He'd do anything to make this up to Rebecca. Anything.

Even leaving her if that's what it would take.

But he didn't want to leave. He wanted to comfort her and hold her and tell her how much he loved her. He'd fallen for her the moment he'd seen her. Before he even knew her name.

He should have left then, after he'd figured things out. But coward that he was, he'd stayed and withheld the most important thing he could tell her. Now, she'd heard it from an old man who got confused, but who also had a memory that seemed as sharp as ever. He couldn't blame this on Shem, though. The man knew what he knew. And so did Jeb. But Shem told the truth in his misguided way.

Jeb had held the truth away because he didn't want to wander anymore. Now he'd have to do that very thing anyway.

He stood in the little building he'd created to show Rebecca how much he cared. Turning, he stared up at the house for a long time, hoping she'd come outside.

But the sun began to set, and she still hadn't opened any doors. Jeb left the letters there on the small counter he'd made for her. Then he turned and headed for the barn. He'd make sure the animals were taken care of for tonight at least. Because he'd be gone by morning's light.

Rebecca heard someone knocking at the back door.

Groggy and confused, she sat up and realized she'd fallen asleep with her clothes on. Outside, the sunset shot ribbons of purple and gold across the lily field. She went to the window and looked down, thinking Jeb was back. The whole place looked like a painting—a painting done by the Master, the One who watched over even the lilies of the field.

Then she noticed the shed.

How was this possible? There had been no shed there when she'd left all those hours ago. Her heart hammered the answer while she tried to ignore it.

Jeb. It had to have been Jeb.

When she saw her brother walking away from the house, she hurried down and came out the front door, so she could speak to him about the new building on her property. And about Jeb.

"Noah."

Her brother whirled as she called from the

front porch. "There you are. We were fearsome worried about you."

Rebecca straightened her *kapp* and wiped at her tear-swollen eyes. "Were you worried when Jeb told you the truth?"

Noah looked so guilty, she almost felt sorry for him. "Why didn't you say something? You were the one who warned me against him."

"I only found out a few weeks ago, not all of it, mind you. But Shem had put things together and asked around. I came to Jeb and confronted him. He told me the rest—about John."

Her anger returned, burning like lightning down her stomach. "You should have told me."

"It wasn't my place, Becca," he said, his hands out. "Jeb promised me he'd tell you everything—after your birthday."

She sank down on a rocking chair. "Why would it matter which day he told me?"

"He wanted… He made you a gift…" Noah stopped. "The man is in love with you, Becca."

As much as those words jolted her heart, she couldn't accept that now. "Well, he has a funny way of showing it—keeping this secret from me the whole time, Noah. The times we worked together, laughed together, chased your goat, ran off deer, every little thing we did together, and he knew, he knew how much this would hurt me."

Noah came to her and patted her shoulder, tears in his eyes. "He did know this would hurt you, sister. He fought with it day and night. He told the bishop and Bishop King urged him to be truthful with you. Jeb was afraid it would destroy you."

"Well, Jeb was right," she said. "I don't know if I can ever get over this."

"But he built you a garden shed."

"That won't help my broken heart," she replied. "Nothing can help that."

Noah nodded and stood. Then he said, "Katie is asking after you. She wants you to have your birthday party."

"I ruined the day for her, didn't I?"

"We explained that you felt ill," he said. "Hannah and Samuel entertained her. Hannah wanted to come and check on you, but I told her I'd do it. We can celebrate another day."

"Tell Hannah to go home. She needs her rest. Or did you know that secret, too?"

Noah shook his head. "She told me a little while ago. Oh, and Adam came over to help Jeb in the barn. I think the boy wanted to find out what was going on. He sure was looking forward to you seeing that shed. We all helped build it. Jeb mapped out the pieces and had it all planned out. We had us a regular shed-raising while you were in town."

"I suppose everyone was in on that, too," she said, her heart too bruised to thank him.

"*Ja*, because we all love you and because we thought—"

"Don't say it." She stood. "I'm going to check on the lilies and then I'm going to bed."

"But it's almost dark."

"I'll just stand on the porch and make sure the fields are quiet."

She watched her brother walking away, then turned and went inside. There was just enough light left for her to go out to that shed and have one look at it. Before she told her brother to tear it down.

Jeb pivoted when the barn door creaked open, hoping Rebecca had come to talk to him. But when Adam stuck his head in, Jeb swallowed his disappointment. Only because the boy looked so dejected. Lily Dog pushed past Adam and ran up to Jeb, barking hello. Jeb rubbed the dog's head.

"Hey, Jeb," Adam said as he moved up the short stable alley, petting Red and Silver as he walked by. "Is Rebecca feeling better? Did she see her shed yet? Is she gonna be okay?"

Jeb swallowed again. "She's still not feeling well, so I think she went to bed. She'll have to see her shed another day."

Adam's dejection held him like a heavy cloak. "We didn't even get to cut the cake and it's a mighty big cake, round and with a lot of high layers. And white icing with sprinkles and Ava Jane even put little flowers on there, like lilies and petunias or something. Things women like, I reckon. Katie's pouting about not getting her piece."

Jeb couldn't look at Adam. He was too ashamed. Darkness shrouded the barn, but he didn't want to leave this shelter. He reached for a kerosene lamp and lit it with the long matches he kept nearby, then set it on the table. The glow from the lamp showed Adam's confusion.

Adam came closer. "Jeb, are you disappointed that Aenti Becca didn't see her pretty garden shed?"

Jeb nodded, cleared his throat. "I am. But I'm more disappointed in myself."

"Why?" Adam asked, moving to help him put away the scrap lumber they'd saved from the shed building. Lily Dog ran back and forth, wondering what to do next.

Jeb was close to telling the boy the truth about why Rebecca was feeling so bad, but when he turned to face Adam, he accidentally tripped over an extended four-by-four board he'd leaned against the worktable. The table wobbled and the kerosene lamp fell to the floor, landing

against some old rags and a pile of straw. Jeb lost his footing and his balance. He went down hard, hitting his head against the thick wooden board. He landed, blinked and saw stars. Then he saw fire running up the wall, before everything went black.

Chapter Twenty-Three

Rebecca stood in the shed, amazed at how beautiful it was. It smelled fresh and clean. New. Two small windows on each side allowed for airflow when opened and…also allowed for seeing both the sunrise to the east and the sunset to the west on most days. The little work counter and the stool behind it were both perfect, and so was the potting table spreading the length of one wall, complete with tools hanging over it and baskets and pots sitting on a rack below. The picnic table off to the side held a lily she recognized immediately. The Farmer's Daughter. Its bright pink petals and soft yellow throat shined against the sunrays covering the yard. How could she forget that day? How could she forget this summer?

But when she spotted the stack of letters tied with a string of twine lying there on the coun-

ter, her heartbeat went into a rapid retreat. Jeb had left her the letters from John.

She stood and took it all in, thinking of what might have been if he'd been honest with her.

And how would she have reacted? Would she have accepted him and let it all fall into place? Or would she have turned him away, her heart still broken over losing her childhood sweetheart? She'd never know because Jeb had not given her that choice. How she wished he would have trusted her enough to be honest with her. Knowing he was John's cousin should bring her comfort, but now it only brought her another kind of horrible pain. The pain of feeling betrayed by a man she'd learned to trust.

What am I to do now, Lord?

Then she heard the dog barking—an urgent, swift bark that sounded different. Rebecca turned, the smell of smoke rising through the air. When she heard a scream coming from the barn, she rushed out the door, Lily Dog barking and twirling in front of her. The dog wanted her to go to the barn.

Her breath gasping, her feet taking her forward, Rebecca cringed and put a hand to her mouth. The barn was on fire.

She glanced around, thinking no one was here to help her. But she'd heard a scream. She heard it again.

"Aenti!"

Adam. Adam was in the barn.

Had Jeb already left?

When she heard one of the horses whinnying in a panic, she knew she had to save Adam—and Red and Silver, too. Asking God to give her strength, she pushed at the half-open door and stood staring as fire licked the back wall with a hungry anger. Then she saw Adam tugging on something.

"Adam?"

"Aenti, it's Jeb." Her nephew's hoarse, breathless shouts sent a cold sweat across her skin. "He tripped over a board and the lamp fell. He got knocked out. Help!"

Jeb. She had to save Jeb.

She rushed forward. She and Adam tried to get him up, but the big board that had fallen kept him wedged between the table and the dirt floor.

"The horses," Adam called. "We have to drag him away." Her nephew started coughing again.

She couldn't let Adam stay here. The fire was spreading too fast, its golden flames sparking and flashing heat over their heads.

"Adam, go and get your *daed*. Hurry. I'll get the horses out and I'll find a way to get Jeb."

"*Neh*, I can't leave you."

"Just go. Now. Run fast. We need help."

Adam gave her one last panicked glance, then hurried out the door. Lily Dog ran with him.

Rebecca lifted her apron over her nose, then searched for a rope. Finding what she needed, she kept an eye on the fire behind the worktable. She had to get to the horses and use one to drag Jeb out. Or he would die.

"I can't let that happen," she shouted. "I can't go through this again."

She loved him. She knew in her heart, she loved him. No matter what, she couldn't let him go.

Right now, she didn't dwell on his misguided deceit. She only wanted Jeb to live. So she dropped her apron and pulled her *kapp* down like a mask, then went to Red and let her out. The roan rushed past her, scaring her almost as much as the fire. Then she found Silver, the gentle draft. Silver, the stronger of the two, would cooperate, she hoped. Grabbing the bit and reins next to the stall, she prayed for God to give her the courage she needed to help Jeb. While the fire clawed its way to the ceiling, she opened the stall and threw an old blanket over the draft's head, then guided him back to where Jeb lay. So still. So quiet.

"Jeb, please wake up."

He didn't move. She'd have to use the rope to tie his feet, but she didn't have time to get the reins and bit onto the horse. She'd have to guide Silver out by coaxing the horse and walking with him.

Rushing around, she steadied the horse with calm words, and threw a rope around Silver's middle, looped it back through to cinch it, then tugged the length of the rope toward Jeb. Silver whinnied and tossed his head back but didn't run away. After tying Jeb's feet, her hands shaking and her fingers working swiftly, Rebecca managed to secure the rope across his work boots. She touched his neck, searching for a pulse.

He was breathing. Somehow, she had to make this horse help her get Jeb to safety.

With a tug and all the strength she had, Rebecca got the heavy beam of wood moved enough to drag Jeb away without hurting him more. When she saw blood near his temple, she went into full panic mode.

"Silver, I know you can do this. You're a *gut* boy." She kept talking in soothing terms to the frightened horse while she tugged at the lasso around the animal's big girth. Clicking her tongue the way her *daed* used to do, she held

the blanket over Silver's head and urged the horse forward, her prayers centered on saving Jeb, instead of fearing she'd get knocked out by the horse.

Silver's fear increased as the smell of smoke and the heat from the fire leaping behind them caused him to balk and lift up his massive front legs.

Rebecca stepped away, her heart dropping. "C'mon, Silver. We can do this. We have to do this. I need to tell him I love him, I forgive him. I don't want him to die."

Silver neighed a high-pitched whine, but when the horse heard voices coming from the yard, he bolted forward, almost knocking Rebecca down. Rebecca stepped back, watching as the rope she'd tied to Jeb's feet held enough for him to come flying up the alleyway.

"No," she shouted, her hands gripping the heavy rope. If the horse went too fast, Jeb would be dragged and hurt even worse. "Silver," she shouted, "wait."

Tugging at the rope with all her might, Rebecca managed to control the nervous animal, her hands burning from the heat and from the rope searing into her palms. But she couldn't let go. Silver practically dragged both Rebecca and Jeb out of the open door.

Then before she knew what was happening, her brother and his three sons surrounded her and took the rope from her.

"Becca, let me," Noah shouted, taking her hand away. "Go, get out of here."

Becca looked into her brother's eyes and then she looked at Jeb. "Don't let him die, Noah."

Adam guided her out into the night air. Gasping, she didn't realize she'd been holding her breath—but not against the smoke. *Neh*, she'd been holding steady for Jeb's sake.

Franny came running and tugged her to the picnic table. The table Jeb had set up for her with the pretty lily centered on it.

Rebecca held to her sister-in-law. "Franny, he can't die. I can't let him die. I have to tell him I love him."

Franny held her tight. "He won't die. He won't. You saved him, Becca."

Katie ran to her mother. "Aenti, don't cry. It's okay. We saved the cake, too."

Becca laughed and took her niece onto her lap. Then she cried all over again, and she and Franny sat and prayed silent prayers while the volunteer fire department came and tried to save the barn.

When the paramedic walked by, Franny ran to one of them. "What about the man in the

barn? My sister-in-law Rebecca needs to know if he's going to be okay."

The paramedic nodded and motioned to Rebecca. "Why don't you go see for yourself. He's been asking for you."

Rebecca hurried to the stretcher they were about to lift into the ambulance. "Jeb?"

He groaned and turned his head. "You're here."

"I'm here," she said, taking his hand. "Jeb, I forgive you. I love you. I'm sorry."

She saw the tears in his eyes, saw the bump over his left temple. "Don't die on me."

"I'm not going to die," he said, his words weak. "I have so much to live for now. I hope you like your shed."

She started crying, her hand touching his smut-covered face. "I love my shed. I love you. I'm sorry."

"*Neh*, I'm the one who's sorry, but, Becca, I love you so much."

Rebecca watched as they lifted him into the ambulance.

"He's going to be fine," Noah told her. "He has a slight concussion and a twisted ankle. You saved his life, Becca."

"And he saved mine," she replied.

A week later

Rebecca stood near the lily field, taking in a thousand scents while up at the house her belated birthday celebration was going strong.

Noah had finally cooked their hamburgers over a firepit grill that Mr. Hartford had sold him. They had potato salad, fresh cucumbers and several other side dishes. Franny had stored the cake at the Campton Center in a big freezer. Jewel had picked it up and kept it there until they were ready.

Today, they were all ready to celebrate. Jewel, with her usual energy, had helped with the whole gathering.

The neighbors had pitched in to rebuild the part of the barn that had burned. It looked new and fresh and strong. Rebecca could step inside now, her old fears burned away with the fire. Silver and she had a new beginning, a bond that brought them together.

A few days ago, Jeb had returned from the hospital, thanks to Jewel picking him up and bringing him home. He'd been resting so his foot and his head could heal. But today, he was well and at home for good.

Home. This would be his official home come this fall.

He'd told Becca in the hospital that he loved her and wanted to marry her.

"But we won't make it official until we're back home," he'd said, after he'd apologized over and over.

"Jeb, I was so angry at you, but I can understand why you did what you did. I loved John and I wasn't ready to let go of him. There was no easy way for you to tell me the truth."

She'd read the letters that night after the fire, and she'd cried with each word. But they had become a gift to her, a gift from the man she'd lost, brought to her by fate, from a man she'd found. She loved both of them.

One man in heaven.

One here on earth.

"What are you thinking?"

She turned as Jeb walked up to her and took her hand.

"I'm thinking about everything. About us, about the future, about the past. I'm so thankful for all of it."

He pulled her close. "I was an idiot."

"I was a bitter *alte maidal*."

"We make a *gut* pair, right?"

"I believe so."

He glanced at the new shed and then back to her. "Becca, will you marry me?"

"Ja," she said, smiling, happy, glad.

"Okay, then. This fall. Meantime, I'm free and clear and I'm Amish again."

"That you are," she replied.

He'd stood up in church just yesterday and confessed all of his sins, including his connection to John.

He was forgiven. They would never speak of this again.

Rebecca wondered about all those who had to constantly pray for forgiveness. She sure had to do her own praying.

But now, she was content and at peace, and she thanked God for his perfect timing.

Only one thing held back her joy.

"I can't give you children, Jeb. I wonder how you feel about that."

Jeb turned her in his arms and kissed her. Then he drew back and smiled. "I'll tell you how I feel about that. *Gott*'s will, Becca. It took me twenty years to find you. We'll just have to see if he has one more blessing planned for us."

"You think?"

"I hope and pray, but if not, then I will still be the happiest man here on earth."

She nodded, unable to speak.

Then Katie and Lily Dog ran up.

"We really need to cut that cake, Aenti Becca. Please?"

"Please?" Jeb echoed.

Lily Dog barked.

Then they all walked together to join the rest of their family as the sun settled over the lily field and the air smelled like a wedding garden.

The Lily Lady had never been happier.

They were married in September, and a week before Christmas of the next year, they had a beautiful, healthy baby boy and named him John.

* * * * *

Dear Reader,

One of my favorite hymns is "In the Garden."
Years ago, I wrote three Love Inspired books
based on that hymn, *When Love Came to Town*,
Something Beautiful and *Lacey's Retreat*. I
loved describing the gardens in those books.
My mama was a gardener and her flowers and
plants brought her a lot of joy, so whenever I
hear or sing that hymn where Jesus walks with
us in the garden, I always think of her.

I love lilies, and not just daylilies, but lush,
fragrant beautiful lilies of all colors and varieties. So it was a true joy to write about Rebecca, the Lily Lady, who tended her plants and
grieved the man she'd lost. But God had a plan
for Rebecca and so He brought Jebediah to her
and showed her the true meaning of forgiveness
and getting over tremendous grief. Jebediah had
his secrets, but he had to learn to trust in God
again to be able to confess his secrets and his
love to Rebecca.

I hope wherever you are and whatever you
might be going through in life, you will take
some time to admire God's beautiful earth. Stop
and smell the lilies. Now I want to plant a lot
of lilies in my yard. Nature has a way of making even the worst of times better. I hope you

find a flower today and I hope you know that He walks with you, and talks with you, wherever you are.

Until next time, may the angels watch over you. Always!

Lenora Worth